Drew Greenfield

Sweeter Than Wine

Published by Magda Green Books 2018

ISBN: 978-1-98054-040-3

Cover image: Bohal, Église St Gildas
© Pymouss/Wikimedia Commons (adapted)

All of a sudden, I'm empty of reason but filled with longings that for six months I've tried to suppress. My resolve is weakening. Something new is happening, something wonderful, frightening and inviting. I'm being trawled into a net of my own making, and from which there may be no escape.

But I don't want to escape. Since those kisses, I've never been so certain of anything in my life.

….. I'm madly, hopelessly in love with him.

Sweeter Than Wine

Bordeaux, France, Early June

1.

Nicole

The bus pulls away, leaving me in the middle of Bordeaux wine country. Vines border the road to right and left, stretching into the distance as far as I can see. The fresh air, laden with unfamiliar scents, is intoxicating.

I stare up at the house. It's built on the only ridge for kilometres around. *Château Ravel.* I know not all Bordeaux winegrowers live in palaces and I wasn't expecting a real castle. But I wasn't expecting this either. My heart gives a nervous flutter. *Chance will be a fine thing*, I think. *What would I give to live in a place like this!*

The house is huge, a long-fronted modern building of brick and decorative stone, two floors, with a landscaped garden. The whole property is surrounded by a metre-and-a-half-high wall topped with a metal railing. It's fronted by an ornate metal gate, which lies open giving me a perfect view. It isn't a typical French house but reminds me of something you would find in the middle of the English countryside. Two cars are parked on the drive, a silver Mercedes saloon near the front door and a small red hatchback half way along.

Everything shrieks of luxury: the neat stone paving, the picture windows keeping watch over the greenery of the Gironde countryside; the perfect symmetry of the shrubs and flower beds. The front door, of solid wood carved with a grape motif, is protected by a stone portico supported on pillars. I wonder whether I'm going to be glad or sorry I answered that ad. *Live-in housekeeper and companion wanted*, it read, and I thought *why not?* I need a full-time job, away from the flat, from *Maman*, Jean and their talk of marriage.

My adventure nearly ends before it has begun. I'm about a third of the way along the drive when a youth on a bicycle swings round a corner from the side of the house and almost knocks me off my feet into the shrubbery. I feel the draught of air as he passes. His muttered *Pardon* is almost lost in the breeze of his going as, head down and pedalling hard, he sweeps out of the gate and onto the road.

I'm recovering my balance when the front door opens and a young woman of around thirty comes out. Looking as if she's swallowed something with a nasty taste, she stomps down the drive. I smooth down my skirt, straighten my glasses on my nose and resume my walk in the opposite direction.

'Good luck with that,' the woman sniffs as our paths cross midway between house and gate. She gets into the hatchback and reverses along the drive. A disgruntled applicant, I guess. In half-an-hour's time, maybe I'll feel the same way.

I catch my first glimpse of my prospective employer. She doesn't *look* intimidating. She offers her hand and then stands aside to usher me indoors. 'You must be Nicole,' she says.

**

2.

I glance round the spacious atrium, its floor tiled with grey slate. Ahead of me is a wide, burgundy-carpeted staircase, to the left of the stairs a passageway leading off towards the back of the house. There are several doors. Through two on my left, I see the colour scheme extends to the rooms. Burgundy carpet, pale grey walls. A second passageway goes off to my right.

Mme Ravel gestures towards one of the open doors. 'Come into my den and we'll have a chat.'

Often, telephone calls are deceptive. Trim, sophisticated, perfect coiffure, business-like; these were expressions I used to build my picture of her during our brief conversation. However, she's not at all like that.

She is taller than me. She has a handsome rather than a pretty face, and thick light brown hair that curls over her forehead and round her ears. I put her age at around forty-five, though I'm not always a good judge. Instead of the snooty socialite, she seems friendly and easy going. Intelligent too, I think; not a woman to be messed with, but certainly not an ogre.

What she calls her den is a spacious room with bookshelves lining the walls on three sides. It has a centrally-placed table-cum-desk and two grey-leather-covered chairs. Mme Ravel sits down on one and motions me to the other. She appraises me silently. My stomach turns over with anticipation.

Though I wasn't sure it was necessary for a domestic position, I took a lot of trouble with my appearance and think I'll pass scrutiny. But she's making me nervous. I see that my *résumé* lies on the table beside her and she's tapping it with her left forefinger. I wonder if she bothered to read it. The job is about cleaning rooms, dusting furniture and washing windows. *Maybe feeding the kids.*

'You have a beautiful house, *madame.*' I feel I ought to say something to break the ice and a compliment seems a good way to begin.

'Thank you,' she says. 'I like it.'

'I love the colour scheme. The grey and burgundy go so well together.' I mean it sincerely and she smiles.

'We have it throughout the house. I'll show you later.'

At least she isn't going to throw me out. I wait for her to begin the interview proper but she's taking her time. Then she smiles again, an encouraging smile, though her eyes resume their scrutiny.

'So, what about you, Nicole? You're nineteen?'

'*Oui, madame.* I'll be twenty in January. I grew up in Bordeaux.'

'And school - you took a year out?'

'*Oui, madame.* I finished *lycée* last summer.'

'And passed the *Bac.*' Mme Ravel taps my *résumé* again. She raises an eyebrow. 'How interesting! Arts and languages. French and English literature - and German.' *So she has read it.* 'And your marks are good - excellent.'

'*Merci, madame.*'

'And a British Council certificate of proficiency in the English language?'

'My grandparents paid for the test. The school recommended it, *madame.*'

'Call me Cathy. *Madame* sounds as if I run a brothel.' She laughs. I'm warming to her. Her eyes are brown and mischievous. I realise she isn't French, though her accent is slight. *American,* I think - *or English.* 'So, what about the past few months? You had a job?'

'Part-time waitressing. Hotel and bar work. But it's seasonal.'

'Twenty-eight years ago, I had the same problem. You want something a bit more permanent.' She nods as if she understands. 'Do you have sisters and brothers, or is it just you?'

'One of each, *madame.*' I begin to relax a little. 'Sophie is thirteen. Bernard's fifteen, a year and a half older.'

'Teenage boys, *eh . . .*' She gives me a friendly grin. '. . . moody and stubborn?'

'Bern isn't too bad.'

I decide to risk a question of my own. I hope I'm being tactful and not too forward. 'Do you have children, *madame* . . . I'm sorry, Cathy? There was a boy on a bicycle . . . when I arrived.'

'*Gerard? Christ*, he isn't mine,' she screeches. 'Gerard's my husband's nephew.'

'*Pardon*. I just assumed.'

'Apology unnecessary! Gerard's OK helping in the winery, but he's hopeless around the house. Yves and I have one son - Andy, past the teenage stage, I'm happy to say. He's nearly twenty-three - .' She pauses before continuing. 'No, there's only Andy. We wanted a daughter too, but we couldn't.' Her frankness warms me to her even more. '*Mais c'est la vie, n'est-ce pas?*'

I nod in agreement, unable to think of a suitable reply. Cathy puckers her lips and pats me on the arm. There is motherly feeling in the gesture, more than I get from Denise - my own mother - and my heart goes out to her.

'The last few girls let me down badly,' she says after a moment or two. 'They were experienced, would you believe. But I want more from a companion.' Cathy leans forward as if sharing a secret. 'I asked the woman before you the title of the last book she read. She gave me a blank look.' She leans back. 'But I like you. I'll give you a month's trial.'

I can't believe my luck and just nod before swallowing a gulp of air. My mouth is as dry as the Bordeaux summer.

'So, I suppose we'd better talk about pay,' Cathy goes on. 'What about five hundred for the trial period? You can start tomorrow! Three days a week and the odd evening for now. I'm looking for a live-in companion so, if we click, maybe twelve hundred a month plus board when you're full time. If you still want the job, that is.'

'*Euros?* But that's . . .' I give another gulp and clap my hand over my face.

Cathy puckers her lips again, considering. 'Well, we might manage a bit more when the trial's over.'

'I didn't mean to . . . That's not what I meant.' Now I'm

flustered. Twelve hundred *euros* is more than I earned in three months of casual work. With board and lodgings included, it's much more than the minimum wage, and way better than was offered at my last interview. 'Twelve hundred is generous.'

'Well, I've said it now so I'll stick to it,' Cathy says. 'No fixed hours but I need you to be flexible about evenings and weekends. We'll work around the idea of two days and two evenings off a week. I teach part time and you'll be alone in the house a lot. My husband is often away.'

'You're a teacher?'

'I teach English in the city.'

'I'd like to do that one day. I love languages, especially English literature.'

'What are your favourites?' She gestures towards the bookcases. 'More than half of those are in English. You're welcome to borrow any time you like.'

'Dickens is my favourite,' I say. '*David Copperfield* and *Christmas Carol*. I like more modern writers too - Daphne du Maurier, Margaret Atwood, and Zadie Smith.'

'We have something in common then. I like Atwood too, though I think her books must be difficult in the English versions for a French student. And there's nothing to stop you being a teacher.' She taps my *résumé* again. 'This is more like a college application than the badly-written stuff I've been getting. You could be at university this year with those marks. Higher education in France is well subsidised, and there are support grants if . . .' She stops mid-sentence and I can tell she is annoyed with herself. 'I'm so sorry, Nicole. That's none of my business.'

'No, it's OK. And I know about the fees and the grants. But I need to do it my way. I want to study in Great Britain.'

'And you need some capital? Well, OK, as I say, the job's yours if you want it. What will your parents think of you moving in with us?'

That's the one question I hoped she wouldn't ask. I don't want to have to explain about Denise. So I tell the plain truth, or as close as I want to get to it. 'My father died when I was twelve. My mother has a new boyfriend. They're going to get married, so home won't be home any longer.'

'You poor soul!' Cathy nods and pats my arm. 'Can you cook?'

'I'm quite a good cook.' It isn't an idle boast. I had plenty of practice while my mother was sick. *Sick. Unwell.* It's strange how easily I voice the euphemisms now.

'There'll be some cooking, though I like to cook too. And there's laundry and cleaning the rooms. Shopping. Putting up with Andy of course - when he's home!'

'I can do that, Cathy.'

'Nothing very strenuous, but I'll expect good value, mind. I didn't see another car. You came by bus? Can you drive?'

'Yes. I've already passed the theory test and booked the practical. I have over 2,000 kilometres driving experience with a friend.' My ex-boyfriend Henri was quite a bit older than me and he jumped at the chance to teach me about cars.

'I'll help you get more kilometres if you like. There's Grandpa Ravel's old car. We'll fix it up and when you pass you can use it for trips to the village, or to visit your family, or friends. Whatever you like.' She opens a drawer under the table-desk, picks up my *résumé* and pops it inside. 'I don't think we need that now,' she says. 'Let me show you the house - and where everything is.'

She takes me on a tour. I'm not one for envy but I catch myself sucking my bottom lip. I fight the growing feeling that life has been unkind to me until now. Our crowded flat in downtown Bordeaux seems so far away and insignificant. Every room here, every passageway, every corner speaks to me of space, comfort and luxury. I want to resist but find myself wallowing in its velvety softness. The vast living-room lies off the hall next to the library where we've been talking. From there, we go into the dining-room, then to the kitchen. A conservatory runs the full length of the house at the back and opens on its short side to a terrace with a swimming pool. The house is oriented so that, in the summer months, the morning sun will warm the terrace, while the conservatory catches the evening sunset.

Beyond the garden and about two hundred metres away is a bank of young trees, through which I catch a glimpse of other buildings. Part of the winery, I guess. Every *château* must have one.

I can see at a glance that cleaning the house will be easy. There are no mouldings or dark wainscoting to gather dust, no dark corners. Cathy tells me all the windows open out and swivel round to permit washing from inside.

We are half way up the staircase when a door bangs somewhere in the house. Cathy stops and grips the rail.

'That's odd!' She turns back and heads towards the passage to the right of the front door. 'Carry on and have a look around by yourself, Nicole.'

I hear the pad of her footsteps on the tiles, the squeak of another door then, a moment later, the sound of her voice, raised and annoyed. 'What the hell are you doing in my house?'

There are more footsteps. Cathy's are accompanied by the clatter of leather heels. A female voice mumbles an apology and something about a key, but I don't catch the rest. The door closes again and I hear no more.

I carry on up the stairs. All five bedrooms boast an *en-suite* WC and shower. The one in the master bedroom has a bath. In addition, there is a separate huge bathroom. I have almost completed my hasty tour when Cathy re-joins me in the final room. She's doing her best to calm her breathing.

'Martha something or other. Would you believe, Yves hired her without telling me? All bosom, legs and heels. It seems she's going to install a computer network for the business. He gave her a key to the office! Not a licence for the rest of the house, the little . . .' Cathy leaves the sentence unfinished but I get the idea.

She leads me downstairs and points to the passageway across the hall. 'The office is down there. You won't have to worry about that. Yves has a woman who dusts his desk from time to time. I'll have to make sure the inner door is locked when both Yves and Georges are out. Georges is Yves' brother. We can't have strangers wandering around the house.'

We go back to the kitchen where Cathy brews some coffee. We drink it and then she shows me where everything is kept - food, crockery, knives and forks, and the rest.

'I've been thinking,' she says. 'I might give you Andy's current room when you come to live in. It's closer to the stairs. He can move into the one at the end of the passage, out of your way. He'll be away from home most of the year anyway.'

'He's at university?'

'Oxford. He graduated from *Pièrre et Marie Curie* in Paris two years ago. A bachelor's in science. He'll be home soon on vacation.'

'Oxford?' To go to Oxford would have been a dream come true. But I have other plans now.

'Yes. He's doing a D Phil. Mathematical Physics.'

'*Formidable!* You must be very proud.'

For a second, I fancy there's a tear forming at the corner of one eye. Then it's gone.

'Yes, Nicole,' she says. 'I am.'

I figure Andy must be studious; you have to be to graduate from *Pierre et Marie Curie* when you're twenty. I picture a lanky, awkward youth with long hair and braces on his teeth. Probably untidy and eccentric, a younger version of the science teacher at my school. Yet, the Andy I meet a few days later is not what I imagined. Andy Ravel is tall, well-built and more than a little handsome. His face bears the softness, the innocence of youth, but these are traits I find attractive in him, as magnetic as the dark brown eyes and arched eyebrows that make my stomach do a flip at the first sight of him.

It's my second week. I'm in the kitchen, preparing something for the evening meal. He opens the door from the conservatory and drops a big suitcase on the floor.

'Who are you?' He reaches across the worktop where I'm working, grabs half the raw carrot I've sliced and begins munching.

'Nicole.' I throw him a disapproving look. 'Your mother hired me.'

'I see,' he says and, still munching, parks himself on one of the high stools at the breakfast bar. 'Is this part of my dinner?'

'It would have been if you hadn't chewed it.'

I collect the chopped vegetables and sweep them into a stew-pan. His eyebrows come together in a frown and for a few seconds we stare at one another. He is first to lower his eyes.

'Now, you'll have to excuse me,' I say. 'I have to finish up here. I have a bus to catch.'

He comes into his room while I'm vacuuming. I've been in the job another seventy-two hours. He towers above me. I've underestimated his height. He must be at least one metre ninety in his socks. I switch off the machine and take a couple of steps back to leave a respectable gap between us.

'Sorry about the carrot!' His dark eyebrows shoot up. 'We weren't properly introduced. I'm Andy!'

'I guessed as much.'

'And you're Nicole.'

'*Bien sûr.*'

'I thought she would have taken on an older woman.'

'Why?'

He hitches his shoulders. 'Oh, I don't know. All the others have been at least thirty.'

'Well, I'm nowhere near thirty and she didn't.' I manage a smile.

He studies me for a moment. I'm quite used to men's stares but this look isn't about sex. It's at once disinterested and, I feel, innocent. But I realise that for some reason I've taken off my spectacles to study him back. He has his mother's eyes, brown with a touch of humour. His hair is almost black, though not a sleek, silky black but rather soft and warm - hair which, in other circumstances, I might . . .

Dieu, I think, I'm not going there. He's my employer's son, for goodness sake. And the last thing I need is another relationship.

'I don't suppose you'll last any longer than the others,' he says. '*C'est bien dommage*! You're quite pretty.'

'Thank you for the compliment.' He hasn't taken his eyes off me and now he's embarrassing me. I put on my glasses, pick up the hose of the vacuum cleaner and reach for the switch. Unlike the machine in our flat, which rumbles, whines and prevents conversation, this one emits only a low hum. 'What makes you think I won't stick the job, Andy?'

'They never do,' he answers. The eyebrows come together as he wrinkles his forehead. 'I don't know much about girls but I think it's the isolation. They want to be in the city, with the cinemas and clubs and restaurants. Here it's just grapes and grass.'

'I like grapes and grass. Anyway, it's only a half-hour drive to downtown Bordeaux, and not much longer in the bus.'

'I suppose.' He smiles for the first time. Now that he's lost the disinterested expression, handsome does him an injustice. Not only is he tall and well-built, he's well-proportioned too. His t-shirt is moulded to his shoulders and arms, and his jeans are tight round his buttocks. I have one of those moments, wondering if he's stopped growing and whether his height might be reflected in his growth elsewhere. Not that my interest is predatory, but simply the natural curiosity of any normal single girl. I'm definitely not going there. Yet I can't rid myself of the thought. *What would it be like - how would it feel to have someone so big . . .?*

'Bet you a hundred *euros* you won't last past Christmas.'

'What?' I snap back to reality. His smile has turned to a boyish grin.

'A hundred *euros* says you quit before Christmas.'

'I'm not taking your bet - or your money. Anyway, I haven't got a hundred *euros*. But for the record, Andy Ravel, I'm not a quitter. You'd be throwing your money away.'

'We'll see.' He sneaks another know-all grin.

'We shall indeed.' It occurs to me that if I fail Cathy's trial he could be right. Though she has shown me nothing but kindness and approval, I still have eighteen part-time days to go.

**

3.

My best friend Amelie leans across her kitchen table, waving a half-empty bottle of Merlot. My third week at *Château Ravel* is nearly over and we've been hanging out in her new bed-sit. She's a trainee hairdresser and beautician in a salon in the city.

'Do you want some more wine?'

I cover my glass with my palm. 'I've had enough, and so have you.'

'You're probably right, *chérie*.' She sighs and puts down the bottle. 'Let's get comfortable and you can tell me the latest gossip about the Ravels. You promised!'

'There isn't anywhere else to sit,' I protest. Apart from the table, two dining chairs, one closet and a bed, there isn't any furniture. 'You need to organise yourself better, Amm. You haven't even got a TV yet.'

'Next week! Let's sit on the bed.' She jumps up and crosses to the bedroom in two strides. 'Come on!'

After my promised room at Cathy's, Amelie's flat seems tiny. Her kitchen is a practical size but the bedroom is no bigger than the closet where I hang the laundry. I follow her next door and we both flop down on the springy mattress.

Amelie hugs her knees. 'Well?'

'Cathy is brilliant.' I copy her pose and we sit facing one another, she at the pillow end, me at the foot. We've shared confidences since before *lycée*. 'I liked her right from the start. She treats me more like one of the family than an employee. Did I tell you? They're even giving me a car. An old Citroen. Cathy has been taking me out on the road for practice. I'm not used to being spoiled like that.'

Amelie flicks back a loose strand of her auburn hair. 'Lucky you! Any more gossip? What about that other woman who works there?'

The IT expert Yves hired, Martha, is in her late twenties, all legs and cleavage, and has a masters' degree in computer science. I give Amelie the details including a summary of her wardrobe. 'She's a freelance contractor,' I explain, 'not a Ravel employee. She's been up at the house a few times checking phone lines and cables.'

'Competition?' Amelie rolls her tongue round her mouth.

'I don't see how. We're unlikely to have much in common.'

Amelie leans over and pats my knee. 'I meant for the son.'

'Andy? He's twenty-two. Handsome, smart and innocent. Martha looks like a dominatrix. She'd have him for breakfast.'

'You can't possibly know that. About his innocence, I mean.'

'It's just a feeling I get.'

'You like him?'

'Not in that way. I didn't like him at all at first, the way he seemed to take everything for granted: his parents' wealth; his Paris education; a place at Oxford. To him, I was just another in a long line of domestics. But we've talked a bit since. He doesn't appear to have many friends his own age.'

'So, you *do* like him?' Amelie has a way of making a question sound like an answer. Whatever I say, she's already decided I have feelings for Andy.

'Don't, Amm!'

'Don't what, *chérie*?'

'You know perfectly well, and I'm not playing! It's possible to like a boy without wanting to jump into bed with him. Anyway, Andy's more like a kid brother than a boyfriend.'

'But he's *years* older you said.'

'Only three.'

'An only child?'

'The Ravels wanted a daughter but apparently they couldn't.'

'That's tough. Maybe Cathy sees you as the daughter she never had. You shouldn't get too close. This isn't the way your life is supposed to be.'

'Actually, I quite enjoy being an employee. And the Ravels, for all their money, are just people.'

'Of course they're people. But you know what I mean. You're going to university. You want a career. You have a *très bien* diploma, for Christ's sake.'

Amelie mostly talks sense, except when she's trying to hook me up with a new boyfriend. I understand what she means about not getting too close, but what else do you do with someone you like? And I sense that Cathy and I could be good friends.

'I haven't forgotten.' I squeeze Amelie's hand. 'Thanks, Amm, for caring. I'll be OK. But I do need to work.'

**

4.

I have packed two suitcases with my clothes and a few other belongings, determined to make as many bus trips as it takes to transport my life to its new home. When Denise discovers my plans, she makes a fuss.

'I don't get why you have to live in.' She tuts and eyes the suitcases. 'There'll be plenty of room at Jean's place.'

'I've tried to explain, *Maman*. Please don't ask me again.'

Bernard and Sophie are as excited as I am, Bern especially.

'I'll have your room,' he announces.

I hug them both. 'I'm not going to the Moon. I'll see you every week.'

Denise realises I won't change my mind and offers to drive me. We manage to squeeze most of my books, my old computer *and* the suitcases into the back of her car, so one trip is enough. There's no one at home. My mother helps me unload.

'You don't have to do this,' she says.

'Yes, I do.'

She turns to go. 'I wish you - we . . .'

But she doesn't finish. She never does and I don't want to hear a lie.

'Don't, *Maman*.' I pick up one of my cases. It's heavy and I need both hands. 'Thank you for bringing me.'

She hurries off. I let myself in and carry my possessions upstairs.

Cathy comes in later to supervise my settling in.

'How do you like it?'

The room is the one at the end of the corridor. Cathy changed her mind about moving Andy. She decided it was too much hassle. It occurs to me he might have put up strong objections. This room is pristine and bears no signs of occupancy. It overlooks the conservatory. Like everything else in the house, the decor and furnishings are amazing. There's the *en-suite*, a double bed, a television and a phone. From the window, I have a view of the swathe of vineyards below. Somewhere beyond the endless greenery is the Garonne. To one side, over the tops of the young trees, I can see what I've learned are the vat room and bottling plant, the heart of the Ravel operation.

'It's brilliant, Cathy. *Merci.*'

'The phone has its own line,' she tells me. 'We installed it when Yves talked of his father living here. Of course, if you have your own mobile . . .'

'I haven't been able to afford one.'

'Well, the line is there if you want it. Is there anything else you need?'

'Will it be OK if I put up some posters?'

'Of course. It's your room. I have some poster pins in the kitchen. You can have those. And there's a spare bookcase in one of the guest bedrooms. And a couple of bookends. I'll move a few magazines.'

I'm always embarrassed by her kindness and never sure how I should react to it. Most of the time, she's good-natured and full of life, but occasionally I feel her loneliness. I doubt Yves Ravel has spent as much as fifteen whole days at home during the last month, and I wonder if he plays around. Already, I've taken an evening meal with the family three times. Although he's always polite, Yves doesn't say much, *except -.*

Father and son argue a lot, and neither seems to mind whether I'm there or not. They seem to disagree about everything. Yves has twice threatened to stop paying for Andy's education. Andy retorts that he doesn't care, though I know his education means everything to him.

There's a pattern to the arguments. The low growls of the alpha male and the challenger are followed by a rapid exchange of words, often indistinguishable. The silence which comes next is the worst part. They glare at one another, short on vocabulary, before the confrontation erupts into another round of accusation and rebuttal. There are expletives - both French and English - then Yves will thump a table or a desk with his fist. Andy will slam a door. I'm always afraid there will be blows.

They have similar temperaments, stubborn and unrepentant. I just haven't discovered what their disagreements are about.

Occasionally, I catch a look from Andy which isn't quite the innocent one of our first meeting. It happens when I reprimand him for leaving his books scattered around the living room after I've tidied, or for throwing a soiled shirt on his bed after I've made it up. He'll hold my glare a bit longer now before lowering his eyes and taking the hint. He certainly isn't beyond redemption.

This morning, he is drinking coffee and reading at the breakfast bar when I go to the kitchen to make a snack for my lunch. The terrace outside is still wet from a shower of early July rain.

'Would you like something to eat, Andy?' I ask. 'I'll make a baguette sandwich with salami or cheese, if you like.'

He glances up from his book. 'Salami, please . . . if it's no trouble.'

'It's no trouble.' I locate the meat in the refrigerator and decide to take some cheese as well. The baguettes are fresh this morning from the *boulangerie*. I slice them in half and cut some salami. 'What are you reading?'

'*Qu'est-ce que la vie?*'

'*Pardon?*'

'That's the title. *What is Life?* It's by Erwin Schrödinger.'

The name is familiar but I can't recall where I heard it. I layer a generous helping of butter on one of the sliced baguettes. 'A science book?'

'Yes. Schrödinger was a physicist, famous for his work on quantum theory.' He grins. 'And the cat in the box experiment. *Schrödinger's Cat*. It wasn't a real experiment of course.'

'Science wasn't my thing at school.' I add the salami to the bread, hand him his sandwich and make one for myself with the cheese.

'Thanks, Nicole,' he says. He gives me one of his nicer smiles and bites into the crusty bread. 'This sandwich is very good.'

We both carry on eating in silence. I brew some coffee while Andy goes back to his reading. After a few minutes, he closes the book, looks up and wrinkles his nose.

'You know, I'm not much good at anything else. Other than science, I mean.'

'I'm sure that's not true. To be fluent in two languages, that's something. And your mother tells me you're quite a good tennis-player.'

'I suppose,' he says. 'But I don't know much about music, or movies. Not much about politics either. Nothing about women or girls.'

I push my coffee mug aside and give him my full attention. A lot of guys know nothing about girls, but they don't usually admit it.

'You can learn!' I feel a blush coming on. 'You must know some girls. Ask one of them on a date and take it from there.'

'There isn't anyone,' he says ruefully. 'I think it's got something to do with boarding school. Boys' school, and very Catholic!'

'I thought religious indoctrination was banned by the government, Andy.'

'Only in the state-supported sector. But it wasn't so much about religion. My parents - my father anyhow - thought a Catholic boys' school would give me the best education.' He rubs the back of his neck and chews his bottom lip. 'So, you see, I missed out. Until I went to UPMC I didn't know any girls at all. And then, most were a lot older than me.'

He is avoiding my eyes, so I sneak a look at him and experience a familiar tug in my abdomen. I've seen a photograph of Andy taken at his graduation, so I can guess his looks at the age of seventeen. At *Lycée François Mauriac*, every girl in the final year would be queuing for a simple *Ça va?* - or to hear him speak her name.

'I did date a few girls in Paris,' he goes on, 'but none of them worked out. What about you - do you have a boyfriend?'

'I recently ended a relationship.'

'I see.' He chews his bottom lip again, digesting my reply. 'How old are you?' he asks.

I can't help laughing. 'Do you always ask girls their ages, Andy? Maybe that's why your dates don't work out.'

He flushes and looks down at his book. 'What do you mean?'

'Maybe it's not the first question you should ask. But if you must know, I'm nineteen. Nineteen and six months to be exact.'

'I thought you were older. Not a lot, maybe a year or two. You seem quite mature and sensible.'

'Well thank you - I think.'

'I'll be twenty-three in a couple of weeks.'

'That's really old.' I steal another glance at him over the top of my glasses, intending to tease. 'Have you ordered a walking stick?'

He frowns but his eyes are warm and hypnotic, his mouth holds the trace of a smile. 'You're making fun of me, *Mlle Durand*.'

'Just a bit, *M. Ravel*.' *Definitely not beyond redemption*, I think. Deep down, there's a nice person waiting to get out. 'Now, if you have a few minutes to spare, why don't you tell me about that experiment with the cat.'

He launches into a lecture on quantum theory, way above my head. The idea that electrons and other tiny particles can be in several places at once - that cats can be alive and dead at the same time - is too weird and goes against common sense. My eyes must be glazing over because he stops mid-sentence.

'I tell you what.' He stands up and runs his hand through his hair. 'There's a book up in my room that explains it better. I've had it since school. I'll go and get it.'

He rushes off. I hear the pounding of his feet as he careers up the stairs, then a minute or two of silence, followed by the sound of him returning.

'There! I've marked the chapter on Schrödinger's Cat.' He hands me a well-thumbed and dog-eared paperback. 'Don't worry,' he jokes. 'The top scientists don't understand it either.'

5.

The weather improves and we're back to the typical Bordeaux summer. Lazy and warm. My work settles into a routine, cleaning the rooms, laundry, shopping and preparing meals. Two of the five bedrooms need very little attention. Both are occupied only when the Ravels have a special function and entertain friends or important clients. Occasionally, one is used by Yves' younger brother and partner, Georges, after a long day in the winery - and an evening when the pair drink more than they should.

Andy has been studying in his room and I haven't seen much of him. But on the morning of his birthday, I see more of him than I've seen before.

He is on the terrace minus his shirt. I have nearly finished with the downstairs rooms, so I decide to have a mug of coffee and take him one. Andy drinks coffee like he breathes oxygen, and I'm forever finding empty mugs in the most unlikely corners of his bedroom.

A few of his books are stacked in a pile in front of him on the all-purpose table by the swimming pool. Two are open, but at the moment he's lounging back in a chair gazing up at the cloudless sky. My shadow falls over him and he turns his head towards me with a start.

'*Bon anniversaire!*' I wink at him. 'No walking-stick then?'

'I've ordered one, but they can't deliver until tomorrow.' His lips curl in a wry smile. 'Thank you for your good wishes.'

I put down the coffee mugs and slide one over to him. 'I'm afraid I haven't got you a present. I only found out at eight o'clock that today's the day.'

'That's OK. I'm not going to buy you one either.' His smile turns into the familiar Andy grin. He fingers the mug then raises it in a mock toast. '*Santé!*'

Until now, the books have obscured my view of his torso. Suddenly, he levers himself upright on the arms of his chair and I get a full view of his upper body. My pulse quickens and I feel a warm glow in my insides. I'm trying hard not to stare but it isn't working. His skin is well-toned. My mind traces lines across his shoulders and down his sternum. He has more hair than I imagined on his chest. Lower, where it spreads out in an inverted V over his firm stomach towards the waist band of his jeans, it's smooth and soft.

I'm embarrassed by my unguarded desire and tear my eyes away before he becomes aware of my scrutiny. The damage is already done; any indifference I may have felt towards him has evaporated. Even if I have no intention of going there, I can't deny that Andy Ravel is a perfect specimen of gorgeous manhood.

I snap to attention as I realise he's still speaking to me. '. . . it's too much sometimes.'

'*Pardon,*' I stammer. 'What's too much?'

'I mean the presents. They overwhelm me with presents. All of them do. My parents. Uncle Georges. Grandfather Ravel. Even Granny Douglas - my mother's mother in Scotland - when she was alive - always sent a parcel.'

'Scotland?'

'Yes. Granny Douglas lived in the Highlands. Mother is half English, half Scottish.'

'I didn't realise.' I sit down opposite him. 'What did your parents give you this year?'

'That's it under the chair. . .' He reaches down and picks up a small laptop computer. I recognise the *Apple* symbol on the case. '. . . a state of the art *MacBook.*'

'Impressive!'

'Grandfather is paying for my textbooks. This lot is only half of what I'll need for my final two years. I'm going to have to buy the rest in England. Actually, the computer is from my mother. Well, it was her idea. My father already gave me a lecture. Thank God it was after he'd forked out half my annual fees. About five thousand *euros.*'

While he's in this communicative mood, I risk the question

that's been burning my curiosity. 'Why do you and your father argue so much? Tell me to mind my own business if you like.'

'No, I don't mind telling you.' He closes the two open books, adds them to the pile and pushes it away. He drinks some of his coffee and licks his lips. 'My father has my life all planned out for me. Private school, university, then the business. Because he's the fifth or sixth generation of Ravels to run the *Château*, he assumes it'll go on forever. Do you know, there actually *is* a castle, about a kilometre up-river? It's a ruin but Father won't hear of it being pulled down.'

'I take it you don't want to join the business. You don't like wine?'

Again, the schoolboy grin. It's so incongruous on the face of someone so mature and handsome. 'In fact, I'm very fond of wine, as long as it's in a glass.'

'I thought as much.' I laugh and he joins in.

'It's the eternal cycle. The thought of devoting my life to *that* turns my brain to stone. The endless round of harvesting, crushing, fermenting and bottling would suck the soul out of my body.'

'I get it.'

Andy swallows the rest of his coffee.

'You know, he even had a wife picked out for me!'

'You're kidding, right?'

'Dead serious! Her name's Irène.' He yawns, leans back again and stretches out his long legs. I tuck mine under my chair, afraid of how I might react if he touches me. 'So that's it basically. I told him what I thought of his grand plan, switched my chemistry course to physics, and we've argued ever since. You'll have heard him say he'll stop my allowance. He's threatened several times but never actually done it. One day maybe . . .'

He fiddles with his mug.

'Let's hope it doesn't come to that,' I say.

I remember I still have a few jobs to do, so I hook a finger round the mug handles and head for the kitchen door. He calls after me.

'How do you get on with *your* father?'

22

Perhaps talking of *his* father has begun to stir my own buried memories, or maybe it's the suddenness of his question. With Cathy, I was prepared. Now I'm not. For the first time in years, I am almost overcome by the dull, empty ache of loss. I feel the blood drain from my face and freeze mid-stride. I catch my breath and half turn towards him, keeping a firm hold on the mugs.

'He died.'

'I'm sorry. I didn't know.'

I go back to the table and lean against it for support. The moment passes and I regain control of my shaky emotions. 'It's OK. There's no reason why you should.'

Andy seems not to have registered the hiatus. 'But you have your mother. That's a good thing, isn't it?'

I'm sure he means well but, good or bad, my mother is not on the agenda either. This time, he notices my hesitation and puckers his lips, an exact copy of Cathy's gesture.

'So you have your family issues too? Your demons?'

'It's complicated.'

'With parents it usually is,' he says. 'So, I guess it's your demons versus my demons, Nicole.'

It crosses my mind that one day I might tell him, but we'll have to know one another a lot better first. My last thought before dropping off to sleep is to wonder what Irène is like.

**

6.

'So, which universities are you considering?' Cathy pops a chocolate truffle in her mouth and holds the box out to me. She laughs. 'Not as easy as choosing sweets, is it?'

I scan the open chocolate box and select one with a hazelnut on top. Since starting work at *Château Ravel* I must have consumed more chocolate than in the past nineteen years. When Yves is at home, I usually read or listen to music in my room. When he's away, Cathy wants company in the evenings and we watch television together or talk about books, often in English. In spite of my British Council certificate, my spoken English isn't as good as I'd like and I'm grateful for the extra practice. I still catch myself thinking in French and translating, something I ought not to do if I'm to study in the UK.

The teachers at *François Mauriac* tried to steer me towards Paris or Lyon, but I had decided I wanted to study abroad. It was Mme Boucher, my teacher at *collège*, and who kept in touch with me all through *lycée*, who encouraged my ambition. My university education is going to cost a lot of money, so I couldn't afford to rush my decision.

I bite the nut off my chocolate and sink my teeth into the soft fudge filling.

'Not easy at all, Cathy. I did consider Oxford or Cambridge. I'm just not sure they're right for me.'

Cathy licks her lips and takes another truffle, the last one in the box. 'Any particular reason? You have all the right qualifications.'

'I think it's a matter of fitting in. You know, Oxbridge is the heart of the English establishment. It's OK for somebody like Andy who's half English already and bilingual. It'd be different for me. I'll have to work extra hard on the social side. On the language too, as well as the course work.'

She rolls the sweet around her mouth. 'That's a problem every foreign student has, I think. Take me, for example. A year at Manchester, then straight to Paris on a scholarship.'

Cathy seems such a comfortable and confident person that I didn't consider what it might have been like for her - that she might have wrestled with the same problems as me.

'Everyone is different,' she says. 'I think you'll fit well into the social climate anywhere. I did. Andy didn't find it so easy, you know. Even in Paris. When he went there, he had no social skills whatever.' She ruffles her hair. 'A year or two out would have done him the world of good.'

He's twenty-three years old and she still worries about him. I guess it's what mothers do.

'He's not that bad!'

'He's come a long way, I have to admit.' She grins at me like a schoolgirl. As with the laugh, it's not unlike the grin Andy gives me from time to time, so maybe he has more of her genes than his father's. 'Especially in the last few weeks. We were worried about him when he went to UPMC, being so much younger than the other students.'

'How did that happen?'

'I shouldn't boast, as it was no thanks to me. I mean, I'm no dunderhead but I never had his passion and commitment. Andy was always a naturally gifted boy. He takes learning in his stride and hungers for more. There was no more school could teach him. He began to out-teach his teachers, would you believe? So, there he was at seventeen, with a *Bac* diploma and a maximum pass mark of twenty in science. He was barely eighteen when he took up his place at *Pièrre et Marie Curie*.'

'He got a *twenty*? That's awesome! He's never said.'

'You don't boast about your marks either, do you?'

'True.'

'You realise you're a positive influence?'

My pulse speeds up and I feel the dryness come to my throat. 'I can't imagine how,' I manage to voice. 'We're getting on OK, though sometimes I'm not even sure he approves of me. He bet me I wouldn't last until Christmas.'

'I'm guessing you didn't take the bet.'

'I told him he'd be throwing his money away. That is, I wasn't - I'm not planning to leave - unless you decide you don't want me any longer.'

'That explains a lot.' Cathy purses her lips. 'You challenge his view of the world, that it revolves around him.'

'Do I?'

'I think so. Maybe it's too late to cure Yves of his obsessions, but I still hope for Andy, that Oxford will be the making of him.' She picks up the chocolate box and rattles it. It's nearly empty. 'No more truffles, I'm afraid. Or hazelnuts. Just two coffee creams. We'll have one each. Now, back to your plans!'

The coffee cream is nice and I suck it so it doesn't disappear too quickly. 'My father always wanted me to study in Scotland,' I say. 'He loved it there; we toured when I was little. So, I'm thinking Edinburgh, Glasgow or St Andrews. Probably Edinburgh. I want to study linguistics as well as English language and literature, and they have the right course.'

'There you are then. It looks like you've decided without any help from me.'

'I considered the financial advantages too. In England, fees alone would cost about forty thousand *euros*. In Scotland, I won't have to pay fees at all. What do you think, Cathy? Andy told me you are part Scottish.'

'Yes, my mother was from Perthshire, though I never lived in Scotland. I think you should go for it. Get your UCAS application in. Apply for all three; leave your options open.'

'I've been working on the form for a few days already -' I grimace. '- between jobs. Getting my personal statement right is a big headache.'

Cathy kicks off her shoes and wiggles her toes. 'So, you've been to Edinburgh?'

'I went to a university open day last September. My friend Hélène came with me. We went to Glasgow too, took the train through the tunnel and a bus from London. Then we hitched rides and stayed in hostels for six weeks. We earned some money waitressing.'

'Sounds like you have it all under control.' Cathy pats my arm. 'Look - why don't you take tomorrow off and finish that application? I know how important it is. Go down to the public library and there won't be any distractions.'

'Thanks, Cathy.'

'No thanks necessary.' She smiles warmly. 'Think of it as a perk of the job.'

But it's much more than that. I can still taste the coffee and sweet chocolate on my tongue. It seems sweeter than before. Knowing I have her support gives me new confidence. Another twelve months here, a bar job during my vacations, and I should have enough for living expenses.

Maybe I'll even get used to the Scottish climate.

**

7.

'This isn't a race, Andy!' He's about fifty metres ahead of me and he turns as I flop down on the grass verge. 'You promised.'

We're into the last few days of his vacation. For the past week or two we've been jogging together before breakfast. A twice daily run round the estate is Andy's main exercise while he's home and he persuaded me to join him on the shorter of two circuits. When I pointed out that his legs are longer than mine, he promised to take it easy. I must have missed the rest of the sentence, the bit where he added *at first*.

'Sorry!' He jogs back at an easy pace and squats down beside me. He hasn't even broken sweat while I'm panting with exertion.

'This isn't working, *mon ami*.' I catch my breath and glare at him in frustration. 'You leave me behind every time.'

'We'll go back then,' he suggests.

'No, *I'll* go back. You carry on and I'll see you later.'

I stroll back to the house, reflecting how things have moved on since I arrived at *Château Ravel*. I've completed the necessary 3,000 kilometres of driving with Cathy and now I only have to pass the test. Georges cleaned up old M. Ravel's Citroen XM and gave it a proper service. I love it. The old man isn't able to drive any longer - he's severely crippled with arthritis - and the car was gathering dust and rust in a spare warehouse at the winery. I thought maybe Andy would want it. However, he keeps a car in England and doesn't seem to need one when he's home.

During the school holidays, I spent my free days with Sophie - and Bernard, when he wasn't lazing about with his mates. We went twice to the *Plage*, saw a few movies and even took a trip to the supervised beach at Arcachon. It'll be so much easier when I have the car.

Now the new term has started, I see them only once a week. I don't exactly have a wild, vibrant social life. Most of my school friends have already gone to university. Others have escaped strict Catholic homes to work in Paris or Lyon. Other than Amelie, only one single girlfriend lives in Bordeaux. Hélène is nearly two years older than me. She took ten months to get over a bout of shingles and had to repeat her final school year. After school, she waitressed with me and worked for a few weeks in a department store. She has now taken a job with one of the other wine-growers to help pay for a course at the Sorbonne.

My friendship with Andy has sort of evolved and, despite Amelie's warnings, I see no harm in it. Because Amelie has a boyfriend and Hélène's days off don't often coincide with mine, I find myself more and more in his company. As well as jogging, we've been swimming together - Cathy said to make use of the pool whenever I want. We've also been arguing about books. He's into non-fiction - science and history. I tell him he'll learn more about life if he reads a novel or two.

But Andy's passion is science and he loves talking about it. I enjoy listening. He goes into college lecture mode, breathless, racing on so I can hardly keep up, about light particles, electrons, galaxies, and a host of other topics I know so little about. It *is* interesting, the way he explains it, not like it was at school. I'm even beginning to understand quantum theory. So much depends on the teacher, I tell myself.

Nearly an hour later, he comes back from his run. He's dripping with perspiration. I have eaten breakfast and started on the downstairs rooms. Cathy is teaching until twelve, so I'll be making lunch.

'What took you so long?' I ask him.

He flicks back his damp hair and grins. 'I went around the vineyard twice. The long route. After that, I jogged to St Pièrre and back.'

'That must be all of fourteen kilometres.'

'Fourteen and a half. I have an app on my phone. Look!' He pulls his mobile from the pocket of his track bottoms and starts to show me.

'Some other time -' He has come quite close and I screw up my nose. 'You need to take a shower, Andy!'

'Sorry.' He looks embarrassed. 'I didn't realise.'

'What about breakfast?'

'I'll make myself something when I've freshened up.' He stuffs the phone back in his pocket and takes off. Fourteen kilometres or not, he manages to take the stairs three at a time.

I finish with the living room and conservatory and go into the kitchen to plan the lunch. Andy comes down in clean shirt and trousers, newly shaved and smelling of cologne. His hair is dry and neatly combed back. I can't deny the tiny flutter in my stomach when he pulls over one of the high stools and perches on it. His face holds an earnest expression.

'Nicole . . .'

'Yes, Andy?'

'We're all right, aren't we? We get along?'

'*Bien sûr.*'

'I didn't like to ask you before . . .'

Now, I get a different kind of flutter. Surely he isn't going to ask me on a date. Then I've got to upset him by refusing. In other circumstances it might be nice to go out with him, but I'm an employee. I swallow hastily. 'You can ask me anything, Andy. I won't promise to answer, but . . .'

'Well . . .' He bites his lip and lowers his gaze to the floor. '. . . I can't help noticing your eye . . .'

'My eye! *Mon Dieu*, Andy, is that all?' I'm a bit annoyed he's noticed, but sort of relieved too. When I was little, I had a bad squint. The doctors prescribed glasses with a special lens. They told my parents the fault would correct itself in time, but the turn in my eye has never completely gone away.

'The glasses help with eye strain,' I tell him. 'But it shows when I've been reading a lot.'

'Right!' He's embarrassed and doing his best not to look at me.

'Or chasing you round a vineyard.' I make a face at him and he relaxes. He laughs his Cathy laugh.

'I guess I asked for that,' he says. 'Anyway, you won't have to put up with me much longer. I've packed and am off to England the day after tomorrow.'

'I didn't realise you were leaving quite so soon. I'll miss you.'

'Like chickenpox?' he asks and makes eye contact again.

This time, it's me who looks away. 'Much worse,' I retort. 'Like bubonic plague!' I don't want him to see sincerity in my face.

**

8.

Cathy

Yves chops the tip off one of his prize cigars, clamps it between his lips and lights up. He blows a cloud of smoke towards the ceiling.

'So, what's going on, Catherine?'

'Going on? I've no idea what you're talking about, Yves.' His smoke curls and dissipates as it is caught by the cooler air from the fans. I would much rather he didn't smoke at all. Apart from its effect on his lungs, his blood pressure is already too high. At least he's agreed not to bring his *Gauloise* cigarettes into the house.

'This girl . . .' He glowers at me over the rims of his spectacles. It's an expression he has perfected over the years we've been together, one that tells me he has something profound to say. *Something he thinks profound.*

The look is more savage than usual and *that* tells me he hasn't forgiven my siding with Andy in their last argument. But the wife-husband scales are balancing well. I haven't forgiven him for springing Martha on me, especially not for giving her the office key without telling me.

'What girl?' I ask innocently.

'Your girl.' Yves drags on his cigar and I watch the tip glow red. 'The new one.'

'Her name's Nicole. What about her?'

'She's very young. Inexperienced.'

He is unbelievable sometimes. 'Have you taken a good look round, Yves? What do you see?'

'What am I supposed to see?' He lets his gaze wander around the living room.

'Nothing! That's my point, Yves. The house is cleaner, tidier than it has been for years. You have your usual meals, whenever you decide to turn up for them. You get clean, neatly ironed shirts for your trips. I suppose someone waves a wand and it all happens by magic. Like Mary Poppins! So I wonder what in the name of Christ has experience to do with it.'

During the school holidays, I was as busy as in term time, giving private tuition in English as well as my voluntary work for the *Bibliothèques Sans Frontières*. The simple truth is, Nicole held the household together, cooking dinners and keeping Andy supplied with coffee and sandwiches during the day, in addition to all the other tasks I pay her to do.

Yves doesn't see the little details. 'You've been spending a lot of time with her,' he grunts.

'The occasional evening - when you're away. No more.' I decide it's best not to mention we've spent the past three afternoons shopping in *Rue St Catherine*. 'So what?'

'This isn't about - you know . . .?' He gives me his other frown, the one where his eyebrows come together and his forehead wrinkles. It's an expression Andy has inherited, all pregnant with unasked questions.

I know what he's referring to. Our beautiful baby girl, the baby we lost. *Emmeline*. Yves won't even say her name. We haven't spoken about her for such a long time and this unexpected mention of her hits me in the middle of my chest.

'No, it isn't,' I snap. 'Nicole is simply the best worker we've ever had. She's great company and I like her.'

Yves takes another drag of his cigar and exhales. 'I don't think you should get too close.' He clenches his jaw. 'Maybe you shouldn't invite her to eat with us so often. She'll get ideas above her station.'

'What utter rubbish! I often wonder what century you're living in, Yves Ravel.'

'And there's André to consider.' He goes on as if he hasn't heard me. 'The boy doesn't need the distraction of a nubile young woman in the house.'

I'm not very good with sarcasm but I can't let a remark like that go.

'Trust you to notice *that*,' I say, putting as much bile into my voice as I can manage. 'It isn't Andy's eyes that are glued on her legs every time she crosses them on the sofa.'

Yves lays his cigar on an ash tray, picks up his financial newspaper and pretends to read. 'I can't help noticing she has nice legs,' he mumbles behind the newsprint. 'But it doesn't qualify her as a daughter-in-law.'

I feel like throwing something at him but have nothing convenient at hand. Instead, I glare at the paper. Could we get so lucky? I can't think of anyone less likely to make a suitable wife than Irène Sonnier. Yet the possibility of Andy and Nicole becoming an item never occurred to me. Silly though it sounds, I think he's rather afraid of her.

**

9.

Nicole

The days pass quickly. I fill in my university application and hold my breath as I click the button to send it off. The Head of Languages at my old school is happy to provide a reference.

I watch the hot summer melt into mellow autumn. Georges tells me the wine harvest looks to be nearly as good as last year's. My fingers are stiff after two days of picking grapes, but I earn some extra cash towards my future expenses.

Martha has been around a lot, doing a final check on the cabling needed for her installation. She seems to have an easy life, coming in around ten and finishing by two. Her tight tops and sweaters emphasise her generous breasts while, more often than not, her lower half is encased in bottom- and thigh-hugging short skirts. The band of flesh between top and skirt, bulging over her waistband, is the least attractive of her attributes. I can tell Yves is quite taken with her, much to Cathy's displeasure, and wonder if she has caught him straying in the past.

I passed my driving test! Not only does the Citroen make my job a lot easier but it helps my social life. I can visit my grandparents without relying on the bus and meet up more readily with my friends. I bought a smart phone with my second full month's salary, which means I can keep in touch with everyone.

It'll soon be Christmas. I can't believe I've been with the Ravels nearly six months.

'I knew a Ravel once,' my grandfather reminisces from deep in his favourite armchair. 'He was a butcher. Louis Ravel. Or maybe it was

Maurice.'

'Maurice Ravel was the composer, *Papi*.' I kiss his forehead.

'Was he?' The old man scratches his iron grey beard and beams at me. 'I was sure he was a butcher.'

'Don't pay any attention to him, *ma chérie*,' my grandmother calls from the kitchen where she has been attending to a pile of ironing. As usual, I offered to help but she waved me away. 'When I'm old and decrepit I'll get a maid.'

'I'm becoming forgetful,' grunts my grandfather. 'So she tells me. It's my age, apparently. I'll be eighty-one next month.'

'Eighty-two!' My grandmother leaves her laundry and comes into the living room. We sit together on the double sofa. She's seventy-six, sprightly and alert, while he's slow and carries too much weight. For all that, I've rarely known him to be ill. I owe them so much and will never be able to repay them. Without their help, I would never have made it through school. *Papi's* government pension paid the bills but it was *Mamie* who managed everything. She dealt with my mother's treatment, gave me a bed when I needed it and made sure I had another place to study while I was preparing for the *Baccalauréat*.

My grandfather won't leave the occupation of his former friend alone. 'Louis was definitely a butcher,' he decides.

'Maybe he was, Albert,' my grandmother concedes, 'but he wouldn't be related to Nicole's M. Ravel. Tell us more about the people you work for, *ma chérie*.'

'Well, I don't see much of M. Ravel, *Mamie*. I work for his wife. Cathy. She's been good to me, helping me with my English.'

'That's nice. You've decided to go to Scotland, haven't you? Scotland's very nice.'

'Edinburgh University next September, I hope.'

'And you'll do very well. I have every confidence in you.' She pats my knee then gives me a knowing smile and changes the subject. 'The Ravels have a son about your age, don't they?'

'I don't think I've ever told you that, *Mamie*.' For no reason at all, I feel heat in my cheeks. 'Let me guess: Sophie!'

My sister has been curled up on a fluffy rug at the other end of the room. She's been multi-tasking, reading a celebrity magazine, watching TV and listening to our conversation all at the same time. At the mention of her name she springs to attention.

'He's called Andy. And Nicole likes him - I mean she really *likes* him!'

I toss a cushion at her and she sticks out her tongue at me. 'You have to stop spreading these rumours, Soph. Suppose Mme Ravel gets to hear them. Or worse, M. Ravel. I'll be fired!'

'Why?'

'I just will.'

My grandfather has fallen asleep in his chair with his head lolling to one side and his mouth hanging open. He looks very uncomfortable. My grandmother collects the tossed cushion, rights his posture and places it behind his neck. 'Is M. Ravel a bit of an ogre then, *ma chérie*?' she asks.

'*Pas du tout.* He's always polite, but he obviously thinks a family servant an unsuitable girlfriend for his precious son. He wants Andy to marry some girl called Irène. She's the daughter of another vintner. Maybe he wants to build the business by taking over the other estate.'

'The Durands are as good as the Ravels any day,' says my grandmother. 'And if the young man lets his father bully him he's not worth a *centime*.'

'Oh, he doesn't; Andy isn't interested in the wine business. The house has been quiet since he's been at Oxford. When he's home, they argue like two bull elephants.'

My grandmother leans across and whispers in my ear. She says my eyes give me away and she isn't fooled for one second. I'm always amazed by how she knows everything that's in my head, even when I don't know it myself. I have no idea why I react that way when Andy's name is mentioned.

Sophie has cocked her head, hoping to hear what's being said, and I rather hope she doesn't.

I'd have to kill her!

Andy has come home for a few days Christmas holiday. He stands, feet apart, with his back to the living room window. His hands are stuffed into his trousers pockets. He has let his hair grow since the summer and it spills over his collar.

'So I was wrong,' he says lightly.

I haven't forgotten his bet and glare at him though I know it's a kind of apology. 'Wrong - really?'

'You're still here.' He grins.

'As you see. Are you disappointed?'

'Quite the opposite.' He bites his lip. 'For one dreadful moment, I fancied you'd been replaced by Miss Longlegs.'

It takes me a second or two to realise who he means.

'So you've seen her? Martha?'

'Is that her name? I saw her getting into a car when I arrived. Who is she?'

'Your father hired her to put in a computer system for marketing and accounts. It was supposed to be finished by now but there was a technical hitch. Martha's going to be around for a while.'

'I didn't know.'

'By the way, I thought men liked that sort of thing.'

'What sort of thing?'

'Legs and short skirts.'

He colours. 'In moderation. She has knobbly knees, your Martha. And too much face paint for me. I'm relieved she hasn't supplanted you in my mother's affections. And it's as well you didn't take my bet. It's been an expensive few months. I hope my father's in a good mood. I have scarcely fifty *euros* to my name.'

'Now you know how the other half of the world lives.'

He shifts his feet and turns to stare out of the window at the darkening afternoon; tomorrow is the winter solstice. I reach for the nearest light switch and turn it on.

'I deserve that,' he says. 'Do you have any plans for the week?'

Cathy invited me to the family *Réveillon* celebration. However, Sophie and I have always spent Christmas Eve with our grandparents, and I already told them we'll be there. We usually stay for a night or two and go home on the Feast of St Stephen. *Mamie* would be hurt if we didn't go. Bern is staying with a friend.

Jean will be there with Denise for the meal this year and I'm hoping the atmosphere won't be too strained. They got married in November and Bern and Sophie moved into Jean's place with her after the wedding. I'm happy for them but I still wonder if they are right for one another. The worst of it is, I don't have an official home any more.

Most of my nineteen years of memories, the good and the bad, are bound up in the flat where I spent my childhood. When they were clearing out, Denise found two boxes, one with all my old toys, the other with books I'd forgotten when I moved in with the Ravels. I collected them in the Citroen and now they're sitting in a corner of my room unopened. I wonder if I've made a mistake taking them; along with my buried memories, there are some things I'd rather not remember.

When I turned her invitation down, Cathy suggested we have a Scottish New Year. I've no idea what that involves but said I'd be happy to join in. Since I'm going to Edinburgh, a course in Scottish culture might be useful.

Andy laughs when I tell him. 'So you'll be here for Hogmanay?'

'*Pardon*. Hog-ma what?'

'Hogmanay.' He spells it out. 'That's what they call it in Scotland - *Silvestre*, New Year's Eve. It's a big event there - bigger than Christmas. People used to visit one another after midnight carrying lumps of coal, and toast the New Year with litres of whisky. Mother takes it very seriously indeed. Last year she got very drunk.'

'It sounds fun. But I can't believe that of Cathy.' I push down my glasses on my nose and peer at him over the rims. 'You're kidding me, right?'

Andy pulls his hands out of his pockets and crosses his heart with a forefinger. 'I swear on the tombs of my pagan ancestors. We used to go to Scotland when I was young. Father too. We'd lock up the house for two or three weeks and give the keys to Uncle Georges. But since Grandfather retired and the business took over my father's life . . .'

I puzzle over the changes in him. It isn't just the long hair. He doesn't avoid my eyes so much and there's a new adult confidence in his manner. *He's met someone?* For a moment I feel intense jealousy. I have no right to possess him, yet deep down, wavering between conscious and subconscious, I experience these churned up emotions of desire and longing. I hadn't realised how much I missed his company.

'I wouldn't miss your Hogmanay for all the wine in France,' I say, and risk a light touch on his forearm. He doesn't draw it away.

**

10.

'Taste this!'

Cathy is in a good mood. She pours me half a glass of a syrupy, golden liqueur. It isn't whisky; that has a distinctive smell, one I dislike.

I take a sip and gasp as the liquid burns my throat. It's sugary sweet and, burning sensation aside, quite a pleasant taste.

'What is it?'

'It's called *Glayva*.'

The men are watching me as I take another sip - Yves with his second or third Scotch, Georges nursing his first of the same and Andy with a red wine. Cathy has poured herself some of the *Glayva* and swirls it around in the glass before downing it in one. Georges' wife Beatrice is there too, and their two boys, Gerard and Thomas. As a special concession to the occasion, their parents allow them to join in a toast with *vin chaud*, but no more than one glass.

It's about ten minutes to midnight on New Year's Eve. The small table in the Ravel living room is decorated with plates of savouries and sweetmeats. The atmosphere is pleasant, friendly. Like my mother and me at Christmas, Andy and his father have decided not to argue. And, like my grandmother, who on Christmas day did a wonderful job keeping us all fed and entertained, Cathy insisted on doing everything herself. There are some *madeleines*, and *galettes* with frangipane, but I have no idea what the other items are.

Andy stretches across the table and helps himself to a handful of bite-sized pastries. He puts one in his mouth and crunches it. A look of pleasure crosses his face.

'You ought to try them, Nicole. Only a genius like my mother can do this with haggis.'

'Haggis?'

'A Scottish delicacy. I won't tell you what's in it but these are delicious.'

'I know what haggis is, Andy.' I reach doubtfully for one of the pastries and even more doubtfully put it in my mouth. The coating is crisp, the filling moist, salty and very tasty. 'Mmm, this is not what I expected at all.'

Cathy looks pleased. 'I made them in your honour. I'm glad you like them. Maybe you should grab a few while you can. Andy is rather fond of them too.'

The old-fashioned pendulum clock on the wall strikes twelve.

'*Bonne année,*' Cathy announces, '*et bonne santé!*'

We clink glasses. The two couples embrace. The boys screw up their faces. I look nervously across at Andy, wondering if I'm expected to participate in this round of good will and if he'll try to kiss me. He shakes his head as if in response to my thought then points to the clock and twirls his finger. I've no idea what he's trying to tell me.

Everyone now toasts the New Year, reciprocating good wishes. We used to celebrate with hot wine and lots of kisses when my father was alive. My grandfather would sing *Ce temps joyeux toujours trop vite passe*, and we would all join in a reprise. *But these people are strangers*, I think to myself. *Maybe I've made a mistake coming.*

Georges empties his glass and claps Gerard and Thomas on the head. 'There are fireworks at St Pièrre,' he says. 'Beatrice and I promised to take the boys. It's always a good display. Do any of you want to join us?'

I assume the celebration is over and quite enjoy fireworks, but Cathy answers for me. 'Not this year, Georges. I've promised Nicole a real Scottish celebration. Yves hates fireworks. Andy can go if he likes.'

'Not me!' Andy lays down his empty glass and delves his hands into his pockets. He flashes a glance in my direction. 'I'm quite happy where I am.'

When he has seen his brother and family to their car, Yves comes back to the living room. He's had quite a lot to drink, mixing his liquor with estate wine and *vin chaud*, and is clearly tipsy. He reaches for the whisky bottle and thinks better of it. 'I'm going to bed,' he says. 'Best not get drunk again, Catherine. I don't want to have to get up and carry you upstairs.'

'Spoilsport!' she hisses and switches on the TV, tuning it to the BBC. 'You realise it's just eleven-twenty in England. We have another forty minutes to wait for *Auld Lang Syne*.'

Andy is hovering at the table and has finished off the haggis cakes. I managed to save only three for myself.

'I lied,' Cathy says. She has drunk another *Glayva* and her face is flushed. She skips off towards the kitchen carrying the empty tray. 'There are more in the 'fridge,' she croons.

Andy leans towards me. 'See what I mean?'

'I'm sorry I doubted.' I shouldn't laugh but I do. 'But as long as she can walk a straight line . . .'

Perhaps the wine and the *Glayva* are getting to me too. I decide to stop at one glass of the latter. Now that there's only the three of us, I relax a bit. Another glass of estate wine will do no harm and I pour one. When I point to the bottle, Andy shakes his head. His glass is already full.

Cathy returns with another batch of haggis cakes. She deposits the tray on the table and sags into an armchair with the bottle of *Glayva* and her empty glass.

'You shouldn't drink any more, Mum,' Andy tells her in English. 'Remember what happened last year.'

'I'm fine. Just a bit merry. If you two helped, there wouldn't be as much left.'

Andy covers his drink with his palm. 'I won't, thanks. I don't like it much, so I'll stick to wine.'

I feel much the same way but, against my better judgement, I allow her to fill a clean glass. When she's distracted I mean to dispose of it among the dregs in other glasses dispersed around the room.

Cathy turns up the volume on the TV. The programme is a review of the events of the past twelve months. She switches off. 'I thought there'd be music,' she says, getting up from the chair. 'We'll have our own. Do you know the words of *Auld Lang Syne*, Nicole?'

'Only the chorus.'

'Come on then!' She starts to sing:

For Auld Lang Syne, my dear,

For Auld Lang Syne.

We'll take a cup of kindness . . .

Her shaky contralto ends in a kind of wail as she sways and clutches her head.

'Too much *Glayva*.' She giggles weakly. 'I must sit down.'

She sprawls on the big sofa, utters an enormous sigh and closes her eyes.

'I warned her,' says Andy. 'That'll be her for the night.'

I bend over Cathy. She has passed out.

'We can't leave her, Andy.'

'She'll be OK. I told you, it's happened before. She sneaks a sip or two - or three - every time she goes in the kitchen. She's the model of sobriety for twelve months then, at New Year - this!'

'If she lies in that position until morning she'll have a dreadful pain in her back, not to mention a vile hangover headache.'

'What do you suggest?'

'We put her to bed.'

'I can probably get her up,' he grumbles, 'but I can't manage the stairs on my own. You'll have to help.'

'Let's do it!'

Cathy doesn't stir as he manoeuvres her into a sitting position. Then with her left arm looping his neck and his right round her waist, he hauls her to her feet. She wobbles and I step in to support her other arm on my shoulder. Cathy is a good six centimetres taller than me, about one-seventy-five, and Andy half a head taller still, so it's a lopsided arrangement as we make our way to the hall and up the staircase.

'Look,' Andy says, 'we can't risk disturbing my father. Relations have been peaceful until now and he's paid the rest of my fees, but I don't want to push my luck.'

The room nearest the stair head sleeps three and I nod towards it.

'In there!'

We haul Cathy a few more steps and into the bedroom, where I gratefully release my hold. My back is aching and I have to sit down. I feel the perspiration in my armpits. Andy lowers his mother onto the single bed and joins me on the edge of the king-size double. His shirt front is damp from his effort.

'*Fuck*,' he says. 'That was fun! Now you have the Scottish Hogmanay in a nutshell.'

The expletive makes me realise we have continued to talk English. He seems to realise it at the same time.

'You're right!' He gives me the benefit of a huge grin. 'We don't usually talk English. Your accent isn't bad. Not bad at all!'

'It has improved quite a lot as it happens.' I frown, but deep down I'm flattered by his approval. 'Cathy's - your mother's influence - everyone has to be fluent in English these days.'

'You and me - we've nearly always spoken French.'

'What else would we speak? I *am* French, not a mixture like you. Anyway, *you* need the practice. Did you know you speak French with an English accent?'

'I don't!'

'Yes, you do. Or maybe it's Scottish. Cathy has the same inflexion.'

'I never thought about it. I grew up speaking both languages so I guess the accents just happened. Is there anything else about me you don't like?'

'I didn't say I don't like it. I do as a matter of fact.' I feel the heat coming into my cheeks. Whether by accident or unconscious intent, we've moved closer to one another and our thighs are touching. There are goose bumps on my arm. 'It marks you out from the crowd. Makes you special - unique.'

'That's the nicest thing anyone has ever said to me, Nicole.'

'No it isn't,' I counter, touching his arm and allowing my hand to linger. 'Don't be dramatic.' Though I've recovered from our trip upstairs, my heart is still beating faster than it ought. My mouth is parched. It isn't just the alcohol I've consumed. The fragrance of Andy's aftershave, which I noticed earlier in the living room, has faded, but the lingering after-scent combined with the sweet musky savour of his skin is making my head spin.

I haven't thought much about sex since Henri left. I've been trying not to think about it and concentrate on my future career instead. Now, suddenly, I have this unexpected need to be touched. To be loved. Perhaps it's my imagination but his eyes seem warmer and more magnetic than usual, his lips more kissable. 'Andy . . .'

For a moment I lean into him. On the other bed, Cathy grunts.

'. . . *auld acquaintance be forgot*,' she croons softly and rolls onto her side, '. . . *never brought to mind* . . .'

I leap up and go to her. 'Cathy?'

A drowsy hand reaches up and strokes my face.

'*Bonne Année, Emmeline*,' she mutters before lapsing again into unconsciousness.

**

11.

Andy shows no sign he is aware of my moment of weakness. I tell myself he isn't interested in me in that way. So thank God nothing happened.

He follows me to the door.

'Thank you!' To my astonishment he stoops to kiss me on the cheek. His lips are warm and gentle and waves of desire surge through me.

'What for?'

'Oh, I don't know,' he says. 'Just for being around. Happy New Year, Nicole!'

His face is well out of reach of my lips so, instead of returning the kiss, I touch his face with my hand. 'Happy New Year, Andy!'

Cathy is in the kitchen when I go down later in the morning. She is drinking black coffee and nursing a monster of a headache. Her hair is a mess and she hasn't put on make-up.

'Christ, I feel awful,' she moans. 'Was it you who put me to bed?'

'Andy helped.' I force a laugh. 'Actually, he did most of the heavy work.'

'Well, that's a first. When it happened before, he left me to my own company. I'm so sorry, Nicole.'

'For what? You're entitled to get a bit tipsy now and again.'

'Did I say anything?'

'Say anything? I don't know what you mean.'

'Did I do anything silly? Say anything I shouldn't. I remember Yves saying *Goodnight*, but that's it.'

'You sang *Auld Lang Syne*. Then Andy and I carried you upstairs.'

'The spare room - that was wise. What then?'

'Well, nothing.'

Cathy hiccups. 'Come on, tell me. I did something awful, vomited over your top?'

She looks so unwell that I decide this is not the ideal moment to ask her about Emmeline. 'Nothing like that. Honestly, Cathy, you didn't *do* anything.'

'Oh God, this hangover is worse than I thought!' She clutches her tummy. Her face is pallid and there are beads of perspiration on her forehead. I think she is about to throw up so I grab an empty pan from the rack opposite. She takes a mouthful of coffee, hiccups and then retches while I hold the pan. It's a routine I performed often enough for my mother when she was sick.

'Feel better?' I fill a glass with fresh water and give it to her.

'A bit. Thanks.' She rinses her mouth and gulps the rest down. 'I think I'll go and lie on the single bed again.'

Half an hour later, Yves comes down for breakfast. He complains of a headache but otherwise has sobered up remarkably well considering the amount of alcohol he consumed. I take some croissants from the freezer, warm them up and put them on the table with some cheese and cold meat. Yves wolfs down two and dilutes them with a large mug of black coffee. I offer to cook some eggs but he declines.

'Is my wife still asleep?'

I decide to keep Cathy's binge and its consequences a secret. Hopefully, Andy won't mention it either.

'She's in the room at the top of the stairs. She didn't want to disturb you in the early hours.'

'Mmmph . . .' He grunts. 'I'll be in the office.'

He's scarcely gone when Andy arrives.

'I didn't like to come in when my father was there,' he says. 'I'm glad you didn't tell him about Mother. You never know his mood after a night's drinking. Did I hear you mention eggs?'

'Two or three?'

'Three! Boiled, I think.'

I cut some bread and do his eggs, plus one for myself. We sit down together at the breakfast bar.

'Who is Emmeline?' My curiosity has got the better of me.

There is a momentary hush before he answers.

'I've no idea.' He dips a finger of bread in the soft yolk and licks it. Some of his eating habits are messy. 'Why do you ask?'

'Something your mother said last night - as she was dropping off to sleep. She said *Happy New Year* and called me Emmeline.'

'I can't imagine why she should do that. She was drunk. Emmeline is probably one of her teacher friends.'

'That could be it.' I'm not satisfied with his answer. I think he knows more than he's admitting. Cathy's words and gestures were affectionate, not like between work colleagues. But, I decide, whoever Emmeline is, it's none of my business.

'Coming for a run?' Andy suggests when we've finished eating.

'No thanks.'

'A walk then?' He flicks his hand through his hair, pushing back a thick strand from his brow. 'I'll take you to see our ruined castle.'

'I'm spending the afternoon with my sister.' I arranged it with Sophie a week ago so it isn't a made-up excuse. 'She's staying with our grandmother again.'

He looks very earnest. 'We can walk there and back within two hours. Your pace. I need some fresh air and I'd like company.'

As I'm still feeling the effects of last evening's alcohol, some fresh air might be good. And it's not exactly a date. '*Bien sûr*,' I say after a moment's consideration. 'Give me five minutes.'

I stash the breakfast things in the dishwasher, fetch a coat and scarf from my room and look in on Cathy. She's back in the spare room and doesn't seem about to wake up any time soon. I decide to put on warm socks too then I join Andy at the front door. He is wearing a short, padded jacket with a zip.

'OK.' I take his arm. 'Let's go!'

It's a chill morning and a light mist hangs over the fields. Our breath is white in the air. With the leaves gone and the canes cut, the vine canopy looks brown and bare. Over the past few weeks, estate workers have lowered the trellises and started pruning. However, today, the vineyard is deserted.

True to his word, Andy allows me to set the pace. He leads me off the road and along a track I've never noticed before because of the abundant greenery.

He talks about Oxford, how he feels so privileged to be one of the small group of graduates taking the course.

'It's pretty intense,' he says. 'You know – equations! I want to do research later - maybe particle physics - though I haven't decided definitely if I want to do it at Oxford.'

Soon, our way narrows further until it's no more than a footpath. For minutes there's nothing to be seen except the denuded vines then, suddenly, the path twists down to the right and I see it in front of me. The *château*.

Only a small part of the original building is still standing and even that is crumbling. The remainder is a shell of broken walls, weather-stained and overgrown with wild grasses.

'I see what you meant, Andy. But there's a kind of romance about it - something out of a gothic novel, where the heroine loses her way and is about to meet the handsome stranger.'

'Come on, it's an eyesore.'

'Then why doesn't your father knock it down?'

'It's a reminder - of how things used to be.' We stop walking. It's bitter out here in the open and Andy zips his coat up to the neck. I wish I'd brought a pair of gloves.

'Father likes the old ways,' he says. 'Having that woman Martha install a new computer system is out of character. That's more like Uncle Georges. I think my uncle planned the programme, Father found the woman.'

I stamp my feet against the cold but say nothing. I've already figured that Georges is the more technical of the brothers. Maybe Yves puts a curvy figure high on his list of essential qualifications.

Andy rubs his ears. 'When I was very young he - Father, I

mean - used to bring me out here. He'd point at the ruin. *That's our history*, he'd say. Then he'd sweep his arm over the rows of vines. *This will all be yours one day, André*, he'd tell me. In those days we lived in the house my uncle occupies now, along the St Pièrre road.'

'It would be a temptation, *n'est-ce pas?*'

'Not to me. The first time, I think I was about five or six years old. Everything was so green. Nothing but green. I liked colours: reds, yellows, blues . . .' He spreads his arms wide. 'The whole spectrum. The rainbow. I wanted to know why the rain and the sun made those arches in the sky.'

'So you decided to study science?'

'I think I was a bit older when I made *that* decision. But I used to go to the public library . . .' He breaks off and delves his hands into his coat pockets. 'Look, we should go back. It's winter out here and I'm boring you to death.'

'Honestly, Andy, you're not boring me at all. I like colours too and even a science dunce like me understands the spectrum.' My coat is calf-length and with my scarf and the thick socks under my jeans I'm still comfortable - apart from my icy fingers. However, I don't want to disappoint Sophie. I copy his action, slipping my left hand into a pocket and my right through the crook of his elbow. I lean against him, feeling the added comfort of his body. Right now, there's nothing I would like more than for him to put his arm round me, to taste his lips, to feel his warm breath on my cheek.

'You're right,' I hear myself say. 'Let's go back. I can explore your ruined castle when the weather's warmer.'

'OK.'

Perhaps it's fancy but for a moment I sense he's fully aware of our nearness. I look up and we lock our gaze. His eyes are questioning.

'Nicole . . .' His voice is velvet.

'*Oui, mon ami?*'

'Do you . . .?'

'Do I what, Andy?'

'Oh, nothing,' he says. 'I just wondered if . . . if you had a good time last night.'

'I did, Andy,' I reply as we start walking. 'I did have a good time.'

**

12.

Surely I can't be mistaken. A spark definitely passed between us. I no longer think of him as an innocent, but either he's afraid of commitment, or he has low emotional intelligence. Come to think of it, most men do. Perhaps Andy *is* more attached to the idea of having a younger sister.

I feel the need for a girl to girl chat so I ring Amelie and arrange to meet up tomorrow evening at Louisa's Café. Right now, her flat is out of bounds for sharing confidences. She has made a few changes over the past few months and her boyfriend has been camping there.

Louisa makes the best coffee in Bordeaux. I've been going to the café ever since my father took me as a child. He and Louisa's *papa* used to sit for hours arguing over the political situation. Sometimes, they spiced their coffee with brandy; sometimes they drank their liquor neat. Occasionally, they shared a bottle of wine. I doubt the old *patron* made much profit from us for, after one or two drinks, whether coffee, brandy or *vin de pays*, the subsequent cups or glasses always came *gratis*.

The place still has the same chequered green and white tablecloths, the same smell of roasted beans and freshly-baked macaroons. And Louisa has the same welcoming smile. She lost her mother when she was eleven. Now the old man, Gaston, has gone too and Louisa runs the establishment with the help of a part-time waitress; I used to do shifts there for pocket money.

When I arrive at the café Amelie is already there. I order an espresso and join her at our favourite table. She is drinking vermouth rather than coffee and trying to spike a cherry that has fallen off the cocktail stick. She pulls it out and licks it.

My gaze falls on her glass. 'What are we celebrating, Amm?'

'Hard day.' Amelie flicks a hand through her silky auburn hair. I've always envied her its colour and texture. 'I needed some extra stimulation. But what about you? You're not wearing your glasses.'

'I don't need them except for driving and reading. And you know my eye's OK when I get enough sleep.'

She throws me a sly look. 'Maybe you left them off for a different reason. A certain physics student maybe . . .'

I shrug. 'He doesn't seem to care one way or the other.'

Louisa brings my coffee. She has put one of her wrapped macaroons in the saucer. Amelie asks her for a *grande crème*.

'Boyfriend talk?' says Louise and beams down at us. 'I'll bring the other coffee. I won't interrupt.'

When we're alone again, Amelie slurps the dregs of her vermouth. 'That's a problem? I thought you'd settled on being just good friends.'

'Still undecided! I think Andy would've liked a sister, so maybe I'm a substitute. We get on. At an intellectual level anyway.'

'*At an intellectual level* - what the hell does that mean? Can you hear yourself, Nica?'

I don't know how else to put it, so I give her a *précis* of what happened on New Year's Eve. 'I nearly kissed him, Amm. Then there was the way he kissed me at the door - on the cheek. It wasn't about sex but it was nice. Intimate - more sexy than sex. And again, yesterday, I had the same feeling, that there's more than friendship between us. But I got nothing back.'

'You have to decide what you want. Is it sex, something more, or are you happy with the status quo? The friendship? You're not exactly a novice, Nica. I mean, even if you ignore that schoolgirl crush, there was Henri . . .'

I'm about to say something when she clamps her hand round my arm.

'*Mon Dieu*, you did actually *do* it with Henri, didn't you?'

'Of course we did it,' I snap, trying to ignore the heat building in my face. Henri was no Casanova. He wasn't much of a conversationalist either, unless the subject was cars or rugby. We had feelings for one another but I can't honestly think of our time together as friendship. 'That was different, Amm.'

'How different?'

'Henri was very physical. Andy is . . . would be . . . I don't know . . . more considerate maybe.'

'You're living in the wrong century, Nica.' Louisa has brought her *grande crème* and she stirs in a sachet of sugar. I've scarcely touched my espresso. 'In this day and age physical is what you get. Most of the time. The man leads - a quick fumble, think of France and aim for the kitty.'

'That's cynical, Amm.' I know she doesn't mean it. Not really.

'Maybe one day when we girls rule the world . . .'

Louisa is hovering. 'Alleluyah,' she exclaims. She hitches her overall provocatively above her knees and drifts back to the counter.

'Honestly, Amm,' I say, 'I don't think men have to dominate all the time. You don't either. Why can't they allow us to dictate the pace? I'd like to experiment, to try something different. Remember the book we looked at when we were fifteen?'

'The *Kama Sutra*. How could I forget? Your eyes were popping out of your head and your face was the colour of Shiraz.'

'And your tongue was nearly on the carpet. I thought you were going to bite it off.'

'We couldn't believe the human body capable of those contortions.'

I passed through my early teens amidst a confusion of old wives' tales about sex and babies. My mother, whilst giving me the obligatory lecture about *growing up*, and the obligatory warnings about pregnancy, always evaded my awkward questions and I was thrown back on the myths and half-truths of schoolgirl chatter. *Mamie* helped a bit, though she has old-fashioned ideas about sex before marriage.

The flowering of my sensuality I owe to Amelie. She grew up in a close-knit family of two loving parents and two big sisters. The elder married at eighteen and by the time Amelie reached her teens, the younger was in a relationship and taking the pill at sixteen. At fifteen, Amelie fell madly for a boy two years older, and lost her virginity in his bedroom.

'It's like nothing you can imagine, Nica,' I remember her confiding, when we were huddled in a corner away from the other students. 'You think it's impossible, but then he does it and there's this amazing feeling.'

I wondered if it hurt.

'It does the first time - a bit. But you get all shivery - I don't know - like tingly all over. Then you want it more and more.'

Amelie has a way of telling a story with gestures and I squirmed as she elaborated her experience.

'We hadn't thought of *capôtes*. We didn't have them so he pulled it out and squirted all over me.'

'*La vache!*' I let out a screech of disbelief and we both doubled over with laughter.

The café is filling up and a middle-aged couple take the table next to ours. I lower my voice.

'Sometimes I feel I'd like to do something daring,' I whisper. 'Something different. Not exactly *Kama Sutra* but, you know, make love in the shower. Or maybe in a swimming pool, or in a cornfield. Other things too . . .'

Amelie sucks in her breath. I can't decide whether she's in sympathy or merely thinks me crazy.

'It's just that I want more from a relationship, Amm. I think anything's possible if it's with someone you like.'

'The old *clichéd* earth-moving thing? You'll be lucky.'

'Maybe. But I want the old *clichéd* thing, Amm. I want the thunder and the lightning.'

'Wow!'

For a few moments we stare at one another without speaking. I wait expectantly.

'And you think Andy would give you all that?' Amelie asks, all teasing missing from her voice.

'Maybe. I know he'd be gentle.'

'Right then.' Amelie strokes her gorgeous hair. 'What about this other girl? Irène?'

'Irène Sonnier. We've never met. I don't think he even likes her.'

'So, it comes down to this: jump him and you might lose his friendship and your self-respect - his respect too probably. Or, you could adopt him as your big brother and never find out what you're missing. There's generally a compromise.'

'Above the neck you mean?'

'Well, maybe a bit of . . . ' She twiddles her fingers. 'Until you're ready. If he's the god you think he is, he won't push it. And if he does - well, you'll know he's wrong for you. What are you afraid of, Nica?'

'Of losing my job!' Her suggestion has much more appeal than either of the other options. 'M. Ravel has very old-fashioned ideas.'

'Nothing ventured, *chérie*. You're not planning to marry *him*, are you?'

'I'm not planning to marry anyone right now.'

'Well then, you have to test the middle ground. Find out if Andy wants the same as you, or if he's happy with the *just good friends* thing.'

'How?'

'You're the one with the *très bien* diploma, for Christ's sake. You figure it out.'

**

13.

I get back around ten o'clock. The night light is on in the hall. A faint odour of cigar smoke floats in the air but there's no sign of activity in the living room. Cathy was out at one of her charity events and may not have come home. I make my way up the staircase. A light shows through the slit at the bottom of Andy's door so I tiptoe past. I need some time on my own and don't want him surprising me. Amelie's advice has my head spinning.

Once in my room, I kick off my shoes, lie on the bed and grab a magazine from the bedside table. I flick through the pages. It offers a distraction while I mull over the options. What middle ground is there? With three or four years of university looming, do I *want* a relationship, especially a long-distance one?

My head tells me one thing, my heart another. *Pulling me apart.*

I yawn. My eyelids flicker and gradually the magazine slips from my fingers.

I'm running towards the café, swinging my satchel. Disappointment, always disappointment. I'm searching for my father, but in his place is a stranger. The old patron, apologising. The smell of brewing coffee but with the taste of blood. Sometimes Louisa too, but a younger Louisa, before she'd put on weight round the hips.

Then a dark corridor, a lit room at the end. A closed door. Hammering. Screaming . . . I can't remember . . . why can't I remember?

I wake with a headache. I'm lying fully clothed on top of a crumpled bedspread, my knees pulled up to my chin. The bed light is still on. The magazine I was thumbing has fallen on the floor. Someone is knocking on my door.

'Nicole!'

It's Cathy's voice, clear but hushed. I sit up, scramble to my feet and grab my phone from the bedside table. It's one-fifteen. My head is pounding and my heart is beating faster than normal.

I cross the room and yank open the door.

'Is everything OK, Nicole?' She's breathing hard. So am I.

'Yes. Why?'

'I thought I heard you scream.' She's eyeing up my dishevelled state. 'Late sitting,' she says. 'I got home a few minutes ago and was on my way upstairs.'

I rub the sleep from my eyes. 'I fell asleep in my clothes. Must have been dreaming. Sorry.'

'No, I'm sorry I disturbed you. So long as you're OK. You can always confide in me - you know, if anything is wrong.'

'Of course.' The details of the nightmare have faded. I don't have them often, and it's the first since I came to *Château Ravel*. 'I'm OK, Cathy, honestly. A bit of a headache, that's all. Too much espresso coffee, I think.'

When I'm alone, I pop a couple of painkillers with a glass of water and in the morning my headache has gone. I haven't decided what to do about Andy but my first thought is, I'll have to be quick. He's going back to Oxford two days from now and I can't expect him home for at least two to three months.

I don't see him until eleven in the morning. He stays in his room, either studying or packing, which means I can't finish vacuuming upstairs. So, after taking a break, I head back along the corridor and tap on his door. He throws it open and beckons me in while jiggling with the handle.

'I thought I'd clean up. The place was a mess.' He gives me one of his best smiles. 'The carpet needs a quick run-over but everything else can stay in its place until after I've gone.'

The room is tidy, tidier than I've ever seen it while he's been at home.

'What's got into you, Andy?' I plug in the vacuum while he waits, still wrestling with the door handle.

'Actually, I wanted to talk to you. I had a call from an old school friend - Pawson. He's a mongrel like me. English father, French mother.'

'*Pau-sonne*? Is that his real name?'

'Boys' school-speak. P-A-W-S-O-N. His Christian name's Alain. We haven't seen one another for a while and he's asked me to spend a couple of nights with him. In Lyon. So, I'm leaving this afternoon.'

His news comes like a punch in the face. 'You're leaving today?'

'All packed as you can see.' He gestures towards the suitcase on the floor by the wardrobe. 'But there was something else too . . .' He reddens. 'It's about New Year's Day.'

My heart gives a little flutter like it does every time he turns those liquid brown eyes on me. This time, the sensation wanders down into my abdomen.

'You can always talk to me, Andy. But maybe we should do it somewhere else. Let me finish up here and we'll meet downstairs.'

'Right,' he says. 'That might be best.'

Fifteen minutes later, we're sitting in wicker chairs in the conservatory. It's bright outside, but cold, and I'm glad I switched on the radiator. Andy has made coffee but I had enough yesterday at Louisa's and wave away the mug he offers me.

'OK, Andy, you wanted to talk.'

'Well . . .'

'*Dis moi.*'

'New Year's Day was weird, the way we finished up, putting my mother to bed. And later too, when we were out walking. I don't always know the right thing to say, and I haven't many friends. Girlfriends, I mean. I haven't had many girlfriends.'

'I kind of guessed that, *mon ami*.'

'It's not a good time with all my studies and research.'

'I know. But too much work is a bad thing if you never relax.'

'I do relax. Well, I try anyway.'

I'm getting strange vibes from him, the sort that tell me we're getting away from the subject he's intent on discussing. At the same time, I feel prickling on my arm. I take off my glasses and stuff them in the pocket of my overall.

Andy begins fidgeting and drums his fingers on his chest. He gets up and goes towards the sliding doors to the terrace. 'Last term, there was this girl - Margie.'

'I don't want to know about your love life, Andy.'

'We broke it off.' He gives a nervous laugh. 'We went out for a while, nearly two months. Margie said I was *immature*. That was why we split up.'

'Why are you telling me this, Andy?' I follow him across the room. We stand side by side looking out at the swimming pool, now covered over for the winter.

'I just wanted you to know.' He blushes. 'There's no one in my life right now.'

'I see.' I turn towards him, sneak him a smile and pat him on the arm, letting my eyes wander over him from crown to toe. Now the heat is coming into *my* cheeks. I have butterflies.

'Look, will you call me, Nicole? Will you text me when I'm in Oxford?' He blurts it out, catching me off guard.

'Of course. We're friends, aren't we?'

'I wondered if we were more than friends.'

'More than friends?' Again, there's that spark between us and my legs grow weak. My pulse is already racing. Is this Amelie's middle ground, I wonder? 'I don't know. Are we?'

'Maybe. I wanted to ask . . . would you have kissed me - upstairs, on Hogmanay, when we put Mother to bed? I thought you were going to . . . then she woke up.'

'If that's what you thought, why didn't you kiss me?'

His eyes widen. 'I don't know. It never seemed right before.'

'Because I'm an employee?'

'I didn't say that. I meant, we're friends and I was . . .' He inches closer and his breath fans my forehead. Another spark ignites as he touches my upper arm, gentle, caressing. The butterflies flap their wings insistently. 'Maybe it's the English part of me waiting for permission. I think I'd have liked you to . . .'

'Shut up, Andy!' I'm a good twenty centimetres shorter and

wear flat shoes so I reach up on tiptoe and put my palms against his cheeks. I lean into him and kiss him gently on the mouth. His breath smells of a mixture of sweet black coffee and peppermint.

'That was nice.' I pull away from him. 'You're not so innocent after all.'

'I guess not.' He gives me the boyish grin. 'You caught me by surprise. Maybe we should do it again.'

He puts an arm round my shoulders. His other hand sneaks to the back of my head, his fingers enmeshing with the hair above my neck. He bends toward me. Our lips connect. Trembling, I press against him and feel him respond. Our tongues meet and my hormones do a somersault.

Kissing him is more than nice. I can feel his rapid heartbeat. Mine is in overdrive and a thrill of intense pleasure passes through me as his body moulds into mine. Countless seconds elapse before I squirm out of his embrace and push him away.

'No, this isn't right. I didn't mean we should . . .'

'What?'

I put my hands to my face. It's burning. I take a deep breath and exhale sharply. 'Make it so real. It was nice, kissing you. But you lied to me about your experience. Or lack of it!'

'It wasn't a lie, Nicole.' He looks hurt. 'I hate pretence. It's only that I haven't had much luck with relationships.'

'You'll get me into trouble and I need this job. Maybe when you get back from Oxford we can talk about what just happened.'

'That won't be at least until spring.'

'You asked me to keep in touch.' I smooth down my overall, take my glasses from the pocket and fit them on my nose. 'I will. Will you?'

'Yes, but . . .'

'I have things going on in my life too, Andy. We both need to think about what we're getting into here, before we get into it. Maybe it was the wine and the *Glayva* - maybe not - but, for the record, you're right! I would have kissed you if your mother hadn't called out. That's all I'm saying now.'

He nods as if he understands then asks if I'll drive him to the airport. On the way, we avoid mentioning the kisses. For a while neither of us says anything at all. Andy pushes back the passenger seat as far as it will go and stretches out with his eyes closed. As we head into Merignac, he comes alive and touches me gently on the shoulder.

'We both have issues right now,' he says. 'I get it. But whatever happens, I want us always to be honest with one another. You need to ask my mother about Emmeline.'

I glance at his face in the mirror. He's doing that thing with his eyebrows, where they meet in the centre, and he looks so unhappy. 'What do you mean, Andy?' I had nearly forgotten the incident. 'What's wrong? Who is Emmeline?'

He shakes his head. 'Ask her! It's time all that stuff came out into the open.'

I pull up at *Departures* and he gets out to retrieve his luggage from the boot. I follow him to the rear of the car, braving the glare of an on-duty policeman. I smile sweetly and sign I'm not waiting. Andy leans down and before I can object - or react - presses his lips against mine.

'On account,' he whispers, and in a heartbeat is through the entrance, leaving me dangling and bewildered.

Of course, it's too late to take anything back - the words, the kisses, the promises. I've probably made things worse rather than better. My feelings about Andy were already all churned up inside and now he's confused too. Yet whether he thinks of me merely as an employee or not, I am one.

But I *can* think about it - about what we said and did, about his hand on my spine, and I imagine it drifting lower, clasping my bottom and pulling me against him. I imagine him rucking up my overall, unbuttoning it, touching my breasts. *His practised fingers brush my nipples. His expert hands explore my belly, my hips, my thighs, delving deep, exciting my wildest desires. I feel the heat of passion, the thrill of intimacy.* It's fantasy, but in fantasy there are no rules.

Now he's in every crazy, erotic daydream. Would he, I

wonder? Would I?

Andy on his knees at my feet - he hooks his fingers in the band of my panties, removes them and casts them aside. I thread my fingers through his soft hair and pull him against me. He kisses me, explores me with his mouth, with his tongue. My body aches, the blood thuds in my ears and my core throbs with need of him. I feel weak, dizzy, unable to breathe, and surrounded by a velvety darkness which promises oblivion or bliss.

These are fantasies beyond experience, far beyond the wildest tales of my schoolgirl years. I come to my senses, hot all over, my thighs damp from the memory of my imaginings.

But it isn't only fantasy. Now that he has gone, Andy is my last thought before falling asleep and my first when I wake in the morning. I relive the best summer days, I replay our conversations and, above all, I remember the touch of his lips on mine.

All of a sudden, I'm empty of reason but filled with longings that for six months I've tried to suppress. My resolve is weakening. Something new is happening, something wonderful, frightening and inviting. I'm being trawled into a net of my own making, and from which there may be no escape.

But I don't want to escape. Since those kisses, I've never been so certain of anything in my life: I want Andy Ravel and don't think I'll want anyone else as long as I live.

I'm madly, hopelessly in love with him.

**

14.

'You did what?' Hélène is incredulous. 'What happened then?'

'Nothing *happened*. I kissed him.' I give her some details. 'There's nothing more to tell.'

'Wait a sec.' Amelie is trying to look shocked, but she has a wicked gleam in her eye. 'You kissed *him*? Not the other way around? That's pretty full on.'

The three of us are together at Louisa's, eating *crêpes* and celebrating my birthday. Though being twenty means I'm no longer a teenager, I don't *feel* any different. My mother sent me a parcel in the mail, a bottle of my favourite fragrance, *Insolence*, a framed photograph of her and Jean on honeymoon in Spain, and a CD from Bernard and Sophie. Cathy gave me a copy of a new book of short stories by Margaret Atwood.

'Well, no,' I say, remembering how it was. 'He was trying to tell me about his awful love life - I think. I told him to shut up and kissed him.'

Amelie puts her hand over mine. 'You found the middle ground then?'

I just nod.

'You truly like this boy?' Hélène clasps my opposite arm and squeezes. 'That's awesome. Does he like you back?'

'As Amm says, *middle ground*. I think he does, more than just a friend, but I can't be sure.'

'Sounds to me like he wants to take it all the way. He kissed you again at the airport.'

'A goodbye peck doesn't count.'

'I'd go for it if I were you,' says Hélène. 'He's stinking rich, isn't he? You know these Ravels are Bordeaux aristocracy.'

'That's it, Lena,' I acknowledge. 'I don't want the Ravels to think I'm after . . . What do you mean, aristocracy?'

Hélène rises to the occasion, a story already on the tip of her tongue. She squeezes my arm again. 'It isn't that the Sonniers - the people I work for - actually *talk* to me. But I overhear things. Five or six generations ago, the Ravel family had a title apparently - *duc* or *marquis* or something.'

'It's the first I've heard of it. Anyway, titles aren't allowed in France.'

'I think they meant before the Revolution.'

Amelie pushes back her hair. 'Go on, Lena, you can't leave it at that. What can you tell us?'

Hélène's exuberance can be overwhelming. She accepts the challenge, lowering her voice to a quiet hiss. 'Not much, except way back, like a century ago, there was a big scandal.'

'What sort of scandal?'

'Well, one of the Ravels, a younger brother, got into trouble. Stole some money and gambled it away. He went to prison. The parents disowned him. They kicked him out of the family home.

'Seems it split the family. There was a sister who thought the younger brother had been treated unfairly. She left home too and married a rival estate owner to spite them.'

'That's just gossip, Lena!' She hasn't let go of my arm and I wrench it away. But I remember what my grandfather said and wonder if there's a connection somewhere.

'That's what I heard.'

'You never told me you worked for the Sonniers.'

'Didn't I?'

'It means we work on adjoining estates.' I think back to the first time I heard the name mentioned. Cathy was talking about our neighbours and used the surname of Andy's supposed fiancée. *He'll marry Irène Sonnier over my dead body*, she said and I laughed with relief.

'Do we? What a weird coincidence. I didn't realise . . .' Hélène screws up her face. 'I wish my employers were as nice as yours seem to be, Nica.'

We're starting on our second round of *crêpes*. 'Are the Sonniers so awful?' I ask.

'They're incomers. New money. Anna - Mme Sonnier - is a tyrant. Marcus, the oldest son, is all right, I suppose. I see him occasionally. Lives in the city and looks after the financial side of the business. M. Sonnier, the father, deals with the trade along with the younger son, Paul. Paul's the sneaky one. He never looks you direct in the face. I don't like him much.'

'What about Irène?'

She looks puzzled. 'I've never met an Irène.'

'That's odd.' I look across at Amelie, who rolls her eyes. 'There definitely is an Irène.'

'Maybe there *are* two Sonnier families.' Amelie suggests.

'I don't think so.' Another idea is forming in my mind. 'I don't suppose you've heard the name Emmeline mentioned.'

'Emmeline? No. Do you want me to find out?'

'It doesn't matter. Don't lose your job on my account. In fact, I positively forbid it!'

Perhaps I should leave well alone but I'll feel disloyal to Andy if I don't ask. I have to choose my moment and I don't have to wait too long for it.

Next morning but one, there's a package for me in the mail. The box is about a metre long and six centimetres by twelve in cross section. I take it into the kitchen, tear out the metal staples holding it together and open it with growing curiosity. My birthday was two days ago and I'm not expecting any more presents.

Inside the box is a carved wood walking stick with a carved bone handle. There is even a gold band round it near the top. I feel my face break into a grin. He hasn't messaged me yet but at least he's been thinking about me. Cathy must have told him about my birthday.

'What's so funny?' My employer peers into the open box. 'That's beautiful! Who is it from?'

'It's a present from Andy,' I tell her.

'A walking stick?'

There is also a note inside, the sort of private message sellers allow you to put with a gift. It's in English:

Mandatory for entrance to the Society of Ancient Hobblers. Enjoy.

Cathy is still hovering and I hold the note so she can read it. 'That boy has the strangest sense of humour,' she says. 'I don't get it.'

'It'll take too long to explain.' I laugh. I feel all warm inside. He remembers - that morning at the breakfast bar, when I made him a salami sandwich.

'I won't ask then,' says Cathy. 'I have some homework marking to do.' She heads for her den but stops at the door and comes back into the kitchen. Her face is creased in smiles. 'A walking stick of all things,' she exclaims and has a fit of the giggles. 'You two seem to have more in common than I expected. The way you both handled my little episode at New Year was masterly. Yves never suspected a thing.'

'About that.' I replace my present in its box and give her all my attention. 'You did say something rather weird when you were - '

'- under the influence of *Glayva*?' She is still smiling. 'Go on, tell me. It can't be any worse than a drunken rendering of *Auld Lang Syne*.'

'Emmeline,' I say. 'You called me Emmeline!'

Her smile vanishes and her face clouds over. She clenches her jaw. I have occasionally seen Cathy annoyed but never truly angry. I wonder what I've said to make her so now. But it takes me only a second or two to realise the look on her face isn't anger but pain. And for several seconds more she stands staring at an invisible spot on the opposite wall.

'Cathy?'

She seems quite unable to speak but, gradually, her face relaxes. She blinks - once, twice and as she does, tears begin to roll down her cheeks.

'What is it, Cathy? What have I said?'

She's still not looking at me but vaguely at the wall. She sniffs and wipes a finger across her nostril.

'Will you do something for me, sweetheart,' she says in English.

'Of course.'

'Give me a hug, will you?'

'Sure.' I go to her and put my arms around her waist while she lays her wet cheek on my shoulder. I feel the dampness through my work overall.

'That's better.' She sniffs again. 'I'm just a big wuss.'

'What's *wooz*?'

'*Wuss*, or *woose*: urban slang for cry-baby,' she says. 'A cowardly, timid person. *Christ*, Nicole, what a great time for an English lesson.'

'If you don't want to tell me . . .'

'No, I do.' She dries her eyes on a sleeve. 'Emmeline was my daughter.'

'Daughter? You told me . . .' I cast my mind back to my first day, the day she told me she wanted a daughter, but couldn't.

Cathy has meantime sat down on one of the high stools, but she gets up, walks across the kitchen floor to the window overlooking the terrace. She stares out into the new day. The morning is bright and crisp and a pale full moon is fading. I can see it from where I'm standing, its companion, Venus, sparkling in the winter air.

'That was true enough, but it was an evasion. My usual one.' She turns and faces me again. She's trying to smile but I notice her lipstick is smeared and there are some black patches around her eyes. 'I need to freshen up. Will you wait here for me? If you see Yves, don't mention . . .'

She comes back twenty minutes later having fixed her hair and face. 'Let's go for a drive. We'll use the Mercedes. You take the wheel.'

'Where are we going?'

'St Pièrre Cemetery.'

She takes the Mercedes out of the garage for me. At St Pièrre, we head along the main street towards the church. It's open. There's a mass taking place. Cathy leads me round the back, into the graveyard. We pass several stones bearing the name Ravel, most encrusted with years of grime and vegetation. She stops at one in white and grey marble with gold lettering:

Emmeline Ravel – 1994 - Avec Dieu

A passing bird has left its calling card, obliterating the gap between *1994* and the *Avec*. Cathy takes a tissue from her handbag, bends down and wipes the surface of the marble. 'There! That's better. I'll get rid of the bird shit later.' She wraps the dirty tissue inside a clean one and returns both to the bag. 'I'm ready to tell you now.

'I got pregnant again before Andy was three years old.' She is fighting back more tears. We're back to speaking French and her accent is more pronounced than usual. 'I carried her nearly full term, but there was a medical emergency. A placental abruption. There was no reason to expect it in a woman my age, but they had to deliver. Emmeline was born at the end of December. She lived for three days and died on New Year's Day.'

'I'm so sorry.'

'I was in a wheelchair and attended by two nurses from the hospital when we buried her. Andy was being looked after by his grandmother. A week later, they told me I couldn't have any more children.' She points to the stone. 'Not that I believe in God - not in any conventional sense. But one must cover all eventualities. I was brought up an English Protestant. Yves has very different ideas. He got the priest to baptise Emmeline. After the funeral he refused to talk about her, wouldn't even mention her name and forbade anyone else to speak it. Thank you, Nicole!'

'For what?'

'It's years since the name Emmeline was spoken aloud in our house. I needed to hear it. After it happened, Yves buried himself in work and I was left to deal with the situation on my own. For a couple of years I used to put flowers on her grave, but I got so depressed I gave up even that.

'Andy found out about her by accident. He was eight. One of his grandparents must have let it slip, or maybe it was Georges. Do you know what he said? *I would have liked a little sister.* Yves got very angry and yelled at him. *Well, you can't have one!* Then Andy went about the house crying *Emmeline, Emmeline!* at the top of his little boy voice. Yves got even angrier, grabbed Andy and shook him. He apologised later of course but it was after that they began to drift apart. I'm not sure if Andy's subconscious has forgiven Yves completely. We sent him to boarding school that year.'

A cold wind is blowing across the graveyard, scattering twigs and small debris over the open ground. We've been standing still and despite my coat and winter underwear the chill penetrates through to my skin. Cathy is motionless beside the simple marble. She seems not to feel the cold.

'I don't know, Nicole. Children are so much better at dealing with crises than we give them credit for.' She takes my arm. 'We should get out of here. You're shivering.'

'I'll be OK if we keep walking. You know, he told me - Andy - that it was time it all came out into the open.'

'Andy told you about Emmeline?'

'No. At first he made something up about her being a teacher. Then he said I'd have to ask you.'

'I'm glad he did - and he's right. Getting drunk at New Year was my way of dealing with it. But I have to stop now - stop grieving and just remember.'

We walk back to the car and Cathy insists I drive again. I'm glad when we're inside and I can switch on and run the heater.

'You like the Mercedes?' she asks. 'Did I tell you it was a present from me to myself?'

'No, but it's awesome. So smooth and purry.'

'I'll let you drive it again. Yves won't approve of course but who cares what he thinks? Would you believe, he accused me of employing you because you're about the same age . . . *as Emmeline would have been.* He has the idea I want to adopt you.'

'Adopt me?'

'It's as crazy as it sounds.'

'I should be flattered. Relations within my family can be difficult.'

'Families are like that. You love them and you hate them.

Sometimes you wish they'd disappear.'

    'I guess so.'

    'Any time you want to talk about it.' Cathy pats my hand. 'And I'm a good listener too.'

**

15.

Yves has been home all week and went early on a tour of the plant. January and February are a slack period. This year, the pruning is nearly finished and the estate workers have started on the *tirage* - clearing the wood. There are no visitors to the vineyards. However, there are always technical matters needing Yves' attention. He is probably in the office by now, so I go down to ask if he'd like coffee and something to eat. It isn't part of my job to look after him while he's at work, but I'm in a buoyant mood.

Andy called earlier to check if I received his present. When I answer in the affirmative, I hear his Cathy laugh at the other end of the line.

'I don't know whether to thank you or not.' I can't help laughing too. It was good to hear his voice. 'I'm going to have to buy you one when you're . . .'

'I bought two,' he interjects. 'The other one I hung on the wall of my room so, you see, you're too late.'

'I'm going to miss you, Andy.'

'Like bubonic plague?' he jokes.

'No, this time it's more like . . .' I hesitate. This is as close as I've come to an admission of the way I feel about him. '. . . a tummy ache,' I finish and wait nervously for his response.

'I'm going to miss you too, Nicole,' he says huskily. 'This term is more intense than ever. We have things to talk about when I manage to get away for a few days.'

'Yes, we do,' I conclude. '*Au revoir, mon ami.*'

The telecom company has finished putting in new cables and Martha has started work on her network. The installation should be complete in a few weeks. Afterwards, she'll work part-time with the brothers for three months to run and test it.

When I get to the office this morning, she is there, leaning over Yves' shoulder as he peers at a computer monitor. She's showing off huge cleavage and a great deal of thigh. Her perfume is powerful and cloying. There is a rip in her stockings, at the back, just above the knee. Though she has been working at the winery for a few weeks now, this is my first opportunity to observe her close up. She is older than I thought at first, maybe early thirties.

'Coffee only, *mademoiselle*,' Yves replies to my offer and gives a thin smile. Always polite, he is a man of few words. After eight months in his home, I still don't know what to make of him.

'Would you do one for me too?' sings Martha, without looking up from the computer. She has a silky voice, cold and patronising. She obviously thinks me on a lower level of humanity to herself. 'Black and two sugars.'

I bristle, but not even Martha is going to spoil my day.

'Yes, make it two coffees,' Yves says. He flashes me a look I can't interpret, maybe his way of apologising for Martha's rudeness. 'Please, if you would be so kind.'

I take their coffees then make myself a savoury *crêpe*. Then I vacuum the living room and other downstairs areas, take the clean towels out of the dryer, fold them and put them away. That leaves preparation of the evening meal which I promised Cathy I'd do. At two o'clock I'm finished for the day and decide to go for a jog in the vineyard.

I shower after my run, make up and dress casually. There is no sunshine and my room has become quite dark so, rather than waste electricity, I pick up my new book and go down to the conservatory where the daylight is better. I'm settling into a chair and have plugged in my earphones to listen to music when I see there's a phone message for me.

Andy has sent me a *smiley* with a picture of his walking stick. It's identical to the one he gave me and is suspended on two brass hooks against a plain cream wall. I imagine its carved handle entwined with mine on some lonely forest walk and feel all warm inside. It's going to be impossible to put him out of my mind for an afternoon, far less a half-semester. I have to think about something else or I'll go crazy.

**

16.

Though Caudéran is a classy suburb, on a wet February afternoon it's grey and depressing like any other quarter of the city. The rain lashes against the Citroen's windscreen as I pull up opposite Jean's house. The wiper blades are useless when faced with this kind of weather. This is only the second time I've been here. When I brought Sophie home after Christmas, I stayed in the car. I'm tempted to do it again. The wind is too strong for an umbrella and I'll be drenched before I can cross the road.

I can't deny my mother has done well by her marriage. Most of the families who live here are professionals - doctors, accountants, bank executives and the like. The houses are smart and clean, and separated from the pavement by low walls and hedges. Some, especially those in the neighbouring street I have just driven along, look expensive. Jean's place is more modest, the left-hand property in a cream and white block of two. My mother's car is parked behind a wooden gate to the side.

The coward in me has been putting off this visit. Until November, I kept my promise to Bernard and Sophie and visited them at least once a week at the flat. Denise's conversation was bland, peppered with references to Jean and what a good stepfather he'll make. There was little sense of a warming in our relations. On the few occasions when we met, I had no reason to fault Jean himself. He was respectful and I sensed that, conscious of my feelings, he was backing off engaging with me other than as a friend of our family.

Denise doesn't do feelings much. It's a harsh way to think about my mother, and I sometimes hate myself for it. She wasn't always like that. I guess she buried her warmth in the grave with my father. There were men but, at least until Jean, sex became a response, an obligation, a payment for male companionship. Whatever they demanded she gave, until she drowned in her own emptiness.

At the wedding, I stayed in the background. I was the elder daughter, the grown-up daughter, fulfilling a duty and no more. How could it be otherwise? Denise's new-found happiness only recalled the sadness of my loss and, with it, the memory of what had come between us. Since then, I've been avoiding them. I feel guilty but I can't help it. Today, it's due to my sister that I'm here at all. She begged me until I could disappoint her no longer.

'Please!' I hear the sigh of teenage boredom in her voice. 'I don't see you often enough.'

'When I go to university you won't see me at all.'

'I know,' she says. 'That's different. You won't be able to come then.'

She does have a point. I'm a half hour away yet have used every excuse I can think of to avoid taking that huge leap into my mother's new life. Now I'm finally here outside Jean's house, only the rain is stopping me.

I take my phone from my bag and dial the house number. Sophie answers.

'Thanks for coming. Where are you?'

'Outside. I'm waiting for the rain to ease off.' In truth, it's an excuse while I gather my thoughts. The prospect of facing Denise in her new home still unnerves me. Against that, a bit of winter sleet is nothing at all.

'Just make a dash for it,' Sophie says. 'I'll be at the door to let you in.'

I brave the driving rain and negotiate an enormous puddle as I make a dive for the shelter of the building. My face and hair are drenched by the time I reach the entrance. The bottoms of my jeans are soaking wet.

Sophie throws the door open, hauls me in and wraps her arms round my damp neck.

'Missed you!'

'Missed you too.' I remind her we've seen one another in town twice since the party at our grandparents. We met after school and she took the bus home.

'Wait, I'll get you a towel.' She wipes the surplus water from her cheeks while I take off my coat and hang it to drip on the tiles of the lobby. I notice there are utility rooms on my left, and an open door which I see leads to a kitchen. A staircase goes off to the right.

Denise is waiting at the far end of the lobby. She hesitates before kissing me lightly on one cheek. Her face has filled out since she came out of hospital. With a bit of make-up, she looks nothing like the pale, skeletal creature of eighteen months ago. I soften towards her but she pulls back to avoid bodily contact.

Sophie arrives with a towel and I dry my hair as best I can. It's a mess but I will fix it when I get home.

'*Ça va?*' My mother ushers me past the kitchen into a big living room. I recognise a cabinet filled with ornaments, and a leather *pouf*, but most of the furniture is unfamiliar. The matching sofa and armchairs, also leather, look and smell brand new. There's a table on the other side of the room, strewn with school work. Bernard sits there with his elbows splayed and his hands covering his face. He grunts something but doesn't look up.

'*Ça va bien, Maman.*' My tummy lurches as my gaze falls on a painting that hangs to the left of the door. It's a copy of a work by Degas - one of his ballet dancer studies - which my father once bought as a birthday present for my mother. It used to hang in our kitchen. There are several girls in the picture and, as I home in on the one who is central to the scene, the girl with a pink ribbon in her hair, a dim memory stirs - my father holding the frame against our wall, searching for the ideal spot to display it. *She looks like you, Denise.* Or did I imagine he said that?

'*Ça fait longtemps, Nicole.*' She is watching me and interrupts my thoughts.

'It's not so long, *Maman.*' My neck is still wet so I give it another wipe with the towel. 'Hi, Bern,' I call loudly. 'Problem?'

My brother swings round in his chair, knocking a book on the floor. He grunts again, bends down to pick it up and squints at it. 'I'll never get the hang of this calculus.'

'Well, I'm useless at mathematics.' It occurs to me Andy might be able to help. Bernard wants to be an engineer like our father and is following the science curriculum. 'Don't ask me.'

'We'll catch up in a few minutes,' Sophie says. 'I have an essay to finish.'

She joins her brother at the homework table and I sit down with Denise on the sofa.

'I've been busy. We've spoken on the phone.'

'It's not the same. You know I wanted you to see the house, and to get to know Jean better.'

'Well I'm here now.'

'*Bien sûr*. But Jean's at work. He's a good man, Nicole. Not like the others.'

I think it's a kind of apology, but an apology doesn't quite make up for the past. She has apologised before - for her addiction, for the succession of men she used to attract, but never for the thing that matters. And the fear the therapy wasn't enough, that she'll relapse into her old ways, makes me cautious. I don't want Bern and Sophie to face the sort of rejection I did.

'I promise to think about it, *Maman*.'

That's all I ask of you,' she says. 'Have you heard from the universities?'

'I'm expecting something soon. An offer from Edinburgh, I hope.'

'The Scots want independence from the UK, don't they?'

'They voted against it, *Maman*. Anyway, my fees will be paid by the SAAS.'

'What's SAAS?'

'The Student Awards Agency for Scotland.'

'I see.' My mother frowns. 'What about money for accommodation? Food?'

'I'll manage. If I have to, I'll defer for another year.'

'You shouldn't wait. Jean would help.'

'I won't let him. You know that.'

'You're twenty years old. You'll want to get married soon, so you shouldn't waste any time.'

She says it so seriously that I burst out laughing. 'I've no intention of getting married, *Maman*. And even if I did, another year is going to make no difference. And Cathy has promised I can stay on until September.'

'And she pays you what . . .' Denise snorts. '. . . a thousand a week? The woman has more money than sense.'

'It's nowhere near! But would that matter if you were married to a multi-millionaire?'

'*Point de prise!*' My mother gives a half-hearted laugh. 'But what about your young man? What does he think - about you going to university in Scotland?'

'I'll murder you, Soph.' I glare at my sister. Suspecting I might throw the wet towel at her, she ducks. She's gone too far this time.

'If you mean Andy, *Maman*, he'll be back at Oxford. And can we get one thing clear; he's *not* my young man.'

A ghost of a smile plays across Denise's face. For a moment her eyes brighten and I see the woman - the mother - she used to be. I feel I ought to hug her and tell her everything will be OK between us, but I can't bring myself to do it. Nor does she make any move to hug me. All the apologies in the world don't make a denial or a retraction of the things she said. Of the things we both did. Is there ever going to be a way back for us, I wonder?

She's yelling obscenities, clawing at my face and hair like a wildcat. I'm fighting back, gripping her thin arms, forcing her away, trying to ignore the trickle of blood on my cheek where a bitten, painted fingernail caught me in her madness.

'My medicine,' she screams, her eyes wild with rage. She rips one arm from my grasp and launches herself at me in a fresh attack. 'What have you done with it?'

I'm ready for her this time. We're the same height and build but the sickness has drained her strength and I manage to dodge her nails and take hold again of the flying arm.

'It's not medicine, *Maman*! They're drugs.' I'm panting with effort, barely able to breathe. 'You're hooked on *drugs!* You don't . . .

don't *need* them.'

'I do. I do.' She's sobbing now, angry, hysterical sobs that wrack her frame and twist her face into a mask of feline fury. 'What have you done with them, you bitch?'

My self-control, such as it is, snaps. I've been studying until late and I'm emotionally exhausted. My temper flares. I shake her hard, too hard. 'How dare you call me that. You're my mother, for fuck's sake.' I can feel the heat of blood in my ears, hear the thud of my heart. 'They're gone. I flushed the whole fucking lot down the privy.'

She began taking the pills after my father died - *to help her sleep*. What she was taking three years later was quite different from the sedative proscribed by our *médecin general*. It began with Marcel, one of her many *boy*-friends. Perhaps she was already addicted, but Marcel provided the fuel for her addiction, first marijuana, then amphetamines and hard drugs. She got worse after he left.

I was sixteen and studying for my finals. When she came home one afternoon she could hardly stand. I assumed she'd been drinking and no doubt she had, so I made her black coffee and put her to bed, hoping it was a one-off. It wasn't.

Denise developed mysterious headaches. She would spend days in bed, which meant she missed work. Soon she began staying out all night and was always in a foul mood the following morning. I had to think up excuses for Bern and Sophie as to why their mother was missing. I cooked them meals. I became quite proficient at invention.

At the beginning, I didn't understand what was going on. I misdiagnosed her condition and looked for signs she had an alcohol problem. There was often a bottle of *eau-de-vie* or Scotch on a high shelf in the kitchen. I suppose my father had once kept it as something special to offer any colleagues he entertained. Denise's men friends drank it now. She rarely did; two glasses of spirits made her violently sick.

We always kept wine in the house, a few bottles in the larder, and I had my eye on that too. However, our stocks were hardly touched. I realised later that pills, not alcohol, were the problem.

Over the next few months, the strain of looking out for her was telling on my school work. I was coping but I needed extra stores of energy to keep up. There were the snatched meals, which were more meagre and less nutritious than previously. There were Denise's persistent headaches and the nights of catching her vomit in a bowl. I was earning a little at Louisa's place and I used my wages to supplement the family budget. Bernard was going through puberty and seemed not to notice. But Sophie was hurting. She did not see her mother as often as before, and when Denise was home she was short with us both.

When I challenged her the first time, that she was using, she made light of the whole thing. She was depressed and needed a pill or two to make her feel better. She was still our mother and wasn't harming anyone.

We'd had an especially bad night when I reacted. Denise was sick twice. I had a headache too, and one of my nightmares. When she went out in the morning, white and hollow-cheeked, and Bern and Sophie had gone to school, I stayed behind and searched her room.

She hadn't made too much effort to hide the evidence. There were pills at the bottom of her wardrobe, some prescription, others bought from the internet. There were others in her underwear drawer, and in a jar labled *cotton wool*, along with three tiny packages of white powder. That was when I gathered it all together, swept it into a plastic bag and went into the lavatory.

'*Salope!*' My mother's mouth contorts. She sucks in some air and spits in my face. '*Fucking bitch!*'

I release her and stagger back in horror. Denise's eyes roll in her head. I glimpse the whites, glazed and red as she turns and makes a beeline for her dressing table. She starts pulling out drawers, inverting them and rummaging in the contents, all the while screeching such obscenities as I've never heard in my life.

When she's done with the dressing table, she repeats the procedure with her tallboy. I can do no more than watch as she crawls among the knickers, brassières and stockings, throwing garments left and right across the room. 'I hate you! I fucking hate you,' she hisses. 'I never wanted children. You were just a big mistake!' She scrambles to her feet and heads for the kitchen. 'I need a drink.'

I follow close behind. Maybe she'll go for the *eau-de-vie* - one addiction on top of another - if I don't stop her. She reaches for the shelf but I'm faster. I seize the half-full bottle, pull the stopper and empty the contents in the sink. Denise is ghastly pale, her cheekbones more prominent than ever, her teeth bared like a wild animal ready to seize its prey. Before I can grab hold of her she swings an arm and her clenched fist connects with the side of my head. As she pulls away, a jagged nail catches me again, on the same spot below the eye as before.

Dazed and hurt, I cling to the table for support while my mother stands open-mouthed, staring at the last remnant of liquor disappearing down the drain. A few seconds pass, tense, silent seconds, while I gather myself for a response. She has never hit me before.

'Nicole . . .'

I don't know what she is going to say. I don't care. My life is over and I'm not going to give her a chance to apologise. I hit her back, with all the strength I can muster, the flat of my hand striking her ravaged face in a resounding slap. Without stopping to see the result of the blow, I storm out, slamming the door behind me.

I can only think of going to my grandparents' house. There is no one else, but I'm terrified they won't understand. I've never heard either of them utter a cross word.

The first thing my grandmother notices is my face. The cut isn't bleeding now but my temple is throbbing above my left ear. I suspect it's bruised, perhaps even grazed by the force of the blow. She bathes my face and applies some disinfectant while I relate to her everything that's happened.

'Where are Sophie and Bernard?'

I struggle to remember. Bernard was playing a soccer match; Sophie was going to a friend's house to work on a school project.

'Go get them,' my grandmother exclaims. 'Don't let them go home. Bring them here and leave Denise to me.'

'. . . *he's not my young man.*' I'm back in the present now.

Even a thin smile is a step forward. There have been too few of those in the past two years. We both have to make an effort. So I smile back, trying to mean it.

My mother's smile broadens a little. She winks. 'But you'd like him to be your boyfriend. Maybe you'd like him to be more.'

'There's nothing between us, honestly,' I retort. 'We're friends, *Maman*, and that's all.'

'You're a bad liar, Nicole.'

You're a better one. But I say nothing. I don't want to quarrel with her now.

**

17.

This isn't the way home. I'm in a dark place, a place I don't recognise, a long corridor with lots of doors. The floor is strewn with broken glass. I'm running towards the door at the end and I'm scared. At first, I thought it was the schoolroom, but it's more like a hospital with lots of signs everywhere, and long medical words that are hard to read.

Why am I in a hospital? I'm not sick . . .

'You don't have to be afraid, Nicole,' my father says.

He takes my hand. But his face is so old he doesn't look like my father at all. I break free of him and carry on running. Behind the door something bad is happening . . .

I wake cold and stiff, my night clothes damp with perspiration. I fell asleep thinking about Andy but I've had one of those nightmares again, vivid and frightening. Psychologists say dreams are a mix of old memories and everyday experience, so maybe I should stop digging in my subconscious for reasons.

I've been stressing about university - whether I will receive offers, where I'm going to live, if I'll be able to cope with the language on a daily basis, whether my money will last. I sometimes think about trivia - the food, the climate - books I have to buy. It's all so silly. I already made a list of all the things I have to do and have more than six months to do them. I stress too over the unresolved relations with my mother. February has turned to March and I worry there may be no way back for Denise and me.

After showering and dressing I feel more like a normal human being. I unhook my work overall from the closet and head downstairs to find Cathy in the breakfast room before me. I instinctively glance at the clock.

'No, it's me, not you.' She looks up, gives me a vague smile and gestures towards the coffee pot that's already brewing on the worktop. 'Couldn't sleep.'

'Something wrong?' I help myself to the coffee, noting it's weaker than I make it. Perhaps that's where the nightmares come from. 'You aren't due at school today.'

'It isn't teaching. Just a staff meeting and PMT.'

'Oh, I see. I'm lucky that way.'

'An old friend rang me last night,' Cathy says. She sighs. 'She's another of the lucky ones. I should've been born with a different body - maybe a man's.'

'You mean, have pleasure without responsibility?'

'That's a very cynical view for a twenty-year-old girl.'

'I think I was joking.' I consider for a moment then shake my head. 'No, I've never wanted to be a man.'

'Me neither,' Cathy says with emphasis. 'All that testosterone.' She gives her familiar chuckle. 'I won't be back until afternoon. Can you cope with Yves for me? Get him some lunch? Martha won't be here today, so you shouldn't have any problems.'

'I'll be happy to do that.' I can't decide if she has experienced Martha for herself or has merely guessed about her annoying superiority complex.

'Still no word from UCAS?'

'Nothing.' I tease my bottom lip with my teeth. 'I can't help feeling I ought to have heard by now.'

'You'll be OK, *chérie*. It's still early days.' She squeezes my hand. 'I can feel it inside.'

'I hope so. It's stressing me out, not being sure.'

Cathy has gone within twenty minutes, well wrapped up in her coat and scarf. The weather has remained unseasonably cool.

Andy rings mid-morning.

'Did you find out about Emmeline?' he asks.

'Yes, we went to the cemetery.'

'I'm glad you know. She was a real person - a real human being, although she lived for only a few days. I know men don't always understand these things - but I think my mother is still hurting. Emmeline deserves to be remembered, and not forbidden in our conversation. I have to do something about it. I'm heartily sick of not talking about her.'

'I can't imagine not having Sophie or Bernard . . .' There's a lump in my throat as I imagine what losing either of them would mean.

'I know,' Andy says huskily.

There's an embarrassing silence at the other end of the line before he goes on talking. 'I have no lectures or tutorials next week,' he announces. 'I'm coming home, so I'll see you then. *Au revoir*, Nicole. Don't do anything silly, like resigning.'

I make a lamb stew for Yves' lunch, followed by a quick dessert, all of which he wolfs down in less than fifteen minutes. He keeps looking at the clock as if he has an appointment, but I think his problem is me and not my cooking. Now that I know about Emmeline, I wonder whether Yves and not Cathy is the one with a daughter fixation. I see nothing sexual in the way he looks at me - when he does look at me. Rather, it's the way he peers over the top of his glasses, searching my face or my manner for something which isn't there.

When he has gone, I take meat from the freezer to thaw, and prepare the vegetables for dinner. I clean the big bathroom and then go into the kitchen and help myself to the rest of the stew, enough to cover a small plate. The afternoons are lengthening. Today has been bright if cold, and I take my coffee into the conservatory to catch the last of the sun. I pick up the new issue of *Match* and am browsing the royal blog on Kate and Prince William when Cathy comes home. She parks her handbag on the table by my side. She's carrying a glass of white wine.

'You look chirpier than you did this morning. You must be having a good day. What have you been up to? Did Yves behave himself?'

'He was the perfect gentleman as always. I think he's still in the office if you want him. Oh, and Andy phoned. He's coming home next week.'

'Typical!' She puckers her mouth. 'He never thinks of telling *me.*'

I fold my magazine and show her the page I was reading.

Cathy scans the headlines as she sips her wine. 'You know, I'm convinced the French love the Royals more than the English do.'

We exchange glances and then laugh.

'There's still time for me to do some heavy shopping, Cathy - if you want,' I volunteer.

'Tomorrow will do for that,' she says. 'I want a word with Yves. I'll see you shortly.'

I finish preparations for dinner then head straight to my computer. For the past week, I've been clicking on the UCAS website twice a day between jobs to track my application. Whilst knowing I can do nothing to speed up the process, I need to feel I'm doing something.

My fingers hover over the keys that will take me to my account and the tracking link. As always, my nerves are taut like the strings of a guitar. My heart flutters like humming bird wings.

I enter my details and a mist forms over my eyes when I see I have a message. I open it, hardly daring to breathe. My forehead is damp with perspiration.

Three unconditional offers. I rub my eyes and read the screen again to make sure it's real. The message is still there. I can no longer contain my pent-up emotions and emit a loud screech. There's no one to hear me.

I call Amelie, Hélène and my grandmother with my news.

'I'm so envious I could spit,' Hélène says. 'If I didn't need the money, I'd drop everything and come with you.'

Mamie is thrilled for me, as I knew she would be. 'Have you told Denise?' she enquires.

'She's on my list,' I tell her. *But not until I've spoken to Cathy.*

Andy! With my fingers trembling I next punch his number. He answers immediately.

'Nicole?'

'Andy.'

'People will talk,' he jokes, and I imagine the twinkle lighting up his eyes in an otherwise serious face.

'I thought you'd want to know,' I say hastily, 'I've heard from UCAS. I'll be going to university next year. I have three unconditional offers.'

'Which will you accept?'

'Definitely Edinburgh. I've already decided.'

'Seriously, Nicole, that's wicked news.'

'What do you mean, wicked?'

'*Street-speak*,' he says. 'It means the opposite to what you think. Wicked is good - great - wonderful.'

I reflect how strange a language English is. Perhaps I'll have to learn a whole new vocabulary.

'How do you feel?' he asks.

'Relieved. Thrilled. If you're coming home soon we'll celebrate.'

'It's not happening now,' he says. 'I'm sorry. I'd love to but my professor has called a meeting right in the middle.'

My heart sinks. It's going to be months before I see him again. 'I'm sorry too.' I feel the disappointment in my throat and can only mumble my reply.

'Can't be helped. But be sure to keep in touch. You owe me.'

'How come?'

Andy chuckles. 'You know perfectly well.' He smacks his lips together. 'On account, remember.'

I send an email to Mme Boucher telling her of my success. Next, I steel myself for the conversation with my mother. I'm never sure how she is going to react. To my surprise, she sounds delighted but again tries to insist that Jean help with the money. I tell her I have things to do and ring off.

Cathy is gone for two hours. When she comes back, I'm pacing the living-room carpet, euphoric and quite incapable of doing any housework. I haven't even logged off UCAS. Every few minutes I go up to my room and look at the message, still unable to believe it's true. *I am going to study in a foreign country.*

'I'm sorry I took so long. Yves was in the winery and I had to go find him. Should I deduct wear and tear?' she jokes.

I'm so overcome with excitement I can't speak.

'My God,' she squeals, 'you've heard from the universities! Edinburgh? All of them?'

I nod my head dumbly and before I can get any words out she seizes my shoulders and squashes them in an enormous hug. 'But that's absolutely wonderful. I'm so happy for you. Fantastic!'

She squeezes again, so hard I think my ribs are going to crack. We dance round the room, hugging and screeching until we're both panting. Cathy is quite as delighted as I am and is acting like a joyful teenager. When our excitement dies down, she fetches a bottle of wine and pours each of us a large glass. *Then another.* We toast everything we can think of and, when we run out of ideas, flop down together onto the sofa. I start to cry.

'Have you thought about where you're going to stay?' Cathy asks after dinner.

'Not yet. There's still time.'

Yves pauses reading his business newspaper. He peers over his glasses at his wife, then at me, suddenly interested in our conversation. Maybe he thinks I've got another job and he'll be getting rid of me at last.

'Nicole is going to Edinburgh University to study English,' Cathy explains. 'The beginning of October, isn't it?'

'Mid-September.'

'Congratulations, *mademoiselle*. It is an excellent university.' Yves gives a rare smile and returns to his reading.

'September will soon come around, Nicole.' Cathy wiggles her shoulders and settles back in her armchair. 'You don't want to be left with the raggle-taggle end of the student accommodation.'

'I won't leave it too long. Actually, I thought of going over to

Scotland in the summer but the flights are awfully expensive.'

'That's a great idea,' says Cathy. 'You don't have to go Air France. There's a budget airline from Paris to Edinburgh. Take a carry-on bag and it's even less expensive. Go now. Take a few days. Have a look round before you decide.'

'You don't mind?'

'Why would I mind? University is your big opportunity. Living accommodation is almost as important as the classes. I can spare you. Take someone with you . . . your hairdresser friend . . . Amelie, isn't it? Or the one who works for the Sonniers.'

'I would love to go and Amelie would too, but she has fixed holidays. And I don't think Hélène's employer is . . .'

Cathy pouts. 'Yes, I've heard the Sonniers can be difficult. That's a shame . . .'

Yves looks up again from his newspaper. 'That friend of yours went to Edinburgh, Catherine,' he remarks, '- the one who married the advocate. Marian something?'

'*Miriam*. Miriam Black.'

'A pleasant couple,' Yves says. 'What was the husband's name again?'

'James.' Cathy turns to me and rolls her eyes towards the ceiling. 'Miriam is an old friend from school. She studied at Edinburgh and married a hot-shot lawyer. Destined for great things was James Black. They visited us last spring . . .' Suddenly she sits bolt upright. 'God, what am I thinking? Miriam! Let me get my diary.'

She reaches for her handbag and peers into it. 'Ah, here we are.' She finds the diary and flicks through the pages. 'I like to write things down.'

'Cathy?'

'I have some free days next week. What if I were to go with you?'

'To Edinburgh?'

'Yes. We could explore together. Miriam is bound to know a few people. She could help you find a room, or a flat. What do you think?' She gives one of her infectious laughs. 'Girls' outing?'

I can't think of anything suitable to say.

'Sorry,' Cathy goes on. 'You think it's a terrible idea. I should shut up and stop interfering. Stop trying to recapture my lost youth.'

'No, it's not a terrible idea at all,' I stutter. 'I mean, I'd love to but do you . . . are you sure you want to go to Edinburgh with me?'

'Of course.' For the second time today, she's as excited as I am. 'I haven't been there for years. Let's have a look at the airline websites. We'll check Paris times and see if there's a budget flight to suit.'

We book to travel on Wednesday, spend three nights in Edinburgh and fly home on Saturday. I insist on paying for the flight and overnight accommodation myself. It's a lot of money but this is the sort of thing I've been saving for. Cathy starts to argue but yields on the fares when I threaten not to go at all.

'But we're staying with Miriam,' she announces. 'I called her. She *does* know people who rent out rooms.'

'Private rentals are bound to be more expensive than the university halls,' I say doubtfully.

'You never know. Some say student halls are best in your first year, though I always reckon you should look at the options. You might be surprised at what's available.' A sudden look of horror crosses her face. 'Oh God, I'm doing it again,' she says. 'Interfering in your life. Maybe Yves is right about me looking for a substitute daughter. Just tell me to mind my own business.'

'No, I don't mind some help. And you're right about checking out the options.'

'If you're sure . . .'

My head is still buzzing but I have to get through a weekend and two more days before we set off. Problems, real and imagined, assail me from all directions. I have nothing to wear; maybe I won't like Edinburgh after all; maybe my spoken English isn't up to standard; Cathy is bound to have expensive tastes in dining while I'm on a budget.

I won't see Andy for another three months!

I drive into the city. With any luck, I'll be able to find an inexpensive outfit at *Galeries Lafayette*. I finish promised errands, stow my purchases in the car and head along *Rue St Catherine*. If that fails I'll try H&M or one of the other boutiques in Mériadec.

At the *Galeries*, I find a navy, knee-length skirt for thirty *euros*. It isn't designer wear but, new, it looks good on me - and I have to wear it only once. They also have a knitted cardigan in cashmere, costing ninety-five *euros* but reduced to half price, so on a whim I buy that too. I can wear it over a blouse and chemise, with or without my overcoat. Edinburgh will be cold.

Satisfied with my bargains, I go to my grandparents'. *Mamie* wants to know more about my study course and about my trip. We chat, drink some coffee and I try on the items I bought for her approval.

She puts on her spectacles and stands back to admire me. 'The whole of Scotland is going to love you, Nicole,' she says sweetly. 'You look beautiful.'

'I feel so nervous, *Mamie*. It didn't sink in yesterday that I'm actually going.'

'No need to be,' she chides. 'You've faced much greater challenges and come out fighting. You'll do very well at Edinburgh, *chérie*.'

'I do hope so, *Mamie*.' I hug her fiercely. 'You know how much I want this.'

'Of course I do. And speaking of challenges, how did it go last time with Denise.'

'We haven't talked so much since she came out of therapy. But there's still this cool wall between us. Whenever I think to cross it, my courage fails me.'

'I think maybe she feels the same. But let her make the first move, my darling. I know she was sick but that doesn't excuse her.'

'I'd like to think she's the same mother she used to be - inside. It's so difficult. I don't know I'll ever forgive her the things she said and did.'

'Give it time, Nicole.' My grandmother releases me from her embrace but she keeps a hold of my hand. 'That afternoon I could have . . .' I feel her gentle touch as she strokes my wrist. 'No, we don't want to drag all that up again. The main thing is, it wasn't your fault. Not any of it. What matters now . . .'

My grandfather, hitherto fast asleep in his favourite chair, starts to snore. The noise wakes him. He grunts, coughs and sits bolt upright.

'Nicole, *ma chérie. Ca va?*'

'*Ca va bien, Papi. Et toi?*'

'All the better for seeing you.'

He holds out his arms to me. I snuggle up to him for a moment and kiss his forehead.

'Why don't you turn on the television, Albert,' says my grandmother. 'Nicole and I are having a chat about something important.'

She turns back to me. 'Come through to my room, *ma chérie.* There's something in my treasure box I'd like to show you.'

'Come back when you've finished,' my grandfather says. 'I have something for you too.'

My grandparents' room is plain without being sombre. There is nothing to suggest it's the bedroom of an elderly lady and her forgetful husband, no frilly pink curtains, no patchwork quilt, no dainty pillowcases. They still share a bed, a narrow double, though I know my grandmother sometimes sleeps in the biggest guest room, to escape my grandfather's snoring. They have a chair each on which to fold their day clothes, while the only other furniture consists of a single wardrobe and my grandmother's dresser.

What she calls her treasure box sits in the middle of the dresser, between neat rows of jars of skin preparations and bottles of cologne and perfume. There is a key in a brass keyhole in the top, but I doubt she ever locks it. *Papi* would never dream of snooping.

'Now, let me see,' *Mamie* slides my grandfather's chair across the room. She picks up the box and cradles it in her lap as we sit facing one another on her side of the bed. She opens the box, takes out a tray of jewellery and lays it on the bedspread. She returns to the box and searches among the remaining contents, which I can see consist mainly of old photographs. 'Ah, here it is!'

She hands me a picture, old, creased and with two of its corners curled in. It's of a woman alone with a baby. I'm looking at the child and it takes me a moment or two to realise the woman is Denise. She's a waif of a girl, her blond hair pulled back in a pony tail, the same as I often wear mine.

'*C'est moi?*' I point at the infant.

'Nineteen years ago. Look at her face, *ma chérie*. Have you ever seen a woman looking happier?'

I study the photograph. My father should be there, I think, and I feel a twinge in the middle of my chest. Then I decide, he probably took the picture. I feel my grandmother's pain too. I think of Cathy - and Emmeline. No one should have to bury a child.

The background is a bit out of focus, a wall of grey, roughcast stone. I focus on Denise. She's seems even younger than I am now. All her attention is on the baby in her arms. Her smile is warm, radiant, as she fingers the edge of the shawl at her baby's tiny chin. I turn the picture over. Something is written there: *Bordeaux, 1995,* and our names - *Denise et Nicole.*

Now, as I study my mother's young face, looking down at my months-old self, I feel a new hope rising in my chest. For the past eighteen months I supposed her drug-addled state had enabled her to confess the truth she hid behind a facade of forced motherhood: that she hadn't wanted me; that she hadn't wanted a child at all. Here, in this picture, I see no sign of indifference, and I remember the good parent she was for the first twelve years of my life. Perhaps, after all, we might find the forgiveness and reconciliation which, until now, I've feared to be impossible.

For a brief moment, something else in the picture stirs a memory, but then it's gone.

'Love, you see.' My grandmother takes back the photo and replaces it with others at the bottom of her treasure box. 'As I said, give her time.'

'How much time should I give?'

'Until you go to Edinburgh, I think. But remember, *ma chérie,* sometimes unexpected good can come from a great wrong.'

When we go back to the living room, my grandfather has taken down a tattered dictionary from the bookshelf and he sits with it open on his lap.

'I don't know why I put it in there,' he mutters.

'What is it, *Papi*?' I go over and sit on the arm of his chair and he slides an old black and white photo into my hand.

'Have a look at *that*,' he chuckles.

I study the picture. It must be thirty or forty years old to judge by the faded images and wrinkled corners. It shows four men seated at a table. One is dandling a small boy on his knee. I don't recognise any of them right away but, despite the changes made since the shot was taken, I do know the place where they are sitting.

'That's Louisa's café!'

My grandfather corrects me. '*Gaston's*, it was then.' He points to the man with the boy. 'That's me. Gaston is on my left.'

I look more closely and sure enough I recognise them both, my grandfather a man in the prime of his life, Gaston old even then, just as I remember him from my childhood.

'Is that my father on your knee?'

'That's Jacques, his older brother. Your uncle. The one who went to Australia. Turn it over.'

I do as he asks. There are names written on the back, in positions corresponding to the seating arrangement in the picture itself: *Gaston Laurent, Albert Durand, Jacques Durand, J-C Poulin*, and *Louis Ravel*.

'I knew I'd remember if I thought hard enough,' my grandfather says triumphantly. 'Three of us were regulars at Gaston's. His wife took the photo. Poor woman died soon after. Jean-Claude Poulin was with the postal service. In those days, Louis had a shop around the corner from the café.'

'I don't remember a butcher's shop there,' I say.

My grandfather thinks for a moment. 'Louis bought bigger premises. He expanded the business.'

'You're a marvel, *Papi*!' I hug him and plant a kiss on his cheek. He isn't quite as forgetful as either of them pretends.

Louis Ravel. I must remember to ask Andy if there's a connection with his family.

**

18.

After the warmth of the Garonne valley, Edinburgh is wintry and miserable. Our spring has already arrived. Theirs is not even round the corner.

We take a taxi from the airport to Miriam's home in Murrayfield, a big sandstone house on two floors with an attic. Miriam works full time at the Scottish Parliament, and has three children and two dogs, playful Labradors.

'I've put a folding bed in Jim's study for you, Nicole. He can do without a home office for three nights. I hope you don't mind. There's only one guest bedroom. Now that the little monsters are growing up, they need their own space.'

'Monsters?' I give her a puzzled look.

'I'm kidding of course,' she answers, laughing. 'Excuse the pun! My husband calls them that all the time. I do too sometimes. The kids know we don't mean it.'

Cathy intervenes on my behalf. 'I don't think Nicole understands the idiom. Some English words can be used in a joking way, or to mean the opposite of what's intended.'

'Like *cool* . . . or *wicked*?'

'So you know that one?' Miriam gives me a crooked smile. 'I think *cool* might be OK. *Wicked* is *uncool*, as it were, I'm informed by my offspring. Or maybe it's the other way around. Teenager slang changes week by week. Sorry, Nicole, I'm confusing you even more. James, my husband, speaks some French, so maybe you can have a natter with him after work. Sorry again! To *natter* is to talk - to chat.'

I can see why Cathy and Miriam are friends. They have the same easy-going outlook on life.

'I'll be very comfortable here, Miriam,' I assure her. 'Thank you for having me at all.'

On Thursday morning, it's so cold I begin to question my sanity in coming, never mind choosing to spend the next four years of my life here. The drizzling rain seems eternal. Whenever we are exposed to the weather, an icy wind whips our faces. As we notice from the antics of the passers-by, umbrellas are useless. The extendible ones are torn inside-out easily by the gust; the stronger, fixed kind are near impossible to control. Although I'm wearing a waterproof coat, the chill penetrates through it, and through the inappropriate French fashion beneath. The hood keeps slipping off my head.

We are walking along Princes Street. Cathy is shivering. She planned the morning as a tour of the Old Town but now she looks as miserable as I feel.

'We can visit the sites later.' She stops suddenly, grabs my upper arm and steers me into a department store. 'Both of us need some extra clothing.'

We manage to find a department selling the last of the winter stock at reduced prices. Nothing fits, but I don't care and buy a thick wool sweater to wear under my coat and over the cardigan I bought at the *Galeries*. Cathy buys one too.

'I don't suppose we'll meet anyone we know.' She grins. Indoors, her face has regained some of its usual colour. 'High fashion is overrated - in this climate anyhow.'

I manage to squeeze into my coat and we brave the weather once more. With all the extra padding, my temperature quickly returns to normal. At the next corner, Cathy hails a taxi.

'Lawnmarket,' she tells the driver. 'We'll start at the Writers' Museum,' she says to me. 'As a student of literature you'll find it interesting.'

We wander the museum's exhibits for an hour. Afterwards, Cathy takes me for a lunch of fish and chips in the Royal Mile.

'You'd better get used to the Scottish diet,' she laughs. 'You've tried haggis, so fish and chips are the next best thing.'

Later, we visit the castle. Cathy is as knowledgeable as any tour guide, and for most of the afternoon she acts the part as she speaks of Edinburgh, and Scotland, and how the history of this proud little country rolls along and entwines with ours.

In the evening, Miriam raises the subject of my accommodation.

'There are the student halls of course,' she says, 'but I have another idea. If you don't think I'm sticking my nose in. I phoned Mrs Hunter earlier. She's a widow who works part-time for Jim - my husband. Last year, she had a houseful of students, but she's hot on good references, and recommendations. The place is within walking distance of the campus, and there's parking space if you need it.'

We go on Friday in Miriam's car. Mrs Hunter's is an old property with two modern extensions and three bedrooms in each. Four of the rooms are already occupied but she shows me the other two, one in each wing. There are two shared bathrooms, a communal kitchen, and a common room with a TV.

The rooms are nice, with comfortable beds, each having a table and chair, a closet and plenty of shelving for my books. Neither is as big as my room at Cathy's, but they aren't prison cells either. The smell of fresh paint hasn't quite worn off. The fitted carpet is newly cleaned.

'I didn't take anyone at the start of last term.' Mrs Hunter juts out her jaw and purses her lips. She's a plain woman with short grey hair. 'I learned by my mistakes after three years that it pays to be selective. I had the place done up. They finished in time for me to find three girls an' a boy for the final term. They're a lovely group. Two of the girls have reserved already for next year.'

'I like the rooms,' I tell her. 'Are they all the same size?'

'A foot or two either way, dear, not that you'd notice. The rent is a hundred and forty a week, although you pay by occupancy. The extras work out at about two hundred and fifty a year each when I have six staying.' Mrs Hunter juts out her jaw again. 'Not like some of the private renters I know,' she goes on. 'They demand fifty-week contracts. *Och*, I can always find a tourist or two in the summer months when the students go home.'

'I don't need a room until September, Mrs Hunter.' I'm doing some quick arithmetic. For thirty weeks of term time, I would be paying less than five thousand *euros*. With the money my father left me and savings from my wages, I already have twenty thousand in my bank account. I'll still have to pay for my food, but pounds are cheap now - and if necessary I can always reduce to beggar status in my third year. I'll have the company of other students too.

'That's fine, Miss Durand. If you like either of the two you've seen, I'll reserve it for you. I'll need a deposit of course.'

Cathy is wandering round the premises checking the facilities. 'What do you think, Nicole?' She nods tacit approval.

I swallow hastily. 'How much will the deposit be?'

'One month's rental in advance will do. Let's say five hundred. That'll cover the security deposit as well. Then you can start paying me at the end of October.'

My stomach sinks. I hadn't thought of that. I changed some money at the airport but I have nowhere near five hundred pounds. My expression gives me away.

'It won't be a problem if you don't have it with you, Miss Durand.' Mrs Hunter says. 'What would the world be like without a bit of trust? As you're a friend of Miriam, just send it to me in the next two or three weeks an' the room's yours. If you're interested . . .'

'I am interested, but . . .'

'I tell you what, Mrs Hunter . . .' Cathy fiddles with the catch of her handbag. 'If Nicole wants the room, what if I pay the deposit now? That'll save a lot of trouble with banks.'

'I can't let you do that, Cathy.'

'Yes, you can.' She has a sterling cheque book in her hand. 'You can pay me back when we get home.'

She writes a cheque, hands it over and I have somewhere to stay for my first year. If I can continue saving most of my salary for the next five months, I should be able to cover costs for three years, provided I don't overspend on luxuries. I try not to think how easy it would be for things to go wrong.

**

19.

Twelve more weeks pass before I see Andy again. The days drag. We talk on the phone but it's not the same as having him here. I tell him about my visit to Edinburgh, about Martha's latest outfits and other local gossip. He talks about his studies and about what's going on in Oxford.

As the seasons advance, I begin to see the Ravel estate with new eyes. The wintering buds swell and break. Tiny shoots appear. Leaves form and tendrils snake out, their delicate hooks winding purposefully along the cordon and the prepared wires. They develop and extend, first to sparse greenery then to the promised verdure of spring.

By May, we see tiny flower clusters form. At first - as Georges tells me - the petals are sealed inside their own shell which, rather like a hatching egg, must be shed before pollination can begin. The grapevine produces both male and female parts, and fertilisation is a simple process requiring little help from forces of nature outside the plant itself.

There have been some changes in the Ravel business too. Martha completed installation of the computer system. Sales and purchases, accounts, inventory, even weather forecasts - indeed, all aspects of estate management are now connected by an intranet. Yves has installed Martha in a small office in the winery for her three-month extended stay with the business.

Georges is proud of *Château Ravel*'s new, modern image and explains the system to me. He takes me on a tour of the winery itself, including the tasting parlour. Parties of tourists are visiting the estate soon and he needs help serving the wine and socialising with the visitors. I'll have to sacrifice two free afternoons but the benefit seems to outweigh the hardship. I'm going to have to buy books, a laptop computer and a new wardrobe more suited to the Scottish climate, so the extra income will be very welcome indeed.

As a *Bordelaise* I ought to know something about winemaking, but I'm ashamed to admit I know almost nothing.

'*N'importe!*' Georges shrugs when I confess my ignorance. 'I'll tell you the basics. It'll be enough. Your main job will be to make the guests feel at home. Serve them their favourite wines. There will always be someone from the estate at hand if they ask an awkward question.'

He lectures me for an hour on growing, harvesting, blending and bottling, and about how the best wines are sold ahead in the market. The Ravel estate grows mainly the Merlot grape, and a much smaller amount of the white grape Semillon. Georges is a graduate chemist. He talks a lot about the fermentation process, the constituents of the soil and how that, combined with the weather, determines the quality of the wine. *Château Ravel* is unusual among small producers. In addition to selling more than half of its wine as futures through three *négociants*, the brothers have opened separate direct sales with retail outlets. One of their customers is an English merchant with an office in Paris.

Instead of being bored, I find the subject interesting, though I doubt I'll remember half of what Georges tells me. It helps distract me from thinking about Andy.

As it turns out, I spend three mornings and two afternoons in the tasting parlour. Georges' wife Beatrice is supposed to be there but at the last moment catches a spring cold. Cathy comes to help instead. By the end of the week I'm drained, though the two crisp hundred-*euro* notes Georges slips into my hand is welcome compensation.

I take Sophie to the cinema in the evening and fall asleep half way through the film. When my sister reports back, Denise gives me an I-told-you-so look. Instead of her more-money-than-sense speech, she castigates Cathy for working me too hard. When I explain about my Edinburgh needs, she repeats her offer of Jean's support.

I have seen my mother three times in the past three months,

including an evening spent with her and Jean. She has put on more weight. Her haggard look has disappeared and, since I saw her in February, so have the purple bags under her eyes. She looks more like a woman in her late thirties than one who is approaching the menopause. My grandmother's final words to me last time we spoke echo round my head - that we'll work things out in the end. Though I'd like to believe we could, I'm not convinced it will ever happen.

Those other words, the ones which cannot easily be taken back, are etched on my brain like engravings on a brass plate - *I never wanted children - you were just a big mistake.* And sitting beside that memory is the image on the photograph my grandmother keeps in her treasure box.

At the beginning of June, Amelie and Hélène come on an evening visit to *Château Ravel*. It's nearly a year since I started working for Cathy.

Hélène gives a shriek when she sees my room.

'I don't ever want to play poker with you, *chérie*.' She climbs on my bed and stretches full length on top of the burgundy quilt. 'You have all the luck of a €uro Lottery winner.'

'Shoes, Lena!' I grab her feet and yank off her flex trainers.

'Sorry!' She jumps off and hugs me. 'This is a palace, Nica. The bed is as big as my whole room. Can I move in with you now?'

Amelie doesn't say anything at first. She contemplates the bed then looks at me quizzically, rolling her tongue round her lips. I shake my head. She turns her attention to my walking-stick, resting against the side of my dressing table, picks it up and strokes it. There is something overtly erotic about the way she fondles the gold band and the bone handle.

'I wasn't sure I believed you about this,' she says and glances round the room. 'But, you know, you ought to display it better . . . '

'Andy has his on a wall.'

'There you are then!'

'You know your fate is sealed?' Hélène says. 'No man would give a girl a present then buy the same thing for himself unless he was in love with her.'

'Be serious, Lena. The walking-sticks were a joke.'

'Not to him, *chérie*. Lena's right.' Amelie sets my walking-stick on top of the bookcase, propping it up on the two underused bookends. 'There . . . you can see it now. These aren't walking sticks, Nica. They're symbols of undying love, even if he doesn't know it yet.'

**

20.

I'm half-way down the stairs and finishing my phone call when Cathy comes into the hall. She can only have heard the last few words on my side, but enough for her to guess it's Andy and that he has asked me to pick him up at the airport.

'You don't have to, Nicole.' It's not quite midday and she's still wearing a baggy tracksuit and slippers.

'I'm happy to go, unless you want me for something else. He's at Merignac now. He'll go for a bite to eat and wait for me.'

'He must have been up before dawn to manage that.'

'He stayed overnight in London.'

'He ought to make his own way. Take a taxi, or a bus.' She looks down at her attire and shrugs. 'But if you don't mind . . .'

She offers me the Mercedes but I prefer the familiarity of the Citroen, especially when there's likely to be heavy traffic.

I make it comfortably in forty minutes. Andy is lounging in *La Brioche Dorée* in *Arrivals*, his long legs stretched out under a table and crossed at the ankles. He jumps up when he sees me. Considering he's come off a two-hour flight, and has been idling away an hour or more waiting for me, he looks surprisingly fresh. I have a desperate longing for his company and conversation, an aching need to be in his arms.

He stoops and gives me a peck on the right cheek. I touch my hand to his face. His chin is smooth.

'I went to the bathroom to freshen up.' Now he puts his lips to my left cheek where they linger a bit longer before pulling away. The electricity courses through my limbs. 'Thanks for coming.'

'No problem,' I say. 'It's all part of the service.'

'I could get used to that,' he quips. 'How are you? What's been happening?'

He wants to drive the Citroen so I let him. I watch him, relaxed and confident as he takes the wheel. He drives fast when he can, all his attention fixed on the road. He's a good driver, not aggressive like some men, and the Citroen is sweet in his hands.

For a while neither of us speaks. I study his profile, relishing the memory of his touch on my cheek, and of his lips on mine when we were last together. Will he kiss me again, I wonder, pick up where we left off five months ago? What if he is merely toying with my affections, with no commitment at all?

I want to ask him, and the question is on my lips when Andy breaks the silence first. 'I've made some decisions.' He flicks a glance to the side and notices I'm watching him. 'Things have to change around here.'

'Change how?'

'With my parents' marriage. You've helped me see that.'

'I'm glad to help, but I don't see . . .'

'It isn't something I thought about much when I was younger - the business with Emmeline . . . That my mother was hurting because Father wouldn't talk about it.' He takes his eyes off the road for a second and I see his brows are knit together in one of his deep frowns. 'Now that I know, I want to do something about it. I need to understand why Father is the way he is. I have to reconnect. Even if I weren't grateful to him for the financial support, I owe it to Mother to try. She's happier than she's been for a while. I noticed it at New Year, the *Glayva* notwithstanding. And I can hear it in her voice when she phones. That's down to you.'

'I haven't done anything.'

'Yes, you have. You were the one to say the forbidden name.'

We turn onto the St Pièrre road. We're nearly home. 'There's more. Emmeline isn't the only family secret. I have aunts and uncles and cousins out there. He won't talk about them either.'

I left the front gate open so we drive straight in. 'What are you going to do, Andy?'

'I haven't quite decided. Maybe I'll start with Uncle Georges.'

'What about your grandfather? He must know about . . .'

'I think Father got it from him - the reluctance to mention family. Something happened . . .'

He manoeuvres the car round to the other side of the house where I usually keep it. 'Thanks for listening, Nicole,' he says.

'Anytime.' I lean towards him, catching his eye in the rear-view mirror. 'I'm always here.'

I'm glad to have helped Cathy deal with the past although but for chance I might never have heard of Emmeline. However, listening to Andy talk about his father makes me realise something else. Despite coming from different backgrounds, our situations are not so different.

I never stopped wondering why Denise was reluctant to look at photographs of herself - why she never talked of *her* parents - why she would never admit her age. It was easier for her to resort to lies than face the truth. Both Andy and I are victims of our parents' decisions. We need to be reconciled to the past if we are to move on.

While I prepare dinner, Andy is closeted with Cathy in her den. The three of us eat together. Yves hasn't come home. Afterwards, Andy catches me up at the stairs.

'I'm going over to see my uncle now,' he whispers. 'But there's something else I want to talk to you about. Tomorrow?'

'Tomorrow is fine, Andy. See you then.'

But we don't get a chance to talk next day. He's being very secretive. He asks to borrow Cathy's Mercedes. All he'll say is, he's driving down to Toulouse to meet a friend. I can't tell if the evasion is for his mother's benefit or for mine.

It's a good three hours trip so he leaves straight after breakfast. Cathy takes the bus to work. I'm left on my own to brood.

I sit up watching television until late, hoping to see him when he comes home. There are things I need to say too. However, by eleven, my eyes are so tired I can hardly keep them open, so I go to bed.

The following morning is wet and humid. It's raining, a typical early summer downpour. Cathy leaves at seven. I'm drinking coffee and watching the rain stream down the window when Andy comes into the breakfast room. He's unshaven and wearing his old UPMC t-shirt and tattered blue denims. His tousled appearance gives me my cue.

'*Bonjour, mon vieux.*' I laugh. 'Did you sleep in your clothes?'

'In my clothes and in a chair.' He hitches his shoulders and rubs the back of his head. 'I got back after midnight. Made the mistake of trying to read. It's the first time I've ever fallen asleep over a book.'

'All work and no play . . .' I tell him. 'Would you like me to massage your neck?'

'Please.' He pulls up a stool and sits down. I stand behind him and put my hands on his shoulder blades, feeling the tension. I press against the muscle and for a few minutes work the heels of my palms along his shoulders into his neck.

'Better?'

'Much. Thanks, Nicole. About New Year . . .'

'You don't have to explain.' I try to sound casual and carry on massaging his neck. His hair is thick and I enjoy the sensation as it glides through my fingers.

'I want to.' He helps himself from the coffee pot but there is only enough for half a mugful. 'We kissed.'

'We did. More than once if memory serves.' I give his hair a final pat and go round to the other side of the table to sit opposite him. Our eyes meet. His are dark and brooding.

'We should talk about that.' He rolls the coffee mug between his palms.

'Not now. Your father will be in for breakfast soon.'

'When?'

The rain has stopped. Over his shoulder I can see the thunder clouds part to reveal a patch of blue sky. There is a rainbow over the winery. Water vapour is already rising from the window ledge. I lean across the table and tap his hand. 'Do you have other plans for the day?'

'I have to go to the public library for a couple of hours.'

'I hope you're going to shave and dress in something more

suitable,' I tease. 'My afternoon's free. Conservatory at one o'clock?'

When I get to the conservatory, Andy is there already, lounging in a basket chair. Relative to this morning, he's made an effort with his appearance, casual but tidy. He is wearing clean Levi's and a new t-shirt he must have bought in England. The slogan on the front reads *Maths is Fun*. On his feet are canvas trainers. He smells of delicious after-shave.

Outside, the clouds are higher in the sky and less threatening than in the morning. I have discarded my work clothes in favour of a dark green pinafore dress and sandals.

'I've made some coffee.' Andy gestures at the huge *cafetière* and two porcelain mugs that sit on a tray on top of the small table at his side. 'There's milk in one of the mugs.'

I help myself from the *cafetière*. Even with the milk it's on the strong side. For a few moments we look at one another without speaking.

'It wasn't all teasing,' he says at length. 'Was it?'

'No, it wasn't.'

'I felt it was more than pretence. It was afterwards - well, that I thought maybe we *were* pretending - that you were leading me on.'

'Pretence in relationships is a cruel thing to do,' I say. 'People get hurt. You shouldn't have to pretend with anyone.'

'No, I agree. With you I don't have to pretend. I can be myself. I'm not used to that. There's been so much pretence in the past. You go along with it all for a quiet life. Maybe things would have been different if I'd gone to a mixed school, or if I'd had a sister at home. If Emmeline had lived . . .'

It's as if I've come into the wrong scene in a play. He's doing that thing with his eyebrows and I have no idea what he's talking about.

'Andy!'

'*Dieu*, I'm sorry. I'm rattling on, aren't I?' He clenches his jaw and spreads his arms in a gesture of frustration. 'I knew I was going to be hopeless at this.'

I lay down my coffee mug, reach across and take hold of his hands. 'Slow down! What are you trying to say?'

He presses his lips to my fingers. 'I like you, Nicole . . .'

'I like you too, Andy . . .'

'. . . I've never known anyone quite like you. You're mature, smart and beautiful. You could have any man . . .'

I want to laugh, though I can't help feeling a little current of pleasure trickling through my limbs. *Maybe you ought to borrow my spectacles, mon ami*, I think. But I bite my tongue.

'There's nothing special about me. I'm just an ordinary girl who wants an education and needs to work to get it.'

'You're not ordinary, Nicole.' He leans forward, blushing. His emotions are not easy to read. I love the way his dark eyes shine with youthful energy, devouring my words - sensuous without being lustful. My tummy tightens.

'Well, normal then. I like to do a bit of teasing occasionally, but we all do it. I like kissing too - when it's with the right person. I guess you learn all the tricky bits as you go.'

'I can handle teasing. There was a lot of that in Paris. I got used to it. I'm not so sure about the tricky bits. I've pretty much messed things up so far with all the girls I've dated.'

'Including Margie?'

'Especially Margie.'

'Are you going to tell me about it?'

I can almost feel the heat in his cheeks as he lowers his eyes. 'Best not. It's over - that's the important thing. Maybe I'll tell you one day when we know each other better.'

He grins, then grows more serious again. His frown returns. 'As I said, I like you, Nicole. I like you a great deal. But you've got university; I've got my post-grad studies. How is that going to work?'

'I don't know. We both have our education and career ambitions. But I'm not planning to seduce you into marriage and babies. We've been doing OK until now. Let's take things slowly and see what happens.'

'But not too slowly.' He smiles and draws his chair closer to mine. 'Maybe if I kissed you again . . .'

'I like the sound of that.' I lean across to him and take his face between my palms. His hands brush my forearms and stop centimetres from my breasts. For a few seconds our lips connect.

We both jump up as the front door opens and closes.

'Anyone home?' Cathy calls.

Andy turns very red. I smooth down my hair and clothes. I find a tissue in the pocket of my dress and wipe the lipstick smear from his mouth. 'That was nice,' I whisper.

'And the tricky bits?' he whispers back.

'Let's not mess up before we've started,' I hiss, and go to the connecting door. 'We're in the conservatory, Cathy!'

'I have some essays to mark.' Cathy pops her head round the door, eyeing the *cafetière* and empty mugs. 'Any coffee left?'

'Dregs only, I think.'

'Oh well, I'll brew some more. What are you two up to?'

Andy is over his embarrassment. He delves his hands into his jeans pockets and answers for both of us, while I pick up the coffee tray and head for the kitchen. I need an excuse to cool my face and slow my pulse rate.

'Discussing the meaning of life, Mum. I think that best describes it,' he says. 'I was about to suggest to Nicole we walk up to the old *château* . . . do a bit of exploring. We meant to at New Year but it was far too cold.' He follows me to the kitchen door. 'How about it?'

'Let's do it,' I reply, welcoming the excuse. 'Five minutes to rinse the crockery?'

'Why did you do that - say that?' I ask him when we're clear of the house.

'It was a spur of the moment thing. I didn't want a lecture. Anyway, you played along.'

'If anything is going to happen between us, I'd like to tell Cathy in my own way.'

'Right!' He takes my hand and we swing our arms back and

forth as we stroll silently between the rows of vines. We haven't had a fairy-tale ending but I'm just happy to be with him.

The day is much warmer than the last time we walked together through the estate. The afternoon sun has peeped out from the cloud cover. I feel it on my face and arms. Perhaps true summer has come to the Garonne valley at last. Though the narrow lane still has a few puddles from the morning's rain, we avoid them easily. Most of the ground has dried off and is firm under our feet.

Growing up in the city, I was scarcely aware of the seasons. Bordeaux is surrounded by vineyards. They even encroach on the city itself. Yet most people never seem to notice they're there. We take our country's major industry for granted. Out here, a few kilometres from downtown, we might be a million away. Though the seasons meld here too, I'm more aware of nature and some of its distinct stages.

In the winter, after pruning, the leaf buds are all but invisible against the dun of the wood and the grey of the earth; in spring, there is the knobbly trunk and cordons with their comical crown of green. Autumn and harvest bring the colours, the verdant shades and the dark purple, almost black, of the hanging grape clusters. Today, almost a year since I came to the estate, the green predominates. Seen in this light with the sun reflecting, however momentarily, from the leaves, nothing else matters. Spring and summer bring the scents too. Here, away from the traffic pollution of the city, you can smell the trees, the vine leaves and the grass.

'Tell me more about yourself,' Andy says.

'You know pretty much all there is to know already. I've told you my age. I went to *Lycée François Mauriac*; of course, we had both sexes.'

'I would have preferred that. I mean, having girls around to temper the conversation. At a boys' school it's so predictable.'

'You've never been a fly on the wall at a girls' get-together, *mon ami*.'

'I guess not.' He runs his hand through his hair. 'So, are you going to tell me? About those female get-togethers?'

'Best you don't know.' I nudge his arm. 'I suppose you think it's all about shopping, clothes and make-up.'

'I've never given the subject much thought, but women talk about their feelings a lot, don't they?'

'Maybe.'

'Men never talk about their feelings. It isn't something we do. We bottle them up and pretend we don't have any.' He pauses and with his forefinger replaces a fallen shoot on one of the trellises. He does it so gently I imagine him pushing a lock of my hair into place. 'That's why I found it so difficult to . . . you know.'

The ruined *château* has just come into view and we head towards it, my head spinning with competing emotions. I squeeze his fingers and lay my head on his shoulder. 'I'm glad you did. I like being with you.'

'I like being with you too.' He bends towards me and kisses me on the forehead. 'What are we going to do about these feelings, Nicole?'

We reach the outer wall and sit down on two adjacent stone blocks.

'I have no idea, *mon ami.*'

'At least we have the rest of the summer to figure it out,' he says. 'That's a good thing, isn't it? Now, do you want to view the family treasures or not?'

I look up at the sky. This isn't the season for thunderstorms but a band of dark grey thundercloud floats near the horizon. Perhaps it was a foolish idea to wander so far from the house. I wonder whether the day will end without more rain.

There isn't much to see here. Only two rooms of the *château* remain intact in that they still possess a ceiling and walls. All glass has been removed from the windows. The floors are compacted soil and gravel. A few others are open to the sky and meadow grass has seeded, providing a soft carpet for our feet. We spend an hour following uncovered passages, climbing over rubble and trying to trace the contours of the former walled garden.

Occasionally, we stop. Andy will sit on a stone block or lean against a wall. He looks at me. I look back, wondering what he's seeing, if he likes it and if he'll make a move. Does he feel the romance of this neglected and unvisited place as I do, or is he aware only of the eyesore that ought to be pulled down?

The sun disappears again behind the clouds. It grows darker. We've gone about a third of the way home when it starts to rain, a few sparse, heavy spots that bounce off the ground.

'We could go back,' Andy suggests. 'Shelter in the ruin until it goes off.'

I survey the sky, which has taken on a threatening appearance. The wind is in the south-east. Away in the direction of Toulouse the clouds are thick and nearly black. 'This rain could last for the rest of the day. I vote we keep going. We can dry off at home if we get drenched.'

'Let's go then.' He takes my hand and we pick up speed. A single raindrop hits my neck and trickles under my collar. Another falls on the side of my nose. A few more, uncomfortable and wet, land on my shoulders and arms. Thunder rumbles in the distance. We are travelling at right angles to the storm but we're not going to make it.

The rain is falling hard now, running down my face and soaking through the cotton of my dress. In a few seconds we are both drenched to the skin. I can tell my hair is a disaster. Andy is pulling me ahead, but his stride is so much longer than mine and I have to run to keep up with him.

'Andy!' I shake off his hand and bend down, my hands on my knees. 'I need to breathe.'

'Right.' He stops and comes back. 'I guess it doesn't matter now. We can't get any wetter.'

I straighten to face him and it's an epiphany moment for me. His t-shirt, tight around his shoulders, hugs his torso like a second skin. His hair flops over his eyes and the water drips from his arms. His jeans hang low on his hips to give them extra length at the ankles. These too are saturated with rainwater.

He is beautiful. Desirable. Despite the coolness of water on my skin, I feel hot all over. Desire courses through my limbs. The falling rain is Eros, moulding my dress and underwear to my figure. He, Adonis-like to my Aphrodite, is touching, caressing me with his eyes.

I want to be free, to give myself to him, to throw my arms around his beautiful body, tear off his wet garments and mine. I want to grasp this Olympian moment, to hold him to my breast and reward him with everything I have to give.

Lightning flashes, followed by a peal of thunder. We reach for one another at the same second. His arms are round me, lifting me clear of the ground, pressing me against him, burying his face in my wet hair. His kiss, when our lips meet, is possessive and hungry. My hunger is no less. I grip his shoulders, feeling his muscles tense. I snake my tongue into his mouth, searching for his, and when they engage, the universe implodes. Surely my heart has stopped beating, or else it is beating so fast that there is no time at all between one beat and the next. His body is hard against my fragility. I wrap my thighs around his hips, feeling the urgency not only of my need but of his. My lips mouth three words though, with the noise of the rain, I cannot be sure there is any sound or, if there is, whether he hears them or not.

Another flash of lightning. More thunder. It's getting closer but neither of us seems to notice. The third clap is so violent it shakes the ground. At the same moment a bolt of lightning, bright and deadly against the black of the sky, strikes the earth a few hundred metres from where we are standing. Sizzling, the current snakes along the rows of vines. There is a crack, the smell of burning wood and smoke rises from the canopy. I feel the energy in the air and a tingling in my arms which isn't libido.

Andy releases me, lowers me to the sodden path. I watch him clench and unclench his fists.

'Fuck this,' he growls and snatches my arm. The rain is heavier than ever. 'That was too close for comfort. Another one of those could kill us. Let's run!'

The house is within sight. We sprint for it and arrive, panting, at the terrace entrance, Andy first, me a poor second. I do my best to keep up but can in no way match his pace, and he is forced to release my arm on the home stretch. There is another crash and, two seconds later, more lightning. The storm is moving away.

There is a bundle of clean, dry towels inside the door and I wrap one of them around my head. I shake off the surplus water from my clothes and, still soaking wet, dash upstairs to dry off and change.

Thunder and lightning. This afternoon wasn't quite what I had in mind when I confessed my feelings to Amelie. I fancy I can still feel the energy in the air of my bedroom, but that may be my desire clashing with my responsibilities. If so, my libido is winning the battle by a margin.

More comfortable now, I check my appearance in the mirror. My hair doesn't look right. I brush it again, refasten it, pushing the clasp closer to the back of my head, and put on my work overall over my clean, dry underwear. The storm has freshened the atmosphere but the air conditioning in my room is set at minimum and it's too warm. I turn the thermostat to medium before checking my appearance one last time and stepping out into the corridor.

Andy is at the door of his room, lounging against the jamb. I freeze, feeling the onset of a blush. The rekindling of my desire does not come without a surge of embarrassment.

He takes my arm. 'Did you mean it - what you said back there?'

'What did I say?' His touch is light and I tremble at the nearness of him.

'I didn't hear, but I'm fairly good at lip reading.' Before I can protest, he pulls me through the open door and closes it behind us. 'Did you?'

A tingle courses down my spine and into my pelvis. Goose bumps come out on my skin. 'I don't know, Andy . . .' I'm mumbling the words. His bed, neatly made up, is five metres away, a magnet, drawing me to the brink of abandon. 'You're confusing me. I don't know whether . . .'

'Just tell me I misread, Nicole, that it was a spur of the moment thing - that you didn't mean it - and I'll back off.'

'Andy.' I put my palm against his chest. What had seemed wonderful and inevitable a short while ago now seems inappropriate in these surrounding. My libido is still winning but I'm beset by doubts. This is Ravel territory and I'm Cathy's employee once more.

'I know what I said but now all this seems . . . *wrong*.'

'How wrong?'

'I'm in a position of trust in this house. *Mon petit*, in this world, for the master to seduce the maid is always forgiven. For the maid to fall in love is not.'

'I don't understand. This isn't the nineteenth century. We're adults.' He frowns. 'Did you mean it or not?'

I move closer to him. My need is real. I want with all my heart to give myself to him, for him to give himself to me.

'What if I did?'

'I think you know.' His arm encircles my waist. He kisses me first on the brow, then the left ear, then the mouth. For a few delightful seconds, my lips linger against his.

'Don't do this to me, Andy,' I say at length.

'Do you know you're stunningly beautiful.'

My insides are in turmoil. He holds me against his chest and I feel the thump of his heart and the pitter-patter of mine. I want him to take me up in his arms. I long to wrap my thighs round his hips again - to surround him and feel pleasure of release that loving him would give. I want the thunder and lightning. I want the tricky bits.

'Don't say things you don't mean!' I rebuke him, but the butterflies won't go away.

'I want you too, Nicole.' He kisses me above my right eye. My brow tingles.

'Andy . . .' In a moment, my fingers are combing his hair. I raise myself on tiptoe and kiss him with eager lips, my tongue seeking his, exploring, wanting.

'Nicole . . .' I love how he repeats my name. 'Nicole . . .'

His cheeks are flushed and his deep brown eyes burn into my soul. He starts to unbutton my overall. *Le bon Dieu* - I can't do this here!

'No!' I pull myself out of the chaos of dream and desire and struggle to free myself from his embrace. I clutch at a chest of drawers to steady myself. All of a sudden, there seem to be too many obstacles to our relationship. 'I can't do this, Andy. Not here. Not now. I'm sorry.' I flee to the door and throw it open. The corridor is empty.

'Nicole . . .'

'I'm so sorry.'

He calls after me again but I ignore him. I run on, refastening my overall as I go, reach the head of the stairs and turn. Andy stands between me and my only private space in the house. His face is the picture of incomprehension and of misery.

The tears come and I can't halt them. *What have I done?*

**

21.

Cathy finds me in the kitchen with a hand mirror. My face is a mess.
Still damp, it's streaked with eye shadow, lipstick and liner.

'Nicole?'

I rub my eyes again and look up, feeling dreadful.

'What on earth's the matter, Nicole? You look like you could use a handkerchief.' Cathy takes a crumpled face towel from a bundle of dried washing. 'Here, use this. No - let me do it.'

She bends over and does her best to wipe the tears and dark smudges from my face. I thank her. 'Now, tell me. *Dis-moi. Toutes.*'

'I can't.'

'Course you can. How long have we been friends?' Cathy pulls up a chair beside me and sits down.

'It's woman trouble,' I lie. 'I don't know why I'm crying.'

Cathy makes a clucking noise with her tongue. 'I've known you for a year, *chérie*, remember. You don't get woman trouble. I do, but you don't. Now, spill!'

'I can't talk about it. Not to you.'

'It's man trouble then. I know the look. Has Yves upset you - said something he shouldn't?'

'No. Nothing like that.'

'What then . . .?' She stops dead mid-sentence as if hit by a truck. Her brow creases. 'No, Andy wouldn't - surely not. He likes you - respects you too much.'

'It wasn't like that, Cathy! If it was anyone's fault it was mine. I led him on.' My tears start again. 'I have feelings for him and I feel so guilty. I should have handed in my notice when I realised.'

'Feelings?' echoes Cathy sternly. 'Tell me about these feelings.'

'I like him. I more than like him.' Without going into too much detail, I summarise events of the past few hours. I mention what happened at New Year.

'I see.'

I stand up and wipe my face with my sleeve. 'I'm sorry. If you want me to leave - to work notice, I'll do it. I'm really sorry.'

'You'll do no such thing. Just sit where you are.' She motions me back to my chair. 'So, you kissed one another. It was mutual. Big deal!'

'You don't mind?'

'Why should I mind? He's a big boy now. Christ, he's twenty-three, nearly twenty-four. You're both adults. It's none of my business.'

'I don't know why you're being so nice, Cathy. It feels like I've taken advantage of your kindness and generosity.'

'I don't see how.'

'By trying to trap him. Because his parents are rich!'

To my astonishment, Cathy gives a roar of laughter.

'What's so funny?' I force a smile through the tears. I said what was in my mind, but Cathy's laugh is always infectious.

'I'm not laughing at you. Gods forbid! Believe me, *chérie*, I can spot a money-grabbing hussy a mile off.' She thrusts the smeared face towel into my hands. 'Here, you need this again!'

'Then why . . .?'

'That was like me nearly thirty years ago.' Cathy is still chuckling. 'I was eighteen when I met Yves. He's six years older than me. I was twenty-two when I married him. Grandpa Ravel didn't want me in the house. He called me *la petite chasseuse*. He thought the main reason I had come to France was to look for a rich husband. I had to work hard to convince him . . .'

'. . . it wasn't true?' I wipe my eyes again with a clean part of the towel, feeling a little less miserable.

'Exactly. And I never for a moment thought that about you either. We're more alike than you realise. I had an ordinary upbringing. I wanted to study in France, like you want to study in the UK.' She rises suddenly, goes to the wine store and comes back clutching a bottle of estate Red. She pulls two glasses from a cupboard, pours a large measure in each and sits down again. 'I was lucky. Thirty years ago, the costs weren't so daunting. I envy you your resolve, Nicole. Your determination . . .'

She swallows down half of her wine and tops up the glass. 'Too much determination maybe. You don't have to do everything on your own.' She puts her hand over mine. 'I'm not your mother, Nicole, but I am your friend. You don't have to hold back with me.''

I shake my head, dab away another tear resting on my upper lip and drink some wine. I've tried so hard not to bring my demons into her home, but Cathy doesn't miss much.

'You know I always wanted a daughter,' she says. 'I couldn't have one after Emmeline. You're the nearest I'm ever going to get now, Nicole. You're much more than an employee to me.'

I can't think of anything to say so I stay silent.

'It isn't only Andy, is it? You are two young and healthy people. There's no reason why you shouldn't . . .'

'It didn't feel right . . . in your house.' I focus on my glass, avoiding her eyes. Outside, the storm has passed. The clear, red liquid sparkles in the afternoon sunshine.

'If that's the way you feel, I get it. But I sense there's something else on your mind. Not worries about getting fired. I've never pried into your family affairs but, if it's that, I'd like to help. As a friend.'

'I can't.' I want to tell her about Denise and the pills, and the men, but I've kept it to myself for too long.

'Yes, you can. I promise it will go no further.' She offers to top up my glass. When I decline she empties another measure into her own.

'I haven't a clue where to start.'

'Start wherever you like. I'm listening.'

'I told you my mother had been ill.' I take another sip of my wine, hoping it will make talking easier. 'That's my favourite evasion when people ask. It doesn't begin to describe what happened. I don't know if I'll ever be able to forgive her.'

'A mother has to do something pretty terrible to turn a daughter against her.'

'Words can hurt more than deeds,' I say and, plucking up courage, tell her about Denise's breakdown - about the sedatives, her headaches and the antidepressants. About Marcel and the other boyfriends. I tell her the whole story, the story no one but my grandmother knows. 'She was about to lose her job and was neglecting us - borrowing money on her credit card for drugs as well as necessities. One day something cracked inside me and I reacted. Denise said some terrible things.'

'What kind of things?' Cathy asks gently.

'That she hated me. That she hadn't wanted me. She hit me and I hit her back.'

'Christ Almighty!'

'If it hadn't been for my grandparents, I don't know what I would have done. They took the three of us in, arranged for my mother's treatment. Denise was in hospital for a month, then a private clinic for eight weeks. Our insurance didn't cover it all. The authorities wouldn't recognise her addiction as a long-term condition so *Mamie* and *Papi* paid the difference. I made it through my first year at *lycée* and began my second. *Papi* has a good pension but I felt so bad about leaning on their charity.'

'I'm so sorry.' Cathy picks up my hand again, rubs the back with hers. 'I can't imagine what it must have been like for you.'

'After the clinic, she stayed clean for three months, Cathy. We communicated but only just. The clinic registered her as an out-patient; she had to attend every week for counselling and psychotherapy. I took control of the household budget, looked after Bern and Sophie. Made sure they were fed. She was happy for me to do that while she was recovering. The pills were gone and money was another temptation removed. I gave her cards to my grandmother, who rationed her spending on non-essentials.

'There had been no men since she came out. One night at a party, she met someone.' I feel the tears coming, and I stop to wipe my eyes again.

Antoine - respectable, mature Antoine . . . Antoine, who fooled me as he fooled her. I can see him as he came into our living room - handsome, looking young for his fifty years, and wearing a jacket and tie. At last, someone who might be interested in more than just sex. A week later, Denise was using again and Antoine was her supplier.

'Then the day came when he touched me. Marcel had looked like a sleaze-bag. Antoine looked like the chief executive of a bank but he was a sleaze-bag all the same. He tried it on in our kitchen; my mother was getting ready to go out. Offered me a good time if I'd go to bed with him. I hit him with a cheese-board.'

'Good for you, *chérie*.'

'When Denise came in, he pretended nothing had happened. He had accidentally bumped into the door frame. I told her the truth.

'She snapped at me. "Don't be ridiculous. Why do you always have to lie?" Then she took his arm and they went off together. It nearly tore my heart out - that she didn't believe me - her own daughter. Three days later, they found her in a bar, unconscious. Antoine - or someone - had spiked her wine with a benzodiazepine and she had reacted badly to it. I gave a statement to the police. They arrested Antoine but the judges said there wasn't enough evidence to convict.

'My mother went back to the clinic. After another eight weeks of in- and out-patient care she was pronounced cured. But the specialists told her she had an addictive personality. She must never drink alcohol or take any kind of sedative again.'

Cathy takes some tissues from her handbag and pushes one into my hand.

'I think she's turned a corner.' I dab my eyes. 'She met Jean during a routine visit to the hospital. He's a psychologist, though not in health care. He works for EDF in personnel, devising tests for prospective recruits. I believe he's different but I can't forget everything that's happened.'

'And with all this stuff going on you still managed to get through school with distinction?'

'Maybe it was the determination in action. I knew I wanted university, a teaching career. Reading and study was an escape from reality. Maybe it was blind luck that got me through. I lived on adrenalin, I think. After school, I decided I couldn't go on sponging on my grandparents. I had to pay my way and this job helped me do that. I owe you, Cathy.'

'You owe me nothing, *ma chérie*. You've earned every last cent I've paid you. So how do matters stand now?'

'Better. At least we're not quarrelling. Jean is well able to support Bern and Sophie through school, but I still feel responsible for them. I'd like things to go back to how they used to be.'

'No financial pressures?'

'Some. But I won't take anything from Jean. My father left a small legacy. There's enough there, and from what I've saved from my wages to fund most of my time at Edinburgh. If you keep me on.'

I wipe my eyes for the umpteenth time. At last I've been able to let go and confide in another human being, and my overwhelming emotion is relief.

'Of course I'll keep you on . . .' Cathy leans over. She hugs me and for the next ten minutes we do nothing else. Her eyes are as moist as mine. 'And all this time . . . Why did you never tell me? We've been friends, haven't we?'

'Pride, I suppose.'

'It's a good pride then. If Andy doesn't fall for you he's a fool.'

'Oh, I don't know,' I say grimly. 'After today, he probably won't want to speak to me . . . ever!'

'Don't worry. He will.' Cathy smiles and puts an arm around my shoulders again. 'And don't worry about my motherly feelings either. I stopped making decisions for my son a long time ago.'

'Thanks, Cathy.'

'No need,' she says. 'Love's a bitch sometimes. Just promise to tell me if you need help.'

'I promise, but I think I'm going to be OK now.'

**

22.

Andy

I wait at my bedroom door until my heartbeat slows, then tiptoe downstairs. The sound of crying comes from the kitchen. I feel terrible, guilty, out of my depth. My stomach is a whirlpool of conflicting emotions. After five years of doing nothing but focus on my studies and career ambitions, suddenly I can't focus at all. Maybe it would help if I knew what I did wrong. After what happened during the storm, I thought we wanted the same things.

The kitchen door is slightly ajar. I can't see Nicole, but my mother is there. I slip past without them seeing me and go outside. It isn't raining now. The sun has parted the clouds and already water vapour is rising from the road. I start running. I break into a sprint and don't slow down until I reach the boundary of the Ravel estate. Out of breath, I stroll back.

Cathy

I hear the outer door slam and the sound of footfall on the atrium floor. Andy has taken his time. I'm guessing he has been out running. When he has a problem, he never broods. But if he knows I'm waiting for him, he'll try and avoid a confrontation. The last thing I want is to act like a fussy mother hen, but we do need to have a talk about his intentions. Though Nicole is an adult, while she's in my house I have a responsibility - duty of care, or something like that.

At last, he comes towards the kitchen door. He hesitates. I can hear his breathing.

'Don't you dare try and slip out again, young man!' I yell.

He comes in, making an effort to appear casual. I pretend to wipe some wine spillage with a tissue then polish the two glasses.

I point to a stool. 'Sit down, Andy!'

'It's not what you think,' he mutters. 'I want to talk to Nicole.'

'You've no idea what I think, so just sit down.' I grab his forearms and manoeuvre him into a sitting position. '*I* want to talk to *you*, and that takes priority.'

'Sorry, Mum.'

'And what are you sorry for, I wonder?' I stand over him. This is one of those times when he looks more like the gangly teenager he was six or seven years ago. *Going on seventeen.*

'I think I've messed up,' he grunts.

'You have.'

'Sorry!'

'If I hear the word *sorry* one more time, I'll make you very sorry indeed, Andy Ravel.' I reach for the wine bottle. It's less than half full. 'Now, tell me about you and Nicole.'

'It's not something I can talk to you about.'

'*She* said much the same thing. Well, let me tell you about *her.*' I sit opposite, divide the remaining wine between the two glasses and slide one over to him.

'Where is she?' He takes the glass and swallows the contents.

'I suggested she spend the evening with her friends. In the city.' I lean across the table and tap him on the back of the hand. 'I don't think you realise it, but Nicole is one of the smartest people I know. And she's done it all without the advantages you had.'

'I don't understand what you mean.'

For a soon-to-be twenty-four-year-old male with a college degree he can be pretty thick sometimes. 'Christ, Andy, I wonder where you hide bits of your brain! I don't suppose you ever asked Nicole about *her* ambitions instead of boring her with yours. Then you expect her to fall into your arms whenever - and wherever - you feel inclined.'

'That's not what happened.'

I finish off the wine. 'Suppose you tell me what did happen.'

'I'm not going to tell you that.'

'Oh Andy!' I just shake my head at him. 'Do you like her?'

'Of course I like her.'

'Tell her, you idiot!'

'I have told her.'

'Well, tell her again. Don't grab and assume.'

I'm being unfair because I know he hasn't done anything very terrible. But I've put him on the defensive.

'It wasn't like that, Mother. You're the one making assumptions. We were getting on really well when she freaked out.'

'She was in your room.'

'We've been there together a hundred times before. I don't understand . . .'

'Your room, Andy - your space!'

He stares at me for a moment.

'Oh God . . .' he covers his face with his hands. 'I *have* messed up, haven't I?'

'It isn't beyond fixing,' I say. 'Look, it's not my job to tell you what to do, and I don't want to argue. I'm not judging you, darling, but I hope you'll listen to some womanly advice.'

'OK. I know I'm hopeless when it comes to relationships.'

'With girls, you have to learn to read between the lines. If you're serious about Nicole, you need to think more about her and less about yourself. Ask her how she feels, what she wants from life. Make her feel special. Women like compliments, little gestures. Pay her compliments. Take her to dinner maybe.'

'What if I've already blown my chances?'

'Grow up, Andy!' I must have said it a thousand times when he was Gerard's age. 'Look . . .' I narrow my eyes, trying to look scary. 'I'm saying no more, except this. For Christ's sake don't make her pregnant or you'll answer to me. I'll disown you. *Capisce?* And that's Italian for *on pain of death.*'

Andy

I go upstairs and knock on Nicole's bedroom door. Perhaps she *has* gone to Bordeaux but I want to make sure. I wait two minutes then try the handle. The door is unlocked. I push it cautiously ajar, take a few steps into the room and look around.

It's been years since I was in here. It was a spare long before my mother took on the first girl. Now only the ceiling pattern and the burgundy carpet, replicated in the corridor and all the rooms on the first floor, are familiar. Apart from the double bed on my right, the main items of furniture are a three-drawer chest, a dressing table which doubles as a computer desk and, next to it, a small bookcase with three shelves.

Two framed photos sit on top of the bookcase, one at either end. Between them, propped on two bookends, is the walking stick I bought for her. Opposite the bed, on my left, are a small television and a DVD player on a stand. There are a few discs on top of the player but I don't investigate.

A plain burgundy satin quilt is folded neatly on top of the bed and turned down to expose part of the duvet. The duvet cover and pillow cases are white, printed with pink flowers. A music player and earphones lie on a nightstand beside the bed. Nicole's bathrobe, also pink with frilled edges, hangs on a hook on the door to the *en-suite*.

I feel guilty at being here; I'm violating her privacy. But I can't contain my curiosity about the photographs. I pick one up. Nicole is around seven or eight years old, sandwiched between two smaller children. The boy is dark and looks nothing like his older sister. He is sticking out his tongue at the camera. The girl is no more than a toddler and sits in the lap of a woman whom I would never mistake for anyone but Nicole's mother. She has the same blond hair, but cut short with a fringe, and the same startling blue eyes.

I take up the other frame. It's a close-up of a couple in wedding clothes, the thick-set man in a tuxedo and the girl in white, holding a bunch of flowers. My heart comes up to meet my throat and my stomach knots. This girl *is* an exact copy of the Nicole I know, down to the ponytail and the same open, mischievous and sexy expression. Apart from the dated fashion, and the slight yellowing at the edges of the dress, the picture might have been taken yesterday. Nicole never talks about her mother, but Denise Durand is beautiful.

Tentatively, I run my fingers along the shaft of the walking stick. I don't know what I was expecting. *Pain? Inspiration?* But it's only wood, and the pain is in my head.

I close the door, go downstairs and leave the house again. Once across the road, I start running. I run and I don't stop. I have some more thinking to do.

**

23.

Nicole

I'm having that nightmare again. In my befuddled dream state, I can't be sure whether the persistent hammering is real or imagined. I force myself to waken. Someone is knocking at my bedroom door.

'It's Andy. Please can we talk?'

I open my eyes, yawn and grab my phone. *Only four hours sleep*. It's going to be a long day. I spent the evening in Bordeaux with Amelie, cooked us dinner and drank far too much coffee. We took the world of life and love to bits and consoled ourselves with chocolates. I arrived home at midnight, couldn't sleep and read a book until I dropped off at two.

'It's six o'clock, Andy.' My throat is dry and I can still taste the coffee in my mouth. 'I'm in bed. You can't come in.'

'I need to see you.' His voice seems deeper than usual, and more sensitive. 'Please.'

'See? Talk?'

'Talk would be a beginning,' he calls through the door. 'I'm sorry about yesterday - no, not sorry exactly, but things didn't turn out the way I meant them to.'

'They didn't turn out the way I meant them to either, Andy. I should be the one explaining.' I look again at the time, slide out of bed, rub the sleep from my eyes and grab my robe. I throw it on over my pyjamas. I look in the mirror, pull a few pins from my hair and open the door.

Andy takes a step back when he sees me. His gaze flicks to the opening in my robe before focussing nowhere in particular on my bedroom wall. I didn't mean to embarrass him.

'Give me twenty minutes,' I say. 'We'll talk in the breakfast room.'

I dress in jeans and a sweater. When I get downstairs, my hair is still wet from the shower. To my surprise, Andy has warmed some of yesterday's croissants, soft-boiled four eggs and laid out a selection of cheeses and sweetmeats. A pot of coffee bubbles on the stove. Two plates, two mugs, cutlery and napkins are set out neatly on the table, with a jug of flowers at the centre.

'You've made me a proper breakfast!' I'm all bubbly inside at the effort he has made. I'm glad he wakened me.

'You've done it often enough for me.' He smiles warmly.

'It's my job. Cathy pays me.'

'I know.' He pulls out a stool, motions me to it and perches on another himself.

'What has happened to you, *mon ami*?' I sit down and reach for a croissant. 'Did you have a brain transplant overnight or have you been taken over by aliens?

He pulls a face that's more like the Andy I recognise. 'Mother gave me a lecture yesterday afternoon . . .'

'. . . and a man always listens to his mother,' I tease.

'No, I'm being serious, Nicole,' he growls in his new Andy voice. 'It was something like *I should listen more and talk less*. I think she also said girls like little gestures. Compliments.'

'Well, they do. And the flowers are beautiful. Thank you.' I layer a croissant with jam and bite into it. I like them best that way. 'You wanted to talk?'

'To apologise for yesterday. I shouldn't have assumed . . .'

'I shouldn't have led you on, *mon ami* - shouldn't have given you ideas . . .'

'The ideas were already there.'

'Me too.' I smile. 'We aren't kids.'

'I think I get it now,' he says, '- what you said about the master and maid. My space, not yours?'

'Something like that.'

'Can we please start again, Nicole?' He fiddles with the handle of the coffee pot. 'Would you like some?'

'I would love some coffee, Andy.' I take another bite of the croissant and help myself to an egg. We eat for a few minutes in silence. 'What will we be starting?' I ask.

'I don't know exactly, but . . .' He draws a deep breath while I wait. 'Will you have dinner with me tonight? There's a great restaurant in La Brède. I'd like to compliment you some more.' I love the way his voice rises and falls when he's excited. 'I'll order a taxi.'

'You're asking me on a date, Andy?'

'I guess I am.'

'And you don't know what we might be getting into?' I tease, but my heart is racing.

'It's just a dinner date,' he says soberly.

'Then how can a girl refuse? Are you sure you can afford it?'

'I should take advantage of my father's allowance while I can. Just in case he does cut me off.'

'He won't do that.'

'Anyway, I don't care.' He leans over and brushes two fingers across my face. 'You had jam on your nose.'

'There wasn't any jam!'

'You're right. I wanted an excuse to touch you.'

'You know, you're crazy, Andy Ravel!' I laugh. 'And I must be crazy too to encourage you. The breakfast was great but I have to earn my keep. Perhaps . . .' I was going to say we could do some more encouraging later but decide not to. *One step at a time, Nicole!*

Later, while Andy is out for a run, I try chatting to Cathy about Edinburgh. However, I'm yawning so much she sends me to bed for two hours - says we can speak later.

By early afternoon, I feel less sleepy so I complete my chores. I'm impatient for the evening to arrive. Will a casual outfit do, or ought I to be a bit more daring? I don't want to keep the taxi waiting while I go to change my dress.

I try a few options: a black skirt with slit, blue and white striped shirt and black sandals; a navy dress that shows way too much cleavage - and heels, before deciding on my black, off-one-shoulder dress that exposes my butterfly tattoo - a moment of insanity when I was with Henri. It has a fluted left sleeve and finishes above the knee. I keep the heels and carry a black clutch purse.

Happy with my choice, I go down to the living room to find Andy has dressed semi-formally too.

'You look nice,' he says when he sees me.

'So do you!' He is wearing a plain white shirt and navy slacks.

Cathy is hovering in the background. 'I could eat you both,' she says in English.

'Thanks, Cathy,' I reply in the same language. 'And thank you again for yesterday. I'll be all right now.'

'I know you will. Have fun and don't hurry back.' She kisses me on the cheeks, French style.

We are in the taxi before Andy says anything.

'You are pretty fluent, you know. In English.'

'Your mother has helped me a lot with conversation and idiom.'

'You told me I speak French with an English accent. Do I really?'

'Yes. But otherwise your French is rather like your father's. More *Académie Française* than Bordeaux. If he was British, he'd be posh. *The rain in Spain stays mainly in the plain.*'

'I never knew that about myself. *Mon Dieu*, I'll have to take elocution lessons in local dialect.'

'Don't bother. I like you the way you are.'

Three hours later I feel lightheaded. I'm not seeing pink elephants yet, but four glasses of wine in two and a half hours is more than I usually drink. My late night and early morning have caught up with me and I'm sleepy and excited at the same time.

The restaurant owner welcomes us enthusiastically. He recognised the name when Andy booked. We take a table on the terrace. Andy tells me it can sometimes be thick with tobacco smoke on busy evenings. Tonight, both the restaurant and the terrace are quiet. I love the decor, the ambience and the trees that shade the tables. Andy orders a bottle of *Château Magneau* and we drink a glass each in the warmth of the evening. Later, we move indoors as the sun begins to sink below the tree line.

We both settle for a lamb entrée. I feel quite spoilt but it's a good feeling, being with him and sharing his pleasure at being with me. It feels like a proper first date.

The smells of cooking waft in from the kitchen whetting my appetite. While we wait for the first course, we hold hands across the table and Andy massages mine with his fingers. His action may be instinctive but it turns me on. My skin tingles at his touch.

'Tell me some more about you,' he says. 'Things we've never talked about before.' His fingers trace little circles on my wrist.

His touch sends little currents of pleasure up and down my arm. The warmth in his eyes is giving me shivers down my spine. *Does he know how much I want him?* I'm thinking about how the evening might end. *Will he try . . .? Will I . . .?*

The first course comes. The food is delicious. I can't remember ever eating so well and in such pleasant surroundings. While we eat, I tell him about Denise and her problems, then about Sophie and Bernard, and finally about Jean. Then I talk about my school and how I came to be interested in languages and linguistics. He asks a few questions and doesn't interrupt any of my answers. I'm waiting for the adolescent Andy to re-emerge and am pleased when it doesn't.

'I was good at languages. It's all about how words flow together. I took German and Spanish as well as English at school.'

'Impressive!'

We select desserts to follow the lamb, me a chocolate mousse, he a concoction of mango and pineapple. 'I suppose linguistics is a bit like physics,' Andy says when the waiter has brought our dessert. He spears a piece of mango with his fork. 'The universe began with the Big Bang. Languages all derive from the first primeval grunt.'

'I never thought of it quite like that. But it *is* a sort of science.' By now I've finished most of the second glass of wine. I laugh; it's more of a giggle. 'Grunt languages.' I hiccup. Andy smiles and indicates my glass. I take a couple more sips.

'Our languages are all descended from proto-Indo-European,' I go on, boasting a little. It isn't my usual style but this isn't a normal situation. The thought crosses my mind there might be a dark side to Andy's character, one he hides behind his boyish innocence. A small part of me rather hopes there is. 'There's a family tree of languages. French and Spanish derive from the branch we call Romance. English, like German and Dutch, belong to the Germanic branch.'

'Cool! How come I never learned any of that at school? Not even for the *Baccalauréat*.'

'Nor me.' I ladle up some chocolate dessert and lick it off the spoon. 'School was about learning the grammar and practising writing and conversation. Linguistics is something I became interested in after school. I started reading English when I was about six years old. There was a children's book in the house. It must have been my father's. He was a good English speaker; he'd worked in Britain and America, as an engineer with the oil companies.'

'Six - WOW!' He stares at me in silence for a few minutes while I tuck into my pudding. 'So you're going to study both literature and language at Edinburgh?'

'And linguistics. It's a comprehensive course.'

'You'll walk it.' He considers, 'but you could have gone to Oxford with me. They're sure to have the same.'

'They do.' I take a gulp of wine. It's giving me false courage. 'I did think about Oxford. Not because you are there. I considered Cambridge too.'

'You would have made it at either. But Edinburgh is cool . . .'

'Very!'

He laughs. 'You *do* have the idiom! I'm happy for you, and only sorry you're not going to be at Oxford . . . with me. Your marks were . . .' He freezes on his last spoonful of mango and grips my hand. I squeal.

'Andy!'

'Christ, I'm not supposed to know . . .'

'Cathy told you about *that*?'

'I sort of twisted it out of her. Sorry.'

'It's no big secret. I just don't like to boast about my school marks.'

'But you *could* have gone to Oxford.'

'Maybe, but I don't have rich parents like you, Andy. In Scotland, the tuition is free.'

He tops up my glass then pours the rest of the wine into his own. 'Mother wanted me to go to Edinburgh, you know.'

'Yes, I know.'

His eyes settle on my bare shoulder and the tattoo. 'We'll be apart.'

'There are such things as phones, *mon cher* Andy. And e-mails. And holidays - if you want . . .'

'. . . to talk?'

'Well, maybe . . .' I finish my dessert then lean across the table to stroke his cheek. *Another step forward, Nicole.* 'I'd like that too, Andy. I'd like it a lot.'

'Maybe I could transfer to Edinburgh,' he says. 'I like Scotland.'

'But you have to complete your *D.Phil.*'

'I mean later. I don't have to stay at Oxford. He drinks the rest of his wine and, calling the waiter, asks for another bottle. 'We should celebrate. Let's have a toast. To Oxford and Edinburgh!'

After that, things become a little hazy. The second bottle of *Château Magneau* comes and I drink two glasses from it. We toast twice. The *patron* - or perhaps he's the manager - comes over to the table and joins us in a third toast. Then Andy kisses me, the waiter kisses me and the *patron* hugs me before kissing me on both cheeks. Then he kisses Andy and there are handshakes all round. I've an idea the bill comes to a hundred and fifty *euros*. Andy pays in cash.

When he joins me in the taxi for the return journey he is smiling happily. I'm tipsy and I know it. He is tipsy too. I slide over and lay my head against his shoulder.

'That was the best night ever, Andy. Thank you.'

'Thank my mother. She made me see what an idiot I was.' He bends his face towards me expectantly. 'It was a great night for me too.'

I take full advantage of the situation. I kiss him lightly on the lips before closing the screen that hides us from the driver. His hair when I nuzzle it has a wonderful recently-washed feel. I inhale the scent of his shampoo and aftershave, neither completely faded. My body tenses as I lean back, and my left leg comes into contact with the muscles of his right. He cradles me against him and strokes my hair. Our tongues meet and my stomach does a double somersault. When we break apart, I can hardly breathe.

'I want us to be more than friends, Nicole.'

'Andy . . .' The seatbelts are in the way but I manage to unfasten two buttons on his shirt. I push my hands inside, kneading the muscles of his chest with the heel of my palms and feeling the rapid beat of his heart.

'Nicole . . .'

'Shh . . .' We kiss again. My body trembles at his nearness. We're in neutral territory now. My false inhibitions have vanished with the alcohol and, I think, may even stay vanished when we get back. *Long enough.*

Too soon, the jolt of two bumps in the road signifies we are home. The taxi pulls up inside the front gate.

'Stay with me tonight, Andy,' I whisper. 'I want you to make love to me.'

'Truly?' He tucks his shirt into his trousers, refastens two of the buttons and reaches for his wallet. 'Because I want it too, but didn't know if . . .'

I lay my finger across his lips to silence him. 'Come to my room.'

'If you're sure. You know I love you, Nicole.'

'Don't say that, *mon chéri* - not unless you mean it.'

'I do mean it. I want us to be together. We have the whole summer.'

'And after?'

'We'll work it out.'

The evening air is now cooler and as I step down from the taxi a breeze ruffles my hair. As Andy pays the driver, I suddenly feel unsteady and stumble on the cobbled stones of the drive. He catches me in his arms, picks me up and carries me to the front door. I don't protest. The downstairs apartments are lit.

'My mother will be watching television, my father reading the financial news. Unless of course they're arguing about me. We'll go this way.' He leads me round the side of the house and I lean on him while he uses his key to let us in through the conservatory.

I suppress yet another giggle. 'It's like sneaking in after a school disco.'

'I've never been to a school disco.'

'*Mon pauvre petit*, you haven't lived.' I squeal as he tugs my hair.

Voices reach us from the living room as we cross the corridor leading to the office and make for the stairs. The conversation sounds friendly.

'Are you making fun of me, Nicole Durand?' He pulls my hair again and, this time, when I don't squeal he bends to kiss my forehead, then my lips.

'I'd never make fun of you, Andy Ravel,' I say, wrapping my arms round his neck, enjoying the softness of his hair. 'But I think I'm a bit drunk.'

'Me too. The sixth glass of wine sent me a wee bit over the edge. I don't usually drink so much.'

'Nor me, and I only had four. *And a half!*'

'But I haven't enjoyed an evening so much for a long time. Perhaps never! I've spent so much time studying and thinking about how to please my father that I haven't had much time for the ordinary things in life, the fun things. So I must be drunk, but I don't give a shit anymore.' He gathers me up again in his arms. I sigh and hold him close, feeling the accelerated beat of his heart and the uncontrollable thumping of my own. My flesh tingles with anticipation as he changes his grip and my dress rides a few centimetres up my thighs.

'You've changed,' I say. 'Maybe it *is* the wine, but you're not the same person as you were that day in the conservatory. The first day I kissed you.'

'How have I changed?'

'I don't know . . . yes, I do. You're more in control. More

forceful, but in a nice way.' *Dieu, how I want this,* my brain screams as we reach my bedroom door. He sets me down gently on the threshold, kisses me again as I reach for the door handle.

'Come in.' I switch on the room lights, the central one on the ceiling and the wall lamps on each side of the double bed.

He hesitates. 'I have to go to the bathroom. Get my toothbrush.'

'Fifteen minutes tops. The door will be unlocked.'

He skips off down the corridor. I wrench open a drawer and select my sexiest night outfit, the print shorts set with lace trim. I snatch my robe from its hook on the door and go into the *en-suite.* Ten minutes later, I'm back in the room. I touch up my face and lips and spray on some *Guerlain Insolence.* I remove the bedspread, take off my robe and slide under the single sheet. The house is never cold and, since the summer weather arrived, I've dispensed with the duvet. I lie back on the pillow, enjoying the sensuality of the shorts and cami on my skin as I wriggle to find the right position. I think of Andy taking them off, fondling my breasts and moving his hands slowly along my thighs.

I switch off the main light and one of the bedside lamps. It creates just the right ambience. It has been a long day, and it's going to be the most amazing night of my life. I yawn. *I love you, Andy Ravel. I want to be with you always.*

The remaining lamp casts its own pattern on the motif of the plaster ceiling. My eyes follow the spiral pattern as it winds its way from a spot above my head into the far corners of the room. Each of the large spirals has a little tight circle at its centre. I wait for the click of the lock that will signify Andy's return.

I love you . . . The little tight circles on the ceiling seem to be spinning. It must be the wine. I'll have to stop at two glasses in future.

The pillow is so soft and downy. I bury my face in it, thinking of his kisses before turning towards the bedroom door to catch a first glimpse as he comes through it. My eyes no longer want to obey me. I close them and feel myself floating, falling and sinking into a velvet lake of well-being and warm contentment.

I imagine the door opening, Andy framed there with the dimmed corridor light behind, but it must be a dream. I'm already asleep.

**

24.

The bleep of my phone wakes me from a delicious dream. I grab the instrument from the night stand. It's six-thirty.

Andy: *RU awake? Made breakfast!*

I throw off the sheet and swing my feet onto the rug at the bedside. *What happened?* I remember getting into bed, the patterns on the ceiling. Then nothing. Well, not quite. There was that dream, the most incredible dream ever. But it wasn't real, and now what will he think of me, promising so much, giving nothing? I hastily tap a text message of my own:

Forgive me! Coming 10M.

I tie up my hair, cover it with a cap and take a shower. I dress as fast as I can, apply some perfume and a little lipstick and run breathless to the stairs. He's waiting in the hall for me. He has shaved and dressed, and his dark hair looks as if it has been blow-dried. My heart does tiny acrobatics at the sight of him.

'I'm so sorry,' I say.

'No, it's OK!' He smiles and kisses me lightly on the mouth. 'Croissants and eggs again? Coffee?'

'*Formidable!*'

We go into the breakfast room. The table is laid much as before - boiled eggs, croissants and cheese - with the addition of a bowl of apples and bananas. There's a new bunch of flowers. Andy has switched on the radio and it's playing a ballade by an American singer I don't recognise. We sit and he reaches for a croissant. He cracks open one of the boiled eggs, spoons the inside onto the croissant.

I don't have much of an appetite but I take an egg anyway. For several minutes we eat and drink coffee in silence. Butterflies don't adequately describe what's going on in my insides; the sensation is more like the flapping of a flock of agitated birds. I take a deep breath.

'Andy, I want to explain about . . . I had only four hours sleep the previous night.'

Andy puts down his second croissant, which he has layered with jam. 'Maybe it wasn't the right time,' he says. He looks sheepish and rolls his eyes. 'The fates are conspiring against us. Maybe we both had a bit too much to drink.'

'I thought we'd agreed on that.'

'Well, I had anyway. I went out like a light.'

'In my room.'

'You knew?' His eyes grow wider and his cheeks redden.

'I thought it was all a dream, *mon chéri*, but you just told me it wasn't. Did you know, when you're embarrassed, your eyes go all innocent? One sort of goes up and the other down. It's a tell-tale sign.'

'I didn't *do* anything. I came back. You looked so . . . so content. I sat down for a minute in your chair to watch.' He hitches his shoulders. 'The next thing I knew, it was nearly dawn.'

'Andy!' I squeeze his hand and press it against my face. 'It doesn't matter. I trust you.'

'Maybe you shouldn't after what happened the other day.' He combs his fingers through his hair, ruffles it. 'I find it difficult to control myself when I'm around you.'

'*Moi aussi, mon chéri.*'

His brown eyes brighten and he colours again.

'Let's wait and see what happens next.' I make a wicked face. 'I'll be finished work by three.'

For the rest of the morning and three hours into the afternoon I manage to hold my thoughts at bay. Andy's simple text is enough to rekindle them. *Main door 20M?* I shower and change into a white summer frock, loose and sleeveless, with a square neck, and blue patterns on the shoulder straps and skirt. It has a pocket in the skirt and is gathered by a cord at the waist.

Andy is wearing a navy shirt, pale blue jeans and tennis shoes and carrying a sports bag. The sight of him makes my heart thud in my chest. My abdomen tightens. Then, as we walk hand in hand away from the house, every casual brushing together of our hips sends currents of delight through my body. Desire gnaws again at my insides and I fight my need to be in his arms.

The air is humid. The temperature is twenty-seven degrees. In the direction of Bordeaux in the distance, a hazy pall of heat and pollution hovers over the invisible city. It's near impossible to look south, the sun is so strong.

'What's in the bag?' I ask. 'We're not going to play tennis, are we?'

'I thought we could have a picnic,' he says, 'at the Rise.'

The Ravel plantation sweeps up in a curve from the edge of the village of St Pièrre, a kilometre-and-a-half away across the fields, though much farther by road. Opposite the house gate, the vineyard dips into a hollow before continuing upwards to the highest point in the district, a brake of trees marking the estate's eastern boundary. The Rise, as the family calls it, is no higher than the roof of the house. In the Bordeaux countryside such hills are a luxury.

'A picnic? Wow!'

'A picnic with a difference.' He grins one of his best grins. 'You'll see.'

The vines are flowering. A few estate workers are clearing weeds from the paths between the rows on the southern side. Otherwise no one else is in sight. It's a lazy afternoon. We head towards the trees. Although the vines shade us partly from the full afternoon sun, before long I can feel the perspiration between my shoulder blades. My hand, held in Andy's gentle grip, is hot and sticky. He's perspiring too, though the temperature doesn't seem to affect him quite as much.

At last we reach the top. I lean my back against the trunk of a tree, enjoying the cooler air and the breeze that rustles the branches. From here, we have a panoramic view of the whole vineyard and the patchwork of fields beyond. I can see the steeple of the St Pièrre church. I tug Andy towards me, rescue my hand and wipe it on my skirt.

He unzips the bag. I just stare as he takes out a tartan picnic rug, a half bottle of white wine in a cooler sleeve and two glasses wrapped in a T-shirt. He spreads the rug so we can both sit on it.

'The rug belongs to my mother. The shirt is clean.' He grins then rummages in the bag again. 'There should be a corkscrew too . . . ah, here it is.'

He uncorks the bottle and pours two glasses. The plastic sleeve has lost its effectiveness but the wine is still remarkably cool.

'My father will probably kill me for taking this but I couldn't resist,' Andy says.

I taste the wine. It's sweet, luscious and rather intoxicating. I feel the smooth liquid warm my inside and peak my senses.

'What is it?'

'It's a dessert wine made from Semillon grapes.' He empties his glass and licks the rim. 'There isn't much of it around.'

I copy his gesture, allowing my tongue to linger until I have his attention. Our eyes meet. There is enough wine for a second glass. I sip mine slowly before delivering my verdict.

'I think it's the most delicious thing I've ever tasted.'

'It sells at forty or fifty *euros* a bottle. I'm sorry I didn't bring some ice cream to go with it.'

'That would've been nice too. But right now I'm just happy to be here with you, drinking this amazing wine. I love it up here. I love the trees, the scent of the vines and the way the sunlight dances on the green.'

'You should see it on a moonlit night. It's quite beautiful,' Andy says. 'I wish the city wasn't so close. I came with my father once. I looked up at the sky and thought: *Where do the stars end? Can we ever travel there and back? Is there anything beyond?* I knew then I wanted to learn how the universe was made. How it worked - if we were the only people in it.'

'Do you think we are?' I pull closer to him and hug my knees, rocking them from side to side and feeling the soft pressure as they connect with his.

'No, I think the universe is teeming with life.'

'Human life?'

'Of course not. But intelligent perhaps. Don't laugh - I'd like to be the first scientist to make contact.'

'I'm not laughing, *mon chéri*.' I take his hands in mine and kiss him. He smells of musk and sunshine. I nip his bottom lip with my teeth and ease my tongue into his mouth, tasting him. He laces his fingers in my hair, pulling me close. After a few moments he breaks away and hauls me to my feet.

'It's too public here - even for this. Come on, there's another place I want to show you.' He hauls me to my feet. While he gathers up the empty bottle and glasses and repacks them carefully, I fold the rug and set it on top inside the sports bag.

We leave the cool of the trees for the narrow country lane bordering the plantation and carry on walking. There is no shade here and I feel the perspiration build again on my back. We are nearing the village when Andy stops at a gate to an empty paddock, surrounded by a hedge of unpruned vines and other overgrown shrubs. This is a part of the estate I have never visited.

'We used to exercise a pony here, many years ago,' he says. 'We stabled her near the other house, where Georges and Beatrice - and my grandfather - live. If the hedging wasn't there, you would see it. I was about seven . . . before I went to boarding school.'

'You had a pony?'

'She was called Wendy. Grey, with a black patch on her left rump.'

'What happened to her?'

'Father sold her. I was broken-hearted.'

'I would have loved to learn to ride. I'm sorry.'

'It was a long time ago.' He lays down his bag, vaults the gate and leans across to hoist me up and over into his arms. The grass is nearly knee high. He lowers me to my feet then retrieves his bag.

'It tickles.' I giggle, smooth down my dress and tug him into the shade of the overhang.

'This is a happy place for me.' He leans close and strokes my hair.

146

It can be a happy place for me too, I think, if we pick up where we left off last night. I encircle his neck with my arm and, pulling his head down towards my face, just touch my lips to his. Then I whisper in his ear.

'*Here*?' His eyes widen.

'Yes.' I undo the top button of his shirt. And the next.

He doesn't say anything but bends towards me and kisses me. It's a long, searching kiss, sweeter than anything that went before. My senses spin out of control. My heart is bursting. I try to think of the happiest days of my life so far and magnify them tenfold, but even that doesn't come close. Fumbling, I undo the remaining buttons and delve inside his shirt, enjoying his warmth and feeling the racing of his heart. In an instant, I've wrenched the garment off and am exploring his body with my hands.

His back is smooth; his skin is soft and slick with the perspiration of the afternoon, and that excites me even more. I know I'll soon have to breathe, but I'm afraid of losing a single microsecond of this precious moment.

At length I have to tear my lips away. Gasping, I suck in a huge lungful of air.

Andy's face is flushed, his eyes bright. 'You mean it?'

I nod.

'Over here, farther away from the gate.' He slings the sports bag over his shoulder, threads his fingers between mine and leads me along the perimeter of the paddock. Without letting go, he pulls me down onto a soft, level patch of grass. His eyes are inviting and I wonder if he sees the hunger in mine.

'You know I love you, Andy Ravel.' I touch his face and play with the cord of my dress, aware that he's following my every move and gesture. 'I've loved you for a very long time.'

'I fell for you the very first moment I saw you, Nicole Durand.'

'You never said anything.'

'No, but I was very rude to you. I stole a carrot.'

'You remember that?' I spread my fingers and lace them through the hair at the back of his neck.

'I remember everything - my stupid bet, New Year, when we

carried Mother upstairs - walking in the rain and thunder - every conversation we've ever had.' His eyes, pools of golden brown, smoulder as he caresses my face. My heart bursts all over again. Time for me ceases to exist. 'And I'm saying it now. I love you. I just never imagined you could love me.'

'Andy . . .'

'I want you, Nicole, but unless you're sure . . . I wouldn't hurt you for anything.'

'You won't hurt me, *mon coeur*. Here . . .' Trembling, I undo the cord and begin to undress. 'I want you too. All of you.'

His arms enclose me and I feel his muscular chest press against my breasts. He touches his lips to my forehead, then to my shoulder, near my tattoo. My fumbling fingers find the buckle of his belt. Undo it. They locate the zip fastener on his jeans and slowly ease it downwards.

The picnic rug is soft under my body. Perhaps I should be worried someone will interrupt us, but I don't care. This seems so right. He is beautiful and I want to hold him in my gaze forever. I want to touch him, feel him grow, take him in and never let him go. But he is patient, considerate, and I need his gentle caresses too.

He kisses me on the mouth, the neck - the throat. His hands cup my breasts. I feel my nipples harden as he rolls his thumbs over my sensitive flesh. His touch is so light and I delight at his empathy with my deepest longings. He seems to know instinctively what I love most.

Now he's teasing my left nipple with his mouth. Then the right. His soft breath fans my hot skin. My spine tingles. My tummy tightens in anticipation. He works his lips along my mid line towards my navel and I feel myself drowning in the sensations. Still my whole being needs and demands so much more.

'Nicole . . .' His voice is velvet soft.

'Oh Andy . . .'

His hands are on my thighs, his fingers creating intricate patterns of delight on my skin, moving ever closer to where I want him to be. I gasp as his fingers encounter the dampness between my legs and begin their hesitant exploration. I feel the rush of intense delight, the hot blood in my veins, the wild pressure building inside me.

His fingers find the nub of my pleasure and I'm overcome by dizziness as he brushes a forefinger against it. My knees tremble as I arch my body into his. Another eternity passes.

Then I'm gripping his hair, forcing his head down until our faces are touching. My mouth seizes his and I kiss him wantonly, savagely, tasting and devouring him in my need.

'*Douce Vièrge!*' I want to scream it but can manage only a husky whisper. There are other words I want to say, but in this beautiful moment they do not come.

I push something into his hand, a blue and silver foil wrapper, thanking whatever gods there are in the sky that I remembered. For how could I possibly stop now? I close my eyes and float, as if looking down from a higher plane of existence, but still hearing the sounds around me - his hurried breathing, his groans of pleasure and the rustling of leaves in the canopy above us. A spasm washes over me, throbbing, tingling, and I inhale the delicious scents of his body as it closes and engages with mine.

I try to hold back a scream, but the scream comes anyway, a cry for release, a mixture of pain and delight which takes my breath away with its intensity. Yet another eternity and I feel the pulse of his climax. *And of mine.*

We make love for a second time and afterwards lie together, our bodies nestling, our thighs touching, until most of our passion has subsided. Later, we stroll back to sit by the trees on the Rise.

For a while, neither of us speaks. The sun begins its descent to the west. I wrap my arms around his neck and kiss him.

'Do you mind you're not my first, Andy?'

'I'm insanely jealous. But I don't suppose I have any right to mind. You're . . .'

I don't let him finish. 'That's unimportant. Do you realise how wonderful you were?' I love him, and his past makes no difference to me.

His gentle gaze drifts to the cord of my dress. He gives me his embarrassed look. 'Could we . . .?'

I shake my head, anticipating the full question. 'We can't, *mon chéri*. Right now, you need to cool down. Kiss me one more time. Then we'll go and find some ice cream.'

**

25.

I make an appointment with my doctor to discuss contraception. There have been some recent scares about the dangers of the newer birth pills, and I don't want to risk blood clots. I want to ask about my nightmares too.

Dr Maria has been my MG since before my mother's illness and is easy to talk to. She gives me a thorough medical examination and bombards me with a raft of intimate questions I would rather not answer. When we've finished, she pouts in concentration and begins typing on her computer. After a few moments, she pushes the keyboard aside. She looks up. Her face is impassive. There is always a moment during a consultation when you think there might actually be something wrong. Your pulse quickens and your mouth goes dry.

'I wouldn't worry about the scare stories too much if I were you.' The corner of Dr Maria's mouth wrinkles in a smile. She picks up a pen and begins tapping her desk. 'Nothing wrong with your heart either - or with anything else as far as I can tell. You are a healthy young woman, Nicole.'

'That's a relief.' My heartbeat and breathing return to normal.

She reaches into a drawer and takes out a pack of pills. 'These should be OK for you,' she says, 'but come back and see me next month. Now, what's this about nightmares?'

'I've been having them a lot.'

'Could be stress. It's been a rough emotional ride for you, Nicole, over the past three or four years. I've known patients collapse under fewer pressures than you've had in your life. Do you remember your dreams when you wake up? I never do."

'Sometimes. My father's in them. And Gaston and Louisa at the café. Or I'm in a hospital. At least I think it's a hospital. Long corridors, lots of doors - and smells. That's the nightmare bit. I don't know why I'm in hospital and being there scares me. That's when I usually wake up.'

'Your father died . . . how long ago? Ten years, wasn't it.'

'Eight.' I feel tears coming to my eyes. 'I still miss him a lot. But the worst is, I sometimes feel it was my fault he died. It shouldn't be like that, should it?'

'In my experience, it's not uncommon for children to feel guilt at the death of a parent. Shock and denial are often the first feelings experienced.' Dr Maria taps the desk again. 'But going to university, especially in a foreign country, will be a huge life change for you. That's bound to be stressful.'

I know what she's saying, though I can't help feeling there's more to my nightmares than that. Something is gnawing in my subconscious, something I ought to remember but can't. It's like the feeling I have when I think of *Mamie's* photograph, of a tiny switch I'm not quite able to reach.

'Memory is a strange companion,' Dr Maria says when I try to explain. 'Damage to the brain can cause several medical conditions, anterograde and retrograde amnesia for example. But it doesn't have to be physical. Even a frightening experience - seeing a fatal accident, or a murder say - can cause bits of the brain to shut down.'

'Like post-traumatic stress disorder, you mean?'

'That's one area of study. Amnesia is a controversial topic. Thousands of papers have been written. New case studies appear every week in the medical journals. There is another dissociative condition called selective amnesia. Patients remember only snatches of the event that caused the lapse.' She closes her laptop and makes a point of laying her pen and notepad neatly beside it. 'But there's nothing like that in your records.'

I wrinkle my nose. 'I've definitely never witnessed a murder.'

'And I hope you never do.' Dr Maria crosses her fingers and smiles reassuringly. 'You know, Nicole, I see lots of neurotic patients. You're not one of them. Unless you have trouble sleeping, try not to worry. My guess is you'll figure out what those dreams are about and they'll stop as suddenly as they began.

'The contraceptive pills are on the house, by the way,' she adds. 'Remember I'm always here if you need me.'

A stirring of air on my cheek wakes me from REM sleep. I feel relaxed and content. In my interrupted dream, Andy and I were harvesting grapes in a vineyard in Oxford. Yves was there too, and they were discussing the rival theories unifying quantum mechanics and relativity. Yves was arguing the merits of loop quantum gravity while I was putting up a good case for string theory.

It was all wrong. I have only a sketchy idea what string theory is about, or loop quantum gravity for that matter. They're just things I've heard Andy talk about, or words I've seen in one of his textbooks while tidying up his room. However, in the dream, our arguments - which seemed to have some connection with the labelling of wine bottles - made perfect sense.

I rub the sleep out of my eyes and open them. Andy is lying on his left side with his face close to mine. His left hand is under the pillow half supporting his head, and his right arm is curled round the small of my back. His breathing is gentle and even. We've been together now for fourteen days and, apart from the days of my cycle, we've made love every night. I can't get enough of him.

'Hi!' Andy strokes my hair. 'You're awake. No bad dreams?'

'No. Why do you ask?'

'You had one two nights ago. You called out in your sleep.'

'I didn't know. They usually wake me.' The single sheet is bunched up in the middle of the bed. My lower half is still covered while Andy's feet and long legs stick out at the bottom. I put my arms round his neck, draw him towards me and kiss him. 'How long have you been watching me?'

'About ten minutes.'

'Why didn't you wake me sooner, *mon ami*? We're wasting time.'

'You want to now?'

I suck my breath as he slides his hand over my hip and repositions it on my left buttock. His eyes are hypnotic. 'What do you think?' I purr. 'But we can't stay in bed, you know.'

'Another ten?'

'No more, I'm sorry to tell you. I promised Cathy I'd help today with the food for . . .' I bite my bottom lip as I climb on top of him. 'I'm not supposed to tell you, but she's planning a special dinner for your birthday.'

'I sort of know already. I didn't want a birthday party, so I invited Pawson and his girlfriend over to hang out. I told you about him, didn't I?'

'The other mongrel? Yes.'

'I saw him about six months ago. We've exchanged a few texts.'

'His girl's called Masson, Cathy said.'

'Elise Masson. I haven't met her but Alain's an OK guy.'

'Am I invited?'

'It wouldn't be my birthday without you.' He nuzzles my left nipple with his teeth. 'You like that?'

'It drives me crazy.' I thread my fingers through his hair. 'Do the other one too!'

Later, we have breakfast together. Andy has made it again, the usual croissants, cheese, boiled eggs, bananas and coffee. He has also tried to grill some sausages, has burnt them beyond repair and attempted to dispose of the evidence. I help myself to a banana, skin it and pretend not to notice the mingled smells of overcooked meat and air freshener.

Cathy breezes in and helps herself to a mug of coffee. She sniffs and gives Andy a pitiful glare.

'Burnt sausage?' She screws up her nose. 'I'd better not ask.'

'Sorry, Mum,' Andy says. 'I did my best.'

'We'll get together at two, Nicole.' Cathy adds a lot of milk to her coffee and drinks half of it in two swallows. 'I'm running late,' she explains. 'Can't stop to enjoy the feast!'

A few moments later the outer door slams behind her. Andy takes one of the eggs, cuts it and spreads it, oozing yolk, on a croissant. He munches it contentedly.

We eat in silence. I glance across the bar occasionally to catch his attention and reward him with a smile, which he never fails to return. When breakfast is over, he wipes egg residue from his lips with a napkin and gives me a winning Andy grin.

'So you're free this morning? Maybe we can do something together.'

'I have to go too,' I tell him. 'I can't get all the ingredients for your surprise in St Pièrre. I have to shop in the city, and I have a date with Amelie and Hélène for lunch.'

'I'll work on my thesis then.' Andy grimaces. 'See you later.'

'You can count on it.' I blow him a kiss and go off to brush my teeth. It's true I have to shop but I haven't told him everything. Apart from the party ingredients, I'm planning to buy him a second present.

A few weeks ago, I ordered a book from Amazon, a science book - *Le dernier théoréme de Fermat*, costing nine *euros*. He might have read it, but I scanned his bookshelves without seeing it there. As soon as the package arrived, I took the book out of the Amazon wrapping, re-wrapped it in some gift paper and popped it under the bed. Andy never came into my room *then* of course, so there was no need to hide it.

Cathy and Yves are bound to buy him an expensive gift, like the Mac last year. Something like a Cartier or Patek-Philippe gold watch. I can't compete with that but I'd like to surprise him with something special. Something that'll tell him how much I care for him.

I have no idea what to buy, but once I've parked the Citroen in the city I head for my favourite jewellery store. They show me watches, priced at three or four times what I can afford - and that's the cheaper models. Then they bring out gold and silver cuff links, which Andy would never wear but which are too expensive anyway.

These are followed by silver watch straps, a silver-plated hip flask and matching cigarette case. I'm ready to despair of finding a suitable gift here when I spot a silver St Christopher on a chain. It's designed as a wrist bracelet but displayed in the cabinet along with fashionable necklaces. It costs twenty *euros* more than I can afford but I like it so much I buy it.

I watch the assistant's fingers as she wraps it for me, long, manicured nails painted alternately pink and mauve, and with left hand matching the right. Between forefinger and middle on the left, her pale skin is stained yellowy brown. I have never smoked a cigarette and have never understood why anyone would want to do it.

We all make choices, I reflect. We all have our demons - and tobacco is hers. Yet she folds the gift wrapping with expert ease, tucking in the edges with a precision and symmetry I have never mastered. I look down at my own fingers, the nails short as I like them, to prevent unwelcome snagging as I work. One day, I think, when I'm at university, I might grow them a bit longer. I might even paint them with one-colour varnish, though never more daring than that.

The woman at the counter finishes wrapping. She ties a neat ribbon round the box, knots it and, having curled the ends with a spatula, hands the gift to me. As I reach for my credit card, I suddenly feel doubt. The book, like Andy's walking stick, would be a gesture, no more, an acknowledgement of our short friendship. This piece of simple jewellery costing seventy *euros* is something else, a commitment beyond sex and love. *Wherever you go I will be with you*, it seems to say. I'm being ridiculous, my rational side tells me; it's only a gift. The irrational, emotional side persists and it scares me to death.

Coming out of the store, I see Martha. She's with a man - smart, elegant suit, maybe a lawyer or accountant I think. I greet her with an unenthusiastic *Bonjour*. She looks puzzled and doesn't respond. I don't think she knows me with my hair loose and without my work overall. As they turn into the next entrance, she looks back. I see the flash of recognition then a brief, animated exchange. The man's eyes follow me as I head for the crossing.

Amelie is already seated at Louisa's when I get there. There's no sign of Hélène.

'She'll be along later,' Amelie explains. 'Her car wouldn't start and your phone was switched off. Again.'

'I think there's a problem with the battery. The charge doesn't seem to last very long.' I reach in my bag for the phone, switch it on then pick up my purse.

'It's OK.' Amelie puts a restraining hand on my arm. 'This is on me. Mind you, I'm expecting lots of news in return.'

I take a seat facing the door. Louisa has a waitress in today and we give her our order. Amelie leans forward confidentially. 'Well? What did you buy for him.'

'A silver St Christopher wrist bracelet.'

'Nice.'

'I paid seventy for it, and it scares me, Amm.'

'Scares you?'

'I still can't believe he likes me. I'm not even sure why he likes me - and I'm scared it won't last.'

'What is there not to like? Have you looked in the mirror lately? You're smart and gorgeous.'

'Be serious, Amm.'

'I *am* being serious.'

The shop door opens, letting a waft of warm air into the air-conditioned cool of the café. Hélène sweeps in, looking flustered.

'Are you avoiding me, Nica?' She frowns at me. 'Why didn't you phone me?'

I try to match my expression to the guilt I feel inside. She has left me two messages in the past week and I haven't responded. 'I'm sorry, Lena. I lost track.'

My two girlfriends lean back in their chairs expectantly. Hélène folds her arms; Amelie plays with her hair. They have known for more than a week that Andy and I are together, so I'm not sure what more they want to hear. And I'm not sure there's any more I want to tell them.

'I *am* sorry.'

'Forgiven!' Hélène air-kisses me then grows serious. 'But there *was* something I need to talk to you about.'

157

I give her a queer look. 'You haven't missed a period, have you?'

'Unlikely for me the way things are,' she snorts. 'No, it's about your employers and mine. Something's going on there. They have history, at least the sons do.'

'What do you mean, *history*?' Amelie asks.

From my seat I can tell none of the other customers are paying us the slightest attention. Hélène takes a quick look round the café anyway before pulling her chair closer to the table.

'*History*,' she repeats, lowering her voice. She latches her hand to my wrist in a conspiratorial fashion. 'You know how you sometimes hear things you're not supposed to. The Sonniers - the old man and Marcus - were talking. They've no idea I have a connection through you, Nica. The old man said something like, *you remember, it's his birthday*. And Marcus said, *who, young Ravel?*'

'That's tomorrow,' I explain. 'What else did they say?'

'I was doing some cleaning and the window was open. They were outside, walking up and down. I couldn't very well go out to listen. But as they passed the window again, I heard Marcus say, *It's awkward for me. Paul can go.* I didn't hear any more but when I saw Paul soon after, he was livid, his mouth all twisted and his fists clenched. He looked ready to commit murder.'

'It could be nothing, Lena.'

'No, there's definitely something. Something in the past.'

'Maybe the Ravels invited M. Sonnier to Andy's birthday party,' suggests Amelie. 'He can't go and wants his sons to go instead.'

'There *is* no party. A couple of friends are coming for a meal.'

'Whatever. I just thought I should tell you. You don't want to get caught up in a fight about male ego.' Hélène squeezes my hand and I give her a reassuring smile.

'Don't worry about me, Lena.' I'm sure she's reacting to something that might be quite innocent. 'But I will watch out for the Sonnier brothers. Thanks for letting me know.'

**

26.

'Bonne anniversaire, mon petit!'

Andy opens one eye and squints up at me. He was awake all the time but he likes pretending. I set the alarm for earlier than usual. It's only six but there's quite a lot of work to do for the party. I kiss him on the forehead and ruffle the hair on the nape of his neck. He seizes me by the shoulders, pulls me to him then flips me over onto my back. His lips find my ear and he nibbles the soft lobe. His thumb massages my neck.

'That's not fair, Andy,' I murmur without convincing either him or myself. 'We can't stay in bed all day?'

'Can't we?'

His thumb pauses at my throat then slowly and gently begins to trace a line along the hollow between my breasts. Desire sparks deep inside me. I half clench my fingers against the bed sheet. Andy's hand moves over my tummy towards my pelvis, his thumb continuing its sensuous massage of my flesh. He slides it under the band of my pyjama bottoms. *'Can't we?'*

He presses his mouth to mine, teasing my bottom lip with his teeth until I open to him. His kiss is everything I hoped. His other hand caresses my face and my hair. My pulse quickens. In the core of my being the spark kindles and flames. I look up into his eyes, liquid brown, and reach out my arms to encircle his body.

'Please, Andy.' I pull him closer and his muscles tense as I run the heel of my palms down his spine and clasp his bottom. He groans and I feel him harden.

My breathing is fast and erratic as I kiss him hard, tasting and taking my fill of him. Now his hands are working, lingering, exploring and teasing each and every part of me. The fire rages inside me. My universe implodes and I part my thighs to take him in.

It's half-an-hour later when he lets himself out of my bedroom but not before checking the corridor is empty. He prefers not to run into his father. The last thing he needs, he tells me, is a row about his sex life.

My body is warm and damp from our love-making. His presents are still under my bed. I'll give them to him later.

The birthday is going well. I've cooked some *madeleines* and covered them with chocolate, and have helped Cathy with the other preparations. I baked some macaroons too, proper French macaroons, the sort baked with almonds and vanilla, crisp on the outside with a soft centre.

This morning, Cathy is as happy as I've ever seen her. Yves is in a good mood too. He seems to have forgotten to argue and embraces Andy affectionately. Their present *is* a Patek-Philippe watch. Not a bad guess on my part and, not for the first time, I feel envious of their wealth. What I've saved for university has been by my own efforts and it vexes me how much riches are taken for granted.

The two guests arrive mid-morning and the four of us have lunch together by the swimming pool. Cathy herself brings in the dishes and wishes us *bon appetit*. It seems the forecasters got it right and summer is here to stay. The top temperature today will be twenty-nine.

Alain Pawson, a year older than Andy, is studying medicine at Lyon. Elise is a medical student too. They met during an open day at the university. She's a dark, southern girl with smoking eyes. I can see she's in love with Alain but can't be certain whether he shares the sentiment. When Andy and Alain are together, they speak English and I do my best to keep up. Alain uses a lot of F-words, though none seem to be with the intention of offending. Sometimes that's the way man-talk goes. I rather like my first impression of him.

I stay out of the men's conversation while Elise is making herself comfortable in the main bathroom, but I'm close enough to hear Pawson remark: 'Half a dozen fucking texts. No wonder you don't have many friends, Ravel!'

Andy's reply is predictable. 'I have a lot of work to get through.'

'So do I! You have a fucking phone, don't you?'

'How about we meet up again before I go back to Oxford?'

'I'll hold you to it. Anyway, how'd a fucking swot like you manage to land a girl like that. You were never any good with girls at school.'

Andy shrugs. 'There weren't any.'

'Jesus Christ, there were plenty of opportunities. Some of us managed OK. But you, Ravel . . .' He lets out a few more expletives. 'Glad to see you're making up for it.'

'What about Elise?'

'She's lovely but I don't know if it's a forever thing.'

'Nicole's special.' Andy looks over and flashes me a smile.

'I'll say she is. She's gorgeous, man. You look after her. Treat her well or . . .' He's nearly a head shorter than Andy but he clenches his fist. 'Or I'll break your fucking arm - and maybe your neck.'

I can't help laughing. Pawson turns towards me.

'So you heard all that, Nicole?' He grins. 'I mean it, you know. If Ravel hurts you, just let me know and I'll . . . Sorry, I use that word much too often. Promise you'll ring me.'

'OK. I've got the message. I promise.'

'Nicole's going to Edinburgh,' Andy tells him. 'To study English Literature and Linguistics.'

Pawson's face lights up. 'That's awesome,' he says, and then begins quizzing me about the course and about my knowledge of Scotland.

Elise re-joins us. 'What's this about Scotland?'

'Nicole was telling us about Edinburgh,' Pawson says. 'She's going to study there.'

'I wouldn't have minded doing that, Nicole. Glasgow has a great medical school. And I love Scotland and all those misty mountains. But my English isn't up to it.'

'I needed some coaching too.'

Elise grimaces. 'A year of coaching wouldn't do it for me.'

'Nicole had the advantage of my mother's tuition,' Andy adds. 'I've just found out she speaks better English than I do.'

'Don't exaggerate.' I punch his arm and he puts it protectively round my shoulders. 'I'll see *you* later,' I hiss in his ear.

'You must have got good marks in the *Bac*,' Alain says.

'I don't like to talk about it.'

'Go on, tell us!'

'I got an eighteen in English language and literature. Seventeen overall, if you must know.' It's boasting, which I hate doing, though I know Andy scored better.

'Christ, another fucking genius!' exclaims Pawson. 'You two are well matched.'

I like Alain and Elise; they accept me without any enquiry into my status in the Ravel household. Not everyone does, it seems. Paul Sonnier arrives at *Château Ravel* in late afternoon. He has a high forehead, prominent nose and small chin. He looks vaguely familiar but I have no idea where I might have seen him before. A thin girl, in her late teens, and with large breasts and attitude, is with him. Though nothing Hélène said disposes me to like Paul, I believe in giving people the benefit of the doubt. And despite her warning I'm willing to be polite.

However, her opinion proves only too accurate. Sonnier offers no conversation but looks at me continually with hooded eyes. Andy bristles, and it's clear my friend was right. They *do* have history. After a brief greeting and what passes for a birthday wish, Sonnier withdraws into Yves' company. The girl, whom he hasn't introduced, stands by the pool, staring into the water or examining her bright red fingernails.

They don't stay long. I'm relieved when Paul shakes hands with Yves. He beckons to the girl and reaches in his pocket for his car keys. As they both turn to go, he gives me a lecherous grin and I'm close enough to hear him remark: *So he's screwing the domestic help.* I don't care what anyone thinks of my relationship with Andy but for a moment imagine insects crawling on my skin. I fight down the feeling of revulsion. Luckily, Andy is laughing at one of Pawson's jokes and is out of earshot.

Something worries me about that remark, not just the insulting way he said it. *How does he know?*

'Tell me about Paul Sonnier,' I ask Cathy when we are clearing up later. She is putting the usable leftovers in plastic boxes. I stack the dirty plates and dishes, while Elise wipes the surfaces of the kitchen units and tables by the pool.

'Paul? Why do you ask?'

'He didn't act like a guest. Andy and he don't appear to like each other. And his girlfriend didn't say much.'

'You noticed? They never got on, even as children. I've never understood why. Some kids hit it off; others don't. And that was his sister Irène by the way.'

'That was *Irène*?' I give a little screech. 'Oh my God!'

Cathy laughs boisterously. 'Would you believe it? She's really a half-sister. Lives with her mother in the city and visits her father once a month. The Sonniers divorced soon after Paul was born. M. Sonnier is on to wife number four. There's an older brother too, Marcus, from a first marriage - an accountant. Paul's the son of wife number two. Confusing that both father and son are Pauls. All the Sonniers are wine growers through and through. Paul is something of a vinologist too, whereas Andy doesn't . . . Well, you know already.'

'I told you my friend Hélène works for the Sonniers. She told me about Paul and Marcus. She didn't know about Irène.'

'Marcus is nearly forty, I believe,' Cathy says. 'He looks after the money side, but he doesn't live on the estate and I don't think he interferes in the practical day-to-day running. Paul is twenty-five. Did I tell you the matchmaking story?'

'Andy did.'

'It's a joke, believe me.'

'That's a relief,' I say. 'Why did Paul and his sister bother coming at all?'

'Paul - the father - probably ordered them to go. There's a sort of fraternity among vintners, and they're neighbours. We must always put on a show of mutual respect.'

'M. Sonnier must have left his respect at home,' Elise sniffs.

'He upset you?'

'I think he upset Nicole.'

Cathy frowns. 'Nicole?'

'He whispered something to Irène. Mild sexual innuendo.' I want to play down the incident. 'It's not important.'

'In my house, it's important to me.'

'No, really. Please forget about it.'

'If you say so.'

When we finish the chores, Andy is deep in conversation with Alain, who obviously intends staying, so I say goodnight and go to my room. I pull the two birthday packages from under the bed and with my heart racing like a TGV sit down to wait. Ten minutes later, Andy knocks on the door.

'Nicole?'

'It isn't locked.'

'I should have told you they decided to stay.' He comes in flush with embarrassment. 'I'm sorry.'

'*Pas du tout*. The guest rooms were made up. Anyway, I've got something for you. I couldn't match an expensive watch, but . . .'

I see his expression change and I register his genuine delight as he takes the presents and unwraps them. It gives me a warm feeling inside.

'Thank you.' He begins folding the gift paper. 'I wasn't expecting anything. These are great, thoughtful presents.'

'Thoughtful?'

'My parents never buy me books. I mean, they pay for textbooks, but not books I want to read - for fun, if you like.'

'You read for fun?' I taunt and he grins like a schoolboy.

'Like this one. I'm looking forward to reading it. And the silver wrist bracelet is brilliant.'

'I'm glad you like it.'

'Being well-off is suffocating sometimes. I've never known anything else. My parents - my father especially - always go for the most expensive things. Like the watch. I was supposed to get one when I turned twenty-one but I was so busy with Paris. Then last year - the computer'.

'I remember last year. I made jokes about a walking stick.'

'You did.' He grins. 'You know, I respect my father for what he's done with the business. He's worked hard to make it succeed. But when I look into his eyes, I always see *euro* signs pop up.'

'*Euro* signs?'

'In his irises. *Euros* instead of pupils, like on those old-fashioned cash registers.'

We both laugh.

'You know I don't care about the money,' Andy goes on. 'But you get used to it, you know. And I have another year of fees and expenses before I can start earning. My Scottish grandmother left me a few thousand . . .'

'Lucky you!'

'I can't touch it until I'm twenty-five.' He's opening up about his domestic situation more than ever before. 'That's what her will says. It would be nice to keep some of it back. One day I'd like my own *Château Ravel* . . . without the winery of course. Maybe a family.'

'My Dad left something for *us* in trust,' I tell him. 'Bernard, Sophie and me. He hadn't got around to upping his life assurance but he managed *that.*' I remember sadly how I discovered the family's relative poverty at the age of twelve. I learned about the trust fund when I was fourteen. Looking back, I'm surprised at the inconsistency of a loving man who took care to provide for his children in later life yet apparently ignored short term needs. But no one, I suppose, expects to die before they're forty. Perhaps it's as simple as that.

'I had access to the money as soon as I was eighteen,' I say. 'But I haven't touched it yet. I wanted to use some to repay my grandparents part of my mother's hospital expenses, but they refuse to take it. The legacy isn't a big one.'

Andy grimaces. 'Nor is mine, though there's also a half share in a cottage in the Highlands of Scotland. She left that to me too.'

'You have a cottage in Scotland?'

'Half a cottage. And it's occupied.'

'I don't understand. She's dead, your grandmother?'

'Yes, a few years ago. It's quite complicated. My grandfather passed away first and Granny Douglas took in a lodger - a woman the same age - for company. Mrs Watson. They became friends. Granny sold her an interest in the house. She had her lawyer draw up the agreement. I get my share when Mrs Watson dies, not that I'm wishing it. She was in the best of health last I heard.'

'So you could be well off in your own right - one day?'

'The cottage is in the middle of nowhere. It probably isn't worth more than a hundred thousand pounds. So, I'd get fifty, at most. I assume it'd have to be sold to give Mrs Watson's heirs the rest.'

'So I could be after your money . . .'

'You could. I don't care. It isn't a fortune. It would soon disappear and I'd be broke. Fifty thousand won't buy much in a city.'

He folds the birthday wrapping into a neat square and fiddles with the edges.

'Don't do that now.' I take the paper from him and slide it under the bed. 'I don't care about your money, Andy. I just need . . .'

He leans towards me, his eyes dark and inviting.

'Come here,' he whispers.

Yves leaves for Bordeaux airport early next day. He is still in a good mood and shares a cab with Alain and Elise, who are returning to Lyon. Andy has to spend the morning studying but straight after breakfast I persuade him to tell me about Paul Sonnier.

'I never trusted him. When we were about seven or eight, Paul stole another kid's toy. He lied about it; said I had taken it. Of course, he'd stashed it in my closet so I took the blame. I gave him a black eye and he's never forgiven me.'

'I can't imagine you doing that,' I say.

'Don't believe it. Every time I see him, I want to do it again.

166

But my father seems wholly won over by his false charm. Paul's good at flattery. Anyhow, give him his due, he knows the wine business and Father values that kind of expertise above everything else.'

'Hélène doesn't like Paul much but I thought she was exaggerating. She called him an upper-class bully.'

'To his face?'

'Of course not! She needs the job. And old man Sonnier seems OK. Marcus too.'

'I'll split Paul's head if he hurts any of your friends.'

'No you won't, Andy. He doesn't knock her about or anything. It's his attitude - you know, the way he speaks to tradesmen and casual labour on the estate.'

I decide to put Paul Sonnier and his smutty remark out of my mind. Men with attitude are not worth the trouble of a response. Cathy helps me clear away a few remains of yesterday's party then suggests we put our feet up in the living room. I sink into one of the armchairs while she lounges on the sofa opposite.

'It's my twenty-sixth year in Bordeaux, you know. I think this summer's going to be one of the hottest.' She kicks off her shoes and wiggles her toes.

'I love our summers.' I sigh. 'But I suppose I'm going to have to get used to a colder climate.'

'Edinburgh? I was thinking the same. Remember what it was like in March.'

'I do remember.'

'It isn't always cold in Scotland. One summer we spent in Perthshire, the temperature reached 32 degrees. Andy was just a wee boy.'

I glance round the room, trying to imagine what Andy was like as a child. There are a few family photographs scattered around the house so I already know what he looked like at eight, and ten, and thirteen, but I'm thinking more about what *kind* of child. Happy, mischievous or both? What would it feel like to grow up in this house surrounded by all the luxuries life with wealthy parents can provide?

'We weren't always so comfortable.' Cathy seems able to read my thoughts. 'The Ravels weren't exactly poor and starving when I met Yves, but the business was in a bit of a mess. Profits were falling and Yves' father was running it into debt. We had a good marriage but the atmosphere at home was stifling. Then Yves took the reins and made a commercial success of it. The profits came rolling in. A co-operative - the one the Sonniers are part of - tried to buy us. Of course, Yves told them politely where to go. The Ravels have been around since before the Revolution.'

'Hélène told me the family once had a title.'

'That's not quite correct. I think the first Ravel - he would have been *de Ravel* - was a *chevalier*. It wasn't strictly a title . . . not like a *marquis*.'

'I've heard the word but I'm not sure what it signifies.'

'Before the Revolution, it was more of a status. *Chevaliers* were professional soldiers in the king's army.' Cathy massages her toes. 'Yves would know for sure. I don't think it could be passed on to the next generation. Anyway, as I said, the family has been around for a while, title or not. The old *château* was a ruin long before Yves was born. You've seen it - an eyesore.' She gives her best impression of a disgruntled Gascon peasant with toothache. 'But, you know, *noblesse oblige*. Tradition is tradition. Who am I to deny it to them?'

She continues massaging her feet. I sit forward eagerly in my comfortable chair.

'Tell me a bit more about Andy when he was little . . . and about Scotland.'

'Curious about everything sums him up best. He preferred animals and gadgets to people. What fascinated him most was how things worked. He preferred taking toys to bits rather than playing with them. And, of course, there was Wendy.'

'His pony?'

'So he told you. She was a beauty, but I'm afraid she had to go when he went to board. Then there was his astronomy phase; around nine or ten, he devoured every book he could find on the subject.

Maybe that was Grandpa Ravel's influence. Well, that was where he got most of the books. With computers, he wasn't so much interested in using them for the usual purposes. No social media and no games. He was more into programmes and logic. Puzzles.

'The two of us holidayed in Scotland every other year until he was ten or eleven. Yves was mostly too busy. My mother had inherited a house from an old aunt. I was born and grew up in Manchester. My father was an Englishman but he liked Scotland and they moved there when he retired.'

'Andy told me about your mother's cottage,' I say. 'He didn't say where it is, except that it's in the Highlands. He told me about Mrs Watson too, how your mother gave her a half share.'

'He hasn't got the story right. Mrs Watson has a life interest only. Andy gets the house when she passes away.'

'All of it?'

'All of it.' Cathy gives me a sad smile. 'My father died of a stroke when Andy was six, my mother three years ago.'

'I'm sorry.'

'That's life, Nicole, as you know. And death. We were quite an ordinary family - and a happy one. Not like the Ravels.'

'What do you mean?'

'Oh, we're happy enough in this house. But the wider family is estranged, scattered around the world. One of Yves' uncles runs a vineyard in New Zealand, I believe. There were three or four brothers in that generation, a sister too. I don't even know their names! The family is more patriarchal than most.'

I'm thinking about what Andy said on the way from the airport. And about my grandfather and the photo taken at Louisa's. Putting it together with Hélène's gossip to make five, I can't resist asking the obvious question.

'I don't suppose one of the brothers was a butcher called Louis, was he?'

'Whatever gave you that idea?'

When I explain, Cathy laughs. 'He could have been. Yves gets irate when the subject of his family comes up. Georges once told me there was at least one murderer and an embezzler in his ancestors.

He could have made it up, for all I know. Yves won't talk about them, and I don't ask.'

'That's so sad.' I nod sympathetically, all the while thinking about my grandparents, and Denise, and the stretch of no man's land keeping us apart. Sooner rather than later, for the sake of Sophie and Bernard - and for my own - it's land I must try to cross.

**

27.

Cathy

Yves' eyebrows come together and his forehead creases in a frown. I know the look. Usually he either disagrees with something he's read in his financial newspaper or he's about to pronounce on the political situation in Europe.

Today it's neither of these.

'What is it with André?' He looks up. Long years have passed since he initiated a conversation about our son.

'What's what?'

'There's something different about him.' He lays down the paper and fishes a small cigar from the pocket in his shirt.

'How different?'

'Less broody. Not so studious. Last weekend I thought I heard him singing in the shower.'

I hide a smirk of self-satisfaction. Since our heart-to-heart in the kitchen, Andy's mood has been buoyant and I've little doubt of the reason.

'Andy can't sing,' I observe.

'Well, perhaps not,' growls Yves. 'It was probably his idea of music. And he actually asked me a question about the business. He's not ill, is he?'

I laugh. 'No, he's not ill. Figure it out for yourself.'

Yves scratches his forehead. The eyebrows separate and he peers at me over his spectacles. 'You don't mean he's got a girlfriend?'

'I believe so,' I say casually. 'Are you blind, Yves?'

'What!' Yves' face reddens and the frown returns. 'Christ, you don't mean your girl . . . *Mademoiselle . . .*'

'You don't even remember her name.'

'Of course I remember her name, Catherine. *Nicole Durand*.'

'She'd make a very nice daughter-in-law.'

Yves' face grows even redder. The artery in his neck stands out. 'Over my dead body,' he shrieks. 'You'll have to get rid of her.'

'Don't be ridiculous, Yves. I'll do no such thing. And it *will* be your dead body if you don't calm down. You'll have a heart attack or a stroke.'

'Little gold-digger!' Yves mutters almost - but not quite - inaudably.

'I heard that, Yves Ravel,' I retort. 'Like me when I married you.'

'Our situation was different, Catherine.'

'Different how?'

'You were just different.'

'Oh yeah? I'm from an ordinary working-class English family. We struggled but I got through school, went to university, got a teaching degree. I had to borrow to go to the Sorbonne. I had to work. Then I met you and married you for your money!'

'You didn't.'

'I know I didn't. I loved you, Yves Ravel. And if you took the trouble to get to know Nicole, you might actually like her.'

'This has nothing to do with liking or not liking. The girl's OK. Pleasant and polite . . . quite pretty in fact.'

'Trust you to objectify.'

'I've nothing against her, but I'm not going to support André and a mistress while he lives it up at Oxford.' His carotid still pulses.

'I wouldn't expect you to.'

'And God knows how many of a brood she'll give him before he's done with his career of learning.'

'So, you'd rather he screwed around in one-night stands with horny undergrads. Or went with whores . . .' He's making me angry now. '. . . risking STDs or worse? This is one relationship you *won't* screw up, Yves Ravel. I fucking won't let you!'

Yves puts down his spectacles on the coffee table and stares at me in astonishment. 'I've never heard you swear like that before,

Catherine.'

'Well, you'll hear a lot more of it unless you see *fucking* sense.' I pick up a cushion and toss it at him. 'Andy's love life isn't any of our business. He isn't a little boy any longer.'

'This is ridiculous,' says Yves. He lights his cigar, inhales and lets out a stream of smoke. It seems to calm him. 'I mean . . . we know nothing about the girl.'

'I know a great deal about her.' His smoke lingers. I cough it away. 'Those are disgusting, Yves! Nicole knows the meaning of hard work. She's smart. Reliable. In September, she'll be going up to university in Edinburgh.'

'I remember. You said.' Yves looks suddenly interested. 'I don't suppose she's doing accountancy and computing.'

'You never listen, Yves! No, English Literature. Why?'

'Martha is taking a week's leave. Has a family emergency apparently. We're behind with the paperwork and I haven't quite got to grips with her computer system.'

'Nicole would be good with the books.'

'She knows nothing about the business.'

'I imagine she knows as much as Martha. She knows about money - managed the family budget, and a younger brother and sister when the mother went through a long illness. And she knows about computers too. Georges can give her a crash course. Ask her. Give her a chance to refuse; you won't be disappointed.'

'I'll speak to her. But it's strictly business, Catherine. It doesn't mean I have to . . .'

'Of course not,' I laugh.

**

28.

Nicole

The days are flying by. Andy has gone back to Oxford for the week. He texted *CU soon XXX* and is going to phone once he's booked a flight from London.

It's Monday morning and I look up from making a bed to see Yves Ravel's bulky frame standing in the doorway. I don't often see him in the mornings; he's in his office and at work by seven. I occasionally make him breakfast but most weekdays he has nothing more than a cup of instant coffee.

'*Mlle Durand.*'

'*Bonjour, M. Ravel!*' Though I call Cathy by her given name I would never dream of calling Yves by his.

'May I speak with you? It will take only a few moments.'

Yves is always polite when we meet or pass one another on the stairs, or when I take him a coffee, but he has rarely if ever requested a conversation with me. Little wheels are turning in my head as I try to imagine what possible reason he can have for doing so today. There was Paul Sonnier's snide remark to his sister at the birthday party - which maybe he heard as well as I - but if he intended to warn me off why has he waited until now? That was a few days ago. Is he going to ask me to leave his house?

'Of course, *monsieur.*' I smooth down the king-size duvet and give him my attention. He's wearing a smart suit, and I notice his airline cabin bag lies on the floor of the corridor behind him. So he's off on his travels again. He's been home only three whole days since the last trip. 'What can I do for you?'

Yves clears his throat with a deliberate cough. He seems embarrassed and gives me that odd, half-apologetic look I've seen once before. 'I have a meeting at ten. Shall we go downstairs?'

I follow him to the living room, where he stops and gallantly holds open the door for me. Cathy is sitting on her favourite sofa with a glass of water. Some financial spreadsheets are spread out on the cushion beside her. She looks up and waves her hand in greeting. The atmosphere is friendly, welcoming. This isn't about Andy after all.

Yves stands in the middle of the room, his hands behind his back. He *is* embarrassed. *Very.* He has something to say and apparently doesn't know where to begin.

'Well, she's here, Yves,' Cathy says. She gathers up the spreadsheets, piles them on the floor and beckons me to sit beside her. 'It's over to you.'

Yves clears his throat again. 'Catherine . . ,' he hesitates. *'My wife* tells me you have some experience with money. You have managed a family business.'

'Only the running of our home, *monsieur.* I'm not an accountant.'

'Nevertheless, I was hoping you might be able to help me.' He glances at Cathy, who has now put on her stern face. 'With the new system and everything, we have a backlog of work. I wondered if you . . .'

'Monsieur?'

'Oh, for Christ's sake, Yves!' Cathy bursts out laughing. 'Nicole, my husband needs a little temporary assistance with his office work. I suggested you might be able to oblige him. For some extra money, that is.'

'Of course, *mademoiselle.* I'm going to be in England for a day or two. My brother will be in charge. But I want someone to deal with mail, sort out the bills so either Georges or I can pay them. Update the computer records. Mark off the ledgers when accounts are settled. *Income. Expenditure.* That sort of thing.' He smiles. 'Maybe run a duster over my desk once in a while, if you would be kind enough.'

'Nothing you won't be able to do with your eyes shut, Nicole,' Cathy adds. She winks at me. 'I'm sure some extra money will come in handy.'

'Of course,' says Yves again. 'Four hundred *euros* for the week.'

'I thought we settled on five,' Cathy says. She winks again. 'Cash.'

'Yes, five hundred,' agrees Yves.

All kinds of weird thoughts are rushing through my head. Five hundred *euros* would come in very useful; it would pay for all my books and more. However, I have no experience of either secretarial work or bookkeeping. But again, Cathy seems to be encouraging me to accept, if not actually driving the arrangement.

'So, are we agreed, *Mlle Nicole*?' Yves smiles pleasantly and extends his large hand. Despite slight misgivings about what I'm letting myself in for, I take it and feel my own hand swallowed up in his firm grip.

I still have only a hazy notion about wine growing and production. During my first months with the family, after harvest, Cathy took me on a tour of the premises. Then, I saw the mechanical crushing process and savoured the aroma of the store where the pressed must is aged in barrels. I sipped *Supérieur* and *Graves* in the tasting parlour where visitors can sample the wines before buying. Then there was Georges' hasty tuition and the four days I spent there as a hostess. There won't be any more picking. Labour costs are high and for this year's harvest Yves has already made the decision to do most of the work by machine. It's quicker and means the grapes can be gathered at night.

However, although hopeless at complex mathematics, I understand arithmetic, money and balance sheets. On the first morning of my new job, Georges Ravel explains the *Appellation* process. He takes me through the accounts, showing me the computer programme Martha put in to handle them. The work isn't difficult and by the second day Georges compliments me on my rapid progress. The extras duties help fill idle hours when, faced with nothing to do, I would fret at Andy's absence. They don't prevent me missing him madly, and these few warm summer nights are long and lonely.

The week passes more quickly than I expect. After two days, Georges leaves me on my own. I establish a routine, two hours in the forenoons, two after lunch. As my job with Cathy has no fixed hours, I manage to tuck in my other work between those as a bookkeeper. *Chateau Ravel* has broken with the traditions of Bordeaux to sell direct to merchants as well as through the *negociants,* so I write a few polite reminders to clients whose payment is due. I send out bills, deal with incoming invoices and mark up Yves' ledgers. He likes to have paper back-up for everything.

On Thursday, I make a trip downtown to deposit twenty thousand *euros* in cheques. It is the largest sum of money I have ever handled. At one of the counters in the bank I am surprised to see Paul Sonnier with an older man, whom I have no difficulty in recognising as his brother. They have the same broody eyes, prominent nose and high forehead. I watch them for a few minutes unnoticed before Paul turns round and catches sight of me.

I steel myself to be polite. '*Bonjour, M. Sonnier.*'

Paul colours. He glances at his brother as if for support before returning my greeting, though he avoids my eyes. Marcus Sonnier - if indeed he is Marcus and not another family member - flashes a look of mild interest. He nods before returning to his business at the counter. But already I have recognised him. I know why Paul seemed so familiar. I realise now how he knew my position in the Ravel household.

Marcus Sonnier is the man I saw with Martha, the day before Andy's birthday, outside the jeweller's shop.

**

29.

Andy returns to France on Friday. He wants me to pick him up at the airport. Cathy tells me to take her car.

When I see him come out of *Arrivals* and wave, my tummy flips. I race across the concourse, ignoring the glares from other travellers, and throw my arms around his neck. He doesn't protest when I give him my mouth.

'Wow!' He grins when we break apart to breathe. 'Do I get to put my bag down now so we can do it properly?'

I realise how much I've longed for him, longed to curl up beside him at bedtime and wake in the mornings with my cheek against his chest. We've been together for no time at all, yet it seems forever. How am I to survive even a single semester at Edinburgh without him when I feel like this after a few days' separation?

'How do you like driving this?' he asks, when we're sitting in the Mercedes.

'This is the second time I've driven it. It's different. Quiet. Smooth and obscenely expensive.'

'It grows on you, doesn't it? Driving is less stressful.'

I start the motor and ease the car silently out of the parking space. 'Much less. On the *autoroute* anyway. Not so much through town.'

'So my father had you as a gofer for the week?'

'It wasn't so bad.' I texted him the details of my new job. 'I can use the money for Edinburgh. And I'm finishing this evening.'

The *Rocade*, the Bordeaux ring road, is heavy with traffic and I have to concentrate hard on my driving. Andy respects that, so we don't say much until we turn off on the E72.

'It'll pay for my books and help with the rent. That's going to cost me about a hundred and seventy *euros* a week.'

'Does your room have a double bed?'

'It does, as a matter of fact, but it's narrow and a bit short by your standards.'

'That'll make my visits so much more exciting.' He puts his hand on my knee and eases his fingers along the top of my thigh.

'Don't, Andy!'

'I've missed you, Nicole. I want you.'

'I want you too, *mon petit*, but not now. You're distracting me from the road. Wait until we're home.'

'Sorry!' He tips back the passenger seat and stretches his long legs into the well under the dash. 'I've been thinking, Nicole. I'm definitely finished with Oxford for the summer. We should go away together.'

'I can't afford it, Andy.' I catch his eye in the rear-view mirror.

'You've got five hundred coming. You don't need it all for books.' His face lights up in an adolescent grin. 'Come on, it'll be fun. No parents to worry about.'

The heat of anticipation has been building in my insides as we drive. Concentration is difficult with him so close. The last thing I want, either home or away, is some juvenile fun. What I want is to wrap my thighs round his hips and press myself against his muscular body.

'You're a natural, *mademoiselle*,' Georges says when I go into the office. 'You have the interests of the Ravel family at heart. That woman is not an asset in my view, but my brother insists she is good for us. He is infatuated, I fear.'

'*Merci, monsieur.*' I blush at the compliment though I scarcely know how to respond to this unexpected confidence. He seems to be confirming everything Cathy is trying to hide.

I decide to tell him about seeing Martha and Marcus Sonnier together.

'I've never met Marcus,' I say, 'but I'm fairly sure that's who he was.'

Georges nods thoughtfully. 'I'm fairly sure too, Nicole. There's no mistaking the Sonnier nose and chin. Typical of old Paul,' he adds. 'Anything we do, he can't wait to do better. The Sonniers will have decided if we can go digital, so can they. And to give credit where it's due, Mme Martha knows her technology. But we'll have to watch that one, I think.'

'Is something wrong, *M. Georges*?'

'Probably nothing, Nicole, but thank you for telling me.'

I like Georges. He is relaxed about most things, unlike his brother who always seems stressed. The odd thing is, I like Yves too. In my year with the family I've had until now little to do with him. Influenced perhaps by his regular arguments with Andy, I supposed him a hard taskmaster. However, after a week exposed to the business, I realise he's quite the opposite. The opinion of the three full-time employees in the plant is that Yves Ravel is the best employer anyone could wish for.

'Catherine tells me you're going to university,' Georges goes on. 'To study languages.'

'*Oui, monsieur.*'

'*Quel dommage,*' he says. 'As a business assistant, there would be a permanent job here for you when you graduate. We brothers should take life at a more leisurely pace, especially Yves. He works too hard. It's bad for his health, and for Catherine. She deserves more. And André . . .' He picks up a thick folder and taps its edge on my desk while fixing me with a solemn smile. 'He has no interest.'

'I know, *monsieur.*' I nod sympathetically.

'But with you -' He lays the file down and pats it as if it were a pet animal. 'But nothing,' he finishes. 'I daydream, Nicole. That is all. We should work.'

His meaning is clear enough and, for the first time since *lycée* I consider the possibility my life might take another path.

**

30.

After a busy week, I have most of the weekend free. On Friday evening, I'm discussing with Andy what we might do together when my phone buzzes. This is a number I don't recognise, but I answer anyway.

'It's Sophie.' My sister is excited. 'Jean has bought us new mobile phones. Bern and me.'

'Cool!' I'm happy for her and try to sound as excited as she is. I feel guilty that I've been neglecting my sister. Schools are closed for the summer but with the extra work in the office I haven't managed to spend even an afternoon with her.

Sophie isn't finished telling me her news. '*Maman* starts a part time job the week after next,' she squeaks. 'You'll never guess . . . at the supermarket, where she used to work.'

'That's good, isn't it?' The best thing Denise can do is face the world of work again, so I'm pleased for her. That she has made the effort is one more indication she has turned a corner and her illness is behind her. However, the news puts pressure on me to fix our relationship.

'I suppose.' Sophie's excitement over, I now recognise her bored tone.

'Look, Soph,' I say on impulse, 'if I come over tomorrow, you can tell me all about your phone.'

'*Formidable*,' she screeches. 'We'll all be here . . . and I think *Maman* will be happy to see you too.'

Glancing over at Andy, I shrug.

'Eleven o'clock? We'll go shopping if you like.'

'That'll be awesome, Nicole.' Sophie puts on her grateful, glad-you're-my-sister voice. 'Love you!'

'Love you too, sis,' I reply and punch the red button.

Andy grimaces. 'Don't worry about me,' he says. 'I have plenty of work to get through. And families are important.'

At Caudéran, Sophie is getting ready. Jean greets me with a handshake. I like the way he looks me in the face and doesn't let his eyes wander over my figure like some men I've known. Denise gives me the warmest smile I've seen in a long while. I ask her about the job.

'A cashier at the till. Three days a week.'

Jean puts an arm round her shoulders. 'I don't want your mother to take on more until she's ready. There will be more shifts later if she wants them.'

'Yes, if I want them,' Denise echoes. 'But I'm dreading my first day.'

'You'll be fine,' I tell her.

'I hope so. I explained to the new store manager about my illness. I didn't want her hearing about it from anyone else. Wish me luck.'

It must have taken guts to take that first step, considering she was close to being sacked three years ago. Then, she was a supervisor. It wasn't a highly-paid job but it covered our expenses - or should have done. Demotion to cashier will be tough to handle.

'I do, *Maman*. Sincerely.'

Sophie has been in her room for nearly an hour experimenting with clothes and make-up. At last, she puts in an appearance. She's not yet fifteen but looks more like eighteen. She has discarded her favourite jeans and scruffy teen looks for a skirt and top. When I saw her last, she had shoulder-length hair. Now it's short, cut off the ear and curves at the nape of her neck. I hardly recognise her.

'What do you think?' she invites.

I'm thinking of the scrawny, nervous girl she was when I took her to the clinic for the first time.

'Who are you, Soph?' I stare back at my soon-to-be adult kid sister, blink twice and give her the OK sign.

'It's too much? Tell me.'

Though she has applied too much eye shadow, it isn't a disaster, so I decide a little white lie is OK.

'No, it's brilliant. Honestly. Shall we go?'

The weather is bright and sunny, but humid, not ideal for walking in the stuffy air of the city. It's one of those mornings when you feel the extra weight of air on your shoulders. However, a promise is a promise and, anyway, the shops are air-conditioned, so I'm looking forward to our day together. I leave the Citroen and we take the bus downtown to mingle with the Saturday crowds on Rue St Catherine. The best shops are outside our budget but Sophie enjoys trying on clothes we can't afford. Eventually, we make for Zara, where she settles for an embroidered top and a pair of frayed denim shorts. I decide to save my money and buy some clothes when I get to Edinburgh. French designers don't tailor summer fashion for the Scottish autumn and winter.

The St Catherine Promenade is busy, so we stroll towards the City Hall, looking for somewhere to eat. After two hours in and out of the sunshine, I regret not wearing a hat. We find a table under an awning at one of the cafés in the square, dominating our view the twin gothic towers of the cathedral. Though it's more than a year since I was there, the scene is one I've witnessed many times, typical of Bordeaux in summer. The north portal is in shade and people are standing in groups round it, taking respite from the glare of the sun. While we wait to be served, Sophie plays with her new phone. I check for messages on mine. There are none and Andy hasn't phoned so I lazily watch tourists mix with locals as they file in and out of the cathedral.

At first, I think my eyes are playing tricks. I left Andy at *Château Ravel* with his computer and books spread over the terrace table. Now, I see him clear as day come out of the north portal of St André's Cathedral, turn right and head away from me in the direction of the campanile. Even at this distance there is no mistaking him. My heart leaps but with the bustle and noise of the square, there is no point in calling out. For a moment the crowds obscure my view. Then I notice Andy isn't alone. There is a woman with him.

They stop. They face one another, apparently conversing. Then she reaches out towards him and kisses him on the cheek. Andy makes no effort to avoid her touch but instead puts his arms round her and they embrace.

In a second, my whole world comes crashing down. I feel lightheaded and my body goes limp.

'Nicole?'

Sophie leans over me, her hand on my shoulder. Nearby stands a waiter, pencil and notepad in hand.

'Are you OK, Nicole? You look a bit pale.'

I look across the square to the spot, uncertain at first if what I saw was real or a hallucination. I'm hoping the latter. There is no sign of either Andy or the woman. But, in spite of the heat and humidity, I know what I saw.

'Do you want to go home?' Sophie asks.

'No, I'm fine.' My emotions are shot to pieces and I'm anything but fine. However, the last thing I want is to spoil my sister's afternoon. If Andy has been cheating on me, it's between the two of us.

'*Mademoiselle* has been out in the sun too long perhaps,' the waiter suggests.

I have no intention of explaining myself to a stranger and give a strangled laugh. 'That must be it. Too much shopping and too much walking. Let's have something to eat.'

We order drinks and salads. My stomach is heaving at the idea of food, but I force myself to clear my plate. Sophie bolts the meal as if she hasn't eaten in a week and doesn't seem to notice my lack of appetite. I am glad she's with me. Her normality stops me from lashing out.

'That was so *weird*,' she hisses when we are on the bus back to Caudéran.

'Weird?'

'You looked as if you'd seen a ghost. I thought you were sick.'

'Probably because I skimped on breakfast,' I lie, and it seems to satisfy her.

'It was a nice day, wasn't it?' She sidles up to me and plants her chin cheekily on my shoulder. 'When do I get to meet Andy?'

'Shut up, Sophie,' I tell her.

I don't want to face Denise or Jean again in my present mood so I say goodbye to Sophie in the street. I turn off my phone and, for an hour, drive round the suburbs, brooding. Cathy doesn't expect me back at work until Sunday evening, so I've already arranged to stay over with Amelie. She won't finish until six. She moved a month ago; her small flat was getting too cramped - after she'd filled it with furniture. Now she's planning to take on private clients and build up her own business.

The Citroen doesn't have climate control like Cathy's Mercedes and by the time I head for Amelie's place I'm a mess. My dress and underwear are sticking to my body and I see from my reflection in the vanity mirror that my eyes are red and my squint prominent. Though determined not to give into tears, I can't help myself. Spells of righteous anger conflate with moments of self-loathing, dejection with eager hope I'm mistaken and that there is an innocent explanation for what I witnessed. I attack the gear changes too harshly and apply the brakes as if I'm on a race track.

I remember Andy's trip to Toulouse to visit his supposed friend. He never did explain what that was about, and after we got together I never thought to question him about it. Now, I'm writing my own story about what happened: a girl from his Paris years - reconnecting - promising to meet again . . . I scream and bang the horn. If I'm arrested for a traffic offence, it'll be his fault. I just don't care any longer.

I want there to be another explanation but I can't think of one. Andy has cheated on me. I can't believe he has been cheating all along; I would have known. But what if he has . . . if it has all been an act? At some stage I'll have to confront him, but I'm not ready for that yet.

I'm nearing my destination when I have second thoughts. I still feel like lashing out. My head is full of anger but I don't want to take it out on my best friend. Amelie would understand, but she doesn't deserve to be the first victim of my mood.

I take another detour, driving north out of the city to the Floral Park. It's beautiful at this time of year and is open until evening. I park the car and go for a walk. It doesn't help. Today, I see nothing of the park's beauty, only the ugliness of betrayal. All I feel is the bitterness of my own naivety.

I head back downtown. When at length I draw up outside Amelie's flat, I collapse against the steering wheel, drained of all expectation, with my head nestled against my arm.

Amelie never judges. She sends me to clean my face.

'You're sure it was him?' she asks when I've unpacked my overnight bag and changed into some fresh clothes. 'You were at the *Café Francais*. By your own admission you were . . . what . . . at least thirty metres away.'

'Of course I'm sure.'

'Maybe it was someone in the family.'

'You know Andy doesn't have a sister. Emmeline, remember. And I know Beatrice, his aunt, and it wasn't her. The two cousins are boys.'

'An old friend from school . . .?'

'Boys' school!'

'. . . or from his time at UPMC?' She is doing her best to console me but it isn't working. 'He didn't exactly have his tongue down her throat, did he?'

'He hugged her, Amm.'

My phone chirps. Andy's name comes up on the screen but I ignore it.

'You'll have to talk to him sooner or later,' Amelie gives me a quizzical look and I nod. 'Ask him straight out and wait for the answer.'

'That's what scares me.' I'm close to tears again. 'I can't help loving him, even if he has betrayed me.'

The phone goes on chirping and I send the call straight to voice-mail.

'Persistent, isn't he?' Amelie twists a lock of her splendid hair. 'But don't go messing up your face again. Let's have a glass of wine and watch some TV. Switch the phone on properly and the next time he rings, give it to me.'

Ten minutes later, Andy calls again and she snatches the instrument from my grasp.

'You have reached Nicole's telephone,' she says in excessively polite, upper class English. 'Her personal assistant, Amelie Jacques, speaking.'

For second or two, I forget my grim mood and clamp my hand over my mouth to stifle a giggle.

'No . . .' There is a long silence. Amelie grins and winks at me. *'I'm afraid Mlle Durand is unable to take calls at present.'*

'A message?' Another wink. *'Certainly, sir.'* She takes an imaginary pad and pretends to write with an imaginary pencil. *'I see. Yes . . . yes . . . of course, sir . . .'*

'What does he say, Amm?' I mouth at her.

Amelie shakes her head. Another long silence. She purses her lips. *'Would you like me to read the message back . . . to make sure I have taken it down correctly?'* Her accent has lapsed somewhat but I have to admire her ability to play it straight. If our positions were reversed, I would have burst out laughing long before this. *'Yes, I will be sure to tell her . . . goodbye, sir.'*

'Well, that was fun.' She ends the call and hands the phone back to me. 'He has a beautiful voice, Nica. It's no wonder you were smitten.'

'Don't, Amm. Just tell me what he said.'

'Why do you care?'

'I don't. But I want to know what he said.'

'I confused him at first. I don't think he knew what to make of me. But he soon caught on. Mumbled something about his name coming up on the screen. Then he played along. He might be a two-timer, Nica, but he's a pretty cool one.'

'Be serious.'

'Well, he apologised for not calling sooner and asked if he could speak to you. Said he would wait until you had finished whatever you were doing. He wanted to know if you'd had a nice day with your sister. And he hoped you weren't angry with him.'

'And?'

'That's pretty much it.'

'What about the stunt with the message pad?'

'That was the bit about you not being angry . . . oh, and would you ring him whenever.'

Right now, I feel I want to crawl into a dark hole. 'I don't think I can, Amm. I wouldn't know what to say.'

'Your decision, *chérie*.' She closes her eyes and blows me a fake kiss. 'But Christ, Nica, I'd give a week of my life for a tiny share of his voice.'

**

31.

I've had another of those weird nightmares. It always happens when I'm excited or stressed, and I'm definitely stressed when I wake on Sunday morning. Amelie does her best to cheer me up and when I leave her at midday my mood has brightened. However, as I turn off the St Pièrre road towards *Château Ravel* it darkens again. I'm hoping Andy isn't home because I still have no idea how to confront him. I even dread facing Cathy's inevitable questions. *Did you have a good time? How is your mother?* Ever since I explained about Denise, she has been eager to learn if our relationship is improving.

Cathy must recognise the grumble of the Citroen engine, because, as soon as I put my key in the front door she calls out to me from the living room.

'I'm in here, Nicole.'

I open the living room door. Cathy is stretched on the long sofa with a box of chocolates on her lap. 'I've saved you some.' She rattles the box.

'Give me a few minutes, Cathy. Let me put my things away first.'

I turn and head for the stairs. Andy is there, already half way down. I don't know what I was expecting - a guilty avoidance of my eyes, a red face, or maybe a pair of horns on his forehead - but he acts as if nothing has happened.

He points to my overnight bag. 'Here, let me take that.'

'I can manage.'

He grins. 'OK, but I'm glad you're back.' He makes to kiss me and I have a sudden flash-back to yesterday afternoon. I avoid him and sprint up the last few steps. On the landing I turn to look back. He is frowning.

'Have I done something wrong?'

'Have you?'

'Have I what?'

'Done something wrong.'

'No. No, of course not. You're behaving very strangely, Nicole.'

'I just want to put my bag in my room and go and have some chocolates with your mother.'

'OK, but there was something I wanted to talk to you about.'

He follows me along the corridor. I'm torn in three. One part of me wants the truth, another torments me to relive everything I saw outside the cathedral. The rest of me insists it was all a nightmare and demands things return to the way they were. The coward's way wins the battle.

'Leave me alone, Andy!' I reach my room and, before he can protest, take refuge inside and bolt the door behind me.

'Nicole! Talk to me, won't you.' He taps the door. 'Are you sick? Should I phone for a doctor?'

'Don't be ridiculous,' I snap back. 'Just go away and leave me alone.'

I dump my bag on the bed, sit down beside it and take a few deep breaths. I hear the soft tread of his feet on the carpet. A minute or so later he's at the door again.

'Is this about yesterday? Are you upset I didn't call you until evening? I'm sorry. There was a reason . . .'

His voice is pleading but the thought he is about to make excuses for his conduct makes me mad. I get to my feet, rush over to the door and bang it with my fists.

'I saw you, Andy. I fucking saw you!' I yell.

'*Quoi?* You saw me. You saw me what?'

'I saw you at the cathedral . . . with that woman.'

'At the cathedral?' he echoes. There is a pause and I hear him suck in his breath. '*Dieu*, Nicole, that wasn't . . . I wasn't *cheating* on you. You know I'd never do that.'

'Do I? Was it her you were meeting in Toulouse? Is she the one?'

'Toulouse? What are you talking about?'

Still torn between resistance and capitulation, I turn back towards the bed. He surely deserves the chance . . . I should give him the chance to explain.

'Nicole! Are you listening?'

I don't reply. Andy retreats once more, his steps now measured and deliberate. I slump to the floor against the bed and contemplate how, in the space of a single day, my whole life has begun to unravel.

The minutes tick away - five, ten, longer, precisely how many I'm unable to tell. I get up and pace the room. Andy's walking stick, once the symbol of our togetherness, screams silently at me from the top of the bookcase. *Betrayal!* I try not to look at it, focussing instead on my parents' wedding photograph to the right.

I must have dusted the frame a hundred times without even looking at the picture. I pick it up, remembering that odd moment while I was studying the photo my grandmother keeps in her treasure box. Something then - about the pose or the background, triggered a switch in my brain, on one moment, off the next. I get the same sensation now, stronger this time, and glimpse what I failed to notice before.

There is no time to dwell on my discovery. Suddenly, Andy is back. He knocks with his knuckles and rattles the door handle. 'You didn't see what you thought you saw, Nicole. Are you going to hear me out?'

I go to the door wearily and slide back the catch.

'I'm listening.'

Andy tests the handle and eases the door open.

'Not here,' he growls.

Before I can protest, he swoops down, picks me up bodily like a naughty child and strides out the twenty steps between my room and his. He sets me down on the chair at his desk and, standing over me like a stern schoolmaster, points to his Mac computer.

'Is that her?' he demands.

I study the portrait on the screen. She bears a resemblance to the woman I saw at the cathedral, although I can't be certain it's the same person. I look up at him and nod dumbly.

'And this one?' He shows me his phone. Someone, a stranger, has taken a picture of them together. I recognise the cathedral campanile.

'Yes.'

'Her name is Monique Li. She is French-Canadian and my cousin. Her mother's name was Adrienne Ravel. Or, more accurately, Monique's my second cousin.'

'Your second cousin?'

'Yes. I thought we trusted one another, Nicole,' he says harshly. 'How could you imagine I would cheat?'

'But you were kissing and hugging. What was I supposed to think?'

'If you were close enough to see, you could have called out, or come over and asked. And let's get a few things right,' he growls. 'She gave me a peck on the cheek to thank me for meeting her. As for hugging . . . well, we all do it - brother and sister, cousins, close friends. It doesn't have to be sexual.'

'I guess not.' I mumble an apology, wondering at the same time if he'll ever speak to me again after doubting him. How can I possibly explain my reasons? I'm beginning to wonder if it was panic, nothing more than the heat, aching feet - and above all, fear of losing him. I didn't think of it at the time but shopping with Sophie can be exhausting. Maybe I *had* been in the sun too long. 'I did think of shouting your name, but you would never have heard. We were at *Café Français* and you were half way to the bell tower before . . . before I saw you together. We were hot and thirsty.'

'That must be well over a hundred metres,' says Andy more gently. 'I suppose you . . . well, I suppose I can see how it might have looked.'

'You're never going to forgive me, are you? For doubting you.'

'I'll think about it.' There is a trace of the Andy grin. 'Maybe I ought to throw you in the pool.'

'You wouldn't dare!'

'Wouldn't I?' He swirls my chair round so we're face to face and pulls up another for himself. 'Do you want to hear my story or not?'

'I want to hear it.'

He leans behind me, spins me round again and taps a few keys. The photograph is replaced by a huge family tree chart. At the top is one name, Georges Ravel, and in the row below five more: Jacques, Yves, Charles, Jacqueline and Paul. Under Jacques, there is a distinct line of descent, ending with his own name, and filled in with other names and dates. A second line under Paul is partly completed. The rest of the chart comprises blank boxes and question marks.

'Good,' he says and adopts his lecture mode. He gestures at the five names on the second row. 'You'll see I've gone back three generations. I got some of this from Uncle Georges, the rest from the library. My *great-grandfather* Georges, who ran the vineyards in the nineteen-thirties and -forties, had five children. Jacques, my grandfather, you know. Yves went to New Zealand; he died young but his family still run a winery there. I have an email address but haven't contacted them yet. Charles had his own business here; I'm researching him now.

'Jacqueline left Bordeaux - married an estate owner in the Fronton region. My uncle told me, and that's what the trip to Toulouse was about. But it was a wasted journey. Both Jacqueline and her husband are dead, and they had no children. I found the estate; it's run by a nephew - no blood relation.

'That leaves Paul. Monique is twenty-six, and his granddaughter. Her mother, Adrienne, is the elder of Paul's two daughters.'

I study the chart. 'There are lots of other names. It looks complicated.'

'You have no idea!' He lowers his voice, more gentle now, and pulls his chair alongside mine. 'I've known about Paul for five years, but I wasn't too interested then. Too busy studying! *Grandpère* got very drunk on my eighteenth birthday and started talking. Father was furious but couldn't stop him. He was rather tanked up himself. Paul got into debt - gambling apparently - and embezzled about twenty million francs from the business.'

'Twenty million! You must be joking.'

'Absolutely not. These were old francs, of course. I'm guessing here but I think it might be the equivalent of something like 500,000 *euros* in today's values.'

'So still a lot of money.'

'Yes. The family kept him out of prison on condition he leave the country. Paul emigrated to Canada. He turned his life around, eventually married and produced Adrienne. Adrienne married Thomas Li, and Monique is their daughter. It was pure chance I met her at all. She grew up in Quebec and studied there for a business degree. About six months ago she decided she'd like to spend time in France so she applied for a job in Paris. She starts next week.

'It was thanks to Alain Pawson that I found her. He suggested using social media to connect with distant family members. Monique saw my profile and sent me a message. Wanted to know if I was descended from Georges Ravel, the Bordeaux vintner. We exchanged e-mails and photographs. I gave her my number and she promised to call when she was in France.

'You had just pulled out of the drive yesterday morning when the phone rang. St André's seemed like a good place to meet. Monique was interested in the cathedral's history. I wasn't much help so we went inside and talked to a priest. You know the rest.'

'Thank you for telling me. I'm so sorry.'

'Me too. I should have . . . I could have phoned you sooner but then I thought how much you wanted to spend the day with Sophie. I tried later but you wouldn't pick up. The strange thing is, we must have missed one another by minutes. Monique and I had coffee at *Café Français* before we went into the church. She would have liked to meet you but she has a flight to catch tomorrow morning. That's what I wanted to tell you when you shut me out of your room.'

I manipulate the slider on the MAC so that the cursor roams over the computer screen, and hover over a few names. 'You haven't found a *Louis* among your ancestors?'

'Not so far. Why do you ask?'

'My grandfather knew someone called Louis Ravel. He has a photograph.'

'I'd love to see that. I think the name *Ravel* is Provençal, though it isn't common in France. I suppose there could be a connection way back. Maybe after I'm finished at Oxford I'll go on researching.'

'So where do *we* go from here, Andy?'

He snaps shut his laptop. His eyes flash and he rolls his tongue round his lips. 'How about we pretend the past twenty-four hours didn't happen?'

I touch his cheek. 'For once we *can* both pretend, but this isn't a good time.'

'I see.'

'It's not *that*. As of this evening, I'm officially back at work, on top of which I have something else on my mind.'

'Can I help?'

'Thanks, but it's something I have to deal with by myself. Relations with my mother.'

'You look a bit pale. Are you sure you're not sick?'

'Quite sure, Andy. By the way, thanks for not throwing me in the pool.'

'That's still an option,' he laughs and snakes out his arms to seize me by the waist, changing direction at the last minute to pull open a desk drawer. He takes out the chocolate box Cathy was nursing when I arrived home. 'I went and got them. Mother's compliments. There are only four left but she said they're your favourites.'

'You didn't tell her about . . .'

'Course not. But you didn't come back so she figured something was going on. By the way, you're off the hook until tomorrow morning. Boss's orders!' He opens the box and I see two of the chocolates are hazelnut. There is one truffle and one coffee cream. Andy picks up the latter between forefinger and thumb and pops it into my waiting mouth.

'I'm having one of the hazelnuts,' he announces.

**

32.

A few more days go by. My routine at *Château Ravel* returns to normal. Yet something has changed. I've become less secure, less trusting of my own emotions and some of my own decisions. Though ever closer to my departure to Edinburgh, I am not a step nearer resolving my relationship with Denise. If my instincts about the two photographs - my mother and father in one, my mother and me in the other – that's one more deception to add to the list.

I have to see *Mamie*'s picture again to confirm my suspicion, but I am fairly sure I'm right. Strange though it seems to think it, *I was at my parents' wedding!* Not only is the background identical but Denise is wearing the exact same dress, masked in the one by my infant self and a shawl. And nowhere else have I seen her with hair arranged similar to mine.

In the twenty-first century, no one cares about such things - children before rather than after marriage. I certainly don't. Being wanted, being loved is of far greater importance. However, it means my childhood was built on an unnecessary fiction, one in which my grandparents, and perhaps even my father too, colluded. Having deceived me about something so trivial, what other secrets might they all have hidden from me?

Andy's success in connecting with the wider Ravel family has made me realise how little I know of mine. In that respect, we are alike, each of us missing what most children take for granted - uncles, aunts and cousins on both maternal and paternal sides. I can always rely on *Mamie* and *Papi* to talk about my father, his childhood, his teenage years and his career in the oil business. However, even they seem ignorant of how my parents met.

And what about Denise's childhood and teens? She never

spoke about *her* family, and always evaded my questions - about her age, her parents, brothers or sisters, school, or any of the other things mothers talk about to their children. When I asked, she would either refuse to answer or tell an obvious lie. I remember being puzzled there was only *Papi* and *Mamie* Durand when most of the kids at school had four grandparents. I can still see the agitation in her face when I persisted in asking why Sophie, Bernard and I had only two. That pained look, and her answer would silence me forever. *They died in a car crash. They're dead. All right?*

My mother consistently lied to me throughout my teens. *Was that a lie too?* How many more are there. I have to ask; I have to know.

There was a moment when my heart felt like a block of ice. And with the chill came an awful suspicion, a sudden terror, that even my fondest memories may be based on a lie. *That Pièrre Durand may not have been my father at all.* I push the notion aside. Half my life is built around memories of a father's love. Those at least are real - those that help sustain me through the darkest days.

But the knot in my stomach doesn't go away.

'All parents lie to their children.' Cathy runs a hand through her ample hair. Over the past six months she has allowed it to grow. Her curls have less spring than before and she has an untidy fringe. 'I must get this cut,' she grumbles. 'Maybe your friend Amelie would do something for me.'

'I'm sure she would. Do you want her number . . . or I could ring her for you?' It cost me two sleepless nights building up courage to confide in her at all. Now that the subject is out in the open I feel as if I'd do anything to avoid talking about it.

'Later.' Cathy purses her lips the way she does when she's thinking deeply about a school problem. 'We were discussing your dilemma, Nicole.'

'I'm sorry, Cathy. I didn't mean to put any of this on you. But I could do with your advice.'

'And I'll give it gladly, though I do wonder . . .'

'Yes?'

'. . . if we're approaching the problem from the wrong angle. As I said, we all lie. Some are tiny lies: *Père Noël*, *La Petite Souris*, the Easter Bunny, or the Garden of Eden. I think they're harmless fantasies. Others are big lies, but then we need to look for the motive, and that's usually to protect our children.'

'Mine are all big lies.'

'Even so . . . if the intention was good . . .'

'I wish I knew what to do, what questions to ask.'

'Let's assume your suspicions are correct. If they are, your grandmother has already opened the door to your questions. Just by showing you the photograph. Perhaps she decided it's time.'

'Time . . . ?'

'Time you knew the truth, whatever that is. Think about it, *chérie*. She must know you've seen the wedding picture.'

'Why would they all lie in the first place?'

'I don't know. Maybe it's a Catholic thing. Even liberals like Yves can't quite cast off the priesthood. Your grandparents belong to a generation with very different values - of purity and chastity before marriage. I still see France from an English point of view. Decades of socialism . . . decades of Church and State haven't made the French less conservative. There's a lot of angst around being a Catholic.

'Mind you,' Cathy goes on, 'my mother was a Scottish Presbyterian, my father C. of E. They had the same attachment to the past. All that guilt . . . And the Protestants have no confession. No absolution.' She laughs half-heartedly. 'I was sixteen when I rebelled. We argued. The rift took a long time to heal.'

'My father was a sceptic,' I say, 'maybe even an agnostic. I suppose I am too. But *Mamie* and *Papi* always went to church. My mother used to go to confession. We kids all went through the rituals - baptism, confirmation, bread and body, wine and blood - all that sort of thing.'

'There you are then. It isn't so much a question of lying as of hiding the truth. We never told Andy about Emmeline. Does that make us liars and bad parents?'

'Of course not. I never thought of it that way.'

Cathy ruffles her hair again. 'I often think a big hug helps.' She sighs deeply and opens her arms to me. '*Dieu*, I'm going to be all weepy in a minute.'

She squeezes me to her and I feel comfort in her embrace. But I try unsuccessfully to find resolution for what I have to do. Having moved a step or two towards a truce - reconciliation - with my mother, I seem to have taken three or four back to where it all began two-and-a-half years ago. I have to deal with it, but another confrontation with Denise while I'm in this mood is impossible to contemplate.

'You know, don't you?' My grandmother takes my arm and draws me into her bedroom. By mid-week I've plucked up enough courage to visit her.

'The photo - yes, I guessed.'

'We'll talk in here. I knew you'd work it out. The dress and shoes are a dead give-away, aren't they?'

'It was the background at first, *Mamie*. Then the dress. Why did you never tell me? This is the twenty-first century; it happens all the time.'

'I don't think I'll ever get used to that,' she says. 'Things were very different in my day.'

I nod as if I understand. Her face seems older, more pained than the last time we spoke, as if she's been worrying about the events she set in motion.

'You mustn't blame your parents. We made the decision together. We always intended to tell you when you were older. Then we lost Pièrre. After that, all kinds of good intentions . . . well, you know, we had other things to deal with.'

'Now I know, *Mamie*, is there nothing else you need to tell me?'

'I don't think so, *ma chérie*. I don't know much more. Your father never talked about how he and Denise met. You must remember we hadn't seen him much in the previous five years. He'd always wanted to go to America. Then he came back and went to work in Paris.'

I'm only half listening. Turning, chugging over and over in my brain like the wheels and pistons of an engine is the question - the dread notion that until a week ago I could never have entertained. I fight down the lump in my throat. The idea of speaking my fears into words makes me feel faint.

'. . . Nicole? Are you all right, *chérie?'*

'*Mamie*, you will tell me, won't you . . . if my father wasn't . . .?'

I'm choking on the words but my grandmother always has an instinct for my inner thoughts.

'*Non.*' She puts her arm round me and hugs me close. 'You must never think that, my darling. There was never any question, not in my mind, not in his. Pièrre never told me why they didn't marry sooner. But he was your real father, *mon petit chou*. I promise you on my life.'

**

33.

It's Friday, and Andy is in the breakfast room, trying to look busy. He has cleared a soiled cup and saucer aside and is laying another place. 'I'll bring you some breakfast in a moment,' he says. 'And coffee. Mother and I drank it all. She went out early this morning. Father too.'

'I've overslept. I didn't hear the alarm. Why didn't she . . . why didn't you wake me? I should've been doing all that.'

'Mother said not to wake you. She said you've been a bit down for a day or two.' He fills the percolator, ladles in some ground coffee and plugs into the socket. 'This isn't to do with . . . you know . . . what happened last week.'

'All forgotten.' I screw up my face. 'Nerves, I think. A few weeks until I go to Scotland and I still have so much to sort out.'

'I can help you with the financial stuff,' Andy says. 'You can use my bank. I'll help you set up an account.' He slices a loaf and puts it on a platter with some cheese and ham from the refrigerator. The coffee is bubbling merrily. 'I've got some Swiss cereal if you like, or some fruit.'

'Fruit, please,' I say. 'And thank you. I accept your offer of help with the banking.'

He adds some apples and a bunch of grapes to the platter, brings it to the bar and lays it in front of me. 'Maybe we could go to Edinburgh and sort it all out. We could even go and see Mrs Watson. Come back via Oxford and I can show you my pad.'

'I promised your mother I'd stay on until the middle of September. There isn't time to go touring round the British Isles. The banking will have to wait.'

'Or we could have a few days at the beach - the *Côte d'Azur*.'

'The *Côte d'Azur* is impossibly expensive, Andy.'

'Not if we stay with *Tante* Lucie.' Andy rubs his chin. 'We'd have to take the Citroen of course.'

'You have an aunt on the Riviera?'

The coffee finishes brewing and he pours me a full mug. 'I found out the details yesterday, when you were visiting your grandmother. Uncle Georges again. He's sick of Father's attitude too and has been doing some digging on his own. You remember the chart I showed you - Charles Ravel. He and Lucie retired to the Riviera seven or eight years ago. Charles died.'

'I see. And *Tante* Lucie will give us a bed for a week - just like that?'

'Just like that. Georges rummaged around in the old man's papers. Found an address and a phone number. So I called her. She was happy I'd got in touch and would be delighted to see us. I'll ring her again . . .'

'You have it all planned.' I punch his forearm. 'What about my job?'

'That's sorted too. Mother thinks you deserve a break. We'll go on Monday - unless you don't want to.'

I'm having my period, so I'm a bit sensitive. For all our frankness about anatomy and biology, Andy has got it into his head I don't want him around. That's probably my fault since, with everything else going on, I haven't explained to him I do. Because of the lack of sleep, and the nightmares, my eye is giving me trouble for the first time in weeks. I wonder how it will react to hours of driving.

On Monday morning, I'm still touchy. We've spent three nights apart and Andy annoys me by referring to the menstrual cycle as *that condition*.

'It's not a disease,' I snap, and he apologises.

Next, we argue about who pays for petrol, agreeing eventually to split all expenses fifty-fifty. It's Georges who cheers me up. Before we set off for St Tropez, he comes in from the office to speak to Cathy. Martha hasn't turned up for work.

'She should've been in this morning,' Georges says. 'There's a fortnight of her contract to run. Yves will be tearing out his hair. He's over in the winery, stressing over last minute questions for her.'

When Cathy explains about our holiday, he kisses me on both cheeks. 'Enjoy yourselves! Martha isn't your problem. We'll manage. But remember what I said about the job.'

I say *sorry* to Andy when we get into the car. He wanted to treat me and I was ungracious.

'Are we OK, *mon chéri*?' I lay my hand on his knee and he squeezes it before starting the engine.

'Of course we are,' he assures me and nibbles my ear. 'The *Côte d'Azur* will be *formidable*.'

We spend Monday night in a hotel near Carcassonne - twin beds - and set out for the coast early the next day. Our sleeping arrangements for the next three nights are settled without reference to my *condition*, and without further discussion. Andy's great-aunt Lucie is a woman in her late seventies, almost as broad as she is tall, with sparkling green eyes and a complexion which seems to defy the years. Her welcome is warm and sincere. However, she views pre-marital sex in much the same way as my grandmother.

'You'll have separate rooms of course,' she announces, and we have to promise her we'll be celibate while staying in her house. 'This one will be yours, Nicole. It's the smaller of the two but it has the best view over the bay.'

She leaves me to unpack and shows Andy to his room, which I discover is next door. Ten minutes later, he taps on my door and comes in.

'*Quelle journée - quelle aventure!*' He faces me across the single bed. 'I'm quite exhausted by all that driving. But mine is a double if you fancy cheating.'

'We gave our word, Andy.' I take off my glasses and rub the corner of my eye. We've been on the road two days - ten and a half hours altogether. I took three turns at the wheel to Andy's two, so I should be the one claiming exhaustion.

'Pity,' Andy complains, flopping down on my mattress. 'This one is quite comfortable too. Aunt Lucie says there's a beach fifteen minutes from the house. Shall we get some walking exercise?'

The sun has retained its warmth and for an hour we simply enjoy the freedom of being in the open air. Although we are several kilometres away from St Maxime, the nearest resort, I can't believe our luck that the beach is almost deserted. When we get back, Lucie is in her kitchen cooking something for us on the grill.

'I had the butcher bring me three steaks yesterday,' she announces. 'We'll have them with a bottle of St Emilion.'

Andy frowns. 'You don't have to go to any trouble for us, *Tante* Lucie.'

'Yes I do.' She beams at us. 'It's no trouble. You've had a long journey and I don't get many visitors.'

'We're very grateful,' I say. 'What can I do to help?'

She flips over a steak with a spatula, then the other two. 'Nearly done! Plates are over there - second shelf - and knives and forks in the drawer below. André, uncork the wine, *mon petit*. Cellar is third door along the hall; light switch on the left and two steps. Mind your head!'

I lay the cutlery in the dining room. Lucie brings in the plates. She has prepared some salad, tossed in olive oil, lemon juice and honey. Andy finds glasses, pours the wine and we sit down to eat. The steak is delicious and I compliment our hostess on it.

'Nothing like a good steak, my husband always used to say. And nothing goes so well with it as a good St Emilion. Now eat it up and bring some colour to your cheeks.'

'Nicole! Nicole!' I struggle from the world of dreams to reality. Someone has hold of me by the shoulders and is shaking me. 'Wake up, *ma chérie*!'

I open my eyes. It's still dark. I have a recollection both my father and mother were in the dream, and that I was a child again. Then I remember where we are.

Andy switches on the bedside lamp. He stops shaking me and holds me close. '*Dieu merci*, you're awake. Are you OK?'

I rub the sleep from my eyes. 'I'm OK. Of course I'm OK.

What's the matter? Why are you here?'

'You were scaring me. I thought you were having some kind of seizure.'

'What do you mean - seizure? You oughtn't to be in my room.'

'I heard you scream loud enough to wake St Tropez, never mind *Tante* Lucie. I'm surprised she isn't here already. When I came into the room you were thrashing about and beating the pillow. Then, when I touched you, you yelled *leave me alone*, or *let me alone*.'

'I was having a bad dream. It must have been the driving. It can't have been the steak.' I'm trying to make light of it, but my pulse is thudding and I have a headache.

'You have nightmares a lot.'

'I don't think so. No more than anyone else.'

'I think you've had this one before. The second or third night we were together. I said at the time . . . I mean, everyone has them occasionally. But I was worried about you there.'

'I'm sorry I freaked you out, Andy.' I kiss his forehead and wrap my arms around him. The detail is fading and I don't want to talk about it. 'Now, find me some painkillers and a glass of water, then go back to your room. There are some aspirins in my handbag - on the dressing-table.'

He passes me the bag and slips quietly out of the room, returning a few moments later with the water. I swallow two tablets.

'Are you sure you're OK?'

'*Bien sûr.*' I nod vigorously.

'My mother always blames the wine . . .' He grins his schoolboy grin. 'And if you need anything . . .'

'What I need is denied me for the next two nights.' I sigh and yawn. 'Now go - go before I'm tempted to sin against the house of Ravel. Goodnight!'

Andy and his aunt are discussing the family. She is showing him some photographs. From time to time, he types a few notes into his phone while stroking my calf with his foot under the table.

'*We had this place as a holiday home . . . get away from the pollution*

. . . children had a twenty percent share each . . . Camille took over the business . . .'

We've spent most of our time walking on the beach and roaming the countryside around St Maxime. This morning we took the ferry to St Tropez. We wandered the quays of the old port. We watched *petanque* in the town square then it was back to St Maxime for a late afternoon swim. Despite our protests that we should take her out for dinner, Lucie insists on giving us two more evening meals. Andy decides I should call her *Tante*, so I do. She seems delighted with the title. I think she's lonelier than she pretends. Her daughter visits once or twice a month - flies to Nice and hires a car there. Lucie has friends among other local retirees, and they socialise during the day. However, with her husband gone, she lacks company in the evenings.

'. . . two grandchildren now . . . live in London . . . Wimbledon . . . oh, I see . . . no . . . a boy and a girl . . .'

Now she's talking about a son who lives in England. I try to remember from Andy's chart where he'd inserted question marks with blanks for names. Was that under Charles Ravel, or was it one of the other great-uncles? I gather Lucie's daughter is called Camille but I don't think she's mentioned the son's name.

'. . . Camille has no children . . . Aristide is an academic . . . no, partner. My son is Giles . . .'

Andy is still stroking my calf under the table and I enjoy the sensation. I continue to drift in and out of the conversation. It's been happening throughout the day. Snatches of our night at the hotel in Carcassonne keep coming back to me - how we pushed the twin beds together but made do with one. How I fell asleep nestling in the curve of his body, his hands caressing my tummy, his lips feathering my ear.

Aunt Lucie is still talking. Occasionally, Andy makes a comment, but mostly he just nods and carries on with his notes. Suddenly, she says something that makes me snap out of my delicious daydream. Andy must have asked the names of her grandchildren.

'This is them with their parents.' Lucie points to one of her photos. 'Chantelle is seventeen. She's at a private school, learning to be a young English lady. The boy is called Louis. He's . . .'

'*Louis?*'

'My grandson. *Louis Adrien*. Named after my husband and my father . . .'

'Your husband's name was Charles . . .'

'*Charles Louis Ravel*. Most of the Ravel men had middle names.' She casts a sideways look at Andy. 'Jacques is *Jacques Francois Ravel*; Yves, the brother who went to New Zealand was *Yves Marie-Ste Ravel*. There were others but I don't remember them all. Maybe even your father, *mon petit.*'

'I don't think so.' Andy does a few final taps on his phone.

'Well, maybe not. Such an obliging young man he was.' Lucie frowns. 'Then he changed. Wouldn't have anything to do with his poor uncle or any of the others. You were still in diapers, André. You were a cute little boy, all chubby cheeks and curls.'

Andy's face colours and he wrinkles his eyebrows. I can't help laughing.

'And look at you now,' I tease, and kick him under the table. 'You were telling Andy about your grandchildren, *Tante* Lucie. I'm sorry I interrupted.'

'I have only met them twice, once when they were babies and again when they came for a holiday two years ago. At least Chantelle was *born* in France. Louis can't even speak French properly.'

I think of my grandfather, the photo he showed me. Five names: *Gaston Laurent, Albert Durand, Jacques Durand, J-C Poulin*, and *Louis Ravel*. 'What was your husband's business, *Tante* Lucie?'

'We had a chain of shops. *Boucherie Charles*. Perhaps you've heard of us if you grew up in Bordeaux. We started there. Now we have five shops altogether in the South-West. Camille is planning to expand to other parts of France. Of course, now that she runs the business, it's more fancy foods than plain old-fashioned cuts of beef and pork.'

My head is buzzing. Of course I know *Boucherie Charles*. I have shopped there many times. They have a lovely delicatessen. How could I have been so dense? *A butcher! Cher Papi, how could I be so unkind as to doubt you?*

'My grandfather told me he knew a Louis Ravel,' I say. 'It was many years ago. To be honest, we thought . . .'

'I can guess what you thought, Nicole,' says Lucie. 'We all have difficulty remembering things when we get older, but it doesn't mean we're senile. A lot of Charles's old friends used to call him Louis. What's your grandfather's name?'

'Albert Durand.'

'Bless me, what an odd coincidence! You're that Durand? My dear girl! Charles used to talk a lot about Albert Durand. I don't think I ever met him. Oh dear, it's more years ago than I like to remember. Must be nearly fifty, when we were first married. Yes, there was Albert, and Jean-Claude, and another man he spoke of. What was his name now? The old crowd, he called them.'

'Gaston?'

'That's it. Gaston Laurent, and Albert Durand. I think maybe Charles and Albert had done military service together. Why on earth didn't André tell me . . . that your *grandpère* and his great-uncle were old friends?'

'He didn't know,' I say sheepishly. 'Nor did I.'

'So your family and mine already have a connection.' Andy leans over and takes my hand. He squeezes it gently.

Tante Lucie beams with pleasure. 'How strange and wonderful life is,' she says.

'Tell me more about the family, *Tante* Lucie,' Andy begs, 'and about my father. I know so little.'

'The Ravel men were always so . . .' Lucie scratches her forehead. '. . . *driven* - I think that's the word. They were so driven. Old Georges Ravel was a patriarchal tyrant. Women were of no consequence. Only the sons mattered. The wine business mattered most of all. There were five boys. One girl!'

'Five?' Andy asks. 'I found only four.'

'Georges, the eldest, died in his teens. Polio. That was in nineteen-fifty, before the vaccines. Then there was Yves - and

Jacques, Charles and Paul. Jacqueline came between Jacques and Charles.

'I already know about Paul and Jacqueline,' Andy says. 'Tell me about the others.'

Tante Lucie needs no encouragement. 'Charles always said Yves loved the industry, but he couldn't face a life dominated by his father. He emigrated to New Zealand in sixty-three, started from scratch and built his own business there. He died ten years ago, but there are children. Charles almost joined him. His father bullied him terribly.' Lucie's face lights up and she giggles. 'But then he met me!

'My father owned a butcher's shop. He took Charles on and taught him the trade. At *Château Ravel*, your grandfather Jacques took over when Georges died in the seventies. He was a true vintner, Charles said, but hopeless as an accountant. After a few years, he began losing money. Charles offered to help. Jacques told him he was a traitor and wasn't getting near the books. They never spoke again.

'All the pressure fell on your father. He studied chemistry and went to business school. *Château Ravel* was his inheritance and his obsession. Its survival lay on his shoulders, to the exclusion of family and everything else. So like Jacques in every way.

'Yves – your father - began to soften after he met your mother, got married, had you. But then there was the tragedy. Your baby sister died, and he was the hard, uncompromising man again. *Pardon*. I shouldn't have said that.'

'That's OK, *Tante* Lucie. It's true. I know how he is. It's only that I never fully understood it before.'

'Your poor mother! Jacques never wanted his son marrying a foreigner . . . then for that awful thing to happen . . .' She wipes away a tear. 'I'm so sorry we didn't try harder to keep in touch.'

'It's not your fault.' Andy puts his arm round his aunt's shoulders and hugs her. 'We're in touch now, and that's what matters. And before Nicole and I leave, *Tante* Lucie, you're going to give me email addresses and phone numbers for all your family!'

'Of course I will. I'm so glad you young people came. I do hope you'll visit me again.'

**

34.

Before we leave, Lucie insists Andy take a photograph to give to my grandfather. The three of us line up and he snaps us with his mobile phone.

'Be sure to send me a copy,' she tells him. 'I don't have one of those fancy phones, but I do have a computer and an email address.'

'I'll do better than that, *Tante* Lucie.' Andy delves into a side pocket of his luggage and pulls out his charging cable. 'If I can use your computer for five minutes, you can have one now.'

'How clever science is!' she exclaims. 'Come down here so I can kiss you.'

We stop again on the way back, at Narbonne, where we book a double room and sleep together for the first time since Carcassonne. I wake to daylight, the chirping of sparrows and the beep-beep of our alarm. The sound has been growing louder, first as part of a fast-fading dream, then as an irritation I can't ignore. We're settled in the sagging centre of the bed. Andy's arm is around me. His head is buried in my chest.

I ease myself from his embrace, sit up and look down at him. He doesn't stir. In the night, he has lost a fight with his pillow - which ended on the floor - but his face now is beautifully serene in sleep.

The past few days have left my head buzzing. Though I have missed the intimacy at bedtime, every other moment of our holiday together has been special and will remain a precious memory. Yet these are the last few weeks we will spend together. So many random thoughts are rattling through my brain. What obstacles or temptations might be put in our way in the course of a year or longer apart? And is our relationship strong enough to overcome them?

Though I've been living away from them for more than a year, I'm going to miss my family too. Most of all, I decide, I will miss *Mamie* and *Papi*. With Sophie and Bernard, our phones and social media will keep us in touch, but my grandparents are not great with modern technology. And what about Denise? I have managed without her since she went into the clinic, so missing her isn't something I've given much thought to. But my conscience will trouble me unless I make an effort to reconcile us before I leave for Edinburgh.

I bend to kiss him on the top of Andy's head, savouring the scent of his shampoo which still lingers in his untidy mop of hair.

'Andy!'

His dark lashes flicker and his eyes open. 'Nicole.'

'I hope so.'

He grins. 'I just love saying your name?'

'I'm glad.'

'No more bad dreams?'

'Nothing that matters. But we can't lie here all day, you know. We have a long way to drive home.'

'*Dommage!* I was hoping we could . . .' He reaches up and caresses my cheek.

I let his hand stay for a moment before pulling my face away and swinging my legs off the bed. My muscles ache. It's the combination of an active few days and long hours cooped up in the Citroen.

'Hope doesn't drive the car,' I say.

Andy does most of the driving back to Bordeaux but I still feel weary when we arrive home in late afternoon. We have been nearly five hours in the car.

'Am I glad to see you!' Cathy is stretched out on a lounger by the pool. She's wearing a wet swimsuit and has draped a towel across her middle. An empty wine glass sits on the patio at her side.

She has parked the bottle out of the sun under the lounger. 'Come and join me. Bring some sanity into my life.'

She looks washed out and not only because her hair is wet from swimming. I drag a chair from the shade to sit beside her.

'I think you're the sanest person I know, Cathy.'

'A week ago, I would've agreed with you.' She wiggles her toes. 'Have a nice time?'

'Wonderful!'

'Everything sorted out? You look happy. One day you must tell me about this Aunt Lucie. Did my little boy behave?'

'Most of the time.' I laugh.

'I just need someone to talk to. This has been a fucking madhouse since you left.' She reaches for the wine bottle and pours herself a generous helping. 'Would you like some?'

I shake my head. 'Not now. You seem stressed. What's wrong?'

'Oh, it's Yves and Georges. They've been at one another's throats - and I mean it literally. Well, almost. If I hadn't stopped them fighting there would've been blows. It all started with Martha . . .'

'Cathy . . . I'm so sorry.' I know she suspects her husband of straying and assume she has caught him out.

'No, it's nothing like that . . .' Cathy shakes her head. '. . . at least, I don't think so. The day before yesterday, Thursday if I've kept proper track, Yves was at a *negociants'* meeting. When he came home there was a furious row.'

'About Martha?'

'About Martha's absence.' Cathy takes a gulp at her wine. 'I've never seen her so wound up. 'You know she didn't turn up on Monday. She didn't arrive the next day either. No explanation; she hadn't even phoned. Anyway, Georges said if she had been an employee, he would have fired her. She was a liability, a techie who knew nothing about how to run a successful business. She had signed a contract and should honour it. As it is, we should deduct ten percent from her fee.'

'Was there something I could have done?'

'You weren't expected to do IT, Nicole. That's what we were

paying Martha for.'

'So what happened?'

'Georges said he would show her to the door the minute she showed her face! Seems she's working at the Sonniers' - I don't know what he suspects her of. *We won't pay her a single euro more.* Yves hit the roof. *You have no right, blah-blah-blah . . . it's a partnership.* A fair point, I have to admit, but I've never known Georges so angry. He slammed the desk so hard I think he's damaged his hand. He retorted he had as much right as Yves had hiring her in the first place without consulting him. That's also true, but both of them forget there are other partners. Beatrice and I each have ten percent shares.'

'What happened then?' In the short time I've known him, I can't remember seeing Georges' outward calm even slightly ruffled. I guess it would have to be something major to make him angry.

'You have to appreciate both of them were pretty fired up. A couple of contract renewals were missed and each blamed the other for the oversight. I heard most of the verbal abuse from the hall but when I got to the office door, Yves had Georges by the shirt front. They were grappling like two grizzly bears. I discovered later Georges had made matters worse by accusing Yves of sleeping with the woman. Then the argument moved on to something else; I don't know what. I screamed at them to stop - accused them of acting like children. Would you believe I had to prise them apart.'

'That was brave of you.'

'I had to do something. Besides, when I heard Martha was involved . . .' Cathy takes another gulp of wine and empties the glass. She pouts. '. . . I took Georges' side. Maybe I'm a vindictive bitch but I don't like the woman much and can't forget how Yves cheated on me once before . . . well, maybe twice.'

I bite my lip. I can't think of anything appropriate to say.

'Yves got mad. You know how his face turns red when he argues. Would you believe it was nearly purple; I'm always afraid he's going to have a stroke. I tried to calm him down but he took off.'

'Took off?'

'Stormed out of the house, got his car out of the garage and drove away. That was yesterday. I haven't seen him since. Georges told me you left things in good order but the office is utter chaos now. The paperwork is always the first thing to suffer when there's a disagreement.' She sighs deeply. 'I suppose I'll have to get my hands dirty.'

I lean over and touch her arm. 'Do you want help fixing things?' I ask.

Utter chaos describes the main office exactly. I start with the correspondence, sorting it into two piles, one which needs immediate attention and another that can wait. The more immediate tasks are the easy part, and I've finished by six o'clock. I'll start on the rest on Monday morning.

'You shouldn't be doing all this,' Andy complains, but looks mollified when Georges slips a hundred euro note into my hand at the end of the evening.

On Monday, Yves comes into the office mid-morning from the winery and acts as if nothing has happened. He must have arrived home after we had all gone to bed. I have dealt with most of the mail, typing invoices and making out cheques Georges will sign later.

'I have spoken to my brother,' he says and gives a polite smile. 'We are both most grateful for your assistance, *mademoiselle*.'

'*Ce n'est rien, monsieur*.' I return his smile, wondering whether he has also spoken to Cathy, and if he knows he'll be paying me two hundred *euros* for a day's work. It also occurs to me to wonder if he has been in touch with Martha.

By mid-afternoon I can see I've underestimated the task ahead of me. Behind the mask of politeness, Yves and Georges are arguing in private, yelling expletives at one another and acting like two boys in the school playground. I can't get near enough to learn what it's all about. *I don't want to.*

On Tuesday, Yves is due at a conference in Tuscany before going off to pursue the overlooked contracts in Paris. His very presence around the premises is counterproductive to my efforts. I'm familiar enough with the system to do all the basic tasks. However, though I do my best, I can't get the computer record to agree with the paper trails. By the time Yves leaves for his conference, there is still a discrepancy.

'My brother is his own worst enemy, *mademoiselle*.' Georges sighs with relief. He picks up some loose invoices and the latest account book. 'We'll sort this mess out in no time now he's gone. If you recheck the digital version, I'll take the paper trail. We're nearly there.'

Close attention to the figures on the screen is making my eye hurt and at the end of an hour I'm ready to give up.

'I could do with a strong coffee, Nicole,' Georges says when another half-hour has passed. The job is almost finished. 'I don't suppose you'd like to make some - for us both. I'm going to check the cash drawer in the safe. Yves has a habit of helping himself without telling anyone.'

I head for the kitchen, texting Andy as I go. He's on the terrace, waiting for me. We arranged to go into the city and I don't want to disappoint him either. I make an instant coffee in a mug and carry it back to the office. Georges is on the phone and it's clear not all is well with the petty cash.

'Nearly two thousand *euros*,' he's yelling. I lay his coffee on the desk and withdraw to a safe distance. I've never seen him like this.

'Don't be more of an idiot than you already are,' he blusters and with a dramatic gesture hits the end-call button on his phone.

'Something wrong?' I venture.

'You could say that.' Georges snatches up the coffee mug and downs half of it in one swallow. Luckily, I added quite a lot of cold milk, 'Thanks, I needed that. Nothing for you to worry about. I'll handle things for the rest of the day. I'll see you tomorrow.'

Since there's nothing more for me to do, I leave him sitting at the desk with his chin resting on his elbows. As I turn into the hall, I hear the click of the land telephone.

Andy is standing at the front door. 'Problem?'

'Not for me,' I say. 'But I think your father has gone off with two thousand from the petty cash!'

'Jesus, he's never done that before. Theirs must have been one hell of an argument. Let's get out of here.'

I take him to Louisa's place for coffee and to meet Hélène. She has her first afternoon off for a week. Amelie is spending a few days with her boyfriend on the coast. Hélène monopolises the first twenty minutes, giving Andy her lowdown on the Sonnier family. I listen for a bit but get bored and go over for a chat with Louisa.

'He's lovely,' is her verdict. 'Have you taken him to meet your mother?'

'I've been dreading the moment.'

'Dreading? Why?'

'My mother can be . . . well, difficult.' I've been telling myself for weeks I don't care whether she approves of Andy or not. Though she's never said as much, I have the feeling she thinks I'm trying too hard to climb the social ladder. When I get to the top I'll probably fall off. Now that I'm on the verge of introducing them, I realise I *do* care. But though I want my family to like Andy, I'm much more worried about something else; that *he* will be put off by *them*!

It also crosses my mind I'll have to make a real effort with Jean, and I'm jittery about that too.

'Come on,' says Louisa. 'It can't be as bad as that. If I were you, I'd introduce him to your kid brother and sister first.'

'You really think that's a good idea?' I twist round to get a good look at the table. They are laughing together and I feel a pang of jealousy.

'The kids are bound to like him,' Louisa says. 'He's bound to like them. Bring them here. I'll make one of those special pastries Bernard likes. Problem solved. My treat! It'll be like the old days when our *papas* were alive.'

New customers come into the café and take a table. The waitress brings their orders over to the bar. Louisa beckons me towards the kitchen. 'I have to do these,' she says, indicating the order slips. 'We can talk while I work.'

I follow her and watch while she sets the coffee machine and ladles in some fresh grounds. She switches on.

Mention of my father, as always, causes a surge of nostalgia. This time, it makes me wonder too about a connection going much further back. *To my grandfather, to Jean-Claude Poulin and Charles Louis*

Ravel.

'I never knew why M. Gaston did that,' I say. 'Gave us free drinks, I mean. You had a business to run.'

'*Look after the Durands*, he used to say. Our families go back a long way.'

'M. Gaston and my *grandfather* were friends too - I learned that quite recently.'

'Further back than that, Nicole! Your great-grandfather, Pièrre Durand, saved *Papa's* life in the war. They were in the Resistance together. So, if it weren't for the Durands, there wouldn't have been any business.' She rubs the side of her nose. 'There wouldn't have been any *me!*'

The light on the coffee machine turns from red to green. Louisa lays saucers and cups on a tray.

'I never knew that, Louisa.'

'*Papa* was over ninety when he died,' she says. 'He was fifty before *Maman* had me. After the war, he'd travelled the world. I think he had another family in America. There were letters. But we never dared ask him.' Louisa closes her eyes and taps her knuckles on the work surface. 'He gave you a book from America once. *Polly* something. You were about six years old.'

With sudden inspiration I visualise the little book which languished for years at the bottom of my toy box. I found it when I was clearing some clutter, just before I went to the *lycée*. The cover was tattered and the pages loose, so I threw it away.

'Yes, I do remember. *Pollyanna!*' I almost scream it. 'Did M. Gaston give me that?'

'He did.' Louisa plants a kiss on my cheek. She pours the coffee and picks up the tray.

I follow her back into the seating area. 'I thought it was my father's. He was in America too.'

Louisa hands the tray to her waitress and resumes her watchful presence, elbows on the counter. I glance across where Andy is still being subjected to and wilting under my friend's interrogation. At some point I'm going to have to rescue him. But there's another question I want to ask.

'Can you remember when my father died, Louisa?'

'I think it was a few days later when we heard. *Papa* was never the same. I think that awful news was the start of his decline. Such a young man!' Louisa cocks her head and gives me a puzzled frown. 'Why do you want to know?'

'I get these dreams. Some things about that day I can't remember.'

'It must have been awful for you. I know you didn't come to the café for a long time after it happened. If you're meant to remember, you will.'

**

35.

I take her advice about Bernard and Sophie. We pick them up on Thursday afternoon and the four of us go to the café. Louisa is as good as her word. Bern scoffs more than his share of the pastries while Sophie makes teenage eyes at Andy. She fires the questions like machine gun bullets.

You live in a proper château? Do you like England? Is Andy your real name - it's not very French? How old are you? And so it goes on.

Andy is being very patient with her.

Are you going to marry Nicole?

I draw the line there and give her a twenty *euro* note to pay for some more drinks at the counter. She goes reluctantly.

'*Jesu Maria*!' Andy swears softly. 'Is she always like that?'

'Pretty much.'

'I like her, but that look she gives scares me. She knows much more about life than she ought at fourteen.' He punches Bern lightly on the upper arm. 'I suppose you do too!'

Bernard gives him a scathing look. 'She knows nothing,' he rasps. 'Well, are you?'

'Am I what?' Andy wrinkles his forehead.

'Are you going to marry my sister?'

Andy flashes me a look which could be either surprise or embarrassment, but which says plainly - *Help!* I think of the two of us I'm the more surprised and embarrassed. Bern sounded more like a protective father than a younger brother.

Sophie has just returned with the drinks and another plateful of pastries.

'We haven't discussed that,' I say.

'No, we haven't.' Andy manages a grin but he lowers his eyes.

'When we finish here, how would you two kids like to have a tour of *Château Ravel?*'

Not having discussed it doesn't mean I haven't thought about it. I feel our relationship intensified during the holiday. However, I'm not thinking of marriage as an immediate priority; I'm not even sure of Andy's views on marriage as an estate, or about having children. I have three or four years of study ahead of me in a foreign country and that's going to take commitment.

Louisa's plan is working out better than I expected. After Georges takes Sophie and Bernard on a winemaking tour, Andy drives us back to the city. Both my mother and Jean are home, and my ridiculous fears are banished. Andy doesn't seem too fazed at meeting them. While he helps Bernard with a science project, and with Jean looking on with interest, Denise hauls me into the kitchen.

'Thanks for the photos!' When we were in the Riviera, I sent her some pictures of the scenery, and one of Andy and me posing outside St Tropez harbour.

'*Ce n'est rien!*'

'You looked happy.'

'I was happy. I *am* happy, *Maman.*'

'That's all I ever wanted for you.'

The warmth in her voice takes me by surprise. My mother can be unemotional, matter-of-fact, and shies away from physical contact. That's probably a result of her struggle against addiction. But now she grasps me by the arms, holds me at a distance for a moment then hugs me. It's a stiff hug, but a hug all the same.

'I'm sorry, Nicole.'

I disengage from her arms but not before noticing the dampness on her cheek. She turns her head away and pretends she has a fleck in her eye. This is a rare moment.

'For what?' I take her hand and press it. '*Maman?*'

'For everything, I suppose.' Her handbag sits on the kitchen table. She rummages in it for a tissue, sniffs and wipes her nose. 'He seems a nice boy; Sophie likes him. Bern has taken to him too.'

'Andy is good at explaining scientific things,' I say.

'I can see that. Are you going to eat with us, or must you go back to work?'

'I did some extra work last weekend while I was still on leave, so I'm taking the time off now.' In fact, I've arranged with Cathy to restart my housekeeping duties on Sunday but decide not to mention it. *One day at a time, Nicole.* 'We'll stay.'

Denise's expression changes to one of pleasure. 'Really? You'll have dinner?'

'*Bien sûr, Maman*! I wouldn't say it if I didn't mean it.'

Andy

I like Nicole's family. Bernard is serious, a thinker rather than a doer, and the only one of the four who is cast in a different genetic mould from the others - as regards looks anyway. He is sturdy, dark and doesn't talk much. Sophie is pert and funny, besides her brown hair a younger version of Nicole, and much too worldly-wise for her age.

Denise scares me on first acquaintance. I feel I know her already and experience the same knot in my stomach as when I saw the photo of her wedding to Nicole's father. She is two decades or so older now but seems to have aged only half of that. At the dining table, they sit together, facing me. Seen side by side, Nicole and Denise are uncannily alike but I'm careful not to pass comment.

'I'm sorry, Andy. I should have prepared you better.' Nicole catches my embarrassment. She and her mother exchange glances. 'People could take us for sisters.'

'Until they get close.' Denise gives a half-hearted laugh. She plays with her wedding ring. 'I'm good at hiding the furrows and the strands of silver. I was very young when I had Nicole . . .'

I manage a non-committal *Oh*.

'Pièrre, my first husband, Nicole's *papa*, was a lot older than me,' she confides. 'Jean is forty-three.'

From what little Nicole has told me about her father, I'm

curious to learn more. I want to help; there are things she can't remember about him. However, Jean glances up from his food and I get the impression he'd rather we didn't talk about Pièrre Durand. Is that a normal reaction, I wonder, or does a shadow of the past hang over the Massy household? Perhaps that's why Nicole is uncomfortable here.

Jean looks like a master I once had at boarding school. I discover he works for EDF at Blaye. He has a degree in psychology and manages the induction and training of new graduate employees. Though I have no plans to join the nuclear industry, I quiz him about his job and his views on nuclear energy and the alternatives. He becomes quite talkative after dinner so I risk asking how he and Denise met. Denise immediately interrupts our conversation, so I'm denied an answer. She would like him to help with washing up. I wonder what it is she's trying to hide.

Nicole

The evening goes better than I feared, or even expected. One sticky moment comes when Andy is curious about how my mother met Jean. He seems quite willing to answer but she seems less than keen that he should. When we're alone I ask her why.

She shrugs and becomes defensive, a mood more familiar than her hug and cry two hours earlier. 'We don't talk about that,' she says.

'Why not?'

'It's private. We don't talk about our private life to outsiders.' She picks at her fingernails, a sure sign she doesn't want me asking any more questions. It's the way she used to be when I asked her about her age, her childhood, or about my father's death.

I think of all sorts of things I might say but instead suggest it's time Andy drives me home. There hasn't been a good time to ask her about *Mamie*'s photograph.

**

36.

Another week passes, another week closer to saying *au revoir* to the people I love. On the Thursday after our dinner with Denise and Jean, Georges asks for my help again. Cathy has no objection so I agree.

Martha still hasn't shown up. As far as Georges is concerned, she's no longer welcome at *Château Ravel*. I have no idea what Yves thinks; he went directly from Italy to Paris to renegotiate the contracts. Cathy is biting her tongue.

I leave Andy in his room at two o'clock; it's the first time we've gone to bed in the daytime. I've promised to clear some paperwork and bring the ledger up to date for Georges to sign off in the evening. Yves isn't due back from Paris until the weekend, but he wants the desks clear and a calm of twenty-four hours before the inevitable storm.

While I put on my underwear, Andy pulls on his boxer shorts and stretches out on the bed, his shoulders supported by two pillows and his hands clasped behind his head. His hair is tousled from our lovemaking and his beautiful body glistens with sweat.

A warm glow infuses my being. The last few days together have been wonderful. Today especially, Andy has been so attentive, so responsive to my need, and I resist the temptation to halt what I'm doing and climb back in with him. We don't usually have the whole house to ourselves. Cathy has gone out to one of her volunteer committees.

His eyes follow me as I pick up my clothes and bag and make for the bathroom. 'You're sure you have to go?'

'Yes, but I'll see you this evening.'

I pull on my pencil skirt and button my blouse. The bathroom mirror is still misted up from when we showered earlier. I wipe away the moisture. Then I do my best to repair the damage to my face and hair before standing back to check I look office respectable. When I go back into the room, Andy has picked up a textbook and pretends to be engrossed in reading. I put on my glasses. Though my eye isn't troubling me, I need them for the paperwork.

Andy sneaks a look at me over the spine of his book. 'You've no idea how sexy you look in that outfit. I do wish you'd come back to bed.'

I make a face as I pick up my phone. 'Me work; you study.'

'*Oui, madame la secrétaire.*'

'*Tais-toi!*' I reprimand, and bend to kiss him briefly on the forehead. '*A bientôt.*'

I go down to the kitchen, put my bag and phone on the breakfast bar, make some coffee and hitch myself onto a stool to drink it. Cathy has left a copy of *Vogue* on the work surface. I flick through the pages as I sip my coffee, doing my best to rid myself of all salacious thoughts. I look up, suddenly alert as I catch an unfamiliar sound from the direction of the living room.

'Cathy?'

There is no reply. I get up, go into the atrium, open the living-room door and look in. 'Cathy!' I call again.

I am answered by a repetition of the sound, but now it seems to come from the hallway leading to the office suite. All through the hottest days, the air-conditioning has been running at maximum power and sometimes makes whistling and other noises as the thermostat clicks on and off. However, this isn't a cooling system sound. It's one I can't identify, more like a slow, heavy and irregular footfall followed by the thump-bump of something being dragged across a bare floor. I go back to the breakfast bar.

'Andy?' Has he come downstairs without me realising and is he now playing some sort of trick on me? Every so often, the adolescent undergraduate emerges. 'Stop it, Andy! You're freaking me out.'

A moment of total silence is followed by a muffled thud. I grab my phone and dial Georges' number. His ring tone is the first two bars of *La Marseillaise* and if he has come back unexpectedly I would hear it. But I don't!

'*Allo.*' He answers immediately.

'Where are you, *M. Georges*?'

'Nicole?' He sounds surprised. 'I'm at home, having a late lunch. I'll be over later. *Qui a-t-il?*'

'It's nothing, *monsieur.* I was about to go to the office and I heard a noise. I'm sorry. I think maybe it was Andy fooling around.'

'Give the boy a good hard slap, Nicole,' Georges says. 'And one from me!' He hangs up.

I look into the living room again. There's no one there. From the window I can see most of the drive. My Citroen is garaged but there is no sign of Cathy's Mercedes. I cross the atrium into the corridor leading to the office suite. More sounds. *Martha*, I think. She must still have a key. Then I remember she weighs no more than sixty kilos and is light on her feet. I dial Andy's phone. Seconds pass before he picks up.

'Are you still in your bedroom?'

'I'm having a shower. Do you want to join me?' he jokes.

'I think you should come down.' I lower my voice. 'We might have an intruder.'

'An intruder?'

'I'm serious.' Knowing he is upstairs, I begin to feel uneasy. 'A burglar, I don't know. Just get dressed and come downstairs right away.'

More sounds reach me from the direction of the office. I definitely locked the door; both Yves and Georges have impressed upon me the importance of doing so. The factory sometimes has unscheduled visitors, especially in the afternoons, and the family don't want anyone wandering into the house by mistake.

Georges is at lunch. Yves isn't due back for forty-eight hours and he, as I've learned, usually lives his life and manages his affairs by the clock. If Cathy had come home, her car would be there and she would have answered my call. Who else can it be but an unwanted guest?

I take a few cautious steps along the corridor. The air is filled with the pungent, unpleasant odour of *Gauloises*. Only Yves smokes and Cathy, though she doesn't object to his cigars, has forbidden him bringing cigarettes into the house. If he has arrived home unexpectedly, he didn't come in by the front door. A distant, vague memory surges into my thoughts. Something is wrong.

As I draw closer to the office, I hear noises as if furniture is being moved, then an angry voice and expletives, all muffled by the sound-proofing of the adjoining wall. The door is open a crack, but not enough for me to see who's inside or what's going on.

'*Monsieur Ravel?*' I'm about to knock when I hear more furniture sounds, the crash of something heavy hitting the floor and the crunch of broken glass.

I push the door open.

Yves is slumped against the desk, holding a more than half-empty bottle of spirits. His eyes are glazed, his face puffy, red and unshaven, his movements jerky and uncontrolled. His shirt has been in a fight with a concoction of beer and tomato juice. The chair at which I normally sit is up-ended, the accounts ledgers and paper correspondence are strewn everywhere in disarray, and splinters of glass are scattered across the floor.

He has cut his hand. Drops of blood mingle with the liquor that spills like a tiny waterfall from the polished surface of the desk. In reaching for the bottle, he must have lost his balance and knocked over a tumbler. I stacked the books and paperwork neatly on a bookcase and he must have stumbled against it, sweeping everything to the ground.

He looks up when I enter but rather than seeing me, he seems to be focussing on a spot on the wall above my head. Then his attention switches to the gash in his hand. He holds it up and stares at it, fascinated, while the blood dribbles freely over the front of his shirt.

'Let me help you, *monsieur*.' I right the chair and move to take the bottle from him. His breath stinks of alcohol and tobacco. 'Give me that and let me attend to your hand.'

He releases the bottle into my custody. Unless I'm much mistaken, he has consumed three quarters of a bottle of Scotch. He likes whisky almost as much as he adores wine, but I've never seen him drunk. I've never seen any man in such a state.

'Martha?'

'Non, monsieur, ce n'est pas Martha.'

'Emmeline.' He mutters the name twice, staring blankly again at his hand. It's going to need stitches.

For a second or two I freeze, wondering what can be going on in his head.

'C'est Nicole,' I say, looking around for something to act as a temporary bandage. 'Do you have a handkerchief?'

'Handkerchief,' he echoes then gives a hoarse laugh. 'I'm *so . . . o . . . oh* pissed!'

The corner of a handkerchief protrudes from the pocket of his shirt. I pull it out and do my best to wrap it round his cut. Meantime, his body has begun to slide sideways along the desk. I try to steady him but he's a dead weight and slumps to his knees.

He groans as he makes an effort to get up. *'Merd . . . duh!'* he slurs as he bangs his elbow on the side of the desk. *Where is Andy when I need him?*

'Try to stand, *monsieur.'* Yves Ravel must weigh a hundred kilos, and a hundred kilos of very intoxicated manhood is more than I can manage. 'Put your hand on the desk. Lean on my shoulder and we'll try to get you to a chair.'

Yves manages to get to his feet, but clumsily, and in so doing loses his balance again. He clutches at my shoulder with his bloody hand and misses. The hand finds the lapel of my blouse and rips it open to the waist.

'Jesus Christ!' Now it's my turn to swear. I make to grab the loose ends of my attire.

Realising he's going to fall, Yves reaches again for support. This time, his flailing fingers catch the cup of my bra and tear it from my breast. He falls against me, pinning me to the side of the desk.

Andy bursts into the office. His eyes blaze with fury. He seizes his father by the forearm, heaves him off me and spins him round by the shoulder. I take the chance to escape, holding the two halves of my torn blouse together at the neck.

Andy balls his fists.

'*Non,*' I shout. 'It's not what you think!'

I'm too late. Andy has swung his right arm. His fist connects with his father's face. Yves totters, collapses on the floor like a rag doll and lies still.

The next few moments are blurred confusion and I can't be sure whether seconds or minutes pass. Andy, horrified now rather than angry, and wearing only jeans, nurses his bruised knuckles. His wet hair flops down over his eyes. His feet are bare. Suddenly Cathy is there too, framed by the office doorway, startled and uncomprehending. Yves lies where he fell, his face a mass of blood and beaten flesh like in some horror film, so limp and motionless I'm sure he's dead.

Memories I have so long buried begin flooding back. Blinded by tears, I think I hear myself scream.

**

37.

Cathy

I've stumbled onto a movie set, one where I have no part. It's a half-run scene which, at first glimpse, and given the amount of blood, makes no sense at all. I take several seconds to realise what I'm seeing. None of the actors moves, as in an old still, shot decades ago and preserved forever on celluloid.

A scream shatters the silence. I can't be certain whether it's mine or Nicole's. She holds her bloody fingers at her throat. Her blouse is smeared red. Andy, shirtless and in bare feet, is staring wildly at the man on the floor. *Who the hell is that?* I think. But then, focussing on the bloody features I realise with horror the face is that of my husband.

I kneel by his side. The smell of whisky and tobacco is overpowering. He's a mess but he's still breathing. 'For Christ's sake, Andy, do something. Call an ambulance.'

'I've killed him. He's dead.'

'Dead drunk you mean.'

Andy fumbles at his pocket for his phone, but he's wearing tight jeans and I can see at a glance he doesn't have it.

'Never mind,' I yell, and reach for the land line. 'I'll do it. Put something on your feet. There's glass everywhere.'

The office phone is programmed with codes for the emergency services. I punch in the number that connects me with SAMU. *Fifteen minutes.* I bend over Yves and examine his injuries. They are bad enough, but not life-threatening unless the shock kills him. The important thing now is, I deal with the situation as best I can. Explanations can wait.

'You know where the first aid is kept, Nicole, would you . . .' I look up and see she has gone. 'Andy! Bandages and disinfectant, and a cloth and fresh water to clean up this mess!'

At last he moves. He darts from the office and returns a few minutes later with the first-aid kit. I have some tissues in my handbag and I use them to wipe the blood from Yves' mouth and cheek. His nose is certainly broken and there's a gaping hole in his upper gum where, when I saw him last, there were two incisor teeth.

'Go after Nicole, Andy. Make sure she's OK. I'll look after your father.' I return to my task, wondering why I bother. If he recovers, I'll kill him myself. This is the man to whom I've given twenty-five years of my life. I've loved him and he has nearly broken my heart with his obsessions and his flirtations. Now he appears to have crossed the line. Maybe he deserves everything he gets.

I pick up the phone again and my fingers hover over the keypad.

Andy

Nicole's bedroom door is ajar and she's packing. Her wardrobe doors are wide open and two drawers from her dressing table lie on the bed. She has changed her top and is stuffing other pieces of clothing into a small suitcase. Her eyes are dry but her make-up is smudged. I've never seen Nicole cry.

'Are you hurt?'

'A couple of bruises - my shoulder and . . .' She rubs the small of her back. 'Here. That was the desk. It's nothing. *Mon Dieu*, Andy, you nearly killed your father.'

'He's not dead.'

'I know. I heard what Cathy said. But it could so easily have been worse.'

'You said it was an intruder. When you called, the water was running. I was covered in soapsuds. Some of it got in my eyes. Then I dropped my phone. I came as quickly as I could.'

'It's OK, Andy. I'm fine.'

'It's not OK. My father hurt you. He tried to . . . *My father!*'

'No he didn't, Andy. It was an accident. He had too much to drink. When I tried to help him, he lost his balance. He just grabbed for a hold. My blouse kind of got in the way.' She's holding back tears now.

'That's no excuse. When I saw his hands all over you, I thought . . . *Christ*, I don't know what I thought. I just reacted. He gets tipsy occasionally but never anything like that.'

'It was Scotch, *mon chéri*, not lust.'

'Oh God, what have I done?' I glance from her mascara-stained face to her suitcase and begin pacing the carpet. My knuckles sting; two are bruised and red; I acted on the spur of the moment and got it wrong. In spite of all our disagreements, I should have known my father would never molest a girl, even when drunk.

'It'll be OK. He'll be OK.'

'What about us, Nicole? You're packing.'

'A few things. For a day or two. You must see . . .'

'So *we're* OK?'

'We're OK.' A tear trickles down from the corner of her eye, the one with a slight weakness. 'I get it, Andy. You were looking out for me.' She takes a tissue from a box on the bed and wipes her cheek, forcing a smile. 'I have to get away for a bit, sort some issues out in my mind. I've called Amelie. I'll stay with her.'

'You don't have to go.'

'Yes I do. This is the wrong place for me at the moment.'

'I don't understand.'

'And I can't explain. Not yet.'

'At least let me drive you.'

'I'll be OK in the Citroen. We'll talk later. Your place is with your family, with your father . . . your mother.'

'You're my family too, Nicole.'

'No I'm not. You have to put things right. When you find your phone, call me.' She points to her dressing table. 'And I've written down Amelie's address for Cathy. It's on a card under the glass tray.'

'I'll tell her.' I make to kiss her but she evades my arms.

'Not now, Andy.' She replaces the drawers, closes the wardrobe and slams the suitcase shut.

I go over to the dresser and slide out the card from under the tray: *Amelie Jacques - Coiffeuse et Manicure - La beauté commence par votre coiffure*. Beneath the print is written in beautiful copperplate lettering a Bordeaux city address and phone number. I'm still staring at the writing when Nicole leaves the room.

Cathy

Paramedics arrive and with them a very harassed doctor. They carry Yves, semi-conscious and groaning, on a stretcher upstairs to the bedroom, where he retches and throws up on his clothes. He can't speak and the doctor thinks his jaw is fractured. He gives him some painkillers and recommends he sober up before going to hospital for surgery.

We manage to get him undressed and into pyjamas. I empty his pockets and toss what he was wearing - trousers, shirt and underwear - everything - into the washing machine. I don't care if it comes out wrong. I certainly can't ask Nicole to deal with it, assuming she ever speaks to me again.

Neither Andy nor Nicole is anywhere to be seen. Nicole's door is open. The room is tidy, the bedspread neatly turned down, all the surfaces dust-free and her books perfectly aligned on their shelves. By contrast, Andy's bedroom is a disaster of creased bedding and crumpled clothes. I'd be a fool to imagine they weren't having sex, and the knowledge shouldn't upset me. However, the proof they've been doing it here, in my house, and in the middle of the afternoon, somehow wounds my sense of propriety.

I go into Andy's *en-suite* bathroom. The shower head is dripping and the floor tiles are swimming with water. A soggy towel lies in the bath. I find his phone in the WC bowl and fish it out.

Tired and depressed, I go downstairs to the kitchen. I need a drink and open a bottle of red wine. One glass, that's all. Enough alcohol has been consumed in the house this afternoon. I go to the living room, take off my shoes and stretch out on my sofa. *What has happened to my once well-ordered family?*

Muddled thoughts whirl around in my head. Perhaps I *should* have called the police but what then? What if Andy is charged too?

As for divorcing Yves, I have a solid case. He's the guilty party so any settlement would go my way. But might he appeal to the court, claim Nicole led him on? I don't believe that of her, yet a tiny, a miniscule suspicion flutters in my mind. What would a clever attorney make of that? I'm not sure divorce is the answer anyway. *Not yet*. I want to confront the man who's hurt me, hear him defend himself, listen to his explanation. *Fucking Hell*. What a mess!

Andy comes in through the conservatory. He's still in his bare feet and shirtless. I decide not to comment.

'I let Nicole out this way.' He hands me a white business card. 'She's gone to stay with her friend Amelie. I didn't want her to get involved with the medics.'

'How was she?'

'I thought she'd be upset at what happened. She is, but not in the way you'd expect. Maybe I don't know her as well as I thought.' He gestures towards the business card. 'That's beautiful writing. Did they take Father to hospital?'

'No, he's upstairs asleep . . . I'm going to have to deal with him when he wakes up. Stay with your uncle for a few days, maybe until you go back to Oxford.'

'I won't be going to Oxford if I'm arrested for GBH. You haven't phoned the police or anything?'

'No, I haven't. I think your father has more urgent . . .' I pause, recalling something odd he said when I asked him about Nicole. 'What did you mean, *not in the way you'd expect?*'

'I don't understand it. She's not at all upset about what happened this afternoon. It's about something else, something I think happened a while ago.'

'You're not making sense, Andy. How could she not be upset? Her employer tried to rape her.'

'That's not what happened. *Dieu*, he and I have our differences, but this . . . ' He flops down on the sofa beside me and puts his head in his hands. 'I'll never be able to face him again. There's something you need to know, Mother. My father may be a drunken idiot but he's no rapist.'

'That was the way it looked to me.' I glare at him. 'You'd better explain what you mean, darling.'

**

38.

Nicole

I don't remember much about the journey into the city. I cry. I drive. I'm remembering little things, then more. And when I reach Amelie's place I sit on the bed and cry again. Flashes of real memory from my childhood mingle with dream images of the last few months. It's all coming together now . . . what happened that day. *Gaston - the café - the hospital. The things Denise never talked about. How could I possibly have forgotten the very worst day of my life?*

'You'll be OK.' Amelie tries to comfort me. 'At least you're not hurt.'

'You don't understand,' I stammer between choking sobs. 'This isn't . . . isn't about Yves Ravel.'

I do my best to explain I've been remembering things about my father.

'Poor you.' She hugs me. 'Such a young man! I don't know what to say.'

'It's OK, Amelie.' I hug her back. 'You don't have to say anything. Just be my friend!'

'Well, look on the bright side,' she says. 'M. Ravel isn't dead.'

'I thought he *was* dead!' I shiver at the recollection. 'He lay there without moving. There was so much blood.'

'Out cold.' Amelie flicks back her gorgeous hair. 'But lucky you to have a boyfriend prepared to defend you like that.'

'I didn't need defending. Yves was drunk; he wasn't molesting me.'

'*Chérie*, he ripped your blouse and tore off your bra.'

'It was an accident. I was trying to help him.'

'When he gets out of hospital he should apologise.'

'I'm more worried about what to say to Cathy. I tried explaining to Andy . . . *afterwards*. I think I got through to him. She saw *only* the afterwards - the torn blouse and the naked boob.'

Amelie laughs.

'It's not funny, Amm,' I mutter, wondering if I need to look for another job for the next four or five weeks. Though I've done nothing wrong, I'm embarrassed and even a bit angry with Andy that he reacted without waiting for an explanation. I remember his arguments with Yves, and that he once punched Paul Sonnier. Is there a hidden aggression in his nature, a quick temper that makes him act first and ask questions later?

Gradually, through the evening, I piece the images together. I guess I didn't cry then and that's the problem. For eight years, I've buried my emotions and my memories in some deep, sealed cavern of my being. I don't know if there's a medical term. *Not really amnesia*, because I never truly forgot. Instead, I stowed away my terror, my sorrow, my helplessness, as if they were pieces of baggage in a railway locker. Maybe that's why I pushed myself so hard through my teen years, read, studied and pretended nothing was wrong. *Maman* was never any use in a crisis but she should have at least told me about my father. She should have told me the truth.

And what about my *other* memories, the ones I've always thought were real? Could they be implanted too, like the lie of my father's heart attack - that he died peacefully in hospital, when I'm sure now he died in my arms: *the beach holidays in the South; the vineyards in Alsace; driving along the tree-lined lanes of middle England; all those things we did as a family when I was little.*

I want Amelie to understand; I want Andy to understand. Nobody can. It isn't physical hurt; it isn't embarrassment. It's something else. The sight of Yves' limp body, the soaked handkerchief and the blood oozing from his damaged face opened the wound. *How my father died.* After eight years of hiding my loss amidst the trials and dramas of growing up, amidst the anger at Denise's addiction, it's comes back to haunt me. First in nightmares . . . then in reality.

Papa lying there - bleeding, clutching his arm, his face twisted

in pain as he gasps for his final desperate breath.
**

39.

I'm swinging my leather satchel from side to side as I skip along *Rue Aristide*. School finished at four and I'm going to meet my father. A light September breeze ruffles my hair. I'm twelve years old and looking forward to my second year of *collège*. Mme Boucher complimented me on the standard of my English. She has given me an extra reader, *Little Women* by Louisa May Alcott. I love reading English and can't wait to start on it when I get home.

I want to be a teacher. I decided when I was eight. My father taught me to read English and speak a few words before I went to primary school. It was through him that I became interested in languages. He had worked in England, America and in Germany before he met my mother and spoke fluent English and German. But Mme Boucher is my true inspiration. An Anglophile like my father, she is encouraging me to read English novels above the level of the rest of the class.

Papa will be at Gaston's. He often goes there after work, to drink coffee or sip a brandy with the old man, and to talk politics. It seems such a boring thing to talk about but Gaston remembers World War II and loves telling Papa how he once met President de Gaulle.

Three tables covered with green and white-chequered tablecloths are set in front of the café, the corners of the cloth flapping in the breeze. There's an awning too, striped with the same colours, to shield customers from the sun. The ashtrays on two tables are clean and empty; a third contains the stub of a half-smoked cigarette. The odour lingers, even in the open air. A stranger is sitting at the table, reading and drawing on a second *Gauloise*. He looks up, gives me a half-hearted smile and returns to his newspaper.

I hitch my satchel onto one shoulder and push open the café door. The ceiling fans are on. I meet a shimmering wall of cool air and rub my arms to counter the newly-formed goose bumps. Gaston sits alone at a table near the counter, filling his pipe with tobacco. There's no sign of *Papa*. I look for Louisa but she isn't there either. We're great friends; sometimes she gives me little treats like freshly-baked *madeleines* or an extra scoop of ice cream.

'*Bonsoir*, Nicole.' Gaston looks up and lays his pipe on the tablecloth. 'I wasn't expecting you today.'

'Isn't *Papa* here?' I glance round the premises, wondering if they're playing a game with me. 'He said he'd meet me.'

'Maybe he has a cold. He was here earlier, but didn't stay long,' Gaston says. 'He felt a bit shivery.' He starts to get up but he must be nearly ninety and has to steady himself on the table. 'I'll fetch my jacket and make sure you get home safely. Strange he didn't mention meeting you.'

'He must've forgotten. He does forget things sometimes. Like *Maman's* birthday.' I draw myself up, trying to look older and taller than I am. 'But I'm twelve, *M. Gaston*. Don't trouble yourself. I can go home by myself.'

I run all the way and by the time I get to the top of our stairs I'm quite out of breath. The main door of the flat is wide open and my father's work case lies unattended to one side. *Maman* must have gone out taking Sophie and Bernard with her, but why would she leave the door ajar? Why would *Papa* leave it like that?

I call out but get no answer. Then I hear noises coming from the living room, scratching and scuffing and the sound of breaking glass or porcelain.

'*Qui est la?*' The sound of more breaking glass is followed by a thud as something heavy hits the tiles in the dining area. I tiptoe cautiously across the hall.

'Denise?' It's my father's voice but he sounds so strange and weak. Maybe Gaston is right. A summer cold.

'*C'est moi, Papa. C'est Nicole.*'

'Come quickly, *ma petite*!'

I no longer hesitate but run into the living room. At first, I don't see him, but I hear him groan.

'*Nicole . . . ici.*'

He's on the floor behind the large round dining table and between it and the kitchenette, half kneeling, half sprawling. His eyes are closed and he's clutching his left arm with his right hand. He has upset a chair and knocked over a glass vase and a jug that normally sit on the lower shelf of our rustic oak dresser. His left hand is covered in blood. When I get closer, I see that a splinter from the vase has lodged in his palm.

'Shall I fetch help, *Papa*?'

'I'm very sick, my darling. I have a pain in my chest. Telephone the doctor quickly. Press *15* for the ambulance. Can you do that? But first . . . if you can, help me to the armchair.'

He's much too heavy for me to lift but I manage to get him onto both knees. Then, with him leaning on my shoulders, I try dragging him towards the chair. His weight makes me lose my balance and we're not half way there before I collapse against the side of the dresser.

Somehow my father manages to get to his feet but he's taken only two steps when he stiffens and clutches his arm again. His face is twisted, awfully twisted. For a second or two he stands motionless. Then he moans, totters and falls his full height on the tiles. The side of his head strikes a corner of the table. He opens his eyes and mouths my name. There's a horrid gash in his temple.

I grab the phone and press the emergency number, give our address, stumbling over my words, my answers. *Papa*'s eyes are wide open now. He's staring at the ceiling. I'm so afraid and I sink to the floor beside him. I don't know what else to do.

I'm sitting there holding his head when a doctor and an ambulance arrive. I've taken out the splinter of glass. My dress is covered in his blood. The telephone is in my lap, the receiver smeared red.

The doctor is a stout man with a beard. I've never seen him before; he isn't our regular doctor. He bends down and feels my father's neck for a pulse.

'We need to treat him now!'

One of the two ambulance people, the woman, takes me by the arm, tries to pull me away, but I won't let go of *Papa*'s head. They bring medical equipment, a stretcher.

'You have to let us look after him,' she says.

'I'm not leaving him.' I shrug off her hand.

'You don't have to, but you have to let go. Your father's very ill. You have to let us treat him.'

The man crouches over my father. He puts two hands on his chest and pushes hard against it.

'Stop! You're hurting him.'

'No, we have to keep his blood circulating,' the woman paramedic says.

Now all three are speaking at once.

'We need to get him to hospital right away.'

'You take the girl.'

'We have to get in touch with his wife.'

'Let's get him to the ambulance. There might still be a chance.'

'Where's your mother?'

'Check the phone.'

'Does your mother have a cell phone?'

'What's your name, ma chérie?'

Dimly, I realise they're talking to me - that they want to contact my mother. I don't know where she is but her number is on a pad beside the land phone . . . beside where it was before I pulled it off the stand.

I point with a bloody finger. One of them, the doctor I think, finds the list. He has a mobile phone himself and punches numbers on the keypad.

More confusing conversation . . .

'Have you contacted someone? The mother?'

'No reply.'

'It's an MI.'

'Any history?'

'Let's get him to Emergency. The daughter's name is Nicole.'

'Looks like he fell. There's blood on the table.'

'He may be concussed. The head wound's serious.'

'Poor kid's traumatised.'

'Not surprised, witnessing something like that.'

At that moment *Maman* comes home. She doesn't say anything; she doesn't look at me. She just stares and screams.

Death is something we never discussed. Old people died, I knew that. But *Papa* was only forty. I don't think I fully understood then what had happened.

I can see my mother's pale face as I silently follow her and the stretcher to the ambulance. I haven't done anything wrong but I sense she doesn't want me there. Her look says *no* but at the last moment she seizes my hand and helps me up the step at the back.

Then the journey. They connect my father to apparatus in the ambulance. The doctor tells me to stand away and then the woman paramedic shocks him. The machine beeps and numbers and irregular lines pop up on the screen.

'Is there a pulse.'

'We're still ten minutes away.'

'Try to stabilise him.'

'The head injury can't wait.'

The rear door opens again. The emergency team are waiting for us with a trolley. My mother still hasn't spoken to me. Her face is pale, her eyes anxious. I cling to her arm but she shakes me off and follows the doctors into the hospital.

The events of the morning - *was that today?* - school, Mme Boucher, Gaston's café, the chequered tablecloths - all are fading into a dream haze. The reek of stale smoke and the sweetness of Gaston's tobacco have been replaced by a different smell, cleanliness, starched linen, bandages and disinfectant. And crowding out those earlier memories are others I don't want to think about. I try pushing them away. *Get out of my head - I don't want you there!*

Now I'm in a long corridor, lit at intervals with fluorescent ceiling lights. There are lots of doors. *Cardiac. Trauma.* At the far end is one open door with a lit room beyond. I know they went that way. I know something is happening there, something that makes my heart thump in terror. *Something bad.*

They'll do CPR, like on TV. He'll be OK. Nobody in our family is ever ill. But I'm old enough to know better. *Real life isn't like television.*

A nurse tries to hold me back but I wrench myself away, start running. As I reach the door, it slams closed. I see silhouettes through the frosted glass. I hammer on the glass until my knuckles hurt.

Let me in! I scream, but no one inside pays any attention. My head is pounding, aching, and my heart won't slow down.

The nurse has a grip of my shoulders but I fight her with all my strength. Then *Maman* comes out of the room with a doctor. I beat them with my fists.

I want to see my father!

The doctor hands me a plastic tumbler and a pill, tries to make me take it. I throw the water in his face. Then the last thing I remember is a sharp pain in my arm and the world dissolving around me.

The rest is hazy. Whether suppressed by my will or simply forgotten, there are still gaps in my twelve-year-old memory. Whatever the doctors injected into me that day, it was strong and I woke up in my grandparents' house, confused, with no idea of the hour or the day. *Mamie* was there - and Denise. They told me to be brave; my father wasn't coming home again. He'd had a heart attack and had gone to Heaven.

I'm standing stiffly beside Bern at the cemetery. A priest is chanting in Latin. My mother is wearing a black dress and hat and is biting her fingernails. Sophie is clinging tearfully to her arm while they lower my father's coffin into the grave. He wouldn't have wanted any of the religion but they had to do it for *Mamie*'s sake.

Did it actually happen that way? I know now it did. *They were trying to protect me, that's all.* But I need to remember more before I go charging around demanding answers.

On Friday morning I don't wake until nearly midday. Amelie said she'd take the day off work to be with me. Her routine alternates between the salon, classes at college and private clients at home.

After I've had a bite to eat, I think about phoning Cathy, but my phone is dead and must have been so for hours. I realise I didn't bring my charger. Amelie tells me to use the land line. I pick up the handset and put it down again. I'm not sure what to say. At some point I'll have to go back. All my books, my computer and most of my clothing - things I need for Edinburgh - are still at *Château Ravel*. However, Cathy will have her hands full with the domestic situation, and I'm a complication she doesn't need. Worse, Yves may still be there and I'd much rather not face him right now.

I'm not much in the mood for talking and Amelie leaves me alone for two hours to watch TV. Four o'clock comes and Andy hasn't called me. Even if he *did* lose his mobile phone, there's no reason for him not using the house telephone. And I left him Amelie's number.

'Would you like me to do your hair?' she asks.

'What is there to do with *this*?' I hold up my ponytail and twist it into a whorl on the crown of my head. 'You mean something like that?'

She laughs, cocks her head and makes a snipping gesture with her fingers. 'I could cut it. New look for Edinburgh?'

I'm so upset about Andy not calling I don't care about my looks, but Amelie has the knack of cheering me up when I'm down. A new hair style might be liberating.

'You know what?' I give her a resigned look and loosen the clasp of my ponytail. 'I'm sick of the old me. Make into somebody else.'

When she's finished, she hands me a mirror. I put on my glasses and study the effect. She's cut my hair at the neckline, and has given me a left parting and a side-swept bob on the right. I hardly recognise myself. My hair looks so much fuller and thicker than it has ever done before.

'Well, *chérie*?' Amelie stands back to admire her handiwork.

'You realise you're a genius, Amm.' I throw my arms around her neck. 'I feel a million times better than I did this morning. Empowered.'

'Hey,' she says. 'Take care you don't mess up too soon. You

look a bit like Emma Watson.'

'Who?'

'*Emma Watson*. You know, Hermione Granger in the Harry Potter movies!'

On Saturday morning, I feel almost normal. Amelie has no work so, after showering, and back in our pyjamas, we sit and chat. She fixes my hair, we have a late breakfast, and then she leaves me to do the washing up. She has a private client in the afternoon and wants to get ready.

My hands are deep in suds when the buzzer on the outer door sounds. Amelie yells to me that she'll get it. Midday has passed and Andy still hasn't called.

'*Qui?*' I hear her on the intercom. 'Come straight up.'

I don't want to be in the way of her business so I drain the basin, take off my rubber gloves and head for the bedroom she's lent me.

'It's him!' she yells excitedly. 'You have a visitor, Nica. It's Andy!'

My heart leaps in my chest and my tummy turns over. Andy is the one person I *do* want to see. I want to see him badly. I want to hear his voice and feel his arms around me.

'I'll be there in a moment.' Quickly, I strip off my pyjamas. I've brought a blue faux-suede wrap skirt I haven't worn in a while. I tie it on, pull on a light sweater, check my face in the mirror and take a few deep breaths. By the time I reach the living room, he's already there.

'Nicole! You've changed your . . .'

I don't let him finish but throw my arms round his neck and press my lips to his in a lingering kiss.

'You look so amazing!' He looks at me approvingly when I let him go and whistles. 'I love your hair. Did your friend . . .?'

'Don't mind me, guys,' Amelie says. 'If you're going to do any of that stuff you'd better go to the bedroom.'

'It's OK, Amm,' I say. 'We just need to talk. Anyway, I

suppose I ought to introduce you properly. Amelie . . . *Andy*, Andy . . . *Amelie.*'

'*Plaisir!*' She strokes her hair and gives him a seductive smile. She's beautiful and I'm quite jealous. 'I heard your voice once. I'm glad to get to meet you at last. You're quite a hunk, aren't you? If you get tired of him, *chérie*, let me know. He's *mine!*'

That's Amelie's way. She doesn't mean it literally but Andy looks embarrassed. 'I'm staying at Uncle Georges' place', he says. 'My father's going into hospital for a few days. It's best I leave my mother to deal with him when he comes out.'

'Why didn't you ring me?'

'I tried.' He grins and pulls my charger from his hip pocket. 'You should have a message from me somewhere. And mother took the business card out with her without giving me a chance to write down the number.'

'I'll leave you alone,' Amelie says. She consults her phone. 'My client is due at one. You now have thirty-five minutes to sort everything out.'

We hold one another. The carriage clock on the window ledge chimes twelve-thirty. The heat is building in my body. It has only been two days but I ache for him - to be with him. I know I'm being selfish, because right now it's mostly physical, a powerful need to be possessed and to forget.

'We still have thirty of Amelie's minutes.' I take his hand. 'There's a perfectly good bed next door, and she won't mind.'

'She might come in,' Andy says. 'We can't!'

'She won't, and we can!' I connect my phone to its charger and plug it into a spare socket beside the TV. Then I lead him into my borrowed room, where I push him down on the bed.

He gasps but doesn't protest. I ruck up my skirt, climb on top of him and straddle his hips. His hands find the tie of the skirt. He cups my bottom and pulls me towards him. The house phone in the living room rings but we ignore it.

'I want you, and a girl's bedroom is sacrosanct,' I whisper as I reach for the zipper on his trousers. The phone goes on ringing, and ringing, then stops.

It isn't the same. Making love in stolen moments in a borrowed room isn't the way it should be - like a couple of kids on their fumbling date. I had that with Henri; I don't want it now. Andy seems to feel my hesitation.

'What's wrong?' he asks.

'You're right. We can't. I need all of you. I want the thunder and lightning again. I want the earth to move for us and I don't think half-an-hour is long enough.'

'Not our own space?'

'No.'

'We could go to a hotel. Tonight. At least that's neutral territory. I won't be comfortable at home for a while and I can't very well entertain you at Georges' place.' He gives a chuckle and the boyish grin spreads over his face. 'Not with two pubescent teenagers in the house.'

'A hotel in Bordeaux won't be cheap, Andy.'

'It's one night, maybe the last chance we'll get.' He grows very serious. 'I did a lot of thinking when I was on my own yesterday. I'm going back to Oxford early. It'll be a busy year.'

My heart misses a beat. All I can manage is a miserable *Oh!* We'd agreed to spend the rest of his vacation together. After that I'd have another fortnight to prepare for Edinburgh. Now he's going to leave me to cope alone with fall-out from yesterday's drama.

'On Monday in fact. I've already packed most of my things.'

'I see. You mean . . .'

My face must be reflecting my inner fear he wants us to break up. *'Mon Dieux, non!'* he says. 'But I can't stay at Georges' much longer. It isn't a big house and the boys need their space. Apart from the Oxford flat, I'm homeless.'

He takes a deep breath. 'I want you to come too, Nicole. The rent's paid until Christmas. We could go to Scotland together - Edinburgh - set you up there. We could get married.'

'Married! Are you absolutely insane, Andy Ravel?'

'I've never been saner in all my life. If I have to start out on my own, I might as well start right away. What do I have to lose? I've blown it completely with my father.'

I can still feel the thudding of my heart and the rapid pulse of the blood through my veins. His proposal - if that's what it was - came as a shock, though with it a thrill of pleasure.

'You don't know that for sure.'

'Yes, I do. We had another argument the day before we went to St Tropez. It was about you . . .'

'What?'

'He knew what was going on, he said, and he wouldn't put up with it, not in his house. I don't know what he thinks we were doing . . . Anyway, I told him to mind his own business. That did it. He got very red in the face. He yelled: *You'd better get a job then, because I'm not paying you another centime!* I nearly hit him then. Maybe I wanted him to try it on with you so I'd have an excuse.'

'You don't mean that, Andy.'

'No, I don't.' He bites his lip and looks very fierce. 'But I was so angry with him that day.'

'What kind of married life would we have, *mon petit?*' I'm thinking about how much I want to marry him. To have his children. Yet I'm torn between my desire, which warms my limbs and my soul like the summer sunshine - torn between that and my sense of what's sensible and doable. 'How will you manage for the next year in Oxford? You'll have to take out a loan against the cottage in Scotland.'

'I'll do it if I have to. I checked today with my grandmother's lawyer about her legacy, and about the market value of the house. There's a great deal more than I thought. The bank will lend me enough for a year - till my next birthday. And I do have *some* savings. We would manage.'

'What about me, *mon coeur?* I love you and want us to be together, but I was counting on another month's wages.'

'I can spare enough to look after you for a measly month.' He is being carried away by his enthusiasm. 'Maybe more. And in Oxford it'll be like another holiday, but better.'

'I can't just pack up my life here like that, Andy.'

'Why not?' he persists.

'You know why not. I've got to think of Sophie and Bernard.' I want to be persuaded but the whole idea is impossible. 'I can't marry you now, *mon chéri.*'

'It's what I want. I love you. I thought you wanted it too.'

'I do. Just not yet.'

He wrinkles his forehead and juts out his chin. His dark brown eyes are touched with mischievous humour. 'Is that a *maybe* - or a *yes*?' he breathes. 'Will you marry me, Nicole Durand?'

I think hard about what I'm going to say. I'm twenty; he's twenty-four. Might we be throwing ourselves into something we'll regret later? Will he want to take back his words in a year's time - in two years - in three? Will I?

I cover his hands with mine then reach down to kiss him. 'I'd love to marry you, Andy Ravel. Give me three years and we'll do it, if you still want me. As far as Oxford is concerned, let me think about it.'

We're sitting in a quiet corner of the kitchen. I've explained as best I can about everything that's been going on in my head, about the day my father died, about Denise, the two photographs and my suspicion that she's holding back more.

'That's huge,' he says. 'What happens now?'

'I need to know what's true and what isn't. And only Denise can tell me. But I know what she's like. If I stomp over to Caudéran, she'll clam up.'

'You mentioned your grandmother . . .' Andy offers tentatively.

'*Mamie* Durand doesn't know the whole story. She doesn't know how my parents met in Paris. She has no idea why they didn't marry before . . . you know, before they had me. And I don't think she knows more about the day my father died than what I've remembered. Other than what Denise told her.'

I play with the bob Amelie has given me. *Mon Dieu*, I'm starting to develop her habits. Andy puts on one of his most intense faces, watching me.

'I like what Amelie has done. I mean, I liked your hair before, but this is . . .' He purses his lips. '. . . different.'

'Good different?'

'Definitely.' He slips his hand behind my neck and strokes it. 'I'm sorry you've been lied to so much. Would you like me to come with you to see your mother?'

'No. This is something I have to do alone. I'll beat it out of her if I have to.'

'Like me, you mean?'

He grins sheepishly and I explode into hysterical laughter. There are times you say things without realising. For a few moments we look at one another, me trying to control myself with a hand over my mouth, him contorting his features to prevent an explosion of his own.

Slowly, I lower my hand. 'That wasn't very funny, Andy, was it?'

'No,' he agrees. '*Ce sont les parents, n'est-ce pas? Qu'on les aime, qu'on les déteste.*'

I want to know about his father. What happened that day in the office - before I found him?

'Uncle Georges hasn't said much. Father was in Paris as you know. I think the firm has lost a contract, maybe two. Father insisted he could fix the problem, whatever it was. That's about it. He couldn't and got drunk instead. I'll try to . . .'

My phone sparks into life. Andy signs I should look. There are four messages: the one from Andy saying he's found my charger, one from my mother, one from Hélène and one from Cathy. I check Cathy's first: *Want to know if you're OK. Please call me.* Hélène's is briefer: *Will try again later.* My mother hasn't said anything. After my welcome voice message, and the beep, comes a three second silence then a click as she replaces the receiver.

The phone hasn't fully charged so I leave it connected to the power. Andy's eyebrows go up quizzically.

'Important?'

'Nothing I can't deal with later.'

'So, what do we do about tonight?' he asks. 'Hotel or under the stars?'

'Hotel, I think, romantic though the stars sound. You've convinced me.'

'I'll try the *Continental*. I have a few last-minute errands before Oxford. Then I'll finish packing. With any luck, I might get more out of Georges about the Martha saga. Or maybe from Aunt Beatrice. Suppose I call you at four-thirty to arrange where to meet.'

He leaves me a few minutes later. Amelie has finished with her client and wants to use the tumble dryer so I go into the other room and ring Cathy. She doesn't answer.

'All good?' Amelie asks when I go back to the kitchen.

'Better!' I waggle my ring finger at her. 'I think I just got engaged.'

**

40.

Cathy

Yves is out of it for thirty-six hours. The doctor comes back the next morning and gives him an injection for the pain. I don't know how well alcohol mixes with painkillers but I guess the medical profession knows its business. Yves can't eat and he can't talk, so I leave him to sleep off what's left of his monumental hangover and the MG's prescription.

I spend most of the day with my lawyer and the manager at my bank. If Yves doesn't agree to my proposition I need to know where I stand. Both reassure me I have nothing to worry about. However, a few hours later, I realise I don't want to end my marriage. I still love my husband, in spite of everything, and would like to save our relationship if I can. I want him back. I haven't forgiven him but if he is prepared to work at it, so am I.

Things could be much worse, couldn't they? Yves has a broken nose, a broken jaw, two missing teeth and a bruise the size of a cricket ball on his face. He'll need extensive surgery, probably over several weeks. He's never going to forgive Andy for that.

On Saturday morning I drive Yves to hospital. They're going to operate on his jaw. He still can't talk, so I talk while he listens. While he's settling into the ward, I write down on a piece of paper the questions I want him to answer. And that includes his version of what happened in the office two days ago, the truth about Martha and his fight with Georges. I give him the pen and when he's finished put the paper in my purse. He swears he never had an affair and I want to believe him.

The situation with the business was simmering well before Andy and Nicole took off on their holiday. Beatrice saw Martha in downtown Bordeaux, dressed to kill when she was supposed to be in the office. And apparently Nicole saw her a few weeks ago with Marcus Sonnier. That was part of the argument I missed. *Christ*, Yves and Georges have fought more in the past weeks than in the previous ten years. There is far too much work for two men to handle. What they need is a full-time business administrator, not a leggy woman who happens to have a degree in computing.

As I leave the hospital and walk to the car, I call Nicole. I still don't have *her* story. Her phone is switched off so I leave a message to call me. I also try the land line number on her friend's card but no one picks up. I hope she'll phone me back; I want to know she's all right.

Andy has called me twice. He hasn't been able to contact Nicole by phone either. He regrets acting so hastily but asks me what a man is supposed to think . . . to do, when he sees his father's hands on his girlfriend's breasts. He hasn't said much else, though I have my suspicions. I think he wants Nicole to join him in Oxford until her term at Edinburgh begins. He'll have the rest all worked out too . . . borrowing against my mother's legacy to fund his final year. And if he's thinking of marrying he'll do it a lot faster if he thinks Yves doesn't approve. I hope they aren't about to make a mistake they'll regret later. Nicole's a sensible girl. Perhaps she'll see the risks better.

Things are different to what they were in my day. *Ironic, isn't it?* The kids know more than the parents. I can still remember my grandma talking about her life in nineteen thirties Scotland. Then, the man was often much older, as *her* father had been, taking a young wife to cook and clean and launder . . . to fuck and make babies until the woman was worn out, drained and old with the drudgery of it all. Sex and love should be better than that. Marriage is as much about liking and companionship and mutual respect. People fall out of love; financial troubles can so easily destroy the best of relationships. I don't want that for my son. I don't want it for Nicole either.

When I get home, the house seems cold and empty, despite the warm August weather. Georges has locked the office and is doing his best to manage the plant and look after the occasional visitor to the winery. I make myself some coffee and heat a ready meal in the microwave. I take it into the living room, put my feet up and watch TV while I eat.

I have a sudden brainwave. *Edinburgh. Why didn't I think of it before?* Am I being silly or is it truly a way to turn crisis into victory, to steer the current situation to the advantage of all?

The house phone rings. I pick up thinking maybe it's Nicole.

'*Ici Denise Massy . . .*' The woman's voice is unknown to me. '*Madame Ravel?*'

'*Oui, c'est moi.*'

It's probably a marketing call. I know no one called Massy and am about to replace the receiver when I remember Nicole's mother's name is Denise. I freeze. My life is about to get a whole lot worse. Something has happened to Nicole and I'm going to be blamed.

'I'd like to speak to my daughter please,' the caller says. 'Her phone doesn't appear to be working. Is she there?'

'Not at the moment, I'm afraid.' She doesn't sound upset or angry but I answer cautiously.

'*Dommage!*' There's a moment's silence then Denise goes on. She seems excited. 'I wanted to give her some good news. Would you . . .?'

'Good news?' I echo, all the while trying to picture the woman at the other end of the line. I've seen the Durands' wedding photograph so I know she and Nicole are alike. I relax. This isn't about my family at all. 'The truth is, Mme Massy, there's been a domestic crisis here,' I say. 'Nicole has gone to stay with a friend for a few days. Amelie. I haven't been able to contact her either.'

'I see.' The disappointment in her voice is so evident that I want to know more. I have a sudden impulse to talk to this woman about whom, despite Nicole's reserve, I already know so much. And I'm only killing time anyway. It would be better to get out of the house.

'I'd really like to meet you, *madame*,' I say hopefully. 'Why don't we arrange something in the city . . .'

Denise doesn't allow me to finish. 'You would? Then why don't you come here? I've wanted to meet *you* for such a long time.'

Half-an-hour later, I park the car in a quiet suburban street in Caudéran.

The former Denise Durand, now Massy, has done well by her marriage. It's a nice neighbourhood, away from the bustle of downtown Bordeaux. The house is semi-detached, on two floors and the Massys occupy the left-hand property. The building has an attached garage to the side. I walk over to the main door, check for the name and press the bell.

'*Qui?*'

'*Ici Cathy Ravel.*'

'*Entrez.*' The door clicks and opens. I'm in a small hallway, stairs to the right, doors to the left. At the opposite end of the hall, a petite woman, an older version of Nicole herself, blue-eyed with just a tinge of grey in her blond hair, holds open a door for me. I guess she's about forty. Though her face is prematurely lined, the sight of her gives me quite a turn. It's as if I've passed through a time portal and am looking at the future as it might indeed be. Nicole in twenty years from now will still be stunning.

She steps to one side to let me enter. 'I'm Denise.'

'Cathy.' I look around. It's a spacious kitchen, clean and tidy, with a round oak table, chairs and a cooking range. There's a big sideboard-dresser, a larder and a recess which houses a fridge-freezer and dish-washer. The only other furniture is a period grandmother clock. Denise ushers me through into another apartment furnished with comfortable - and new - chairs. Two teenagers sit on the floor surrounded by books and writing materials. The boy, who in my eyes looks more like eighteen or nineteen rather than sixteen, has clearly inherited his father's genes. He is well-built, tending to overweight and has brown hair. The girl is another Denise copy, though her hair is darker.

'*Dégagez!*' Denise waves impatiently at the children who scoop up their books and flee to another part of the house. She turns to me and I feel her silent appraisal. 'You're not at all what I imagined,' she says.

'Whatever did you imagine?'

'Oh, I don't know. More sophisticated maybe, more stylish, perfect clothes . . . ' She colours. '*Mon Dieu*, what am I saying? I'm sorry; I'm no good at this. I mean, you are . . . not that you don't have these things.'

'Offence not taken - I think.' I smile. 'Whereas I've seen your photograph . . .'

'Which one?'

'The wedding. With Nicole's father.'

'Oh,' she says and ushers me into a chair already smothered in cushions, velvet and print covers. 'So, what's the crisis? Have they broken up . . . your boy and my Nicole? She's dumped him . . . he's dumped her?'

'Quite the reverse actually. They're thinking about moving in together. At Oxford. Until Nicole goes to Edinburgh. I'm worried it's too much too soon.'

'If you think I'll interfere, you're wasting your time. Nicole does her own thing. I've never had much influence with her. Maybe I haven't been the best of mothers. We're not as close as mother and daughter should be, not since . . . ' She hesitates. 'No, I'm lying; I can't help it. I've been a *terrible* mother.'

'I find that hard to believe.' I feel I have to say it although, on the basis of my gathered knowledge, I believe what she says is true. Yet I'm beginning to think my preformed opinion might be just a small part of Denise's character. I hadn't expected such frankness. And I *had* been prepared to dislike her.

'Believe it! I've been a depressive, a drug addict, a kept woman. If I could turn back the clock I would. It wasn't the kind of home any teenage girl should have to grow up in. Bern and Sophie were too young to understand most of what went on. The pressure was all on Nicole. She's probably told you.'

'She told me you'd been ill, but I don't know all the detail.'

'It's best you don't. But I've been lucky to get a second chance, with a decent husband and a nice home. And now . . . I suppose I can tell you . . . ' She claps her hands to her face, emitting a little screech. 'What am I thinking? I should offer you something. Coffee? Wine?'

I shake my head. 'I've had my fill of coffee today. And best not alcohol when I have to drive back.'

'I can't drink alcohol, *tu comprends*.' Denise smiles a sad smile. I notice she uses the familiar address for the first time. After more than twenty years of coming to terms with French formality, that's unexpected. 'Alcohol wasn't my problem, but apparently I have an addictive personality, so it's best I don't touch it. Drugs nearly destroyed my life.'

'I'm sorry.'

'Don't be,' she rejoins. Her face brightens. 'I know what! How would you like a cup of English tea and some cake?'

I swallow my surprise at the offer. 'I'd love some tea,' I say.

Denise pulls a small table out from a corner and lays it with an embroidered cloth. 'A present from my first husband,' she says as she smooths it down and carefully arranges the folds of the overhang. 'He bought it for me when we were on holiday in England.'

While she's busy in the kitchen I take the opportunity for a closer look round the room. The chairs and carpet are quite new while some of the other furniture shows signs of wear and tear. I'm guessing Denise wanted to keep a few of her own favourite pieces. Against one wall is a display case, rather old-fashioned, the wood walnut and the glass framed with pieces of intricate carving. It has a mirror at the back, creating the illusion of space, and one shelf is filled with framed photographs. Nicole and her siblings feature in several, and there is one of Nicole alone holding her *Diplôme Général*. I see none of Nicole's father but I hadn't expected to. The centrally-placed picture was obviously taken at Denise's recent wedding. She stands beside her new husband and the couple are flanked by the two younger children, Bernard and Sophie. On the wall is a framed print of a Dégas masterpiece. I recognise the style though not the title.

'I keep the older photos in my special drawer,' Denise says. She comes in carrying a tray with two china cups and saucers, a china teapot, milk and sugar and a huge plate of sweetmeats. 'It doesn't seem right to . . . you know.'

'Another present?' I ask, indicating the china. I'm impressed. The French are not great tea drinkers.

'*Oui*. Pièrre bought it for me in London. We only had Nicole then. Does she ever speak about her father?'

'Some. She told me he encouraged her reading and learning English. She's mentioned he used to pick her up from school . . . and about a holiday in Great Britain. She remembers being in Cambridge, and Edinburgh.'

'She won't remember the London trip in '97. She was two.' She pours the tea. It's the best I've tasted in twenty years of French experimentation, made with real tea leaves. At home, I occasionally pop a tea bag in a mug but it isn't the same.

'This is good,' I say, and she beams Nicole's smile at me. 'Where did you learn?'

'We went to Hong Kong once. For a few days. Pièrre had business. Nicole was a baby and stayed with Madeleine and Albert, Pièrre's parents. The waiter in a tea-garden taught me how to make it properly. I know you're English and I wanted to impress you.'

'Why?'

'I think it's because I wanted you to see I've turned a corner. I'm no longer the woman I was back then. Oh, I know she's told you, Cathy. About the pills, the drugs, the debt and everything. And now I'm going to have another baby, Jean's baby.'

'You're expecting a baby!'

'That's my good news. The reason I phoned. *Mon Dieu*, Cathy, I'm not far off forty years old.' She giggles like a schoolgirl. 'I'm going to have another baby, and I'm scared of what my twenty-year-old daughter is going to say!'

'Nicole will be delighted.'

'*Peut être.*'

'Of course she will.'

'I shouldn't have said. Please don't tell her. I want to do it myself.'

'I won't if you don't want me to. But you'll have to tell her soon.'

'I will. Nicole didn't want me to marry Jean. But he's not like any of the other men I went out with, or brought home. He'd love to help her with her university expenses, but she won't hear of it.'

'Nicole is proud, Denise. Independent.'

'Stubborn more like. I know she looks a bit like me when I was younger but she's her father's daughter in other ways. I'm flighty. Unreliable. A liar. A soft touch when it comes to men. She's serious, strong. Sometimes I feel she can't be my daughter at all. When Pièrre died . . .'

I notice there are tears in her eyes and reach for the china teapot to refill her cup. She pulls a couple of soft tissues from a box on her chair, dabs her eyes and blows her nose. She drinks some of her tea. 'Thank you. I don't know what came over me. I've never been able to talk about this to anyone else. About Pièrre.'

'*Your* parents died, Nicole told me. In a car accident.'

Her mood changes, becomes colder, more rigid. 'Should I be sorry?' she mutters, more to herself than to me. 'People die.'

'Sadly, they do,' I say. She sounds harsh but I don't want to judge her without knowing the facts.

'You shouldn't hate people,' Denise goes on. 'But I hated them, most of all my father. He was very controlling. They both refused to have any more to do with me when I got pregnant. They were strict Catholics. Very religious. They believed in Heaven and Hell, and Purgatory. I had sinned against God and the Church, they said. I was no daughter of theirs. They kicked me out of the house.'

'I'm sorry.'

She softens suddenly, fetches another tissue from the box and dabs her eyes again. 'Pièrre was seven years older than me . . . no, that's another lie. I can't help myself. He had a whole other life before he met me. He was agnostic. He hated the Church, the priests and all their works. But we were happy. Nicole was the light of his life. His short life!'

I lay down my cup and saucer and lean over to touch her

259

hand. 'He died of a heart attack, didn't he?'

'Forty years old!' she says bitterly. 'And that's the truth. He had a valve defect . . . something like that. It wasn't hereditary. He'd had rheumatic fever as a child. No one should have to die at forty. I didn't get to say goodbye to the man I loved. I wasn't able to cradle him in my arms.'

This is such a private memory I'm uncomfortable sharing it. I feel I should interrupt, prevent her from going on, but Denise has no such qualms. The anger has gone and her sad smile returns. For a few moments she absent-mindedly picks at her fingernails with the opposite thumb. Realising what she's doing, and that I'm watching, she stops and throws both arms to her side. I'm guessing she once bit her nails mercilessly.

'He had a good job, you know . . . had been all over the world. England, America, the Middle East. Shall I pour you some more tea . . . or would you like to do it? My hands are shaking a bit.'

'May I?' I pick up the teapot. I'm no expert in china but I already recognised the Spode logo on the bottom of the cups when she set down the tray. It's a delicate grey pattern, unlike the strong blues often associated with the make.

'There were six cups and saucers,' Denise says. 'One cup and one saucer got broken.'

'*Dommage*. This is such a beautiful set.'

I've been here less than an hour and already there are so many inconsistencies. I'm beginning to realise what a private person Nicole is and how little I know about her - how little I know of her home life. What sort of man was Pièrre Durand, a man who bought his young wife expensive porcelain? All my instincts are telling me that, until his death, theirs was a happy, loving home. Yet death happened and depression turned this petite, sensitive woman into a raging hellcat who spurned and abused her daughter and, unless I am deceived, drove her to deny all motherly feeling for her. Or did it begin earlier with her own uncomfortable childhood? With parents so rigid in their beliefs that they put their pregnant teenage daughter out on the street to fend for herself. I think of my own happy teenage years and of the freedom I was given to think and act for myself. I think of Emmeline, and my own loss, and wonder, if circumstances had been different, and I had lost Yves instead, whether . . .

I pour tea for both of us, set down the pot and pick up my cup. Denise reaches for hers and then seems to change her mind. Instead, she goes over to the display cabinet and, opening one of two drawers in the base, takes out a photo album. She slides the tea tray to one side and lays the album on the table in front of me.

'Would you like to look? We didn't have a digital camera in those days.'

'I'd love to.' I open the album at the title page. It's inscribed *Pièrre et Denise* in copperplate and, below the names, someone has drawn a heart and coloured it in red.

'Nicole writes like that sometimes,' I remark and begin turning the pages.

'I taught her when she was little,' Denise says. 'I took a course.'

All the photographs are captioned and dated. The first few are of Denise, or of Pièrre, or of the two of them together: *Paris 1994*; *Bordeaux 1995*; *Hong Kong 1995*. One of the Bordeaux pictures is the wedding photo I have already seen, the one Nicole keeps in her room. *Denise*. If I didn't know better I would swear every shot is of Nicole - Nicole as I know her now and have done for the past fourteen months. The resemblance is uncanny.

On the page opposite the wedding picture is an empty frame and I guess that once, perhaps, it held the other . . . the one Nicole told me about, the one her grandmother keeps in a box in her bedroom. I thumb through the book carefully, forming a picture in my mind of a happy, contented couple, very much in love. Of a woman who was reviled but then loved.

The later photos are of the children, and of the family together: Nicole with her father; Nicole with her mother; Nicole at two, at four; in her school uniform; with Bernard; with Sophie; all three siblings together. The last picture of all is of a group: Denise, Pièrre and the three children, together with an older couple whom I take to be Nicole's paternal grandparents.

Denise is watching me over the rim of her teacup. 'You must

be wondering . . . *where did it all go wrong?'*

'No.' I close the album and hand it to her. 'I was thinking if . . . no, it's none of my business.'

'Truly, I'd like to know.'

I don't want to hurt her after she has been so hospitable, so I choose my words with care.

'It's like the Spode porcelain,' I tell her. 'Sometimes things break. They have to be put together again. But it isn't always easy to find the proper adhesive.'

'You're right!' For a moment, her eyes light up and I recognise the small part of her, until now well hidden, she has passed on to her daughter. Then the sad expression that I've already seen several times returns. 'I don't know how to ask for her forgiveness. There were so many lies. So much guilt.'

'You'll find a way.'

'But it means I have to tell her everything: about my mother and father, and what they did to me; how I lied about my age; how we didn't get married until . . . *tu comprends, after* she came.'

'Nicole knows about that. She doesn't care!' I say impulsively. 'I think her worst fear - her nightmare is that her father wasn't . . .'

Denise's eyes now show nothing but horror. *'Douce Vièrge,'* she exclaims. 'Not that, never that! You must tell her, Cathy. You *have* to tell her! Pièrre was her father. There was never anyone else. You have to believe me.'

'I believe you, Denise, but telling Nicole isn't my job.'

'I guess not. There I go again, ducking my responsibilities. I never considered the possibility she'd think . . . it's too . . . *unthinkable.* She'll *never* forgive me now. I can't even forgive myself.'

'I'm sure she will. You said things you didn't mean - words hastily spoken in a moment of madness. Tell her, Denise.'

'You don't understand. I can't even tell Jean!' She plays again with her fingernails. 'It wasn't all a lie. And because of that I'll never find absolution.'

The teapot is cold. Most of the sweetmeats are untouched because we've been talking. I know I should go. However, I can't help my curiosity, my desire to learn more, to understand this self-hate, to discover what kind of parents throw their child on the street when she's in trouble. Perhaps in Denise's situation I too would have pretended life was all one big lie. Not only that, for Nicole's sake I feel a responsibility to ascertain the truth and put things right if I can.

'Then make me understand, Denise,' I say. 'What else have you done that's so terrible?'

'I didn't want a baby. I hadn't even had sex before I met Pièrre. He was working in Paris and lodging with a neighbour in the next block. I had grown up there. I was seventeen and had left school to go to technical college. Pièrre was twenty-seven – just a cradle snatcher.'

'My husband is a few years older than me. I was eighteen when I met him.'

Denise gives a wry smile. 'But you know how we can look much older when we're made up. I pretended to be twenty-one. We were in a relationship for six months before he found out. Then I got pregnant. I was in the middle of exams. I was terrified to tell Pièrre in case he rejected me and even more terrified to tell my parents. In spite of their Christianity, they were the kind of people who thought boys could do what they liked; girls had to be pure and chaste.

'I had to go to church. Sundays and saints' days. Confession on Fridays. Dress demurely - no mini-dresses or tight tops. The pressures were always psychological. It sounds mediaeval but that's the way they were. They'd had a good old-fashioned Catholic upbringing and wanted the same for me. It was refreshing to meet someone who didn't care about religion. But I felt guilty all the time, waiting for God to punish me for my wickedness. I had to sneak around and lie to see Pièrre. I'd pretend to be staying with a friend. That was allowed.

'Pierre said he loved me and quite liked the idea of being a dad. We should get married. The funny thing is, it was me who was against it. I was a month or two short of eighteen, so I couldn't without my parents' consent. Anyway, I didn't want to tie Pièrre down. I thought he'd get tired of me - and the baby. He had seen the world; I hadn't been anywhere.

'Anyway, my parents told me to pack my bags. We moved to

Bordeaux. It was his home city. And *his* parents would help when the baby came.

'I hadn't wanted her, but as soon as I saw Nicole I loved her. Twelve wonderful, amazing years, Cathy!' She sinks back in her chair with a pathetic sigh.' It should've been me there with him that day. Me, not our daughter! But it was Nicole who was with him at the end, and she doesn't even remember.'

Denise feels the outside of the teapot with her hand. She lifts the lid and inspects the contents. 'Leaves,' she announces. 'Shall I make some more?'

She's as changeable as the British weather, wallowing in self-pity one moment, friendly, good-natured hostess the next. I want to understand her. I need her to explain her last enigmatic remark about Nicole.

'Not for me, thanks,' I say. 'Please tell me more about Pièrre, if it's not too painful.'

'No, it's OK, Cathy.' Her mood changes again, dry-eyed and reminiscent. She goes back to picking her fingernails with a thumb then, as before, stops abruptly. 'Life can throw some big rocks at you. You have to get up and carry on. I loved Pièrre, but he's gone. Now it's just me and Jean, and the children. I get these weepy moments now and then, you know.'

'You said something about Nicole not remembering . . .'

'It was my fault I wasn't there. Nicole . . .' She gives a start as the clock in the next room chimes a half hour. '. . . Nicole was at school, Pièrre at work. Bern and Sophie wanted to visit their grandparents. So I took them. With the traffic, it's about twenty minutes in each direction, sometimes more. On the way back, I did some shopping. I was gone maybe an hour and a half.

'When I got home, I found them. A doctor, two paramedics. The ambulance could only have been minutes ahead of me. Nicole was just sitting there . . . squatting on the floor. She was cradling Pièrre's head and shoulders in her arms. There was blood everywhere, on her hands, on her dress, on the carpet. Even on the telephone receiver. The doctor was holding that, but Nicole must have phoned SAMU. One of the paramedics was trying to coax her out of the way so they could treat him, but she was yelling at them not to hurt him.'

I feel uncomfortable and fidget in my chair. Half of me wants to hear what she has to say, the other half knows these are not things she should be confessing to a stranger. Has Nicole relived her father's death, and is that what Andy meant when he said she was upset but not in the way he expected? Did the incident in the office trigger something in her subconscious? I can't begin to imagine how a child would feel after such an experience. To relive such a horror after blotting out the memory for eight years is more than I would ever wish to contemplate.

Denise is determined to continue her story. 'At first I thought it was the massive head injury. Later, they told me he had an MI. Nicole never uttered a word, not until we got to the hospital. Then she had hysterics when they wouldn't let her into *Resus*. She wouldn't stop screaming. They had to sedate her. I don't know what they gave her but she was out for hours. I had to break the news to Pièrre's parents of course. They took Nicole, Bernard and Sophie so I could clean up the house. When Nicole woke up, she seemed not to remember anything. She couldn't, or wouldn't, tell me what had happened. She was always asking *me*; I told her he'd died peacefully in the hospital. Eventually she stopped asking.

'It became a taboo subject. I never got the whole story, only what the doctors and the paramedics told me. Some kind of amnesia the *psych* doctor said. He said not to worry; it wasn't uncommon after a traumatic experience. Her full memory would come back in its own time. As far as I know, it never did.'

**

41.

Nicole

I have this mad impulse to go shopping. I should be saving money but if Andy and I are to spend the night in a good hotel, I need something to *wear*. Amelie decides to come with me. Before we go, I try Cathy's number again, both her mobile and the house phone. She doesn't pick up either and I get her messaging service. I feel guilty about not letting her know I'm OK but it can't be helped.

'What are we shopping for?' Amelie asks with a grin as big as the Louvre. 'Do I have to buy my wedding outfit now?'

'It isn't that sort of engagement.' I tell her what we're proposing and she pretends to look shocked.

'Underwear then,' she says decisively. 'You want to look your best both in and out of bed.'

'Maybe a new dress.'

Bordeaux isn't the fashion capital of the world but we manage to find a boutique in *St Catherine's* that sells a wide range of fashion underwear. Red doesn't suit me and black seems too sombre for the occasion. Eventually, I choose a pale blue set, a lace bra with front closure and a matching thong. I preferred bare legs in summer but I also buy a pair of thigh length stockings which complement the lingerie. My skin tingles as I imagine Andy's hands rolling the tops along my thighs and easing them over my knees. The bra and thong are *Armani*, the stockings *Trasparenze*, and the total bill comes to seventy-five *euros*, which is money I can't afford.

'*Bon Sang!*' Amelie exclaims when she sees my purchases. 'Do you want him to have a heart attack?'

I ignore her. Amelie is as prone to exaggeration as she is to mild expletives. We go looking for a dress. It's one night, but if it's to be our last night together I want to say goodbye properly. It takes a while but after three stores I find a dark blue number that is a perfect contrast with the shade of the stockings. I try it on with the bra, and it's just right. Close fitting, short and zipped down the back, it shows my figure to advantage without looking too tight - or cheap.

Back at the flat, I try things on again. I feel good - ready - but at the same time apprehensive.

'Is it too much, Amm?'

She shakes her head. 'I was joking before. It's perfect.'

Andy rings to tell me everything is arranged for the *Continental*. I'm surprised how easy it was. At the weekend, you expect the hotels to be busy. He'll book a taxi and pick me up at six-thirty. Maybe we'll have some food brought up to the room.

I go into the bathroom to get ready. Already, I'm shaking like a schoolgirl before her first date. I bathe with a shower-cap; my hair tends to revert to its original set, but this way I'm sure Amelie will be able to fix it in no time with one of her special combs. Back in the bedroom, I put on the underwear, enjoying the slinky feel of the satin as I fasten the bra and pull on the thong. I apply some make-up - *not too much! Bon Dieu, don't let me cry* - and reach for my dress.

I check my appearance in the long mirror beside the bed, toy with my hair, debating whether I ought to try my own fix. I decide to do nothing and slip into the dress.

Shoes!

I packed two pairs, flat casuals for everyday wear and dressier black courts with medium heels - and just as well I brought them. They go with everything. Finally, I do a last-minute inspection to check nothing shows, and I'm ready.

Amelie knocks on the door.

'Come in, Amm, and tell me how I look.'

She bounces down on the bed and eyes me from top to toe.

'I hope Andy has told you how beautiful you are,' she croons. 'One tiny suggestion . . .'

'Well?' I wait on tenterhooks, wondering what I might have

missed.

'Something to draw attention to the throat - and the cleavage.' She bounces back up, makes a dive for a top drawer in the dressing table and rummages for a moment. 'I know! You can borrow this if you like.'

She pulls out a string of pale blue glass beads.

'I've never seen you wear those, Amm.'

'I don't. Wrong colour, but on you . . . And if we fasten like this . . .'

She loops the beads round my throat and fixes the clip to make a drop necklace. I rather like the effect.

'Now you *are* perfect,' she says.

**

42.

Our hotel has no restaurant, so we dump our overnight bags and go for a light meal at the nearby bistro. The evenings are cooler now, but still warm enough to eat at a table outside. Andy is wearing grey slacks and a casual shirt that hugs his shoulders, tummy and hips, and he smells of aftershave.

'Have I said how amazing you look?' He strokes my fingers across the table. 'Better than amazing - beautiful!'

'You look nice too. How's your father? Have you heard?'

'Better than he deserves.' He avoids my gaze. 'There's no excuse for what he did - drinking himself senseless and pawing you when you tried to help.'

'You know he didn't mean to paw me.'

'Deliberate or not doesn't matter. Anyway, the latest news is, Martha is engaged to Marcus Sonnier.'

'That's a joke, right?'

'No joke! They've been engaged to be married since the beginning of May.'

'Well, I did see them together.'

'So my uncle told me. It seems Beatrice saw them too. Father, stubborn as usual, said it was all a misunderstanding. Everything's sorted out now. Georges went over to Sonniers' yesterday and demanded answers. Martha was there. Contracted to both enterprises at the same time maybe isn't criminal, but it's unethical.'

'You mean this was about industrial espionage?'

'You know how sensitive the *châteaux* are about guarding their secrets.'

'I thought they were all the best of friends.'

'It's a mask. Behind it they are bitter rivals. And I mean cut-throat bitter! But there was no deliberate intent, *they say*, and Martha didn't have access to our trade secrets anyhow. She apologised and agreed to accept a four thousand *euro* cut in her fees. Old man Sonnier will pay her that. He apologised too; he hadn't known she still had two weeks of her contract to go. Nor did she apparently!'

'I don't understand what Martha had to do with your father getting drunk. What could possibly make a man drink himself into that state?' I reach across the table and clutch his arm. The image of Yves, unconscious and bloody, flashes into my mind. With it comes again the other memory, more horrible yet more precious, of my father and his last moments.

'Nicole?'

'Sorry, I was thinking about something else. Go on.'

'It wasn't all about Martha. She was the catalyst. A couple of contract renewals were due and were overlooked. Father is usually more careful. He went to Paris to try and rescue them - saved one, lost the other worth a quarter of a million a year.

'But Georges reckons that was just another flint to spark the tinder. Contracts have been lost before and the business will survive. The drinking spree had more to do with the other thing they argued about - well, us . . . and Emmeline!'

'They argued about *Emmeline?*'

'Georges said he was sick of the silence. My asking about the uncles and cousins made him realise how bad it had become. He told Father he should think more of his wife's feelings. They had lost a baby and he wouldn't even talk about it. They went on to talk about me - and you. I'll spare you the nice things my uncle said but, in summary, he also told my father to butt out of my private life.'

'*Mon Dieu*, that is huge!'

'Monumental! Georges thinks he got through. He made Father feel guilty . . . guilty about relying on Martha, about the fight, about his own stubbornness - well, you can imagine. Father realised what an idiot he'd been and went on the binge. A drink or two turned into three or four, or ten. The result you saw. *Un trou du cul* was the expression Uncle Georges used. *There's no fool like an old fool*, as the English say.'

'Don't be too hard on him,' I beg. 'You need a father. My father's death left a huge void in my life. I can forgive. You should too.'

'I don't know if I can. And he'll never forgive me. *Dieu*, I broke his fucking jaw and knocked out a tooth or two.'

I put my fingers against his cheek. 'He'll forgive you. That's what fathers are supposed to do.'

'You are such a good and wise person, Nicole.'

'No, I'm not. Let's not talk about this anymore.'

Although the meal isn't expensive, I have already calculated our special night together will cost a hundred and twenty *euros*. Andy shakes his head when I insist on paying half.

'The hotel is all settled,' he says. 'A bottle of wine included.'

'What do you mean, *all settled*? We haven't even explored our room.'

'It just is! Forget about it.'

I force a great sigh and give in, but then he relents and lets me pay for the meal.

We return to the hotel at eight-thirty. Our room has a big double bed with bedside tables and lamps on both sides. A widescreen television hangs on the opposite wall and there is a *wi-fi* connection if we need it. The décor is fresh, the colours subdued. We have a WC and shower-room - and a mini-bar. A bottle of red wine and two glasses sit on one of the tables.

We brush our teeth. Andy re-opens our door and hangs a *do not disturb* sign on the outside handle.

'There!' He turns to face me.

My shoes give me height but I still have to stretch to reach him. Stretching is well worth the effort. His fingers graze my cheek as his mouth melds with mine. I kiss him tenderly, allowing myself to lean into him, feeling his heartbeat through our clothing and enjoying the closeness and hardness of his body. After a few moments bliss, we lean back to look silently at one another.

'I love the way Amelie did your hair,' Andy says at length. 'I know I said it before but wanted to say it again. And that dress! I've never seen you in it before.'

'I bought it today.' I kick off my shoes. The carpet is fairly new and the pile soft under my feet.

'I think I like it better than the one you wore at the restaurant in La Brède. I'm having naughty thoughts.'

'Me too. Later, you can take it off and tell me about your naughty thoughts.' I pat the bed, climb on top of the bedspread and pull up my knees. 'I think I'd like to sit here for a bit, Andy. We can talk about Oxford, or about the cat in the box, if you want. Or we can quietly enjoy one another's company. Watch a sexy movie. Maybe some extensive foreplay.'

'OK.' He joins me on top of the bedspread and we link hands. The television control is within his reach on the bedside table to his left and he gives it to me. 'You choose!'

I switch on and scan down the hotel's list of films. There are some classic French comedies and a couple of American thrillers. None of those appeal. They also have *Titanic*, which I have seen three times. It isn't all that sexy, except for the scene in the vintage car. Another is *L'Histoire d'Adele H*, an old Truffaut movie set during the American Civil War, based on the true-life story of a daughter of Victor Hugo. I've seen that too and remember it has a sad ending.

'What about the Truffaut?' I suggest. 'I'll probably cry all over your shirt but if you don't mind . . .'

'I don't mind. Shall I open the wine?'

'Please, but don't let me drink more than two glasses. I want to stay sober tonight.'

We pour the wine and settle down on the bed, with our backs against the headboard, to watch the ninety-minute-long film. Before a half hour has passed, I can tell his heart isn't in it. Nor is mine. From the beginning, the closeness of him, the scent of his aftershave and the warmth of his hand in mine is a distraction. And when he begins to nibble my ear and stroke my hair, I know I'll have to give in.

I switch off the television and, bending over him, press my lips to his.

'Make love to me, Andy!'

He responds by teasing my bottom lip, catching it between his teeth and nipping lightly. I open to him, offering him my tongue. He allows one hand to drift down my spine. I gasp as he spreads it over my bottom and draws me towards him.

He presses his sweet mouth against mine in another slow, amazing kiss. I close my eyes, let my head fall back, feel my heartbeat accelerate with every second that passes. *Dieu!* I don't want this to end.

Warm desire courses through my blood, my breasts and my belly. 'Unzip me, *mon coeur,*' I breathe when an eternity has passed. There are so many things I want him to do to me tonight.

He releases me, sets me gently on my feet and springs up to tower over me at the side of the bed. A brief moment of confusion follows as he reaches for the fastener and our arms become hopelessly entangled. Why am I so nervous? We've made love before, among the vines and in my bedroom.

'It's stuck . . .'

'Wait.' I extricate my arms from his and turn away from him. He tugs at the fastener and eases the zip along the curve of my back. 'What are you doing, Andy?'

'Enjoying the moment.' I hear his soft chuckle. He rests his chin on the top of my head and I feel the pressure of his arousal as his hands caress my buttocks and the backs of my thighs.

I spin round to face him, scarcely aware the dress has already slipped from my shoulder and is resting on my hips. He enfolds me again in his arms. I fumble the buttons of his shirt, wrench at it clumsily and draw him towards me, feeling the pleasure of his naked chest against my skin. His breath is sweet with the aftertaste of wine. We are alone with the low hum of the air-conditioning and I'm trembling all over.

My back is now to the bed and I take a step nearer to it, my calf making contact with the mattress. I pull back the covers. Andy bends his head towards me, kisses my eyelid and then my ear, the touch of his lips no more than a whisper as they move over my neck and throat. A tiny surge of electricity passes through me as he unclips my bra. I dig my fingers into his thick hair and gasp as his mouth finds a nipple and begins teasing it with his teeth.

Everything is different tonight. No matter how much I denied it to myself, we have always been on Ravel territory. Now we're on neutral ground, in our own space. I realise we can give ourselves to one another without reserve of any kind. Andy is all mine; I am all his.

His hands brush my stomach, rest on my waist and begin wrestling with the folds of my dress.

'You have to let me . . .' I reach behind. The fastener isn't wholly unzipped so I tug it along the last few centimetres. The dress slides off my hips and falls to the floor.

Andy raises his head and looks at me, his cheeks flushed, his eyes bright. 'My beautiful Nicole . . .' His voice holds a soft huskiness. 'I've never wanted anything as much as I want you.'

'I want you too,' I hear myself say as I slide onto the bed.

He steps back to unfasten and remove his slacks. They fall and he kicks them away. Then his boxers. I have never truly appreciated him before. I have looked but not seen how beautiful he is: handsome, strong and infinitely desirable. The muscles of his chest, his stomach, his arms are taut and inviting. His erection swells under my gaze.

I kiss him slowly and deeply. He hesitates a moment, his thumb hooked in the band of my thong. Then, with his face still close to mine, he draws the flimsy garment down over my limbs. I chose it with care, for him to see. He has seen - and it no longer matters. I no longer want it between us.

Now the stockings.

The outside world - the real world of time and space - is collapsing around me. I can no longer hear; I can no longer think. I close my eyes, half-open them, and then close them again. It doesn't matter I don't see him. His touch is exquisite and I lose myself in the sensations. Electricity runs in my veins. I'm floating, falling into that other realm, the one where we become like gods. *Adonis and Aphrodite.* I lie back and allow my thighs to surrender to his need.

I find my tongue. 'I love you, Andy. I want you, *mon amour*. I need you, my dearest darling.'

'Nicole. Nicole . . .' He speaks my name several more times before his lips fasten again on mine, now stifling my moans of pleasure. His hand slides between my legs, his thumb moving back and forth over my delicate flesh and gently parting the folds of my femininity.

'*Jesus Christ! Andy . . . Andy . . .!*' I free my mouth. The core of my being responds to every nuance, to every subtle motion, to every wonderful caress of his fingers.

Heat, already so much heat. Wetness too. His skin glistens with moisture, on his neck and in the groove of his chest. *And not only there.* He bends again to kiss my lips and my breasts. Then, growling quietly, he shifts to the side. I moan and lift my hips against him, feeling the ache of greater need as his penis replaces his stroking fingers.

My body stiffens. My fingernails dig into his shoulders. *Please don't let it happen too soon!* At first, there is resistance, then the indescribable stretching as he thrusts inside me. For the first time, there is no pain at all, just the luscious warmth of acceptance and surrender. He moves, and shivers pass up my spine - tension and release in one glorious sensation. *Not yet*, screams the voice in my head. *Please not yet!* He moves again and I take in all of him until there is no more to take.

Douce Vièrge! The pressure inside me is intense. The spring is fully wound and I know there is nothing in the universe to prevent its unwinding. The first spasm hits, forcing an animal sound from my lips, then another. My heart is pounding. My body tingles. My fingers grip Andy more tightly than ever and he groans, eclipsing my moans of fulfilment. I push my hips against him one final time.

The climax of his release rocks me back on the pillow, flushed, helpless, yet overcome by new and wonderful feelings of freedom. Never in my life have I felt so alive. With a sigh of pleasure and his breath hot against my skin, Andy folds his arms around me and lays his head on my breast.

'*Dieu*, did we actually do that?' He eventually releases me. He leans on his elbow, his chin supported by his hand, and stares at me with his beautiful brown eyes, the pupils wide and bright. His chest is heaving from exertion and sweat glistens on his forehead and neck. My nostrils are filled with the scent of him, a musky mixture of cologne, warm skin and passion.

'*Vraiment.*' I lever myself upright, still panting from the unexpected strength of my orgasm. My body is covered in perspiration, my inner thighs damp. I straddle his hips. 'I think I'm in love with you, Andy Ravel.'

'Think?'

'Maybe I need convincing.' I pin him by his shoulders to the bed and bend to kiss him. He could easily wrestle me off but doesn't try.

'You don't mean . . .? He leans his head back on the pillow, feigning exhaustion. 'I could lie here forever if you were with me.'

'Who's the stronger now?' I tease. 'That was the thunder; now I want the lightning.'

'We had both long ago, I seem to remember. We got very wet!'

'I'll never forget.'

'Nor me.' He kneads the insides of my thighs with the heel of his palms. 'We had a moment, didn't we?'

'We did.' I caress his fingers. 'Well, are you going to convince me or not?'

Without warning, he throws me over onto my back so that our positions are reversed.

'That was so unfair, Andy,' I screech.

'You wanted thunder and lightning,' he grins. 'You can have it on one condition.'

'What condition?'

'That we have the rain too. I'm prepared to convince you but I want to do it in the shower.'

There's little enough room in the shower cubicle for one, far less two, and with the door shut we are squeezed like city commuters at rush hour. And with the cascading water slick on our naked bodies, the glass screen misted by condensed water vapour and our accelerated breathing, the atmosphere is tropical.

Andy slips his hands behind me, one encircling my waist, the other cupping my bottom. 'What we did back there was amazing. I didn't know it could happen like that. Together.'

His touch sends sparks through my limbs. I put a free arm round his neck and suck in another damp breath. 'I wasn't sure it would, but when you love someone I guess anything's possible.'

His grip on my buttocks tightens. He lifts me up against him and presses our foreheads together. The shower water trickles down my back, warm and sensuous. I feel his arousal and my insides do their usual flip. 'So you love me?' he murmurs.

'More than you can ever know. No pretence.'

'No more teasing. I love you, Nicole. I love you forever.'

My mouth meets his and I part my lips to his tongue. My feet are already dangling half a metre from the floor of the cubicle and as I give myself to his kiss, I wrap my legs round his hips. Andy shifts his grip, supporting my thighs and buttocks with his palms and wedging me against the smooth side wall of the cubicle.

I manage to free my other arm and slide my hands between us. He hardens quickly to my touch. I gently encircle him with thumb and forefinger. His lips find my throat, my neck, my ear, and he kisses each in turn. My core throbs with need.

'Take me, *mon coeur*. I need you . . . I need you inside me again.' I thrust myself against him, on him, feeling the resistance, the stretching as before, and the same painless relief of full penetration. I'm so wet inside with desire for him that he fills me smoothly and quickly. *Dieu, mon Dieu, Andy!* It's like nothing I've ever experienced before. He groans as, using my legs as support, I ride him, panting with every stroke. Though I feel the strain of the position, he's strong and holds me, his muscular arms tensed, his fingers biting into my flesh.

'Don't stop!'

I forget the shower, the misted glass, the cascading water - everything. There's only my erratic breathing, the racing of my heart and the pulsing of blood in my veins. Then I'm contracting, tightening over him, and he is pulsating inside me. I didn't think the pleasure could be so different, nor can I explain why it is so. However, when he at length lowers me onto my feet I'm trembling all over. I lean my back against the slippery wall and allow gravity to do the rest.

**

43.

Sleep is far from my mind. However, in the comfort of Andy's embrace, and despite the humming of the air-con, tiredness overtakes me and I fall asleep anyway. A drop in the temperature wakes me. Andy has rolled away, taking our light duvet with him. However, my left arm is trapped beneath his left shoulder-blade. I ease it out in an effort not to wake him. The circulation surges back but it's a while before I regain proper feeling.

A grey dawn filters through the gap we left in the curtains. Gazing down at Andy's sleeping form, I realise how hard it will be to say goodbye. I'm not ready. I won't be ready tomorrow and I won't be ready four weeks from now. We haven't talked about Oxford at all and in a way I'm glad because I haven't been forced to make a decision. I'm caught in a no-win situation. Letting him go now will be heart-breaking enough, yet if I spend another month in his company the wrench may be impossible to bear. Moreover, though my finances are much healthier than they were a year ago, another month's wages would - with economy - seal my comforts for at least half my course at Edinburgh.

I can't have access to the duvet so I reach for the bedspread, dangling loosely from the end of the bed, and wrap it round me. So many random thoughts course through my mind. I try to think in English. It seemed so easy before but I wonder how I will cope for weeks on end without my native language to fall back on. Even when I was estranged from Denise, I was never on my own. There were always familiar faces and voices around me - Bernard, Sophie, Amelie, Hélène. *Mamie* and *Papi* Durand were always there to support me when life seemed so grim. There will be those goodbyes too and for the first time in my life I will be totally on my own.

And my mother. In all my time at *Château Ravel* I have never known her ring me. Even if there was no message I should have called back. There are words to be spoken, however hard they are to say.

I must have dozed off because the next time I open my eyes it's full daylight. Andy is still asleep. I check the time. It's eight-thirty. I get out of bed, go to the bathroom and take another shower. Afterwards, I do my best to fix my hair, pack my new dress and underwear, and put on the spare clothes I brought in my overnight bag - a pair of jeans and a casual top. I'm about to wake Andy when my phone rings.

It's Cathy. I swallow hastily and answer.

'I'm sorry I couldn't take your calls yesterday,' she says. 'There was a good reason.'

'I should be the one to apologise, Cathy, for taking off. How is M. Yves?'

'He's not talking much.' There was a trace of amusement in her voice. 'I assume Andy has told you the situation. Or some of it. But what about you? Are *you* all right?'

'I'm OK now. I sort of relived something that happened to me once. I'll tell you about it later. Is it OK if I come home today?' It's strange how the idea of Ravels' as *home* comes to me so naturally now. 'Amelie's boyfriend is coming back to Bordeaux and I'll be in the way.'

'Why don't you come now?' she says rather brusquely and I wonder at the change of tone, still amused yet expectant and almost commanding. 'Don't worry about Yves. He'll be in hospital for another twenty-four hours.'

'OK, Cathy.' Out of the corner of my eye I see Andy stretch and run his hands through his hair. He looks up with a question on his lips. 'Let me collect a few things.'

Andy rubs the sleep from his eyes. 'My *mother*?' he mouths.

'Right,' Cathy says. 'Now, will you put my son on, please. I'm pretty sure he's with you. And before you ask, it wasn't difficult. He isn't at Georges' place and I already know you're not at Amelie's . . .'

I manage a stuttered *Oh* before she continues.

'Look, never mind. I'm not prying or anything; you have your lives. Just tell him: I'd like to see you both . . .' I hear the familiar laugh. ' . . . whenever you can get him out of bed.'

She rings off.

'What on earth does my mother want?' Andy grunts.

'She wants to see us both apparently.'

'*Pourquoi?*'

I shrug.

'Well,' he says. 'We'll have breakfast before we pick up the car. I'm hungry!'

Cathy hugs me and for minutes we stand there in the atrium without saying a word. Then she hugs Andy too before leading me by the hand like a small child into the living-room. He makes to follow but she stops him.

'Please, Andy. I'd like a few moments with Nicole alone. Go into the kitchen and shut the door. Make some coffee.'

She cocks her head and stares at me.

'Your hair . . .,' she says. 'It's . . .'

'. . . different?' I finish for her. 'Everyone says so.'

'It suits you. Would you like some chocolates?' Cathy's escape from crises alternates between chocolates and wine. This morning it's the former. She rummages in a sideboard and brings out an already opened box of *Z Truffles*.

'Only one. It's a bit early and we've just finished breakfast.' I take a truffle and bite through the soft, dark exterior into the central mixture of cocoa and hazelnut paste. These chocolates, like all Cathy's luxuries, belong to another planet.

'Your mother phoned me.' She blurts it out before I can even say *thank you*. 'I've been to see her!'

'*My mother?*' I almost choke on the truffle.

'When she couldn't reach you on your mobile she tried our house phone. She said she'd like to meet me, and I'm afraid my curiosity got the better of me.' She stuffs two chocolates into her mouth at once. There are three left in the box. I look at them, tempted, but decide to abstain.

'*My mother?*' For the moment I'm capable of no response other than a muttered repetition of those two words. I've always supposed Denise to despise the Cathy Ravels of this world and all they stand for.

'I'm sorry. Maybe I should have waited until I could ask you.'

'No, it's cool,' I say. 'It comes as a shock, that's all. What did you talk about?'

'What do two middle-aged women always talk about? Their children.'

'You talked about me?'

'And Andy.'

'You mean as an item?'

'That was mentioned, but mostly we talked about you. Rather, Denise talked about you. I listened. You should call her soon, better still go over to Caudéran and see her. I get the impression she has a few things to say to you. What I want to talk about won't take long.'

She picks up some papers lying beside her phone on the coffee table, shuffles them. There's one I recognise.

'My *resumé*! You kept it.'

'It's in pristine condition. I thought you might want it back.'

'I have the file on my computer. But thanks.'

Cathy gestures at the document. 'I have some questions. One is about *that*. There's a paragraph headed *Career and Life Objectives*. I wondered if anything has changed.'

'My career plan? No, I don't think so . . . well, I can see there may be other options after graduation, but teaching is still at the top of the list.'

'Teaching is very much a skill in its own right. Perhaps an art. Once you know how to do it the subject doesn't much matter. When I went back to it, for a wee while I used to teach some geography and mathematics as well as English. As I see it, you could teach English to French children or French to English children.'

'Well, I'm hopeless at maths.' I start playing with my still-unfamiliar hair style. I fixed it as best I could though it falls short of what Amelie can do. Cathy has a mischievous glint in her eye, and I wonder what this conversation is leading to. *My resumé - my mother.*

'Nevertheless . . .' She closes her eyes. When she reopens them she immediately changes tack. 'You know, that cut really suits you, Nicole. Like Emma Watson. I saw a photo of her some time back in a fashion magazine.'

'*Merci*, Cathy. That's much like what Amelie said. You said you had several questions.'

'I do.' She purses her lips. 'So Andy has asked you to go to Oxford with him.'

My cheeks burn and I have a prickly sensation all over my body. Surely he hasn't discussed his marriage proposal with her . . . that would be too gross.

'He told you?'

'Not in so many words. But I know my son. Though he doesn't talk about his feelings, he sometimes drops very subtle hints. He tells me things without telling me, if you know what I mean.'

'I'm not sure if I do.'

'When you have a son. you'll understand. But, to move on . . .'

'You want to know what my answer was? I thought you'd agreed I could stay another month.'

'I did, and of course if you want to hold me to it, I won't argue. But I wondered how you'd feel if we made a different arrangement.'

'You *want* me to go to Oxford with Andy?'

Cathy shakes her curls. '*Christ*, this is becoming more difficult than I imagined. No, that's not what I'm saying. I'm saying I have no objection if you do. I have no right to object.' She hands me one of the other documents she has been holding. It's an electronic airline ticket for two, Paris to Auckland, New Zealand, dated three days from today.

'New Zealand?' For one crazy second I think she's offering it to me. 'What's this?'

'I have always wanted to go there,' says Cathy, 'so we're going together, Yves and me. He's had one operation. He'll have a second when we come home. Our marriage has been rocky for too long. We're going to try and rescue it.'

'I'm glad. The holiday sounds wonderful.'

She tells me her plans for the trip: three days in Auckland, two weeks touring the North Island, another two in the South. She hopes Yves will look up his cousins and their families.

'This isolation from other members of the Ravel family has to stop,' she says. 'There's no sense to it.'

'Has he agreed?'

'Yes. That's what is so strange, he seems to have had a change of heart overnight. I can't be sure whether it was his fight with Georges or Andy's fist . . . or what happened with you in the office that afternoon. He's willing to talk about Emmeline. Agree on a proper memorial to her, maybe light a candle on her birthday. Or fresh flowers again on the grave – instead of a plain shitty stone in an old churchyard.

'And for things to work, I'm imposing a few other conditions,' she goes on. 'Less business travel from now on - and he must appoint a competent executive assistant to take some of the strain. No interference in Andy's personal life. And there's the apology to you, of course.

'I'll pay you for the month as agreed, and if you want to stay on here meantime you can . . .'

I smile. 'Or go to Oxford with Andy.'

'Exactly. However, I do have another proposition for you. Do you remember Miriam in Edinburgh?'

'Of course.'

'Her two girls are studying French at secondary school. Miriam feels they would benefit from extra tuition. Especially conversation practice. Actually, I made the suggestion and Miriam jumped at the idea.'

'I definitely benefitted from English conversation with you.'

'You had a good start.' She smiles. 'How would you feel about doing a bit of tutoring yourself? In French.'

'What?'

'How would you like to tutor Miriam's girls for a month? Maybe even longer. It would give you a chance to get used to Edinburgh and earn some extra money at the same time.'

'I have no teaching qualification.'

'It doesn't matter. You just have to talk French. Easy as sucking chocolates. No pressure, Nicole.' She picks up her phone. 'There! I'm sending you a text with Miriam's number. All you have to do is call with an answer. It's up to you to agree your fee.'

Andy taps on the kitchen door.

'I've made some coffee. Can I come in now?'

'*Oui, mon chéri,* you can. We'll have coffee and Nicole can talk to you about Oxford.'

She tells Andy about the holiday and then allows me to explain her proposition.

'But don't you see?' he exclaims. 'It's the perfect solution. My time is flexible so long as I do the work and complete my dissertation. We can do both: you come to Oxford with me; I go to Edinburgh with you, see you settled. We'll drive in the Citroen.'

'I can't take the Citroen to Edinburgh, Andy,' I object.

'Why not?'

'It doesn't belong to me.'

Cathy affects a cough. 'Excuse me . . .'

'That doesn't matter.' Andy interrupts her. 'There's no point in it rusting away here in France.'

'Will I be allowed to drive in Britain?'

'I don't see why not.'

We both carry on talking as if Cathy isn't there and she coughs again.

'*Children!*'

We both stop and turn towards her, synchronising our apologies.

'What were you going to say, Mother?'

'First, Nicole can drive in the UK for the next fifty years as long as her French licence remains valid. Second, *chérie,* the car does belong to you now. I thought Georges had told you. It was in his name and you paid him ten *euros* for it.'

'I did?'

'The paperwork says so.'

'You see!' Andy gives me a thumbs-up sign. 'So, there's nothing stopping us.'

My first duty is to phone Denise. Cathy has a few jobs set aside for me but she insists I do that first. I arrange to drive over to see my mother in the evening. Next, I call Miriam to say I accept her offer. She has done her research and says she'll pay me the going rate. Qualified teachers can expect to earn upwards of twenty-five pounds an hour. She offers me fifteen and I accept. The challenge and the experience will be its own reward.

The three of us go out on the terrace to catch the best of the morning and, later, Andy and I go for a walk in the vineyard. The vines have hardened off. *Veraison*, the ripening, is almost complete and the estate workers have begun stripping leaves from clusters that are not ripening evenly. The Merlot grapes have turned a delicious, silky, dark blue, the colour from which they derive their name *little blackbird*. Their powerful plum-like aroma hangs over the trellises. For some reason, it reminds me of Cathy's rich chocolates. I can almost taste them in the air.

Cathy will pay the month's salary she promised me in Sterling pounds, which I can deposit in my British bank account as soon as I have one. She assures me the business will do the same with the money it owes. I don't know what to say and feel tears springing to my eyes. I want to hug her but she forestalls me by wrapping her arms round my shoulders. She hides her face but I think she is crying too.

Andy is brimming with ideas for our journey: a stop in Paris, two days together in Oxford, three days in Scotland - later changed to three in Oxford, and later still to four in both cities. Wonderful though that might be, I suggest five days altogether is more practical, otherwise neither of us will do any work at all.

We still haven't decided when I get into the car to go to Caudéran.

**

44.

My mother opens the door for me. She is wearing a blue dress and light make-up. I have difficulty believing this is the same woman as caused me so much hurt all those months ago. She looks happy and waves to me as I lock the car.

'Come into the kitchen.' She pats my arm. 'I made us something to eat. We can go through to the living-room afterwards. We have the house to ourselves. Jean is visiting a work colleague. Bernard and Sophie have gone out too.'

She has cooked her version of a *cassoulet* stew, with duck legs and plenty of beans. Luckily, I haven't eaten since mid-afternoon on the terrace and feel hungry.

'You used to like this as a little girl,' she remarks as she ladles onto two plates.

'I still do, *Maman*.' I savour the aroma of the food and have to admit it smells good. 'But you needn't have gone to any trouble on my behalf.'

'It wasn't any trouble. I wanted to do something for you. I wanted you to see I've changed.'

We sit facing one another at the kitchen table. As we eat, I watch her between mouthfuls of *cassoulet*. Occasionally, she smiles and I smile back, as if we are two different people, meeting and engaging for the very first time. Since her remarriage she *has* changed but it seems I'm seeing for the first time how significant the changes are. She has taken more care with her appearance, perhaps for Jean's sake and because she wants to be a different person. Yet I can't help feeling that today she has done it all for my benefit.

Her hair, long enough to be worn in a ponytail like mine, is neatly collected and fastened into a bun at the back. During her time in the clinic I began noticing strands of grey, and now she has made the most of those using, I guess, a streaking brush. Rather than ageing her, the pleasing result, platinum highlights in her dark blond, seems to have the opposite effect. Instead of being twenty years or more my senior, she could be a woman in her mid-thirties and might at a glance pass - I realise with alarm - as my older sister.

I glance at her hands as she delicately cuts her meat and raises the fork to her mouth. As long as I can remember, my mother chewed her fingernails. Now, though still short, they are neatly manicured.

My grandmother always refers to her as *Denise*, even in the presence of Sophie and Bernard. For so long, she has been *Denise* in my mind too; I think it helped me bury the horror of what she did to us. But maybe that part of my life is over. *New beginnings?* No longer *Denise*, but *Maman* again. I wonder - but hope dwells in my brain.

'Are you enjoying the stew?' She puts down her cutlery and risks another smile. There is something different about her eyes too. Instead of pill-induced brightness, they have a sparkle which suggests neither desperation nor self-loathing, but genuine *joie-de-vivre*.

'*Formidable.*' I push the last of my food onto the fork and nod furiously. '*Merci, Maman.* It was exactly what I needed.'

'I'm glad.' Her smile broadens as she eyes me up and down. 'There are some things I need to say, important things. But before that . . . '

'What? Why are you looking at me like that?'

'You look happy. I never wanted anything else for you.'

'I know, *Maman.* You look happy too.'

'I'm pregnant!'

She comes straight out with it and I spring out of my chair, knocking the salt and pepper set onto the floor. I feel as if she has stabbed me with a hot needle.

'Pregnant! How . . . ?'

'The usual way, *ma petite* . . . '

'But you're . . .'

'What . . . old?' Her face falls a little and she speaks sharply,

288

though there's no bitterness or anger in her tone. 'I probably deserve that, considering all the lies I've told about my age. But it's true. I found out for sure three days ago. I'm twelve weeks gone.'

'Wow! I think I'd better sit down again.'

'Come through.' She picks up the fallen condiment set. 'We'll pack the dirty dishes in the washer, make some coffee then sit down for a talk.'

Recovering slowly from my shock, I carry two mugs of coffee into the living-room. That my mother might want more from her marriage than companionship hadn't occurred to me. It's hard enough to come to terms with a parent's sex life, but a *baby*. I briefly close my eyes and form my lips in the shape of a silent expletive. *La vache!*

I'm going to have another sister or brother. By the time they're my age now, I'll be forty.

'You would never tell me your age, *Maman*,' I complain. 'So how can you blame me for guessing?'

'I don't blame you.' She takes a mug from me and sips the liquid. 'It's a bit hot for me. I'll let it cool. Sit down, Nicole. Over by the window - where we can see one another properly.'

I do as she asks, taking one of the pair of armchairs matching the new sofa. My mother pulls over the other and sits so that our knees are almost touching.

'You want the truth,' she says. 'I always lied about my age . . . long before I had you. I wasn't quite eighteen then which means I'm only thirty-eight now. But I couldn't lie when it came to getting married; the state always wants proof. So your father and I didn't - until afterwards. That's what you wanted to know, isn't it?

'I was a little innocent, Nicole. I didn't know much about sex and babies. And I can't deny you came as a surprise bundle, but I never meant the things I said. None of them. You must have hated me . . . '

'Yes.'

'. . . and maybe you'll always hate me, but I hope you might begin to forgive me in time. Say you'll try, *ma chérie*. I'm truly sorry for all the things I did and said. Please say you'll try.'

I reach across and take her right hand in my left, pressing it lightly. Something else I notice is the ring on her thumb. It's distinctive, a plain white gold band but with milgrained edges. I recognise it immediately as her wedding ring, the one she wore for my father, the one she took off when I was about thirteen. She sees me looking.

'Yes, it is,' she says. 'I had it resized. I wasn't sure what Jean would think if I wore it with his on the fourth finger. It doesn't mean I don't love him, but I don't want to forget either.' She strokes the surface of the ring with her forefinger. There are tears in her eyes. 'About your father, Nicole - there was never any doubt.'

'I know. *Mamie* said . . .'

'Madeleine never understood. She doesn't even know the whole truth. My parents kicked me out when I got pregnant - told me I'd made my own bed and would have to take the consequences. How could I know the consequences would bring me so much happiness? You, Bernard, Sophie, and until your father died . . .'

'You should have told me, *Maman*. It might have made a difference.'

I wonder if she is telling the whole truth now. To disown a seventeen-year-old daughter may even be against the law. Perhaps there are other dark horrors which have made her what she is. *More big lies*. I decide I don't care. I'm sorry her parents are dead, but past is past. A few sincere words and we've come a long way in mending the rift between us. A new baby - a new life - is a new beginning - for us and for me.

'That doesn't matter now, *Maman*. What they said - what they did, what we said and did. You hurt me and I think I did hate you for a while. But a *baby*! You're going to have another baby. That's the future.'

'You're not angry . . . jealous?'

'Why would I be? You took me by surprise, that's all.'

'I'm sorry.'

'No need. I'm happy for you.'

'You mean it?'

'Of course. But I haven't told you my news. I'm leaving for England the day after tomorrow.'

'I thought we had longer.'

'A last-minute change of plan.' Briefly, I tell her about Cathy's trip and what Andy and I have arranged.

'I see.' My mother sighs. 'He's a lovely boy - Andy. Are you sleeping together?'

I have no reason to lie to her. 'Yes.'

'Taking precautions?'

'What's with the inquisition? But, if you must know, yes, I am.'

'That's good.'

'I've been remembering things too, *Maman* - about the day *Papa* died.'

'Cathy - Mme Ravel said you'd had nightmares.'

'I call her Cathy.'

'That's very modern of you.' My mother wipes her eyes and again there's a trace of a smile on her lips. 'Or maybe I've realised you're not a kid anymore.'

'No, I'm not.'

'I want everything to be all right between us. I'd like to hear about your memories, when you're ready. And I will try to give you honest answers.'

'One day soon, I promise!' I go to her, lean over her chair and kiss her on both cheeks. 'I have to visit *Mamie* and *Papi* now. Then I'm going to pack. But I'll be back tomorrow to say goodbye to Bern and Sophie.'

My mother reaches up and clasps me round the neck. 'I've missed you, *ma chérie*, and I'm going to miss you more when you're in Edinburgh. Make your father proud, Nicole. Make us all proud.'

Papi is delighted with the photograph of Aunt Lucie. He never met her but he remembers seeing a picture of her once, when she and Charles - Louis - got engaged. *Mamie* makes a fuss, asks if I need any money and makes me promise to come home at Christmas. She shows me the mobile phone she has bought.

I am learning never to underestimate elderly people. If they are forgetful at times it's because they have more to remember. And they are as willing to accept new technology as their children and grandchildren. Lucie Ravel has her computer, and now my grandmother is embracing the smart-phone. Maybe it's the ages between that are stuck in the old ways: Cathy, who keeps a diary; Yves, who prefers dusty old ledgers to computer-generated spreadsheets, and who still addresses me as *mademoiselle*.

'Sophie is going to teach me about emails and texting,' *Mamie* says proudly. 'We're going to keep in touch, you and me!'

**

45.

We have loaded up the Citroen. My clothes are packed in the boot in two suitcases, my choice of books crammed in a cardboard box beside them. Another two boxes go in the rear seat with Andy's bag. I can't take everything; the car isn't big enough. I'll use the money earned for my office work - what we didn't spend on St Tropez - to buy an Edinburgh wardrobe. I ordered my course books on the internet, to be delivered to my room at Mrs Hunter's. There will be enough left over for a small laptop to replace the one at *Château Ravel*.

We have planned the journey to Edinburgh over five days. Our first stop is Paris. I'm going to meet Monique after all. She has a sofa bed we can use for one night. It's nearly six hundred kilometres but we'll be on the A10 *autoroute* most of the way and Andy reckons we should do it in six hours plus time for breaks, if we share the driving.

After Paris, we head for Calais and the Eurotunnel shuttle. From the south of England, it'll take another three hours to Oxford. We'll stay at Andy's flat and spend a whole two days in the city before heading north. How long he stays will depend on Mrs Hunter. My room is ready but we don't know her views about male guests.

Yesterday, I had the car serviced and declared fit for the trip, so we're keeping our fingers crossed. Driving in Britain will be a new challenge.

'Nothing to it,' Andy quips, 'as long as you remember you're on the wrong side of the road.'

The French countryside flies past. When I'm driving, Andy mostly sleeps or lies back with the seat tilted and his eyes closed. When he's at the wheel, he talks a lot while I listen and look out at the changing scenery - trees, fields, vines and concrete. Sometimes he pays me compliments; sometimes he touches me on the thigh and I reluctantly brush off his hand, telling him to concentrate; sometimes he drops into lecture mode. In six hours, you can say a lot about Erwin Schrödinger, cats and String Theory. But it's not all physics now. He has learned to talk and ask about the things I like - novels, music and languages. In a few short months he has become quite knowledgeable about Jane Austen and George Eliot.

We've been on the road for three hours and are approaching Tours when I remember the envelope. Cathy gave it to me before we got in the car.

'It's for Andy, but not until you are well on the way.' She slid it into the side pocket of my handbag. 'I don't want an argument. You'll understand when you read it.'

We pull into the next rest stop to eat and change drivers. Andy stretches his long legs and takes in a lungful of not-so-fresh air. The motorway is close enough to surround the services area with traces of exhaust fumes.

'You'd better have this now, *mon chéri*.' I rub my stiff neck.

'What is it?' He turns the envelope over and opens the flap. It's unsealed. Inside is a folded sheet of blue paper. He reads quickly and then, grinning, hands it to me.

'Good news?'

'I suppose - though sometimes she forgets I'm twenty-four. Read for yourself.'

Half of one side is filled with Cathy's scrawl. She has written in a hurry but the note is still decipherable.

Andy! I read. *Don't go and do anything silly with Granny's money. And for Christ's sake don't think of borrowing on your share of the cottage. Though your father might not forgive you easily for what you did to him, he'll cool down eventually. For all his bluster, deep down he's very proud of you. I know you have some other money but you're going to need at least something towards the rental of the flat. I have an old account with the*

National Westminster Bank in England and have transferred nine thousand (£) into yours. That should help. Don't forget what I told you back in June - if you can't be good be careful! Love, Mother.

He's doing the thing with his eyebrows but seems unsure whether to frown or laugh.

'What's that last bit about?' I ask.

'Nothing for you to worry about. Maybe I'll tell you one day.'

He puts his arm round my waist, kisses me on the top of my head and we walk slowly towards the restaurant.

** The End, For Now **

Acknowledgements

I would like to thank all the people who have helped me bring *Sweeter Than Wine* into being, especially:

To Nan Johnson for her valuable comments on the narrative and her editing skills. If I haven't always taken her advice, the responsibility is entirely mine.

To Beryl Lockhart for proofreading the novel and picking up more errors than I really want to admit.

To all my friends and colleagues at Creative Minds Writing Group for their suggestions and advice. Again, if I haven't always taken the advice, the responsibility is mine alone.

Drew Greenfield
May 2018

Printed in Great Britain
by Amazon

85468726R00173